MW00974964

# THE BIG-TIMER

## BY
## CONRAD BAILEY

*Bookman* LLC
*Publishing & Marketing*

www.bookmanmarketing.com

© Copyright 2004, Conrad Bailey

All Rights Reserved.

No part of this book may be reproduced, stored in a
retrieval system, or transmitted by any means,
electronic, mechanical, photocopying, recording,
or otherwise, without written permission
from the author.

ISBN: 1-59453-375-X

Memory is a crazy person who hoards rags and throws away food.


# PROLOGUE


A flash of brilliant lights, searing pain, then nothing
For one brief instant before that "nothingness" claimed him,
he was outside and above his body. All action was slow-motioned.
All screams emptied into a black pit of dark silence.
And with this emptying, all memory was lost...

Club fighter Sully Hawken's life was reduced to a book without print the night he and his best friend were accosted below the streets of Atlanta. Jigs Moran, his manager and mentor for years was murdered during the encounter. He wanted to know why. Remembering nothing of the attack, he vowed to track down the men responsible and rip the answers from their throats. While recovering from his wounds in the hospital, Hawken learned that his bank account had grown to heights he'd never imagined possible. But there was more coming; a lot more. He was in for the shock of his life as Christmas of 1949 approached. It would be quite a trip for a person who had grown up in the slums of northwest Atlanta.


The greatest weakness of all is the inability to distinguish need
from greed.

# CHAPTER ONE

On October the eighteenth, 1949, the first truly cold morning of fall came to Atlanta; for weather like that to appear at such a late date was highly unusual. As a rule, chilly days began weeks earlier and stayed until freezing temperatures arrived in late November. The sudden drop to 32-degrees had caught most of the populace unprepared.

Among those surprised was Doctor Thurman Haygood when he stepped from his four year old Packard at five-thirty that morning. With a deep breath, he breathed the chilly air in the hospital parking lot before continuing. For some reason, the cold front had left him strangely exhilarated; a feeling that had eluded him in recent months. Walking toward the front steps of the hospital, he glanced above the main entrance and looked at the magnificent marble threshold he had witnessed for the first time as an intern in 1942. Seven years later, it still held its' high degree of luster. The words, "Crawford W. Long Hospital" were engraved deep into the Georgia marble, letting the world know they were entering one of the finest medical facilities in the state of Georgia. It was second only to Emory University, a college known throughout as one of the top-ranked hospital in the nation.

Four years earlier, the forty-two year old doctor had shocked staff members when he had chosen to stay with the Intensive Care Unit after his internship. Foregoing a lucrative private practice by not leaving the hospital, at the time, was deemed by most of his colleagues as a very foolish move. Now under constant pressure from problems other than the medical field, second thoughts of his original decision began to intensify. He knew that hindsight was not always the best policy, but, if the opportunity were to present itself in the future, it would definitely be given serious consideration. Enjoying the brief tranquillity while it lasted, Haygood knew things had to change when a particular patient came under his care at the hospital. He was not surprised when thoughts of leaving suddenly became a priority.

Stepping into the lobby, Haygood glanced down the dimly lit corridor. That early in the morning, the only person on the floor was the elevator operator leaning against the wall and reading the morning newspaper. He stepped into the elevator and spoke softly as was his nature, "Morning, Ralph! How was your night?"

The elderly black man had worked the night shift at the hospital most of his adult life and recognized the doctor immediately. He followed Haygood in the elevator, dropped the hinged seat and sat down. "Not too good, doc. Ain't been getting' much sleep since my fan broke. May be better now cold weather heah." He closed the outer gate easily, then pulled the inner gate to and pushed the control handle up. The elevator lurched, then began to rise.

At the fifth floor, Haygood turned to the operator after stepping out into the hall. "Stop by the nurse's station before you go home," he said. "I'll leave something there for you."

"Appreciates that, Doctor Haygood. I needs somethin'."

Haygood stepped into the doctors' lounge down the hall after delivering several instructions at the nurses' station. Quietly, he opened the locker and pulled out a clean smock. He proceeded to fill the coat with the tools of his trade: a stethoscope, watch, pad and pen, organizer and other necessary odds and ends. With it all firmly in place, he was prepared to make the initial round. He poured a cup of coffee and downed what he could before stepping into the hallway.

"Good morning, doctor," a nurse said softly, meeting him with an armful of clipboards. "Is there any particular pattern you want me to arrange the charts?" She fanned out the numerous boards in preparation for his answer.

Doctor Haygood answered without looking back, "Put the patient in "2" on the bottom...I want to see him last."

"Mister Hawken?"

Haygood nodded in agreement.

The nurse removed the chart and placed it on the bottom. "Have you been informed of the update concerning Mister Hawken?" she asked. "He went through quite a lot last night."

"...Not yet."

"He started having spasms just after three this morning. He was jerking violently and his exposed eye began blinking rapidly. He held onto the bed rail so tightly, his hands couldn't be pried loose."

"Who was on the floor?"

"Doctor Greenbaum!"

"How did he handle it?"

"He elevated the bed to thirty degrees and stationed a nurse there with a tray of ice…She stayed with him the rest of the night."

"Was there any response?"

"Not at first, but he began settling down about fifteen minutes later. Then he opened his eye and looked around."

"Did he say anything?"

"I was told he tried, but the vocal cords were too raw to cooperate. He couldn't make a sound."

"What's being done now? Ice chips for the soreness? Swabbing saline? Maybe something to ease the pain?"

"All of those! Doctor Greenbaum said he wanted you to see the patient before doing anything further. He felt you would be the better judge of how to handle the situation at this stage."

"I appreciate his confidence in me. Since there aren't very many patients to survive a bullet in their brain, you can never be too careful. Coming out of a long coma can be delicate in the beginning."

Doctor Haygood moved through the ward methodically and completed the round, with the exception of the patient in the final cubicle. As a person of privacy, no one knew of the doctor's association with the man. Stepping inside the small room, Haygood stopped short of the bed. He was surprised that Hawken was staring at him through a narrowed eye. The left eye was heavily bandaged, but the right eye moved about easily with each motion in the room. There was a futile attempt at speech without success.

Haygood ignored him momentarily while scanning the chart, wanting to make sure of the patient's status before going any further. He leaned over the bed to be heard clearly. "Hawken!" he said a little loudly. "Can you hear me? "…Do you know who you are?"

Hawken tried to answer but couldn't. He nodded yes.

"Good! Don't try to talk! Just nod if you understand."

Hawken nodded he understood.

Haygood pulled up a chair and sat beside the bed where he could be seen easily. He reached over and placed the palm of Hawken's hand around his left thumb. Now, what I want you to do is squeeze my finger once for *yes*, and twice for *no*...Can you do that?"

Hawken squeezed once.

"You indicate that you know who you are. Is your name Sully Hawken?"

"Yes," he squeezed.

"What was the day you last remember? Was it after January, 1949?"

A quizzical look crossed Hawken's face; he squeezed the doctor's thumb twice.

"Was it after July of 1948?"

"Yes!"

"After August?"

"Yes!"

"September?"

Hawken squeezed twice for "No."

"All right, we've narrowed things down to September of last year. Now, let's try for a day? Was it before the fifteenth of the month?"

Hawken nodded "No," befuddled by the huge loss of recollection.

"Was it after the fifteenth of the month?"

"No!"

"Then September the fifteenth is the last day you recall?"

"Yes!"

Haygood removed his thumb from Hawken's hand. "I think that's enough for now. It's obvious that your faculties are coming back, but it's best not to rush these things. You have lost the memory of the last thirteen months, and in most cases, it's only a temporary problem. In time, flashbacks will occur unexpectedly. Don't become alarmed when that happens. It will seem like a dream while you're awake...It's common in traumas like you've experienced. Sometimes a person will recover all their memories at once, and there are times they won't. You could wake up recalling everything as if nothing happened, but I wouldn't bank too heavily on it. What I'm trying to say is, there's no set pattern to rely on...Just let your memory recover normally; let nature takes its' course. If you put yourself under pressure by forcing it, the brain could respond negatively. It might depress some memories forever. So, a certain amount of caution is necessary during the period of coming back."

Haygood returned to the doctor's lounge, satisfied that Hawken was going to recover fully. What was expected to be a lengthy visit with someone on the brink of death for three months, lasted a mere twenty minutes. He walked out of the hospital at 4:30, which as a rule, was early for him. Any other day he would have been on the floor as late as 9:00 PM.

Through for the day, Doctor Haygood left the hospital. He drove north to the corner of West Peachtree and Ponce De Leon Avenue and parked. He walked a block west of the Fox Theater and entered a small eatery on Spring Street. The restaurant was empty at that time of the day. The retired seniors, who lived at the Georgian Terrace Hotel up the way, usually waited until after six before coming in. Haygood had frequented the restaurant for years; living ten blocks from the hospital on Fourth Street, it was halfway between work and home. And, since excellent food was served there daily, it was an added amenity. By 5:00, he was seated and had a meal placed in front of him. Then he did something unusual: He spent an hour and a half savoring the food as if it were his last meal, then quietly got up and left. He drove slowly down Peachtree to Fourth, and turned right. He stopped at the curb by his apartment and parked. He sat quietly as if in a trance for a moment, as sinister thoughts began flooding his mind. He basically understood their presence, and quickly shut down the dark feelings. He stepped from the vehicle, walked up the steps to the front porch and went inside. He slowly ascended the hall stairwell to his 2nd floor flat. Inside, he walked to the sliding glass doors leading to the verandah, opened them and stepped outside. The time approached 7:00 and dusk was almost gone. He took the pleasant view in briefly, then returned inside and went to the bedroom. He opened the drawer to the night table and stared momentarily at the Smith and Wesson revolver lying there. He picked the weapon up and walked back out on the verandah and sat down. He took a deep breath as a cold wind came from nowhere unexpectedly. He laid the pistol on his lap, then calmly stared at it. He laid his head back on the chair with a sigh. An hour later, he raised the weapon to his temple but was unable to squeeze the trigger. The thoughts of his wife being surrounded by a constant parade of men were devastating, but not to the extent of taking his life. There had to be another solution. The crisis over, he went inside and laid the .38 by the bed…He had made it through another day. He stretched out across the bed and tried to sleep, but it was useless. When the alarm went off, he was already showered and dressed; it would take a lot of coffee to keep him going today.

# CHAPTER TWO

Sully Hawken laid still, deep in sleep. A nurse nudged him gently on the shoulder. "Mister Hawken!" she said smiling. "It's time to check your blood pressure and draw blood. I know you hate to be disturbed right now, but bare with us and we'll be out of your hair in a minute."

Squinting through his one good eye, Sully looked at the nurse and pointed to his wrist as if asking the time.

She smiled. "You going somewhere?"

He motioned to his wrist again.

The nurse placed the blood pressure wrap around his arm. She looked at her watch and deadpanned the answer, "Six o'clock!"

The absurdity of his wanting the time sank in and he grinned. "...Sorry," he said with a scratchy voice. The single word was like a knife searing his throat. Holding his throat with both hands, he tried to speak again. "...I—need—to talk—to—a friend."

"What you need is rest," she chastised playfully. "Whether you realize it or not, you've been in a lot of trouble the past three months."

Sully acted as if writing on his hand and spoke through the pain, "Pad!"

"Tell you what," she said. "The doctor will be in at ten. I'll talk to him and we'll see what he says."

Sully eased back on the bed and pointed to his temple. "...Headache," he said, then swallowed trying to override the pain.

The nurse began removing the IV lines from his arm. "You won't be needing these anymore, and since the side effects are headaches, let's unhook it...In about fifteen minutes things will settle down."

"...Need—pad," he said again.

"All I can do is ask the doctor," she replied. "Now do yourself a favor: Avoid talking. That sore throat will go away a lot quicker. Now, as quick as the doctor gives an okay, I'll bring a pad and pencil."

Sully squinted through the one eye. He looked hard at the name-tag pinned to her blouse and tried to focus. *"Beverly?"* he asked unsure, then coughed and grabbed his throat from the ripping pain.

"You see what I'm talking about?" she barked. "You shouldn't be talking at all for a few days; it's too punishing...And the name *is* Beverly."

Sully nodded his head just as another nurse entered the cubicle. She was pushing a cart full of medical supplies. She came to the bed, lifted Sully's arm and wrapped a second rubber band around his arm. "Make a fist," she said politely while tightening it.

She withdrew the sample and Sully returned his attention to Beverly, still standing to the side. "...Favor?" he rasped out.

"You're not *listening* to me," Beverly replied curtly. "You're not going to be able to take much more if you don't stop. Now relax until I can talk to the doctor." She left briefly and returned with a pad and pen and placed them beside the bed. "I didn't get to see the doctor; I guess this is all right...But, under no circumstances are you to talk...Those are my orders!"

Sully immediately began scribbling on the pad. *"Jigs Moran...In telephone book...Address—The Prado...Find him if you can... Important I talk to him."*

"The doctor may not want me to do that," Beverly said, concern crossing her face. She hunted for the right answer. "You need to talk to him first."

*"I have to see Jigs,"* Sully printed. A cramp gripped his hand. When the pain subsided, he began writing again, *"The doc shouldn't object to that."*

"I know you have questions, but now isn't the time. I'm sure everything will work out in time...Why don't you wait and talk to the doctor. I'm sure he has some answers."

Sully wrote vigorously. *"Why are you giving me the run-around? I'm not asking for the moon."*

"Don't get so upset," she said calmly. "Just wait until the doctor comes in; he'll explain everything to you."

Sully's throat became irritated from the strain. *"Not mad, okay!"* he wrote,? *"Look at this from where I sit...I* **was** *6'2"— **healthy**...Woke up like this."* He waved his hand down at his shriveled body. *"How am I supposed to feel?"*

Beverly stood silently; there wasn't an answer. "We'll talk about it later," she said, then turned to exit the cubicle.

Sully slapped the pad to his leg and got her attention. He wrote hastily and pointed his finger at her. *"Tell me now!"*

"What happened isn't a big secret," Beverly said. "It's just not my place to say anything." She waited in the doorway for a response and when it didn't come, left the room.

Sully laid back on the pillow and gritted his teeth from the ache in his throat; he chewed an ice chip. As his mind wandered, he thought angrily, "S*omebody better get me some answers—and be damn quick about it…*He turned over on his side and was asleep within minutes.

# CHAPTER THREE

Sully awoke to the sound of three nurses moving about hurriedly in the cubicle. Why was everything in such turmoil? It became clear when a fourth nurse came in pushing a wheelchair: He was being removed from the Intensive Care Unit. He was going to a private room. He winced in pain as they brought him to a sitting position on the bed. Dizziness and nausea followed immediately.

"You all right, Mister Hawken?" a nurse asked.

"I'm fine! Give me a second!" he said and lowered his chin on his chest. He noticed that the pain in his throat was almost gone.

A nurse leaned over. "Are you uncomfortable sitting up?"

"It's not bad," he said with agony on his face. "Quick movement is what gets me...My head can't catch up."

"Bare with us," she said, then left the room. She returned shortly with an ice bag and placed it at the base of his skull. "Let's hold this here a minute...We'll put you in the chair when you're ready."

Weary from distractions, Sully asked a nurse, "I know you're taking me to a room; is it for good?"

"It looks that way now, but your condition is still guarded. We'll keep an eye out, but everyone thinks it best you have a room of your own."

A sense of urgency entered Sully's mind. "What time is it?"

"Ten fifteen," she replied.

"Can we put things on hold a while? I was supposed to talk to the doctor this morning."

"It's not morning," she smiled. "Except for a few minutes earlier today, you've slept around the clock."

"But the doctor!...Beverly said he'd be here."

"He was! You were sleeping so soundly; he didn't want to disturb you unnecessarily. That's all I heard."

Sully was seated in the wheelchair after the dizziness subsided, then rolled out of ICU. Approaching the elevator, he turned to the nurse pushing him. "Is there any way you can get Beverly to drop by? It's important I see her."

"I'll tell her," the nurse replied, "but it won't be tonight. She's on the day turn. Maybe tomorrow! Don't bank on it, though! The majority of the time she's tied up until dark...She's a busy lady."

Sully had little to say when the elevator stopped on the third floor. He felt the sensation of flying while being rushed down the hallway before it stopped. He glanced upward while being rolled through a doorway; the room number was 351. The nurse helped him in bed, then made certain he was comfortable. She placed all accessories within reach. She gave instructions on how to control the bed and how to contact the nurse on duty, then left. He breathed a sigh of relief from the rigorous trip and drifted off almost instantly.

Sully was awakened again by a gentle nudge. "Wake up, Mister Hawken, it's Beverly," she said. "The girls said you wanted to see me...Is everything all right?"

Sully looked at her groggily. "My eye's matted over...Could you get a rag?

Beverly quickly stepped to the sink and wet a rag. She returned and cleaned the eye.

Sully looked at her intensely for a moment, then became embarrassed because of the awkward attraction. Uneasy that she might pick up on his feelings, he looked away. He was afraid that it was no longer a mystery why he asked for her. It certainly wasn't because she'd been so kind to him. The first time he laid eyes on her, chemistry developed that disturbed him. Being a stunningly attractive woman, the intimidation had been present from the very beginning. The urge to hide those feelings engulfed him.

"I haven't got much time," Beverly said, looking at her watch. "I have to be back on the floor in five minutes."

Sully blinked his eye several times before it cleared. "...Someone needs to tell me what's going on," he said. "I haven't heard from Jigs and you're the only person that's bothered to pay me any attention."

Beverly took his hand and whispered softly, "I know I shouldn't be telling you this; I hope you can take it."

Sully stiffened. "Take what?"

"Mister Moran is dead; you were together when you were shot. He wasn't able to survive...I'm sorry!"

Sully's face went ashen. "I was shot and Jigs is dead?...*Why?*"

"I'll tell you what I know, but please don't ask more...I have to get back on the floor. It was in the news that you and Mister Moran had left the Kimball house at night, heading for the parking area underneath the streets. Someone stopped you as you were going to the car and tried to kill both of you. Whoever it was, did it in a way you couldn't possibly survive."

"Did they shoot Jigs in the head too?"

"No!...Now I have to go."

"Where, then?"

"In the heart," she said, stepping to the door. She stuck her head back in for a moment. "I'll stop by on the way home if you like, but no more questions."

"I'll be here," he said, pleased with the possibility of seeing her again.

Sully's curiosity was aroused to the point that his adrenaline was flowing at a fierce pace. He was now wide-awake. Not only had he been shot, but also Jigs had gone down in the same fashion. *Why would anyone do that?* Sully could handle someone trying to kill him, but not his friend. Jigs was a gambler and a gentleman; maybe a money hawk, but he wasn't devious about what he did. If anyone lost money to him, they knew all the risks beforehand. Some people went out of their way, knowing what the final results would be. They simply enjoyed the association. Besides, Jigs was a wealthy man. He would never take a person's money unless they could afford it. Monetary gain couldn't be the blame for Jigs' death and the possibility of a female being involved, was definitely out of the question. He had his share of women, but they never hung around for any length of time. He was a rich forty-eight year old bachelor, who showered the ladies with gifts or anything they desired; just as long as they stayed out of his private world. That was the mistake women always made with him; they tried to get involved. Sully was sure there wasn't a woman in the picture. If Jigs was seen with a woman more than twice, it meant one thing: Money was involved. The female aspect wasn't considered: Jigs had other priorities. There were two major interests in Jigs' life: Training him for upcoming fights and gambling. Both were handled at Big Town's poolroom and gym. The gym, located beyond the south wall of the poolroom, was where the majority of time was spent. Keeping Sully in peak condition was probably the most important aspect of their relationship, but it went much deeper than that. Their friendship was the reason he followed Jigs around like he did. Jigs Moran had been like a father to him since he was a kid. Sully had always made sure Jigs was safe, but something had gone terribly wrong this time; his friend was dead. The answer was locked somewhere in his mind and the thought of losing it forever, was beginning to frighten him.

Sully was distracted when a nurse walked into the room with a tray of food. "Good morning," she said pleasantly, then placed the tray on the table. "Are you ready for some solid food in your stomach?"

Sully ignored the cheerfulness. "What about the doctor? When does he get here?"

She cranked his bed up high enough where he could feed himself. "He'll be here shortly; he's just down the hall…I think he's looking forward to seeing you."

Sully said nothing but wondered why the doctor was interested in him.

"Try and get some of that food down before he comes in," the nurse said, stepping to the door. "I know you have questions."

He watched as she left the room, then picked up his spoon and dipped it into a pudding of some sort. It tasted like tapioca but he wasn't sure. He did know it was delicious and continued eating very slowly. He knew better than to stuff himself after being fed through a tube for so long. He looked at what seemed to be boiled spinach and took a bite. He never liked spinach when he was a kid but took a bite anyway; he hadn't changed his mind; it still tasted the same. Cream potatoes, a small portion of beans, and small chunks of beef and gravy rounded out the meal. He ate a few bites of each item, took a few nibbles at a biscuit and washed it all down with a swig of tea. An indication he'd had enough was obvious when his stomach became swollen.

The doctor walked in just as he pushed the eating table aside, "I see you've made an effort to eat," he said. "How'd it go?"

"It didn't take a lot to get full..."

The doctor slowly began removing the bandage from Sully's eye. "Don't worry about it," he said. "In a few days you won't be able to get enough. You'll be eating everything in sight...First of all, let's take a look at this eye. It won't take long...Then we'll get the nurse to re-bandage it."

Sully remained quiet as the doctor finished removing the bandages. With the gauze absent, he opened his eye and blinked incessantly from the burning sensation.

"Can you see anything?" the doctor asked, placing his thumb on the top lid and forcing it upward while shining a light throughout.

"I see movement, but it's blurry. That light feels like a torch. It's a burning sensation, if that means anything."

"It does; it means that you'll regain some of your eyesight in that eye. Twenty-five percent, maybe more. Don't set your sights any higher than that. On top of surviving this ordeal, by all rights you should be blind. You should accept the fact that you've been extremely lucky; the head wound alone warrants that. The good part of this is you *will* gain full use of your right eye. And there is a *chance* for the left eye as well."

"How long will I be here?" Sully asked.

"That depends on you...Once you're eating and walking regularly, we'll re-evaluate. You have to be able to make it on your own."

"You got a ball park figure?"

"Two weeks, maybe three. If you have a relapse, maybe longer."

"What do you think could happen?"

"You're still a way from total recovery and a number of things could happen. Blood clots, infections, pneumonia. All of those could be trouble."

"Then, why aren't I still in ICU? They're geared for that sort of thing."

"These are only possibilities. If anything goes wrong, I assure you it's where you'll be...At the moment, your chances of walking out of here in a couple of weeks are excellent. Believe me, your health is amazing considering what you've been through...When you first came to the hospital, there wasn't a physician here who thought you'd come out of this. It was quite a surprise that you survived. Our staff was so stunned they had to call a conference to figure out how you had accomplished it. The remarkable condition you were in was their final analysis."

"Sounds like you don't agree."

"Oh, it was a major factor but there's more to a recovery than being an outstanding physical specimen."

"What do you think it was?"

"Mental strength. A lot of things point to your subconscious being stout enough to take over in the coma; it refused to let you give up. I've seen men in excellent condition as you were, that gave in to death without a struggle. By all rights they should've lived, but they didn't."

"That sounds complicated."

"It really isn't! If you were a confident person when you were hurt, that mentality stayed with you throughout your ordeal."

Satisfied with the explanation, Sully felt an irritation in his throat. "You got something for this?" he asked, rubbing his neck. It tends to get uncomfortable when I do too much jawing. I talked to the nurse; she said she'd ask..."

The doctor placed a small spray bottle in Sully's hand. "She said something; I didn't forget. Use that as often as you like...It's very soothing. If you have more questions, I'll be here until late this evening. If not, I'll see you in the morning."

Sully took the bottle and asked without looking up, "Do you have time to answer a few before you leave?"

"I'll do what I can."

"Have the cops found out who did this yet?"

"Not that I know of. I talked to some detectives last week and they had nothing at the time—or so they said."

"You talked to them?" Sully asked. "What did they say?"

"They were just checking on you. They wanted to know if you'd improved any...Which reminds me, I was supposed to call them when you came around."

"Could you call now? You'd be doing me a favor."

The physician looked at him a moment. "...I'll make a note."

15

When the doctor turned to leave, Sully asked, fearful of the answer, "Am I going to fight again?"

"Never!" the doctor replied flatly. "If you received a blow to the head anytime in the future, it could blind you permanently. It may take years for you to get back to normal...Not even taking into consideration that your life would be in danger."

A disgusted look crossed Sully's face. "What about after that?"

"You'll progress to a certain stage, then it stops. You'll be stronger and able to take more punishment, but the possibility of a lethal blow will always exist. My advice is not to take that chance."

Sully was crushed; it was not news that a professional boxer could take lightly.

# CHAPTER FOUR

Sully jerked violently from the gentle shake by Beverly; it awoke him instantly. When she had left earlier in such a hurry, he had thought she was just patronizing him. Her being there surprised him. He gazed at her and grinned thinly. "I didn't think you'd come back today. I had it figured you were being nice just to shut me up...Looks like I was wrong."

Beverly smiled. "That was yesterday...I wasn't here last night. Don't you remember anything about the last twenty-four hours? The walks down the hall, the meals, any of that?"

"None of it comes to mind," Sully said. "The truth is, I feel like I'm wandering around in a dream. Everything's all mixed up." A strange sensation ran through his body for the second time in as many days when Beverly sat on the edge of the bed and clasped his hand.

"I wouldn't be too concerned about it if I were you. Not being able to recollect things is normal with the IV you were on. The doctor did have you on some very powerful drugs. With all that in your system and your body wanting some time off, will probably keep you disoriented for another week or so. It'll take that long for the medication to get out of the system."

"That's all there is to it?" he asked, then accepted the confusion that was swirling through his head. "I figured it would be more complicated."

"Don't take what I say too seriously; it's just what I think! The doctor is the person you should talk to. I do know this: The length of the coma has contributed the most to your confusion. Between the drugs and the long coma, your body clock has difficulty knowing when things actually happened A combination of those two has a tendency to scramble the process in your brain that keeps events in order."

"I thought a coma would be like taking a long nap? Aren't you supposed to feel rested after something like that?"

"The best way to put it is, it's the wrong kind of sleep. You're just worn out. Your gray matter has been keeping you alive for so long that it's ready for a break."

"Then I'll have to make an effort to remember things in the order they happen from now on," Sully said, looking at the closed blinds in the window. It was difficult to tell whether it was day or night. "What time is it?"

"Eight thirty-five!"

"*AM?*"

"Yes!"

"That means you don't have a lot of time."

"I'm not that rushed," she said, "I still have another ten minutes. Is there something you want me to do?"

"If you wouldn't mind? It might take a couple of hours...And if I'm taking advantage, give me the word. I'll shut up right now."

"You're not, and I don't mind. I'm off the entire day tomorrow."

"You have a car? I don't want you riding all over town on a bus."

"I have an old Ford...It's been a while since it's been on the road. I'll have to get someone to look at it."

"I hate to ask you this, but there are some things stuck in my head that I can't figure out. It's my house: I want you to find out if I still rent the place. I don't have a clue whether I still live there or not. I wasn't the type to move around before, but that was a year ago. There were only a handful of people who knew where my place was. One is dead and I don't know how to get in touch with the others. My reason for this is, I'm going to need a place to go when I get out of here."

"What's the address?"

"You know the Grant Park area?"

"Some! I used to live on Cherokee Avenue."

"What about Atlanta Avenue on the east side of the park?"

"I've been there on the way to State Patrol Headquarters. Can't say I paid much attention, though."

"Do you remember the long hill going down Atlanta Avenue away from the old fort on Boulevard?"

"Yes! It dead-ends at Confederate."

"A block before you reach Confederate, is Marion Avenue; that's where I lived. Take a right there; it's the second house on the left. If I still have the place, fine! But, if the landlord let somebody else have the house, I'll understand…They don't owe me a thing."

"Does the landlord have a phone? Maybe I could call?"

"No phone. They use a neighbor's. At any rate, their names are Billy and Josie Jordan; they're retired and in their seventies. They live on Confederate, about a block from the house."

Beverly took a pencil from her blouse. "What's the directions?"

"When you go down that steep hill on Atlanta, take a right on Confederate and their place is the third house on the right."

Beverly put the information in her purse. "Just so there's no confusion, the Confederate Soldier's home and the State Patrol Barracks are on Confederate Avenue, right?"

Sully grinned "If you wind up there, you've gone way too far. That's five miles past where you want to be."

"I have to get back," Beverly said with a silly grin on her face. She knew she had asked a senseless question the moment it was said. Logic dictated the landlord's house was just three blocks from the park. "I'll drop by later if I can. If not, I'll be by when I have some answers."

"One more favor?" Sully asked. "Could you call me Sully? *Mister* makes me uncomfortable." When she turned to leave, he watched closely as she walked away. When she went up the hallway, he mumbled angrily, *"What the hell am I thinking?"*

# CHAPTER FIVE

Sully's throat irritation had completely disappeared by the time he awoke the following morning. *At least that's one ache out of the way,* he thought, cranking the bed up to a sitting position. A nurse walked in with breakfast and he wondered how he had managed to sleep so late. "What's the time?"

"It's after 8:00 o'clock," she said. "You don't mind a late morning every now and then, do you?"

"Beats waking up to a sharp needle," he said cockily.

"Did it help?"

"Feel like a new man," he said, easing his legs over the side of the bed.

Meticulously placing the food where it was easily accessible, the nurse left the room. A giant black orderly stepped in as she walked away. "Mornin' boss! My name Fred," he said amicably. "It gon' be my job to take care of you fo' a while. We gon' walk you 'round the halls 'til they turns you loose. An' we gon' do it 'bout three times a day…Or long as you can stands it."

Sully looked at the huge man and grinned. He thrust his hand forward. "Hello Fred! I'm Sully Hawken."

Fred took his hand and shook it just as two shabbily dressed men stepped in. Both wore uncoordinated ties that were loose around their necks. A dark brown fedora sat loftily on each head. They were recognized instantly as detectives.

"I'm Smith from homicide," the taller of the two said and then pointed to his partner. "This is Jones. We're here to talk to you about Jigs Moran, and the night he was killed."

"Smith, Jones?" Sully asked. "Is that really your names?

Neither detective offered a reply.

Fred went to one knee and eased Sully's feet into his slippers. He looked up at the taller detective. "Don't mean to interrupt anythin' boss, but it time for his walk down the hall. We be back shortly if you folks care to wait." He turned to Sully. "You 'bout ready, boss?" he asked.

Jones, the smaller, but heavier detective, put a heavy hand on Fred's shoulder. "Get this straight, burr-head," he growled viciously. "He's gonna be tied up with me an' my partner for a while."

Fred brought his huge frame up to its full height and looked down at the policeman with contempt. He was very close to going after the arrogant detective and the anger was evident..."Let *me* tell you somethin', *boss*! We *ain't* down on Decatur Street where you does as you please. You's at Crawford W. Long Hospital, an' the folks heah say Mister Hawken gots to take his walk. Now you go 'way an' come back when he done walking."

Jones looked at Smith. "Can you believe this smart-ass clown?" he spat out angrily, then turned back to Fred while snatching a leather slapjack from his belt. "You fool with me, *boy*, an' I'll split that woolly head of yours open."

Sully intervened before things got any worse, sensing Fred might be in over his head, "Lighten up a bit," he said softly to Jones. "The man's just doing what the hospital expects him to, that's all."

"And what's his job?" Jones barked. "Givin' us a problem?"

Sully felt the hair rise up in the back of his neck and was surprised by his reaction. He had been taunted in the ring time and again by other fighters, but had always been able to remain calm; Why was he so angry this time? The best retaliation had always been to undermine someone's hostility by ignoring their comments. It was an attitude he needed now for Fred's sake. Losing his temper could take him out of the picture and put the friendly Negro in a precarious position. If the two detectives were angered to the extent they took Fred to jail, he would be at the mercy of the two cops. There was no way he could help then.

Sully kicked off the slippers and spoke to Fred trying to calm him. "Tell you what, Fred...Lets walk after these nice policemen ask their questions."

Fred glared defiantly at Jones and refused to budge.

An angry nurse charged into the room, furious that the disturbance had become so loud. She chastised the entire room for disturbing other patients on the floor. "I don't know what's going on here," she said heatedly, "but it's stopping right now...Do we understand each other?"

Fred clinched his fists tight and eased his elbow back. He was about to take a swing at Jones.

"Fred," Sully said loudly, breaking his train of thought, then waved his arm wildly at him and the nurse. "Both of you; get out of here! I'll take care of this."

The nurse turned on her heels in a huff and headed for the door. "*Remember* what I said," she spat over her shoulder. "Another peep and everybody's out of here."

Fred stepped to the door reluctantly and looked back at Sully. "You needs me, boss, I's right down the hall," he said sharply, letting the policemen know they were not as superior as they would like to think.

"I'll call," Sully said, "You can *count* on it."

Fred stood in the door a moment, still not wanting to leave.

When Fred finally did leave the room, Jones smashed his slapjack into the palm of his hand. "That *boy's* lucky he got out of here when he did," he said nastily, "I was just about to make him a new face."

"I'll call him back if you like," Sully said icily. "But, if I were you, I'd call for some help. I don't think you can handle him alone."

A chill settled over the room after those words. Smith, the taller of the two detectives, used a more peaceful approach. "We've got a job to do, Hawken, and people like your orderly don't understand what we have to go through on a daily basis. It can get pretty frustrating at times."

"Getting the job done and being a pain in the butt are two different things," Sully said. "If your buddy would take off the storm-trooper boots and relax, maybe something would be accomplished on occasion. I think Jones owes Fred an apology."

"Like hell," Jones growled. "I ain't apologizin' to no damn darkie."

"Have it your way," Sully said, then turned to Detective Smith. "Let's get this over with. I've got walking to do."

Smith thought a minute. "On July 11th, the night you fought *'Bull' Gerklin,* you and Moran left the auditorium for a celebration party at

York's pool hall. York told us the party lasted the entire night. He said Moran put up a good front, but it was pretty obvious something wasn't right."

Sully looked hard at Smith. "Mister, I have no idea what the hell you're talking about…Have you bothered to talk to anyone about my condition?"

The two cops exchanged glances. "We're here for answers, Hawken. We haven't been able to get any while you were in a coma."

"Well, I hate to disappoint you, but, except for the last few days, I don't remember a thing that happened the last thirteen months."

"We *were* told you had amnesia," Smith said. "We just didn't figure on it hanging around to this extent."

"Well, it has…When I woke up, to me it was September 16th of last year. There's nothing beyond that. The doctor told me that everything should come back in time, but there's no set time-table."

"What are we hanging around here for?" Jones snapped abruptly. "We ain't getting nothin' from him."

Sully did not want them to leave so hurriedly; there were several questions *he* needed answered. The most important was what took place the night he and Jigs were gunned down. "Give me a minute before you leave," he said. "Maybe we can help each other…Walk me through what happened that night? It could break some memories loose? It certainly wouldn't hurt."

"One condition," Smith said pointedly.

Sully was desperate and replied adamantly, "Name it!"

"…Answer every question I ask truthfully, and promise to call me the minute you remember anything."

"That's two things."

"I don't give a damn if it's a dozen," Smith said flatly. "That's the way it's going to be…Take it or leave it."

"You going to call me when you find out something?"

"I don't see why not," Smith said, looking at Jones. "You got any objections?"

"Not a one," Jones replied, without expression.

Sully knew they were lying, but didn't care. All he wanted to know was what happened the night in question. "Okay, let's have it… What happened?"

"…Well, to start, the night of the fight had a bizarre atmosphere from the outset. When the news broke that you won the fight, the town went crazy. You and your friends wound up at a party at York's afterwards. Moran was the only sober person there, and he stayed that way all night. That's when York said something had gone haywire; Moran wasn't the kind to shy away from celebration. Before daylight, something else happened that was unusual."

"What was that?"

"It's common knowledge that Moran's parties are open to everybody. That particular night, for some reason, he shut people out. The strange part happened when a couple of guys beat on the door downstairs wanting to get in. Moran told York not to let 'em in. York got suspicious because Moran was white as a sheet."

"Did anybody see them?"

"The only person who saw them was Moran, and he took it to the grave."

"Nobody else was even curious enough to look out the window?"

"That's the question we wanted you to answer," Smith said. "I suppose it'll have to wait now."

"If Jigs and I were shot the following night, where did we go after we left York's? There's a lot of time in between."

"…After the party, Moran dropped you off at your place…*But*, he never went home. He came back and picked you up at four that afternoon then the two of you headed for the Kimball House. You parked underground at the railroad tracks, walked around to Prior Street and came in the back way. You bypassed the steel steps up to the hotel's Peachtree entrance. It was like Moran was dodging somebody. We wondered what the reason was for not taking the direct route. When you went into the poolroom, Moran wasted no time in pulling some of his cronies off to the side. They were all heavy gamblers; we checked it out the next day."

"Where was I all that time?"

"At the bar, still celebrating."

"Then I might not know what was going on?"

"Either *that,* or you didn't care."

Sully took offense. "Get this straight: If Jigs was in trouble and I knew about it, I would've backed him up. If I didn't know, it was the way he wanted it…"

"You *did* have a good reason to party," Smith said. "But it was *definitely* under odd circumstances. During the first five rounds, Gerklin had pounded you to a pulp. Then, in the sixth, you dropped him with a solid right from out of nowhere, He was down two more times after that, but it was all over…And this guy was supposed to be the third ranked Heavyweight in the Division. There was talk of your getting a shot at the big time after that. A lot of fight people took notice. You had a real future…Too bad it got all screwed up."

"I'll probably never remember any of it anyway…The last memories I have are of fighting with some canvasbacks. I usually won those fights, but the way I recollect things, it was always a struggle. It's hard to believe I was knocking out top heavyweights a year later."

"That night!" Smith said, going back to the incident. "…When you and Moran left the Kimball House; it was right at 10 o'clock. It couldn't have taken over ten minutes to leave the poolroom and walk down to the underground parking area. It was only fifteen minutes after you left the hotel that a vagrant found you in a pool of blood; he thought you were both dead. What I'm driving at *is,* whatever took place happened very quickly. And, the last people to see you and Moran alive were standing at the head of that stairwell. They were less than a hundred feet away and never heard a sound. It's been a dead-end since then."

Sully thought a moment. "…I'm having trouble understanding why I didn't see something wrong. Jigs would've told me if there was trouble. It's strange that other people saw what I couldn't."

"How long were you hooked up with Moran, kid?" Smith asked. "And what about the money? Did you ever know how much of it went on to other gamblers?"

"Jigs put me in the ring when I was nineteen. I've been with him ever since. He took care of the money and I didn't complain…I always came out okay."

"Where did you first meet Moran?"

"At Joe Cotton's Rhythm Ranch...A few years before that, my mother and I had moved into Techwood homes. I tried to keep my nose clean, but being a newcomer, challenges were thrown my way. A tough nut named Womack took notice when I won the fights and wanted my scalp. I was at Joe Cotton's that night, and Womack came after me. He was the baddest guy in Techwood about then, and took it personal that I could take care of myself. Anyway, he had it in his head that I had to be put in my place...He felt it was his job."

"Well, I'll be damned," Jones said, looking at Sully. "That was why Womack left town so fast. If it ever got out some snot-nose kid cracked his head, there would be no living it down. That punk was in Chicago the day after he got out of the hospital. A month later, somebody put a bullet in him."

Sully wondered when it would be Jones' time.

Smith took up the conversation again. "After you and Womack fought, how did Moran get into the picture?"

"He saw what I did to Womack and thought I could be a boxer. So, he came to Decatur Street and bailed me out of jail. The first time I laid eyes on him was at the turnkey's desk. He had me believing I was going to be the greatest heavyweight in history the next day. But, that was a long time ago. I'm guessing we were still friends when we were shot...?"

"I'm sure nothing changed," Smith said. "...I've been told that you also watched over Moran outside of the ring. The only way he could keep out of trouble was when you stood over his shoulder...Now, the money? Do you remember any of that?"

"I remember that Jigs always footed the bill getting me ready for the ring. It was a year before he started getting anything back."

"Then you don't know about Moran using you to line his pockets?"

Sully bristled at the remark. Though Jigs was dead, he was not going to allow anyone to malign his friend. "At last count," he blurted out, "I had eight-thousand dollars in the bank. That ain't bad for a *pug* like me."

"Got a flash for you…According to the bank, fifty grand is in that account. *And*, if you think that's a nest egg, guess what your buddy, Moran, pocketed over the past year? A quarter of a million bucks."

"Jigs didn't make *that* kind of money from my fights…Maybe gambling?"

"Think what you like," Smith said, "but as far as Moran was concerned, you were nothing but a meal ticket. And he was well rewarded for the effort…Seems like everybody knew he was a crook but you."

Sully grimaced, again taking issue with the derogatory remarks,. "Fifty-thousand bucks doesn't *sound* like I was cheated…It's more than I ever thought existed."

Smith sat on the edge of the bed. "Look, Hawken!" he said trying to be convincing. "During a period of twelve months, you had four fights with one tough opponent after the other. You won them all by knockout. It increased your value in the boxing world considerably. After each one of the first three fights, your bank account grew by twelve thousand dollars. Moran pocketed *eighty thousand* a fight. That smells…Then, what was supposed to be the most profitable fight of all, was when things went crazy. The Gerklin fight was the *only* time you made more money than he did…It was just five hundred bucks, but the funny part was, he didn't deposit a dime into his own account. We haven't been able to figure that out, but we're dealing with people now who might shed some light on things."

"Who are you talking about?"

"The *money people* Moran pulled off to the side that night at the Kimball House. So far we haven't been able to get anything out of them, but since you're out of that coma, things are warming up."

"What does *that* have to do with it?"

"Beats me," Smith said, "but somebody believes you know more about Moran's business dealings than you let on…The natives are getting restless."

"What you don't understand," Sully said pointedly, "is that Jigs didn't get wealthy by telling me how he went about it. He didn't need my advice…Besides, he was filthy rich before I knew he existed. His family had Coca-Cola stock from the day it was put on the market.

Jigs didn't have money like the Candlers or the Woodruffs, but those people gave him the respect he deserved...Unlike you."

"You need to face reality, Hawken...I know you think Moran was your friend, but the guy never saw the day he was anything but a cheap hustler."

"Yeah, Jigs was a hustler, all right," Sully said, his face turning crimson, "but there was nothing cheap about him. What you can't comprehend is, in our world, he was considered a gentleman. Manipulating people and money was a trade in our circles and no one had troubles dealing with it."

Smith turned to Jones and thumbed at the door. He glanced back at Sully. "Don't forget our deal, Hawken...I'll be in touch!"

Sully didn't return the look or make a comment. He'd had enough of the two detectives for the day.

# CHAPTER SIX

Sully sat quietly on the edge of the bed after the two detectives left. He stared at the empty wall while thinking of their bullying behavior. Tolerating the more reserved Smith wasn't a problem, but his partner Jones was another story; his arrogance defied all reason. Easing his legs off the side of the bed, he eased his feet into his house shoes. He stood momentarily, waiting for the dizziness to subside. With stable equilibrium, he held the bed rail a moment before taking the short walk to the chair by the window. Every bone in his body is aching now. His thoughts turn to Jigs once settled in the chair, and how the confident little man had run his life. When Jigs was alive, there *were* no problems too difficult to deal with. All was accomplished without hassles, threats or insinuations. Jigs had a way of presenting his thin, five-foot-four frame, that made it clear that he was in control at all times. He had been a respected gentleman among a closed throng of millionaires, gamblers and con men.

Sully never minded watching over Jigs at the time, but now, the tables had turned; there were problems that weren't there in the past. A twist of fate had suddenly turned his world upside down and it was a mystery how he would handle it.

Fred stepped into the room moments later and it was a welcome interruption to the dark thoughts raging through Sully's head. "Ready for yo' walk?" the huge Negro smiled. "Saw them polices leaving; figured I could come back without havin' to hurt one of 'em."

Sully didn't reply right away. Thoughts of how Jigs had died were still churning away in his thoughts. When he did speak, it was with a thin grin. "…And there's no doubt you could."

Three days later, Fred entered the room to help in a scheduled exercise.

Sully was sitting on the edge of the bed waiting. "I'm trying the halls today without help…You mind?"

"Fine wit' me, boss," Fred said. "But I gon' tag 'long jus' in case. It's what I gets all them bucks fo'."

Sully laughed; it was impossible to be irritable when Fred was around. "Then, let's let you earn your money."

Fred slid Sully's slippers on, then helped him stand erect. He waved his arm in mock politeness toward the hall. "A'ter you, boss."

"You mind not calling me *boss*?" Sully asked, stepping to the door. "It makes me uncomfortable."

"I thought white folks liked that?"

"Some might, I don't. Besides, you don't have to cow-tow to anybody. I saw how you handled those cops the other day. Not too many people could've walked away from that without their heads cracked..."

"It ain't over yet; them police will have their day. They don't forget nothin'. Next time I gets in jail, this uppity ol' nigger gon' get beat good."

"That doesn't bother you?"

"Naw! They done it before...Never could beat me down. I just laughs at 'em...Them slapjacks don't hurt me none."

"I'd think making a joke about it would make them madder?"

"That's why I does it. The harder they hits, the happier I gets...They's so upset befo' they quit smacking me, they fit to be tied."

Sully stepped out into the hall. "What do they pay you here, Fred?"

"Sixty cents an hour."

"What do you think about coming to work for me?"

"I won't fo' no sixty cents an hour."

"How about a hundred a week?"

"...You serious?" Fred asked suspiciously.

"Dead serious," Sully said. "But, is your work here secure?"

"They puts me back to work no matter what I gets into. I pull six months down Tatnall County an' they lets me back. It won't be no different next time."

"You have family?"

"Jus' mama, but she do fine when I ain't there."

"You think she can handle your being with me twenty-four hours a day? It'll take a while to get the legs back."

"She do fine! She always *do*, when I's in the lockup."

Sully was concerned when Fred mentioned for the second time about his being behind bars. "How often are you in jail?" he asked "...I'll be in a lot of trouble if you're in a cell when I hit the streets...I'm going to be upsetting some people and I'm expecting you to keep the peace."

Fred smiled. "Don't be worrying, boss. I's one fella who gets in trouble only when *he* want to."

"You mean you *wanted* to spend six months at Reidsville?"

"That weren't my fault, boss...I got caught with this man's wife and he pulled a knife an' started sticking me...Had to shoot him."

"You killed him?"

"Weren't no choice. 'Fore I could explain that fool went crazy. I couldn't jus' lay there an' do nothin'."

"Sounds like he had good reason to be upset?"

"Well, he *didn't*," Fred said stiffly, not appreciative of Sully's evaluation. "That woman come to me with nothin' but a lie. She say she broke up with him and it weren't no problem. When he walk in that room, screaming and hollering about her being so sorry, was the first I knew they's still married. When he start cuttin', time for talking was done. That woman tried to make her man jealous, and all she wound up doing was gettin' him dead?"

"What kind of shape were you in *afterwards*?" Sully asked.

"Spent two weeks at the Grady 'fore bein' taken to Reidsville."

"You only spent six months on a murder charge?"

"They decided to turn me loose when they got the truth out that woman,. They said it were a justifiable killin'."

"Justifiable Homicide," Sully said as they stepped back into the room. "How about the pistol? Do you still have it?"

"The police wouldn't give it back...Said I's too dangerous to have a gun."

"We'll get another one," Sully said, getting into bed and pulling the blanket up over his legs. He rolled over and was asleep almost immediately.

Sully awoke day's later with a ravenous appetite. Glancing at the small clock on the table, he noticed it was eleven-thirty. No wonder he was so hungry. He looked back at the clock. *Where had it come from? It wasn't his?* He jerked nervously when he noticed a figure standing at the foot of the bed. Seemingly from out of nowhere, Beverly had appeared holding a small bag. *That explains the clock*, he thought.

Sully noticed the rigid frown on her face. "Is everything all right?"

"There fine," she said, laying the bag by the window. "Thought I'd drop these clothes by so you'd have something to wear...I'll leave them over here."

"You sure you're okay?"

"I'm perfectly fine," she said, noisily placing a cold breakfast tray in front of him. "Why do you ask?"

"It just looks like something's bothering you...I haven't seen you for a few days and I thought I'd hurt your feelings somehow..."

"I'd rather you didn't think like that...It gives the impression that there's more to our friendship than there is. I already feel that I've misled you somehow and you've attached yourself to me...It has to stop."

Sully voice was calm but cold. "Do I have a house to go to, or do I have to find another place?"

"You're fine where you are," she said just as coldly. Your rent is paid up to May of next year. The landlord said you paid a year in advance in the spring; he said you liked to do that...Something else!"

Sully stared at her with a blank expression.

She ignored the look. "He told me that the day after you went in the hospital, two policemen went into your house and ransacked it. They put everything back in place, but a few days ago, it happened again. It was right after you came out of the coma. Somebody broke in and left things in shambles. Whoever did it had to be looking for something special the way everything was strewn about. We cleaned the mess up with the help of a neighbor."

"What neighbor?"

"The one on the corner."

"Gabby?" he asked with a scowl.

"Yes," Beverly said, then walked out of the room without saying another word. It was obvious she was angry about something.

Sully rammed his fist down on the night table, sending food containers clattering over the room. He knew exactly what had happened.

Seconds later, Fred came rushing into the room to see what the commotion was. "Everythin' okay, boss?" he stammered, seeing food everywhere.

"Sorry," Sully said, settling down. "Didn't mean to make such a mess."

"No trouble...I's here for accidents like this."

"...If you're going to look after me like I'm an adolescent, at least you should get paid for it...You're on the payroll starting now."

Sully sat alone after Fred left the room; his thoughts went to what had transpired during Beverly's visit to his house. He was sure the talkative, twenty-year-old girl next door had said something offensive. Gabby had been his neighbor for several years as far back as he could remember. She had ruined her life by marrying and having two kids before her eighteenth birthday. Her husband, a truck driver twenty-five years her senior, had contributed to their problems heavily by his constant absence from home. Leaving a young woman like Gabby alone was an invitation to disaster. It shouldn't have been a surprise to anyone when she showed up at his door looking for attention.

The first time Gabby had came to his house her husband was on a lengthy trip. She had dropped the children off at her mother's and returned home alone. The excuse was she needed a night of rest. It was a far cry from what she had planned. What *was* on her mind was Sully, who was sleeping soundly next door. It was no secret that Sully never kept the door locked and the house was easily accessible. Even if it were, anyone could get in by using the key dangling on the door facing.

Sully awoke to a strange noise coming from the living room that cool September night; it was well after midnight. He slipped quietly out of bed, grabbed a rusty iron poker by the bed, and then moved slowly to the front room. Peeking around the doorway, he drew the poker back, ready to attack the person there. He stopped just in time when he saw Gabby standing there; she was completely naked. There was no mistaking what she was there for.

He remembered her words when he dropped the iron poker to the floor. "I ain't wasting another minute of my life being alone all the time," she said, defending her actions. "And I ain't apologizing to nobody."

The incident set a trend. She showed up at the door every week after that. The nights her husband was on the road and she had access to her mother as a baby-sitter, she had came knocking. Sully had gullibly taken Gabby's word that their trysts would never escalate beyond friendship.

But she didn't keep her promise. Somehow, during her conversation with Beverly, she managed to deliver the message that he was off limits. It drove a wedge between he and Beverly. Gabby would be the first person he would talk to upon leaving the hospital.

# CHAPTER SEVEN

The doctor was seemingly preoccupied when he walked into the room. He was thumbing busily through the contents of a large folder. He pulled several reports from the folder, closed it and then began examining the sheets. He returned the documents to the folder. "I have good news for you, Mister Hawken," he said. "Everything indicates you'll be leaving the hospital today. If you're ready, I'll set it in motion?"

"I'm ready to leave," Sully replied. "…No doubt about it…Been ready for a week. Once my vision came around, I started getting antsy."

"Before we do anything rash, just to be sure, let's administer a final evaluation. If everything works out all right, we'll have you out of here in an hour. But, everything has to be right before we send you away."

"Wouldn't want it any other way," Sully said. But, he was more than just anxious to get away from the hospital. The reality of remembering only the last seventeen days of a complete year was gnawing at him.

The doctor checked his blood pressure, took his time with the heart, then inspected the face wound. He took a small flashlight with piercing brightness and put it close to Sully's eye. "Everything seems to be in order," he said, "and if the other eye is okay, you're free to leave."

Sully looked at the clock by his bedside; it was a few minutes past ten o'clock. He still wondered if Beverly had placed the clock in the room. With all the confusion in his head, he couldn't remember.

The doctor almost touched Sully's damaged eye with the light, then moved it from side to side. "Look up!" he said, pealing the top lid from the eye.

Sully looked up.

"Looks good…Now down!"

Sully looked down.

"To the right…Now left!"

Sully was getting nervous. The time it took the doctor to examine the bad eye was causing concern. "Anything wrong?" he asked shakily.

"It looks fine," the doctor said. "...And the prognosis is you were extremely lucky. You'll regain normal strength in the right eye, but the left one—I'm not sure. It may never be right. It could be capable of sixty percent in time; I doubt any more than that...It'll probably take as long as two years to get that much."

"What about boxing? Will I be able to get in the ring again?"

"No, that's definitely over," the doctor said. "You have *Detached Retinas* in both eyes and *very* fortunate you aren't blind as it is."

"Then a hard shot to the head could permanently blind me?"

"Exactly! Any blow in that area would be dangerous."

*"Then I'll have to watch my step,"* Sully thought, thinking of what lay ahead.

The doctor handed Sully a business card. "In about a month, I want you to drop by the office. Call the nurse and work out an appointment. In the meantime, if you have any questions, my office is just down the street...If there's nothing else, I'll call someone in to help you get ready."

Sully was dressed by the time a nurse walked in with the discharge papers. She smiled at his nervous anticipation.

Sully didn't return the smile; he wasn't *intentionally* being rude but his mind was mulling over other things. "The clock in the window?" he said pointing. "Did nurse Beverly give it to me?"

"Yes! Along with some slippers and pajamas."

"Do you know her last name? The least I can do is send a card; something for being so nice."

"Her last name is Johnson...I remember a man asking for her at the desk one day; that's the name he used."

Sully tried not to look confused; the idea of Beverly being attached never dawned on him. For some reason, he had assumed that she was available. He politely thanked the nurse for the information, and would thank Beverly properly another day. "I guess the next thing to do is check out," he said, looking around the room. "Then I'll have to see about getting the bill paid."

"It's already been taken care of."

"I don't understand!" Sully said, withdrawing his insurance card and driver's license. "Won't they need these?"

"It won't be necessary," she said. "Miss Moran came by earlier this morning and took care of everything."

A mystified look crossed Sully's face. "Are we talking about Virginia Moran, Jigs Moran's sister?"

"Yes sir!"

Sully couldn't imagine Virginia Moran giving him the time of day, much less leaving her sanctuary and coming there to pay his hospital bill. The few times he'd been in the Moran mansion, the woman had hardly spoken to him. He definitely wasn't considered as one of her friends. He wondered why she would go to such lengths for him, and planned to ask her at the first opportunity.

The nurse called downstairs for a wheel chair after gathering Sully's belongings. She put everything in a paper bag and laid them on the bed.

Sully was surprised when a different orderly came in pushing the wheel chair. "Where's Fred?" he asked. "I thought he was taking me downstairs?

"He take off 'bout an hour ago," the orderly replied. "Say he had somethin' to take care of; somethin' 'bout his mama...Tol' me he won't be back fo' a while."

Sully was silent while being transported to the first floor. He was disappointed Fred had let him down on the very first day. Downstairs, he stepped into admissions on his own and signed the release papers. Walking out of the lobby to the front steps, he looked in every direction; he halfway expected Fred to come walking up. In a sudden afterthought, he wondered if he had any money. Checking his billfold, he found he hadn't, which was a definite setback. He felt for change in his pocket. There was only thirty-five cents and a rusty pocketknife. He wouldn't be taking a taxi anywhere. *"What luck,"* he grinned wryly. *"I've got enough for the trolley home and if things get worse, I can cut my throat with the knife."*

Sully began to walk east toward the trolley stop on Peachtree. Twenty feet from the corner, a loud noise caused him to jump back from the curb. An old Ford with its tires screaming in agony came sliding up.

"Better gets in, boss," Fred yelled over the loud engine. He reached across and opened the passenger door. "...Pretty cold out there. I know you's wonderin' why I's late, but we needed a way of getting' about. This ol' car'll take care of that. If we takes a trolley to yo' place, wouldn't be no talking 'tween us at all, you sittin' up front and me to the back."

Sully glanced at the ragged automobile and was amazed that it was even running. No vehicle in that shape should be allowed on the street. Reluctantly, he got into the front seat. He took notice of the one good feature of the car; they were sitting on it. Fred had had the civility to put a clean blanket over the smelly seat.

"Where to, boss?" Fred asked, ignoring the inconvenience.

"Take me to the house first...I want to pick up the bankbook. We'll need some money to get by on."

"Don't mean to be pushy, boss, but since I on the payroll, could you give me somethin' up front for mama. It could help while I's gone."

Sully liked Fred's frankness; he smiled. "I'll give you a week's pay providing you quit calling me *boss*."

"Can't do that, boss," Fred said. "If you gon' pays me to do a job, it gon' take respect. That means *you* the boss, and that's that."

"Let's compromise," Sully grinned. "If you won't call me anything but boss, and I won't let you call me Mister Hawken, let's go for something else. How about *Mister Sully?* Is that all right?"

"If I remembers," Fred said easily. "...Now, where you live, boss? We needs to get moving afor' this old car die on us."

Sully began yelling loudly over the engine noise giving instructions on how to get to his house in Grant Park. He turned around quickly when a bone-chilling breeze hit the back of his neck. He noticed the back window was missing on the driver's side; no wonder he was freezing to death.

Fred was apologetic. "Sorry, boss! I'll put some cardboard in it when I gets the chance."

Sully slid down in the seat shivering. "You got a heater in this thing?"

"Naw suh! Weren't no good when I bought it...Only give forty dollars for it to begin with...Can't 'spect everythin' to work."

Sully covered his head with the blanket. "Shake me when we get to the house," he said, closing his eyes. "Got a lot of things to do today."

# CHAPTER EIGHT

Sully felt like he was in the confines of a cocoon with the blanket loosely wrapped around his head. Fantasies and reality mixed as he dozed lightly. The darkness under the blanket was comforting to a degree but there was no peace; thoughts of Beverly kept disrupting the tranquillity. Constantly visioning her beauty; her face, the brown hair, the eyes, the white uniform with mystical curves. It all seemed to be ever present. It had to stop; it was too hard to deal with along with everything else.

Fred shook him from the slumber. "We here, Boss."

Sully eased the blanket from his head and noticed that Fred had parked on the wrong side of the street in front of the house. But it was of no consequence. The only other vehicle sitting by the curb on the small, narrow street had been there for years rusting away. He gazed at the small porch where *39 Marion Avenue* was roughly painted on the steps. It had taken a long time but he was finally home. He opened the door to the Ford, stepped into the street, then crossed over to the opposite sidewalk. He stepped up onto the porch and glanced around to the shrubbery. He wondered how the small yard had gotten so neatly trimmed. He remembered the kid who used cut the grass during the summer months. The boy must have taken care of things while he was in the hospital. He probably owed the kid for four months of lawn care.

Fred stood beside Sully, wondering why his employer did not go in the house. "You gots a key, boss?" he asked. "We gon' need one."

Sully mumbled softly, "Over the door."

Fred looked at him quizzically. "You okay, boss?"

"...I'm fine," Sully said. "...Let's take a look inside."

Fred took the key from above the sill and opened the door. When they entered the living room, a distinct, musty aroma hit their nostrils. It indicated that the house had not been aired out in a while. He opened a few windows. "We needs a little air in here, boss...Dis' smell could gag maggots."

"You're going to freeze us to death," Sully said, rubbing his hands together. "That wind came right off the North Pole."

Fred looked at the radiant gas heater in the small living room. "You wants me to stoke 'at heater?" he asked.

"I think it's a good idea, don't you?" Sully said, then stepped into the back bedroom. "The matches are over the stove in the kitchen."

The gas heater was more than enough to heat the four rooms and bath in the coldest of weather. The house was indecently small.

Sully was accustomed to living in tight quarters without difficulty. For years, it had sustained his meager existence. It gave him a sense of stability to have a place of his own. He was comfortable there and deliberately avoided telling people of his life away from the ring. Jigs Moran was one of the select few who had ever entered the front door. He was irritated at the two homicide detectives who had invaded the premises without cause. He became angrier thinking of their ripping through his possessions. He returned to the living room shortly with an aged cookie tin, then backed up to the tiny heater. "How much longer you going to keep those windows open? I'm supposed to be careful of pneumonia, so the doc says."

"Well, you don't needs none of that," Fred said, closing the windows.

Sully lifted the lid from the tin. There were two ten-dollar bills still lying on top where he had left them. He thought of the burglar who had broken in recently. He was certain of one thing: Whoever came in the house definitely wasn't a burglar. No decent thief, large or small, would leave anything of value behind. He knew many thieves and was aware of their mentality; a buck was a buck, no matter how small.

Sully lifted his bankbook from the tin and opened it to the last transaction; his eyes bulged. Detective Smith had been right; a balance of forty-nine thousand, three hundred and twenty dollars stared back at him. He had no recollection how the money got into the account. He had a dumb-founded look on his face.

Fred noticed the detachment. "You all right, boss? Ain't too cold now, is it?"

"I'm fine," Sully said. "I don't think I'll *ever* be cold again."

Fred didn't inquire further.

Sully walked into the bedroom and placed the tin on a closet shelf. He dropped the bankbook into his jacket pocket and returned to the living room. "You know the C&S Bank at Five Points?"

"Across from the Kimball House?"

"That's our next stop. I need to make a withdrawal."

Fred cut the gas off to the heater. "You wants to open the windows back up and let it air out in heah?"

"Wouldn't hurt," Sully said, stepping out on the front porch.

Fred opened the windows again then followed Sully out and closed the door. "I guess we ready?" he said, placing the key above the door. Stepping into the yard, he glanced skyward. "Boss! This don't look good!"

"What's that?"

Fred put a hand palm up. "It gon' rain!"

"So what," Sully said. Then the thought hit him. "...Don't tell me; no windshield-wipers."

"Sorry, boss...I get 'em fixed soon as I can."

"Can you see to drive without them?"

"I gets some Coca Colas to pour on the windshield," Fred said, cranking the engine. "The water jes slide off after that." He raced the engine slightly to warm it.

Sully swore that everything within a quarter of a mile was startled by the sound of the motor. "You figuring on getting a muffler too?"

"Been wantin' to...Jes' ain't got around to it yet."

Sully shook his head. As strange as it was, he was beginning to understand the make-up of this procrastinating giant who didn't have a worry in the world.

Fred pulled up just feet from the entrance to the bank and stopped in the driving rain. Traffic behind him came to a complete halt. He was blocking the busiest intersection in downtown Atlanta. A patrolman half a block away, came running down the sidewalk screaming obscenities.

Sully quickly stepped in the bank and wondered how Fred would handle things. The question was answered when Fred gunned the Ford and left with tires smoking.

Sully went straight to a teller's cage and laid the bankbook on the counter. He placed his identification inside the book. "I want to withdraw five-hundred dollars."

The woman teller was unaccustomed to handling such large amounts of cash. "Excuse me, please," she said nervously, looking around for her supervisor.

"*Now what*," Sully mumbled under his breath when she left her station.

The supervisor returned moments later with the teller. "Mister Hawken?"

"Yes," Sully replied, agitated at the delay."

"Please understand that we express caution before handing this kind of money over to anyone. A withdrawal this size naturally gets our attention."

"Is my identification in order?"

"Yes sir!"

"Then, would you please give me the money?"

The supervisor instructed the teller to count out five hundred dollars.

Sully counted the money and put it in his billfold. He returned the supervisor's concentrated glare. "Is there something else?"

"No sir," the man sputtered, "...I just thought—you were dead."

"A lot of people did," Sully said, then walked to the exit. He had trouble understanding why the man's statement bothered him. Stopping outside, he looked for the patrolman who had been so angry at Fred. He didn't see the policeman and began walking toward Broad Street, a block over. He hoped Fred would come looking for him when he wasn't at the Peachtree entrance. The minute he stepped onto Broad Street, Fred pulled to the curb and swung the door open. "Better gets in, boss. That cop still on the war path."

Sully was soaked to the skin when he got in the car. He began shedding the wet cloths as they sped away in the drenching rain. He wrapped the dry blanket around his shoulders, then withdrew his billfold and counted out a hundred dollars. He handed it to Fred. "Drop by your mother's house first," he said. "Then, we head for the Governor's Mansion."

Fred's eyes got big. "You knows the Governor?"
"No, but I know a neighbor of his."

# CHAPTER NINE

Sully sat in the car quietly waiting for Fred to step out of the house.

Fifteen minutes later, the huge bodyguard came out on the porch with a crooked smile on his face. "Mama ain't never seen that much money," he said, settling into the driver's seat. His weight dropped the vehicle dangerously close to the mud-laden alleyway. "...She goin' shoppin'."

Sully smiled. "It's nice you do things like that for her...Let's get to the Governor's Mansion before it gets too late."

Fred cranked the engine and a loud noise from under the hood shook the vehicle.

Sully looked nervously out of the window when a cloud of dark smoke came from under the front fenders. "What in the *world* was that?"

"It do that sometimes," Fred said, making light of the noise. "Ain't serious!"

Sully shook his head. "You figuring on looking into that one of these days too?"

"Thought about it," Fred said, easing onto Auburn Avenue in the direction of Five Points.

Sully yelled over the roaring engine just north of town, "Do you know where the governor's house is?"

"I knows!" Fred replied, turning off the main thoroughfare where the Peachtrees merged. "It jes' down the street heah."

"Okay! When you get a block past the governors place, slow down; I'll show you which driveway to turn in."

Fred went past the governor's mansion driveway slowly and waited for instructions. He stopped the car when Sully told him to.

Sully pointed to a rusted, weather-beaten, wrought iron gate that was mounted on concrete pedestals. "That's the entrance over there?"

"You wants me to pull in?"

"Yes, and go around to the front of the house."

Fred dropped the Ford in gear and swung in the driveway. He stopped at the front door and stepped from the car onto the gravel driveway.

Sully lingered in the soft rain for a moment; he was still mesmerized by the aged, but beautiful, ivy-covered Moran home. It did not look as well as it once did though; the grass, the shrubbery; the complete exterior was in an unkempt condition. The house was a far cry from what it was when the elder Moran was still alive. In his day, the house was *the* showcase of the Prado. Next to the governor's quarters a block away, there was no match. Sully stepped out of the rain up onto the huge marble porch, then glanced upward at the three story high pillars that supported the massive roof overhead. The sight had always held him in awe. He looked back at Fred. "Let's get this over with," he urged.

"If it's all right wit' you, boss, I jes' stays out heah."

"You're always supposed to be with me, Fred...That includes now."

Fred shuffled his feet stepping away from the automobile "You sho' 'bout this, boss?" he asked, walking up the steps to Sully's side.

"I'm sure," Sully said, raising the huge brass ring on the door and bringing it down hard three times.

A full minute passed before footsteps were heard walking down the hall. It was a delicate tapping sound on the hardwood floor. The huge oak door opened slightly and a short, wispy, black woman peeked through the crack. Sarah, the housekeeper, smiled broadly when she recognized Sully "Miss Virginia said you'd be by..."

Sully figured it had something to do with her paying his bill at the hospital. "Is she home?"

"She in the study trying to make some sense of Mister Jigs' papers. Said she had a lot to talk to you about."

"If she's looking for information about Jig's affairs, I can't help her. He kept his dealings to himself...And I was glad of it."

"Don' know nothin' 'bout that," Sarah said. She turned and began walking down the long hallway. "Wipe yo' feet—the both of you," she barked, as if talking to two small children. "I done cleaned this hall one time today because of nasty feet, and I don't intend to do it again."

Sully wondered who could have visited Virginia Moran. She wasn't exactly the type to invite people into her home. She was widely known for her inability to socialize. Whoever had been there, had to have come by unexpectedly.

Sarah stepped into the study, stopping short of the desk where Virginia Moran sat. "Mister Sully here, Miss Virginia. You ready to see him?"

Virginia Moran motioned for Sully to enter and Sarah left the room. The elderly woman sat exploring a mountain of papers without looking up. Several minutes passed in silence. "Sit down!" she eventually said, still not bothering to look up.

Sully and Fred sat, wondering what held her concentration so greatly. They waited for the attention of their host.

Seemingly finished with her study of the papers on the desk, the white haired, hundred pound woman stared at them with a blank expression. She stood stiffly and stretched, then walked around the mahogany desk and extended her hand with a smile. "It's good to see you again, Sully," she said. "It's been a while."

Sully got to his feet and took her hand. He was somewhat surprised at the warmth in the greeting. They stood in silence a moment before she released his hand and stepped back around the desk.

Seating herself, she looked hard at Fred. "Who's this?" she asked menacingly.

"This is Fred," Sully replied politely. "He works for me."

"Doing what?"

"Right now, he's taking care of things I can't."

"Like beating up on people you want him to."

"That's one way of putting it, I suppose. I'm not capable of taking care of myself just yet, so Fred has to do things for me. You never know; somebody might want to finish what they started a few months ago?"

Virginia Moran took a disgusted look at Fred and blurted out angrily. "You!...Did you wipe your feet when you came in? Sarah has enough to do around here without chasing after people with muddy feet."

Fred did not like her curtness. "We done what Miss Sarah told us," he said aloofly.

Sully knew by her rude behavior that some things would never change. No guests, by her standards, would ever be welcome while visiting the Moran household. And his being Jigs' friend didn't help the situation; she had always looked down on him because of that. Uncomfortable with her mean-spirited attitude, Sully stood to leave. "I just came by to thank you for taking care of the hospital bill," he said. "...I want you to know I appreciate it."

"Sit down, Sully," she snapped. "We're not through."

Sully reluctantly sat back down. "Look, if this has anything to do with Jigs' and his business affairs, I can't help...I know he made a lot of money from boxing...But that's about it. Away from the ring, all I did was look over his shoulder."

"I'm aware of what you did, Sully, and I know you wouldn't have done it for just anybody. You did it for my brother...Probably the only real friend he ever had. I *do* admire you for that."

"That was a two-way street...With Jigs around, I was always taken care of. The fights, the gambling, the money changing hands...He took care of everything. I was just along for the ride."

"Now that Jigs is dead, do you have any plans for the future?"

"I'm not rolling over and forgetting about it, if that's what you want to know."

"What does *that* mean?"

"It means I'm going to find out who killed him and make 'em pay."

She stared at Sully quietly for a moment. "...If you do go after the people responsible, I want to help...I know you think of me as some cold-hearted bitch looking at the world with arrogance, and you're not far from wrong. But this was my brother. He was the only family I had, and he's gone. I want what is just." Her face rigid, she gathered some papers from the desk and handed them to him. "This is a twenty-five thousand dollar life insurance policy that Jigs drew up some years back. You are the primary beneficiary." She handed him a business card. "Contact these people and they'll instruct you on what to do."

Sully took the papers and the card and fell silent; he was at a loss for words.

"There are other things you should know," Virginia said.

He waited quietly for her to continue.

"The police came by this morning…They were asking a lot of questions about you and Jigs. They knew about his safety deposit box, and they knew about the large amounts of cash he kept there."

"I knew about the box," Sully said, "but I didn't know anything about any money stashed in it."

"Jigs kept close to a hundred and twenty-five thousand there all the time," she said, "along with jewelry worth almost that much. I opened that box after his death, and it was empty."

"How did the cops find out about the box? Jigs wouldn't have said anything. He told me a few things, but that was it…I was the only one."

"As far as I know," Virginia said, squinting her eyes, "I'm the only person, other than my brother, who knew what was in that box…I can't imagine."

"It has to be somebody at the bank," Sully said. "They must have watched him when he laid everything out. That's always done privately, so it had to be a bank official. There's no other explanation."

"You're probably right…I can't imagine how else they could have found out. At least they know nothing of the insurance policy or your being in the will."

Sully looked at her, confused. "What will?"

"Jigs' will stipulated you receive fifteen thousand dollars plus the Buick," she said, handing him more papers. "The lawyer's address who will handle things is there on top. He'll fill you in."

"This is a lot of money…You sure this is right?"

"I'm sure! And one more thing before you leave."

Sully looked at her in silence.

"Stay in touch, Sully…I might be able to help find Jigs' killer. I know a lot of people at City Hall who owe me."

Sully did not understand the sudden show of interest; it was certainly out of character for a woman like her. He suspected an ulterior motive was behind the actions. "I'll be in touch," he said, standing.

"Your car's in the garage...The chauffeur serviced and cleaned it when it was brought to the house. You can pick it up on your way out," she said, then returned to the papers as if he didn't exist.

Sully walked away after being dismissed so abruptly. He left with no option but to go directly to the chauffeur's quarters. In the garage out back, he and Fred approached a man working under the hood of a vehicle. "Pardon me," he said. "Miss Moran said I should pick up the Buick out here."

"Yes sir," the man said. "She said you'd be coming by."

"When did she tell you that?"

"Just a minute ago," the man said, opening the stall door in front of the Buick.

Sully smiled at being so suspicious. He looked at Fred under the roof extension outside. "Head for your mother's house...I'll be along shortly."

Fred said he would, then walked toward the Ford. Moments later, the Ford was running and noisily went down the driveway.

Sully cranked the '39 Buick moments later and took the same route. A block away, in front of the Governor's Mansion, Fred was standing behind his automobile in the driving rain. He was soaked to the skin. Sully pulled alongside. He rolled the passenger side window down. "What's the matter?"

"She quit, boss...Plain out died. Made a loud noise and locked up."

Sully shook his head. "...Anybody know you own the car?"

"Never bought a tag for it if that's what you mean."

"How long you had it?"

"Five years."

"Get in," Sully said. "The county can take care of it."

Fred got in from the downpour and pulled the door to behind him. "I's tired of that car anyways," he said disgustedly. "Nothin' never did work."

# CHAPTER TEN

Sully left the Governor's Mansion and turned south on Peachtree Street. He drove down Spring to North Avenue and pulled into the Varsity. He pulled to the rear of the building and parked. "I need something to chew on," he explained. "You hungry?"

"Wouldn't hurt...Ain't eat since mornin'."

"We can use curb service if you like?"

"At's all right, boss. You go on up front and eat...I jes' stays here with the coloreds if it all right wit' you?"

"I'll join you," Sully said.

"You won't like it back here, boss. Sometime coloreds gets ugly when white folks come in heah."

"Does it bother you that I want to eat back here?"

"That ain't it, boss...I jes' don' want nobody messin' wit' you."

"I'll be all right," Sully assured him. "...They're bound to have enough sense to be peaceful while you're with me."

"I s'pose," Fred said, shaking his head.

Sully followed him into the dingy room reserved for blacks and took a seat to the side. "You mind ordering for us?" he asked.

"Don' mind at all...What you want?"

"A couple of dogs and a coke."

"You don't want no onion rings?"

"No, just dogs will be fine."

Fred stepped to the counter and ordered their food, then sat down beside Sully. He looked around the room menacingly. Other customers avoided his message-filled stare.

They ate their meal without incident, emptied their trays in a trash barrel, then stepped out in the drizzling rain. Sully started for the front of the building instead of going to the car. "I need to go up to the pool room...I'm looking for somebody."

Fred looked sheepish. "You wants me to go in there?"

"It's what I pay you for," Sully said.

"I understands that, boss, but some of those white folks gon' get madder n' a wet hen. They ain't gon' like me being there."

"They'll have to get used to it! I'm not going anywhere without you. If anybody takes offense, then we'll deal with it. Besides, I'm not taking you in there to *aggravate* anybody…You'll have a purpose for being there."

Fred followed Sully up the stairwell leading to the Q-room over the Varsity. He was resigned to the unpleasant task of provoking white people.

An enormous fat man greeted Sully with a broad smile. He sat behind a wrap-around counter in the middle of the room. "Well, I be dammed! When did you get out of the hospital?" he asked, gasping for breath.

"Hello, Fat Man…I Got out this morning," Sully replied. "You all right?"

"I'm okay! But it looks like you lost a ton of weight…With all of them muscles gone, I almost didn't recognize you."

"I'll get back to normal eventually…Might take a couple of months though."

"Who's that with you," the fat man asked, obviously not bothered by Fred's presence in the all-white establishment.

"This is Fred. He's taking care of me until I get on my feet."

"Would you look at the size of this guy," Fat Man said, staring at Fred. "He's bigger'n me…Couldn't blame a body for turning tail if he had to face this one. He's enough to scare anybody off."

Sully eyes narrowed. "What's that mean?"

"Words out, Sully. They're gunning for you."

"Like who?"

Fat Man raised both hands in front of him and shook them negatively. "You're an old friend Sully, but I don't get mixed up in other people's problems."

Sully looked around the huge poolroom to see if anyone was within earshot. The two teenagers playing on a table by a window were the only customers in the building. "I need information, Fat-Man…If you know something, let me have it."

Fat Man looked around nervously. "I'm not giving names," he said, sweat pouring down his cheeks, "but take my word for it, there are people looking for you."

"You know why?"

"It has something to do with Jigs."

"Names?"

"C'mon, Sully, I can't do that."

Sully's face went grim and turned to leave. Mounting the steps leading downstairs, he turned to the fat man. "I need to see G.W. Spence...You seen him?"

Fat Man didn't like being in the middle of anything controversial and was becoming jittery from the questioning. "He was in earlier...Said he was going out to Red Ward's place in Hapeville. The way he talked, he had more on his mind than playing a little pool. I think somebody was going to meet him there."

"What time did he leave here?"

"Around three...Couldn't have been any later than that."

Sully took the first step down and spoke over his shoulder, "Appreciate the help, Fat Man. I'll do something for you one of these days."

Fat Man replied easily, "No need for that...We'll just call it even after that last fight. Promise me one thing though: Don't bring my name up in any conversations. Somebody might get the wrong idea."

Sully stepped around to the passenger side and looked across the hood of the Buick. "You want to take the wheel for a while, Fred? I don't need to be pushing things so hard the first day out of the hospital."

"You relax, boss, and tell me where you wants to go."

"You know where Hapeville is?" Sully asked, laying his head on the seat.

"Been there a few times."

"Well, head south on Stewart until it dead-ends at the railroad crossing. Georgia Baptist Children's Home is just across the tracks. When you get there, give me a shake...I'm taking a short nap."

Sully awoke thirty minutes later to a gentle nudge.

"We's here, boss," Fred said. "You awake?"

Sully looked out the window somewhat disoriented. He vaguely remembered that it was daylight when they left the Varsity earlier. It was now pitch-black. "Where are we?" he asked, rubbing his eyes.

"In Hapeville, boss. At's where you wanted to go. Don't you 'member?"

"I remember now," Sully said, sitting up. He rolled the window down and took several deep breaths of the cold air. He pointed his thumb down the railroad tracks. "You see that red light?"

Fred nodded.

"That's Virginia Avenue; take a left at the light. About a mile from there, we'll pass the Hanger Hotel. It sits across the street from the entrance to Candler Field. A few hundred yards past that is Ward's Poolroom. It's on the right in an old army Quonset hut...That's where we want to go."

Fred smoothly changed gears while pulling away from the muddy shoulder. He veered left at the intersection, then drove past the hotel and turned into Ward's. A downpour covered the area just as they went onto the lot.

When Sully stepped from the car, it was almost impossible to see anything through the heavy rain. A single fifty-watt bulb over the door did little to help. Sully pulled the jacket over his head, then raced ankle deep in water to the entrance overhang. He waited at the door while Fred parked the car.

They entered Ward's together. The pool room was an old Quonset hut; a long, rectangular structure full of pool tables. The building was a pre-fabrication unit that the military used during the Second World War. Except for the few people at the rear of the hall, three men playing on the front table were the only people there...They were playing a game of nineball. Red Ward was one of them.

Ward leaned against the wall with a cigar dangling from his mouth. When he recognized Sully, the cue-stick was slid into the rack. "Never thought I'd see you again," he said softly. "...It's been a long time, Sully."

"Hello, Red!"

Red stepped behind the small counter where he kept the cold drinks and tilted his head in Fred's direction. "You guys want a Coke?"

Sully and Fred indicated they wanted one.

"Been reading about you, kid," Red said. "Never figured you'd get out of that hospital alive."

A thin grin crossed Sully's mouth. "I heal good!"

"What brings you out this way? It's been a few years."

"I'm looking for G.W. Spence...I was told he was coming here."

Red paused a long time before answering. "...What do you want with him?"

"Business!"

"And I know what kind," Red said stiffly.

"Do you know where he is?" Sully asked, ignoring Red's irritation.

Red was again slow to answer. "...You don't need to be dealing with his kind, Sully. But if you have to, he's at the hotel down the street."

Sully finished the Coca-Cola and placed the bottle in the rack. "Hate to run, but I've got some things to take care of...Maybe one day when things settle down, we'll mull over old times." He received an icy stare upon stepping out into the pouring rain.

When Sully reached for the car door handle, Red called out from behind. "Sully!" he said loudly. He was soaked to the skin. "You need to think about this...You need to let it go. I know how you felt about Jigs, but dealing with G.W. Spence ain't the answer. That's nothing but trouble."

"I appreciate the concern, Red, but with everybody in town afraid to open their mouths, I don't have a choice. I'm the only person in town who doesn't know what's going on. This is the third time today somebody's warned me of the danger I'm in."

"You might not have a problem if you let me handle things."

Sully stared at him coldly and did not answer.

"I know some of these guys, Sully. Maybe I can put a stop to what's going on...Give me a few days."

Sully sneered. "You know the bastards who are after me?"

"Let me make a call...They may listen to reason."

"Get one thing straight, Red. If they killed Jigs, I'm not letting it slide. Nobody walks away from this…I don't care who they are."

"I don't know if they killed Jigs, Sully, but I *do* know who's looking for you." Red said. He knew there was only one way to stop what was about to happen, and it had to be done quickly to keep things from getting out of hand.

Sully and Fred stepped on to the verandah of the Hanger Hotel in almost total darkness. Like Ward's place, the front was lit up with a single bulb, making each step a hazard. Sully opened the French door that led to the corridor inside. Behind a large bar-like counter at the opposite wall, a night clerk sat quietly reading the newspaper by a dim light. The darkened hallway had a rancid odor, probably coming from the filthy floors that looked as if they had never been cleaned. It had been years since he had set foot in the hotel and the place still turned his stomach.

The clerk dropped his paper on the counter and looked hard at Fred. He turned to Sully and snarled, "What you two birds want?"

"Not what you think," Sully said equally nasty. "…I'm looking for G.W. Spence. I understand he's got a room here."

"See him 'bout what?"

"That's mine and G.W.'s business," Sully said, then pointed his thumb at Fred. "Now, if there's a reason you don't like the way I'm asking these questions, you can talk to my friend here? You won't like the way he does things."

"Smart ass," the scrawny man said under his breath, then rang the bell on the counter top for a bellhop.

A tall, thin black man with a pronounced stoop in his shoulders came out of a room behind the counter.

"Take this bird up to Spence's room," the surly clerk said. "He's in 215." He shook his finger angrily at Fred. "You wait out here, boy."

Fred looked at Sully. "What you want me to do, boss?"

"Stay out here," Sully said. "I won't be but a few minutes…That old bastard's probably looking for an excuse to shoot somebody anyway."

"That's exactly what's gonna happen if'n you don't watch it," the clerk growled."

Sully knocked softly on the room 215 door. "Open up, G. W…It's Sully!"

After a moment, the latch clicked and the door opened until the chain caught. A pair of suspicious eyes stared through the crack. "What are you doing here?" G.W. asked, releasing the chain then looking both ways down the hall.

"I'm looking for you," Sully said, stepping into the smelly room and closing the door. He saw two young women sitting on the bed. "We need to do business, G. W…And we don't need ears."

"Out, girls!" G.W. said strongly, thumbing at the door. "Take a break or something…See you in about half an hour."

The moment the prostitutes left the room, G.W. whirled around. "Dammit, Sully, what are you trying to do, get me killed? If certain people even thought I was selling you hardware, I'd be a dead man."

Sully suddenly realized that if they were able to frighten G.W. so easily, they were probably capable of doing a lot more. He was definitely in a lot of danger. "All right then, don't sell me anything… Just give me a name."

"Are you crazy? *That'd* be like cuttin' my own throat."

"How about selling a couple of guns to my friend downstairs? Nobody will ever find out where he bought them."

"What's the matter with you, Sully?" G.W. said angrily. "Have you listened to a word I've said? If those guys figure out what's going on, they're probably writing my obituary right now. How many people know you've been looking for me?"

"Just Fat Man and Red Ward, that's it…You won't have to worry about them; they'll keep their mouths shut."

"What about that old man downstairs?"

"I don't think he knows me."

"You're putting me in a vise, Sully…All for a few lousy pistols. It ain't worth it…Do me a favor and get out of here before you get me killed."

"I need something to defend myself with, G. W...If they killed Jigs, they won't be satisfied until they're finished with me."

G.W. picked up a shirt at the foot of the bed and slipped it on. "I shouldn't be doing this. It's a move that *could* get me buried...*But,* wait here 'til I get back."

Sully laid his head back on the chair and closed his eyes. He needed to know why everyone he talked to was so fearful of helping him. Finding the people responsible for Jigs' death was not going to be easy if that kind of resistance continued. It could be an even greater task if his life was in jeopardy.

G.W. returned to the room five minutes later with a large paper bag. He placed it on a small table. "Here's a couple of Singer .45s and a box of shells...You ain't gonna find a more reliable piece anywhere."

"How much?"

"Hundred and fifty for the pair."

"Done," Sully said. "Now, *what's* a Singer .45?"

"You know *anything* at all about guns?"

"Don't think I ever held one in my hand."

G.W. uncovered one of the pistols. "...This is a forty-five caliber, automatic. Singer Sewing Machine made them for the military in the Second World War. It'll knock a man off his feet up close...Watch closely how I load it!" He mashed the release button behind the trigger housing and the clip fell in his hand.G.W. filled the clip with shells, then shoved it in the grip until it clicked firmly in place. "Everybody has a preference...Me, I like to keep a round in the chamber all the time." He pulled the slide back and jacked a shell in the chamber. He then placed a thumb on the hammer and pulled the trigger without letting go and eased the hammer down. He thumbed a button to the right of the trigger housing. "That's your safety. It won't fire until it's pushed back."

Sully looked at the gun thoughtfully. "When I get ready to use this, all I have to do is push the safety to the side?"

"Except for one thing."

"This isn't complicated, is it?"

"Just squeeze the gun tightly when you pull the trigger. There's a bar on the back of the handle that keeps it from accidentally going off."

Sully gathered up the two weapons thinking the meeting was over, paid for them and walked away.

"Judson Fletcher," G.W. said quietly when Sully reached the door.

"What?" Sully asked, turning around.

"It's the name you wanted. He's small potatoes, but he has all the answers. When you find him, watch for a .45 Derringer hidden up his left sleeve...He's as dangerous as they come, so be careful."

Sully was quiet a moment. "You didn't have to do this, G. W...I would have found out soon enough."

"Yeah, but you'd always think of me as the rat who wouldn't help you when you needed it...I wouldn't like that."

Sully stepped out into the dimly lit hallway. "I won't forget it," he said

"I'd rather you did," G.W. said, closing the door behind him.

# CHAPTER ELEVEN

Sully rolled over and looked out the window. He was disoriented by it still being dark and wondered why the sun wasn't up. It was past 2:00 o'clock when he had laid down. He had to have slept six or seven hours. It's impossible to feel so refreshed with only a few hours sleep. He checked the time; it was 5:00 o'clock.

A small light in the kitchen was shining into the living room and someone was moving about. Sully sat up on the edge of the bed. "Who's there?" he yelled a bit too loudly; he had forgotten about Fred being with him.

"It's me, boss," Fred said easily. "I was jes' about to wake you up."

"It's not even daylight yet," Sully protested. "Why so early?"

"It's time for breakfast...You done slept a whole day away."

Sully yawned and stretched while gathering his thoughts. "I've slept around the clock?" he asked, almost whispering.

"Yassuh! You figuring on getting up, or are you gon' lay back down?"

Sully walked slowly into the kitchen across the cold floor. "I'm staying up...Any hot coffee in here?" he asked, sitting down.

"Be a minute...Put a match to it soon's I heard you stirring."

"How much longer?"

"'Bout five minutes. I'll put on some eggs while we waitin' on the coffee."

Sully rubbed his eyes and walked back into the bedroom. "I'm going to take a shower and get dressed. Give a yell when it's ready."

Showered and dressed, Sully sat down to his meal and thought thoroughly of the next step. "You know anything about guns?"

"Yassuh, a little...Why?"

"I bought a couple in Hapeville the other night. Thought we might need them one of these days."

"Is that what we's doin' at that hotel?"

"Yeah! You know anything about army .45's?"

"Sho do! Carried one durin' the war."

Sully was impressed. "You were in World War Two?"

"Yassuh, from Normandy on...I drove an ambulance in the Medical Corp."

"I would've thought somebody as big and strong as you would've been a stretcher bearer on the line."

"Oh, I was strong enough...Jes' too slow afoot. They put them bucks what could run like the wind on that job."

Sully walked into the bedroom and returned with a paper bag. He laid a .45 on the dining room table. "Load this up and stick it in your pocket...We have to go to the Kimball House this morning."

Fred loaded the powerful automatic with a worried expression on his face. "...Boss, sooner or later, you's gon' have to tell me what goin' on. I ain't figured out yet who we's after or why...I need's to know if I gon' do you any good."

Sully knew he was right. Up to that point, he had thoughtlessly failed to inform Fred of any details. He immediately began making up for lost time. He carefully explained the entire picture to Fred once they left the house. He finished as they drove up Edgewood toward Five Points.

Sully jerked his finger at an available parking spot when they reached Courtland Street. "Pull in there," he said. "We'll walk the rest of the way."

Fred looked confused. "We still gots fo' blocks, boss. Howcum' you want's to park way down heah?"

"I don't know," Sully said easily. "Maybe I'm wary about going there...Because it's where Jigs was killed?"

They walked into the Kimball House using the Prior Street entrance, then took the stairway to the basement. They made their way down the long hallway to the billiard room on the Peachtree side of the hotel. Sully Stepped in the billiard room first and nodded at some elderly men in pinstriped suits. He knew every one of them; they were all Jigs' people. Jigs had liked them the most because they were fat with money and power. Sully wondered why they were there at eight o'clock in the morning? He stepped to the bar and sat down. He scanned the sixty-foot long mahogany bar, beautifully decorated with brass rails. There was a feeling of stepping into the past. The walls were covered with 19<sup>th</sup> century paintings and a magnificent mixture of glass, mirrors and stainless steel. History had ground to a halt in the ancient room.

The bartender at the far end of the bar wiped several glasses and placed them on a shelf. He looked at Sully, then at Fred, then walked toward them with a scowl on his face. "What's on your mind, Hawken?" he asked angrily?" Without waiting for a reply, he focused on Fred. "There's *rules* around here, boy...Personally, I don't give a damn, but the people who pay me don't approve of mixing."

Sully stared at the bartender with the same blank expression. "They can object all they want...Every step I take, he goes with me."

"I just work here, Sully," The bartender said icily. "I do what I'm told, or I'm out of a job. Now, tell me what you want, then you and your friend get out."

"I just want to know if you were working the night Jigs was shot?" Sully said.

"I was here...Stuck around answering a bunch of questions for those cops. They talked to everybody here that night."

"What cops? Street cops? Plain clothes? What?"

"Two homicide dicks. If I remember right, their names were Smith and Jones."

"Figures! What'd they ask about?"

"They wanted to know who you talked to before leaving and how you acted."

"How we acted?"

"Yeah, they wanted to know if you guys acted bothered or afraid of something."

"What'd you tell them?"

"I told 'em what I saw: Jigs spent his time with some friends while you were at the bar drinking like a fish. They were all huddled up in the corner and nobody could hear what they were talking about. Then, they started arguing like crazy. Things settled down after that; Whatever the problem was, they worked it out."

"Did any of them follow me and Jigs when we left?"

"You're barking up the wrong tree, there...Those guys wouldn't hurt Jigs; they were his friends. All three of 'em were at least seventy...You know 'em."

"Who were they, Barney?"

"Well, Charley Benson ain't around no more...He died a few weeks ago. Ol' man Bradford went into hiding, scared to death about something. Ain't nobody seen him since the night of the shooting."

"Who was the third man?"

"Milton Elliot. He's probably the best bet?"

"I know Elliot," Sully said. "Nice man! Jigs thought a lot of him ...Has he been around lately?"

"Not much," Barney said, shaking his head negatively. "When he does show up, it's only for a few minutes. He talks to his buddies a little then he's out the door. He's always looking over his shoulder— like he's scared of something too."

"When's the last time you talked with the cops?"

"Four days ago...They wanted to know if I'd seen Elliot or Bradford, and I told 'em the same thing I told you."

"You haven't heard anything from them since?"

"Not a word."

"You have any idea where Elliot is now?"

"Same place he's always been, I suppose: At the Georgian Terrace!"

"You tell the cops that?"

"They didn't ask—I didn't offer."

Sully looked hard into the bartender's eyes. "One more thing before we leave: You know a guy by the name of Judson Fletcher?"

Barney was noticeably upset. "Uh, uh, yeah! I know him," he stammered. "So do you...So what?"

"Was he in here that night?"

Barney's face went flush. "What the hell are you trying to do, Sully, get me involved in this crap?"

"Never mind that! Was he in here?"

Barney started to sweat profusely. He was obviously shaken by the questioning. He glanced around the room nervously, making sure no one would overhear. He leaned over the bar and whispered, "You gotta give me your word, my name ain't going to be mentioned."

"You have it."

"Well, this Fletcher character and some gorilla named Tony, came to the bar that night. It was just minutes after you and Jigs showed up. *And*, it was like I said before, Jigs was at the far side of the room and you stayed at the bar. Anyway, those two goons called Jigs over to yap about something."

"Could you hear anything?"

"Naw, they stuck pretty much to themselves. They made sure nobody was listening. They didn't talk but just a few minutes...I'll tell you one thing, those two were mad as hell about something. I thought they were gonna' bash Jigs right then and there."

"What happened after that?"

"Nothin'! They just up and left...But they were still hot."

"Do the cops know about this?"

"I don't know...I know I didn't say anything. I wasn't about to get those two on my case if I could help it."

"Does Fletcher and this Tony come by any more?"

"Hardly ever," Barney said, then looked at Sully quizzically. "That crowd hangs out at Big Town's...Hell, you ought to know that."

Stepping away from the bar, Sully said quietly, "I'm going through a bad case of forgetfulness right now, Barney. It's why I'm asking the questions; I can't remember what happened...Sorry if I was rough."

"Just take your boy and leave—*please!*" Barney said, pulling dirty glasses from the sink. His hands were shaking. He watched as Sully and Fred walked away, hoping he had seen the last of them.

# CHAPTER TWELVE

Fred turned off Ponce De Leon onto Peachtree, then pulled into the Fox Theater parking lot; it was after ten o'clock. He looked across the street at the Georgian Terrace Hotel. "You gon' be all right heah, boss?" he asked. "If you is, I need's to make a run by the house."

"Troubles?" Sully asked.

"Nawsuh! Jes' need's to see mama…It been a few days."

"You have someone you can call instead?"

"*Could* call the folks down the alley…They's always good enough to watch over her while I ain't there…Jes' hates to bother 'em."

"Take your time, then," Sully said, stepping from the car. He looked back through the window. "I don't know how long I'll be here, but when I'm finished, look for me on the steps out front."

"Appreciates that, boss. I won't be gone long," Fred said, and pulled away.

Sully crossed the street, then walked up the front steps of the hotel. He stopped on the marble verandah, ten feet above the sidewalk. The ferns on the frontal deck had not been taken in for the winter and he wondered why they were still out. A couple of cold nights and they would surely be victims of neglect. The porch chairs were out also, rocking gently in the chilly wind. Someone had yet to concede that summer was no longer in the air. He entered the well-lit hotel lobby, noticing numerous guests lingering in the warm interior of the foyer just beyond. It was ten-thirty, but for the men gathered in the hallway, the day was just beginning. He mulled momentarily looking through the throng, then stepped over to the night clerk behind the counter. "Could you tell me if Milton Elliot is in?" he asked.

The clerk responded politely, "Sorry, but Mister Elliot left strict orders not to be disturbed, day or night…Perhaps another time?"

"It's important I talk to him…Ring his room and tell him Sully Hawken's here. See what he says!"

"I can't do that, sir…Mister Elliot has been quite emphatic about his privacy for months now."

Sully folded a twenty-dollar bill and slid it across the counter. "Maybe he's changed his mind by now?"

"Sorry, sir," the clerk said, pushing the twenty back.

Sully added another twenty. "At least check...It won't hurt!"

A victim of greed, the clerk looked around and crammed the two bills in his pocket. "I'll make the call, but I don't think it'll do any good. Mister Elliot hasn't had any visitors for quite some time."

"*Nobody*?" Sully pressed.

"Just the police!"

"I'm betting I know who they were," Sully said under his breath.

"Sir?" the clerk asked, not understanding.

"Just talking to myself...Give Elliot that call and see what he has to say."

The clerk picked up the phone and dialed Elliot's room. The conversation was short and to the point.

Sully didn't hear what was said and waited patiently for an answer. He wondered what Milton Elliot was so frightened about. Why would someone so confident issue orders to isolate himself? Then the question arose of what to do if Elliot refused to see him. Having to sit in the lobby until Elliot came downstairs seemed to be the only alternative if that happened.

The clerk hung up and turned to Sully. "Room 604," he said. "He'll be waiting for you...Would you mind not revealing our transaction? Mister Elliot wouldn't appreciate why I chose to call."

Sully assured the clerk their secret would be kept, then moved quickly to the elevator. "Six," he told the operator and then stepped to the rear. On the sixth floor, his feet sank deep in the plush hallway carpet. He was impressed with the simple elegance of the hotel. The Georgian Terrace was definitely for the elite. Rooms 614 and 616 were directly across from the elevator. The smaller number was to the left so he went in that direction. He knocked gently on the door of 604 and waited. He heard movement inside and stepped back.

The door swung open and a small, frail man in his seventies, stood there nervously. He was immaculately dressed in a dark blue, pinstriped suit. "Come on in, Sully," he said, his voice quivering. "...Been expecting you."

Sully wasn't sure what Elliot meant but it was definitely something to question while there. He stepped inside and found a chair. He sat silently as Elliot mixed a drink.

"Care for something?" Elliot asked.

"Nothing for me, thanks."

Elliot pulled over another chair and sat across from Sully. "I'm guessing this is about Jigs? Is that right?"

"I've got a problem, Mister Elliot…I've lost my memory…I don't remember the first thing about the last thirteen months."

"And you need someone to fill the gaps?"

"I was hoping *you* would."

"You're putting me in an awkward position by coming here, Sully …There are people who won't appreciate it if they find out."

"Just tell me what you feel comfortable with…I'll find out eventually anyway. All I want is a shove in the right direction. So far, everybody's been too terrified to talk to me. They think I'm poison. I'd like to know the reason behind it."

"What have you learned so far? Maybe I can add a little something."

"I know Charley Benson and Lyle Bradford were with you the night Jigs died. And you were the last people to talk to him that night. I understand it a was heated conversation…You want to tell me what that was about?"

"*You don't know?*" Elliot eyed him suspiciously.

"That's why I'm here. From the way things are shaping up, I figure money was involved somehow."

Elliot was quiet a moment, considering how to approach the subject without exposing himself to danger. He wanted to help Sully, but at the same time, he had to look out for his own interests. He did not like the possible consequences that could follow. "You're right," he finally said. "We were *all* upset with Jigs that night, and it *was* about money—a *lot* of money."

"Did Jigs owe you guys?"

"He didn't owe us the money, Sully. But, there's more to it than that…Let me go back further. Do you remember anything about the Gerklin fight?"

"Not a thing! I was told that I took a beating for five rounds, then caught him in the sixth. They said he was out of it for forty-five minutes."

"*That's it?*" Elliot pressed. "You know nothing about the odds, or any of the heavy betting that went on?"

"I heard the odds were three to one against me and people won big bucks when they bet on me."

"You aren't aware of Jigs losing a small fortune on the fight?"

"Jigs bet against me?" Sully said sheepishly. It was like a slap in the face. "Why would he do that?"

"It's nothing but speculation and I prefer keeping it to myself...I'll say this: He was so sure of the outcome he came to Benson, Bradford and myself before the fight, and told us to go with Gerklin."

"That's what you were arguing about?"

"Basically! We just couldn't understand why Jigs had enticed us to bet against you...He was so sure of things."

"Had he ever done anything like that before?"

"No! He would never steer a friend wrong."

"You think Jigs was your friend then."

"Positively! When he insisted on covering our losses, I knew something had gone terribly wrong. He was in a state of shock...He had talked for days about that fight being the big one...How you two would be on easy street. When you knocked that palooka out, everything changed."

"Jigs was already on easy street," Sully said. "Why would he say that?"

"I'm sure it was just an expression," Elliot offered. "He was like that when he scored big or expected to. It was the excitement of winning that made him go."

"How much were you guys out?"

"Close to thirty-five grand apiece, but Jigs was out a lot more than that. When we followed him into the restroom that night, he had a money belt crammed with thousands of dollars. But, he said we'd have to wait for ours; that was for someone else."

"Then he had the money on him when we left the hotel," Sully said softly. "He was supposed to have a lot of jewelry also…Did you see that?"

"…I'm not sure, but when he took his jacket off, there was a leather pouch hanging over one shoulder and under the arm. It could have been jewelry. I didn't give it much thought at the time."

"What about the cops? Did they find anything? Virginia Moran said they knew about the money *and* the jewels."

"I probably shouldn't say this, but those two detectives investigating the crime never mentioned the money or the jewelry. They focused on who Jigs had talked to that night. It was never mentioned in the papers either."

"Did they question everybody at length, or did they make short work of it?"

"Oh, they took their time…And they were pretty rough about it. When they didn't get a right answer, they got ticked off. They finally searched everybody and confiscated what we had on us. It took three lawyers two months to get our money back."

"Why would they do that? Witnesses had to have told them you hadn't left the poolroom. There's no way you could have had anything to do with the murder."

"Well, they did, for whatever reason…And got away with it."

"The cops who questioned you; was it Smith and Jones?"

"Yeah, but there were more. The place was full of detectives… How'd you know about those two?"

"I'd heard that they were the first to arrive at the hotel…Are they the ones who've been here? The clerk said some cops have visited you at times."

"They've been here *too* often if you want the truth. They act like I know something about the murder."

"Did they say specifically what they were after?"

"Never did! Actually, their questions gave me the impression that they already had the answers. It was like they were hiding something and they wanted to find out if I knew what it was. They harassed me to the point, I thought of leaving town."

"One more thing before I leave: What do you know about a guy named Judson Fletcher?"

"He's a dangerous man," Elliot said softly. "And he definitely has something against me. Our paths have crossed a few times since Jigs' death, and every time, he and his friend act as if they want to cut my throat. It's like I did something to offend them…For the life of me, I don't know what."

"I was told I know this Fletcher…You got any idea how?"

Elliot hesitated. "…About a year ago, he came to town brandishing a lot of cash. He hung around the gyms all the time, betting on the club fights. He didn't seem to care how much he won or lost. He saw you in the ring one day and talked to Jigs about promoting a fight. He was going to match you with a known heavyweight. Jigs was all for it, *but*, you didn't cotton to Fletcher or his pal. I was standing right there when you told them to keep their distance. Neither one of them liked it much, but they weren't about to tangle with you. At any rate, a couple of days after that, I saw some hoods huddled around Jigs at Big Town's. Somebody said they were from Chicago. A month later, you were the main event at the sports arena. You knocked your guy out in the third round. That was the beginning. You knocked two more top contenders out after that. Those thugs always seemed to show up right after you fought, and then, they'd take off in a few days. I'll tell you something else: Fletcher isn't so tough around those people. If he'd have worn lipstick, their butts would've been blood red."

"You figure he's just an errand boy then?"

"I'm sure of it! But that doesn't mean anything…He's not very high up the totem pole, but he still demands a lot of respect. Ain't no doubt about it; Fletcher and that friend of his would kill at the drop of a hat."

"What about the Gerklin fight? Does anything unusual or out of place come to mind? Everything seems to focus on that one fight."

"There was a lot going on that wasn't right; you could smell it. Those people from Chicago that always left a couple of days after your fights? This time, they didn't. They hung around town for over a week. I don't know what it was, but they were sure stirred up about something."

"Money is the only one thing that draws that kind of attention," Sully said. "Somebody *snookered* them and they were after who was responsible."

"You think it was Jigs?"

"It doesn't sound like him, but it was his nature to chase a buck. He might have been caught up in the middle of something and couldn't turn loose."

"You think they lost money and blamed Jigs?"

"It might have happened that way," Sully said, standing to leave. "But if they killed him because of it, this is far from over."

"You'd best be careful," Elliot said, following Sully to the door. "There's only two of them around now, but there's an army of 'em in Chicago."

"I appreciate the talk, Mister Elliot," Sully said, stepping into the hallway. "And don't worry about this—it won't go any further...I wouldn't cause you any trouble."

"Never crossed my mind, kid...Jigs was my friend too."

# CHAPTER THIRTEEN

Sully stood patiently on the verandah in front of the Georgian Terrace Hotel. He was shivering from the cold wind that cut unceasingly through his jacket. He was at the top of the steps an hour and Fred still wasn't there. Since Fred had no way of contacting him or if there were unforeseen problems, it might be hours before there was an explanation. He fought the cold winds by rubbing his arms and stomping his feet until the chill forced him back inside. In the lobby, it was a half-hour before his limbs thawed. Ready for another trek outside, he moved quickly across the street to the bus stop at the Fox Theater. The time was 12:25. He had until one o'clock before the last bus left the downtown area. He was a half an hour away from being stranded since the streets were barren of taxies. When a bus pulled up minutes later, he boarded and dropped the token in the box. He sat on the empty bus behind the driver. "Looks like a slow night," he said, rubbing his legs and arms.

"Yeah," the driver replied. "The last run is usually like this. You're the only passenger I've had since leaving Buckhead while ago. When I drop you off, that's it for me...I'm heading for the barn...You gonna transfer when we get to Five Points?"

"I'm taking the trolley to Grant Park if there's time."

The driver looked at his watch as they edged past Baker Street. "You should make it; it'll be twenty minutes before they make their last run."

"Is it always this slow at night? I figured there'd be more people."

"There's a few stragglers, never more than that. When I do have a load this late, it's a bunch of drunks goin' home."

"Why does your last ride stop in downtown and the Grant Park ride doesn't?"

"The Grant Park run ends a couple of miles from the barn. The driver just heads for Dekalb Avenue when he's through."

Sully stepped to the front exit as the bus approached Marietta Street. He steadied himself by holding onto the pole, "Enjoy your night," he told the driver as the bus came to a halt.

The driver ripped off a transfer ticket. "Might need this; it'll save a token."

Sully took the transfer, stepped from the bus, then shivered when the wind hit him. He began walking briskly toward Hunter Street.

He rounded the corner at Hunter and trotted slowly toward the last bus parked a block away. He looked at his watch; there was still five minutes. He stepped up on the sidewalk and slowed to a walk. When the vehicle pulled away, he whistled shrilly. The bus stopped and the front door opened with a whoosh. He stepped up inside the bus and handed the driver the transfer. "Pulling out early, aren't you?" he said, not trying to hide his displeasure at almost being stranded.

"Not by my watch," the driver countered evenly.

Sully looked at the driver's watch when he put both hands on the steering wheel; it was clearly five till one. He chose to ignore the incident and looked for a seat midway of the bus. He closed his eyes and laid his head on the back of the seat. The realization of doing too much, too quickly, came down hard. He was not adjusting well to the lack of strength or stamina. He tried to get back what was once taken for granted, too quickly. The progress was far too minimal to be appreciated.

Sully sat upright when the bus started down the steep hill on Atlanta Avenue. He was two blocks from home. He pulled the cord when the bus approached Marion Avenue. He stepped to the curb when the bus came to a halt. He didn't move for a moment, blinded by the pitch-black night. Dimness of the crescent moon, added to the broken streetlight above, forced him to wait until his vision adjusted. He immediately became suspicious of the streetlight being out. It had worked perfectly the night before. His hand shot into his jacket seeking the .45 there. He jerked the weapon out, cocked it, and then eased it to his side. An automobile sitting conspicuously two doors up from his house had caught his attention. He began walking slowly up the opposite sidewalk, never taking his eyes from the vehicle.

Sully saw fogged over windows in the car, which meant the car had to be occupied. He made his move just feet from the parked car. He sprang across the street and jerked the door open. He grabbed the man in the driver's seat, threw him to the pavement, then viciously jammed the .45 against the back of man's head. "You've got one second before this thing goes off! Who are you and what do you want?"

"Dammit Sully, knock it off," a quivering voice said.

"G.W.? What are you doing here? For God's sake, man, I came within an inch of putting a bullet in your brain."

"I was waiting on you...I dozed off."

"Did you bust the street light?"

"I had to...It lit things up. I didn't want to be seen."

"I saw you."

"Yeah, but you had reason to be looking...You got even more of a reason now."

"Has this got anything to do with Fred's not showing up tonight?"

"I don't know nothing about no Fred," G.W. said, then stood up and brushed himself off. He sat down in the automobile. "Get in the car! I'm getting nervous out here in the open...I feel like a sitting duck."

Sully walked around the car, opened the door and sat down. "Sitting duck?" he asked. "What are you talking bout?"

G.W. rolled down the small hill and cranked the car as it moved. "...Red Ward's missing...He never showed at the poolroom today. Something's happened to him...I went by his house tonight. The car was gone and there wasn't any lights."

Sully thought for a minute. "I talked to Red before I saw you last night. He was going to talk to some people for me. I told him to forget it, but he wouldn't listen. Besides, I'm not sure I want these people to go away."

"If you knew who he talked to, you wouldn't say that."

"How do you know who they are?"

"Because they came looking for me tonight, that's how...And I know why. Somehow or other, they squeezed it out of Red that you came to the hotel looking for me. You know they went after you when you got out of the hospital, don't you? When I sold you those forty-fives, it cut the odds down...That's what turned 'em in my direction."

"...Are you sure about this?"

"Yeah, I'm sure! Judson Fletcher and that goon friend of his came into York's place looking for me tonight. I knew nothing about it until I stepped in the door. When I was told about their coming after me, I damn near panicked. Up until then, I figured Red hadn't opened the poolroom because of family troubles or something. He had to tell 'em about me selling you those guns. It's the only way he could've saved his skin."

"You think they busted him up?"

"They're mean ones, Sully. I wouldn't put anything past them. That's why I'm leaving town. I got a sister in Florida; she's been wanting me to visit for a long time. I'm going to take her up on it until this blows over."

"How're you fixed for money? I've got a few bucks if you need it."

"I got a couple of hundred on me, but the quicker I see this town in the rear view mirror ain't too soon. You've always been straight with me, Sully...That's the reason I've hung around tonight. You need to know what's going on. I've told you, now I'm taking off after I take you home."

Sully pulled out his billfold and withdrew close to two hundred dollars. "Take this," he said, putting it in G.W.'s shirt pocket. "We can square up when you get back."

G.W. looked sheepish. "You know I'm good for it, Sully...Under any other circumstances, I wouldn't take it. But things are different now...Hey man, I've got a couple grand in the bank that I'm too scared to go after."

"If you'll hang around till morning, *I'll* go with you to the bank. If Fred shows, he can tag along."

"Thanks anyway," G.W. said, pulling up in front of Sully's house. "If those two catch me, especially in your company, my life ain't worth a plug nickel...I'm heading south, right now."

Sully stepped out onto the sidewalk and watched G.W. speed off into the night. He suddenly felt vulnerable standing alone in front of his house. He became even more unsettled when he thought that Red's disappearance might be his fault. He began to wonder how Red knew *who* to go see in the first place. A lot of people knew a lot of things, but nobody was talking. He had to find somebody willing to open up to him. His work was cut out for him.

# CHAPTER FOURTEEN

Sully sat on the side of the bed with swollen eyes dreading the day ahead. His body was aching from lack of sleep. Red Ward's disappearance, combined with not hearing from Fred, had him tossing the entire night. He did finally doze off somewhere around three in the morning, but awoke a few hours later with a splitting headache. He quickly downed four aspirin, followed it with a cup of coffee, then dressed and left the house. He walked briskly up Confederate Avenue heading for the nearest telephone at the drug store. He stepped into the drug store after the four-block walk and laid a half-dollar on the counter. "I need some change for the phone," he said, then added as an after thought, "and fix me a cherry coke." It had been a long time since the delicious drink had quenched his thirst.

The soda jerk handed him forty-five cents in nickels and a cherry coke. "Appreciate the business, champ," he said smiling.

Sully, not thinking of himself as a celebrity, slid the coins into his pocket and took a small sip of the drink. "Do I know you?" he asked. "...Been a little forgetful lately; I have a hard time remembering people."

"You've been here a few times, but that's about it," the soda jerk said. "We've been neighbors five years and I guess this is the first time we've spoke...I read about your troubles after that last fight; how you were laid up in the hospital and all that. Good to see you back; we were rooting for you."

Embarrassed by the unexpected attention, Sully thanked him, then stepped outside to the phone booth.

He laid the phone book up on the small counter, then began looking for the hospitals. Grady Memorial was the first hospital to call since Atlanta directed all its emergencies there. Red Ward had not been admitted there over the past forty-eight hours. The next call was to Crawford Long; Red wasn't there either. He made subsequent inquiries to St. Joseph's, Piedmont, Emory, and the Veteran's Hospital. Every call produced the same result. If Red *was* in a hospital, it had to be outside of Atlanta. He stepped back inside for more change and began making long distance calls to the hospitals away from the city. He gave up after checking the Spalding Hospital in Griffin and the Newnan Hospital. He made one final call to the City of Atlanta Police Department.

On the fifth ring, a deep voice answered. "Atlanta Police Department"

"Missing Persons, please," Sully said.

"What's the problem?"

"I have a friend who came up missing a few days ago. I was wondering if it's been reported? Or if you know what happened to him?"

"The name?"

"Mine or his?"

"The missing person's!"

"Red Ward," Sully said. "I don't have the address but it's somewhere in Hapeville;

"Your name?"

Sully hesitated a moment. "...Willy Walker," he finally said, reluctant to give his right name.

"Address?"

Sully gave him a fictitious number and street on the north side.

"Hang on a minute," the officer said.

A few minutes later, someone else came on the line. "Mister Walker!" a voice said pleasantly. "I understand you're inquiring about your friend, Red Ward. Well, if I could get you to..."

Sully cradled the phone softly, hanging up on Homicide Detective Smith. The only reason homicide would field calls for a missing person was if they were dead. He had no intention of talking to Smith under those circumstances. He would wait until things were more to his liking.

Sully walked up the street to the bus stop and waited patiently for the next bus. When the bus arrived, he stepped on board, dropped a token in the box, then found a seat and sat down. He got off downtown at Houston Street, then walked quickly to five points. Then he headed east on Auburn Avenue, hoping he could remember where the Gregory home was. Eight blocks later, he found the alley he was looking for. It was an unpaved alley with a lot of muddy potholes; there was no doubt it was the right place. He walked through the mired mud carefully, trying to keep his shoes clean; the attempt was without success. Just as he approached the Gregory driveway, the Buick at the rear of the house came into view.

Sully stepped onto the porch and glanced at the mailbox by the door. *Alice Gregory*, was printed neatly on it. He knocked on the door.

Shuffling footsteps were heard inside just before the dead bolt slid open. The door partially opened. A gentle voice asked, "Yes?"

"It's Sully Hawken, Mrs. Gregory. I'm looking for Fred."

The door opened further. "Please come in, Mister Hawken," she said and offered him a seat. "You probably haven't heard what happened 'round here last night."

"No ma'am," Sully said, sitting. "When Fred didn't show up at the hotel, I took a bus home...Is he in trouble?"

She offered coffee or tea and Sully politely declined both. He had one thing on his mind at that moment, and that was to find out about Fred. He leaned forward on the sofa. "About last night, Mrs. Gregory?" he urged, "If I'm going to do something, you need to tell me about it."

She eased back in the chair and sighed. "I don't think you can help him, Mister Hawken...The police gon" make sure of that...When he came home last night, he put your car out back so's nobody would bother it. Then he came in to talk for a spell. He give me some money and said he see me in a couple of days. We sat 'round 'bout half an hour, talking 'bout one thing then t'other, then some folks started making a lot of noise outside. Fred went out to see what all the commotion was about, and 'fore I knows it, he on the ground in handcuffs. The police shoves him in a car and starts calling him a murderer...My boy ain't done nothin' like that, Mister Hawken; he ain't no killer. If he was, he wouldn't have been so happy when he come in the door last night. I would've seen it on his face."

"For what it's worth, I don't think he killed anybody either. Something smells here, and I intend to find out what...How many policemen were there and what did they look like?"

"They's four or five in uniform and two who weren't...And they's all white."

"Those not in uniform? Tell me about them?"

"My boy got into a fight with them right off."

"Did they say anything before they started fighting?"

"Nothing I could understand," she said, shaking her head from side to side. "They's too much hollerin' an' screamin' going on."

"Do you remember anything about the two detectives Fred was fighting with? What they looked like?"

"I don't see too well at night," she said, "and it *was* dark... Everybody was moving so fast, it was hard to tell what anybody looked like. 'Bout the only thing I recollect is, one was tall and t'other was short."

Sully knew who he was dealing with now. "I'm going to Decatur Street shortly, Mrs. Gregory," he said. "Maybe I can get this straightened out. I have an idea what's behind it and why it's happening." Sully stepped out to the porch, completely forgetting about the Buick in the driveway. He was distracted by the thought of Fred being held out of vindictiveness.

"Mister Hawken," a soft voice behind him said. "You'll need these." She handed him the car keys. "...Fred left 'em on the dresser."

Sully took the keys and smiled at his forgetfulness. "It *would* be hard driving without them, wouldn't it?"

# CHAPTER FIFTEEN

Sully parked across from the Decatur Street station, then stepped from the car and put a coin in the meter. He glanced at his watch; it was ten after two. He ran to the other side of the street, dodging the dangerous traffic. Two patrolmen took notice of the complete disregard for the laws on jaywalking. He waved as if he knew them. "How's it going, ol' man?" he shouted and kept running.

The officers looked quizzically at each other. "You know him?" one asked. "…Probably got us confused with somebody else."

Sully walked up the marble steps smiling; a few distracting words had avoided a jaywalking ticket. He entered the lobby and walked toward a double door entrance that led into a large chamber. He stepped into the beehive of activity, full of both uniformed and plain-clothed policemen. A sign was on the counter by the entrance; it directed all visitors to the desk sergeant. He stepped to the counter and rapped softly to gain the attention of the officer there.

The sergeant gave Sully a nasty look like he had been unnecessarily disturbed. It was several minutes before he looked up again. "Okay, now what can I do for you?" he asked nastily.

"I need to talk to someone in Missing Persons."

The sergeant pointed to the rear of the room. "Against the wall," he said. "Peters handles those."

Sully made his way through the throng of people and quickly found Detective Peter's nameplate on a desk. He looked around and seeing nothing but uniformed policemen, took a seat and waited.

Peters walked up several minutes later and sat behind the desk. "Sorry to keep you waiting," he said, thrusting his hand out. "I'm Peters! Sarge says you want to talk to me about something."

"I have a friend who's missing," Sully said. "I was just wondering if you knew anything…Or maybe check around and see if he's all right?"

"How long has he been gone?"

"Just a couple of days, but…"

"That's kind of quick to consider him missing," Peters said. "We usually find those guys off on a drunk or laying up somewhere with a woman…They usually show up on the third or fourth day, wanting to apologize to everybody…I'd give it a few days if I were you."

"Red wouldn't do that," Sully said. "And he certainly wouldn't up and disappear without telling anybody."

Peters stared at him as if it were all a bother. "What's his name?" he asked. "I'll see what I can do."

"Red Ward! He lives in Hapeville…I'm not sure of the address."

"Wait here," Peters said, then walked away without giving Sully a chance to explain that he was pressed for time.

Sully watched as Peters moved across the crowded room until he was no longer in sight. Turning back around, he relaxed, expecting to be kept waiting for a while. Peters returned a few minutes later with Detectives Smith and Jones, and for some reason, he was not surprised.

Peters stood to the side, extracting himself from the conversation as the lanky Smith took control. The heftier Jones sat on the edge of the desk.

A sarcastic smirk came across Jones' face. "We've been looking for you."

Sully ignored the remark, noticing both of the homicide detectives had numerous cuts and bruises on their faces. Fred had probably worked them over before being taken down. Jones was the worse of the two; both eyes were noticeably blackened and his trying to hide them with sunglasses tended to make him look foolish. Smith, on the other hand, had one eye slightly darkened underneath and a large bruise on his cheek. He made no attempt to conceal the wounds.

"You listening to me?" Jones asked sarcastically.

"I'm sorry," Sully said politely. "I wasn't paying attention…Your face had me wondering what happened."

"I said, we've been looking for you," Jones growled, then added quickly, "and what happened to my face ain't none of your damn business."

Sully kept the innocent face. "I'd have to say, if you were looking for me, you didn't go about it the right way. I'm *not* that hard to find…I'm home most nights and you know exactly where I live."

"Who says I *know* where you live?" Jones barked.

Sully was no longer amused by the arrogance of the detective. "My landlords," he snarled, *"that's who!"* They said you two ransacked my place while I was in the hospital. If you'd have told me what you were looking for to begin with, I probably could've saved you a lot of trouble."

"Don't you get smart with me, you…"

Smith cut him off mid-sentence. "Shut up, Jonesy," he snarled. "I'll do the talking from here."

Jones protested vigorously before being stopped the second time. It was done this time by a chilling stare; it was not an idle threat.

Sully logged that information in the back of his mind; it was quite clear who the mastermind of this duo was. If there ever were a confrontation with these two, Smith would definitely be the one to deal with first.

Smith didn't waste words. "We fished Red Ward out of the Chattahoochee late yesterday. Preliminary reports from the coroner indicate he was beaten badly; but that wasn't what killed him. His lungs were full of water; he drowned. When they got him on the bank, his arms and legs were hanging loose. The person who did it had thrown him in the river alive. Whoever did it tied a weight around his waist to sink him, but it came undone before he touched bottom. If it hadn't, it would've been weeks before we found him…Maybe longer? No telling how long he would've stayed down."

"I get this feeling that somehow you're trying to tie me to this… And what's this about charging Fred Gregory with murder?"

"You know about that, huh?"

"I found out from his mother; she's pretty upset about it…Who's he supposed to have killed?"

Smith looked sternly at him. "Red Ward! And the fact that you and Gregory talked to Ward the night before he disappeared makes you both prime suspects."

"If you've locked Fred up for the murder, why aren't I in there with him?"

"Because Gregory is booked with more than murder."

Sully's face turned crimson. "What else are you charging him with?"

"Other than 1$^{st}$ degree homicide, drunk driving, speeding, running a dozen red lights, drunk and disorderly, resisting arrest, six counts of assault and *attempted* murder. There's another charge of murder pending until we get more proof."

Sully stared at the detective in disbelief. "...We both know this is nothing but garbage. Any lawyer in town could make a meal out of this in court. They'd cut this to shreds the very first day...And what about this second murder? Who's he supposed to have killed now?"

"A friend of yours: G.W. Spence."

Sully's mouth flew open with surprise. "G.W.'s dead? When?"

"We're not sure yet, but we've learned that after you talked with Ward that night at his pool room, you went to the Hanger Hotel and hooked up with Spence. Neither one of them has been seen since. You and Gregory were the last ones with them and that puts you at the top of the suspect list."

Sully relaxed. "There's nothing wrong with G.W. He's left Atlanta...He had it in his head somebody's out to get him."

"When did he tell you this?"

"Last night! He stopped by before he left, and told me about Red disappearing. He said that if he didn't go while he had the chance, the same thing would happen to him...I gave him some money and he took off."

"That's kind of odd," Smith said sarcastically. "A man with thousands in a bank comes to you for money...How do you explain that?"

"He didn't come to me for money. I gave him what I had because he was afraid to go into Atlanta. I offered to help, but he wouldn't have any part of it. The last I saw of him, he was headed for Florida; he has a sister down there."

"And you don't know where, right?"

"I didn't want to know…If I did, I'd be put in a position to say where…He wouldn't like that, and neither would I."

"What about the guns you bought from Spence?" Smith asked. "Do you have one on you?"

Sully stood and raised his hands above his head. "Check for yourself," he said. "…I'm not that stupid."

Smith waved his hands, indicating for Sully to sit back down. "What about your car? You have anything in there?"

"It's out front on the other side of the street. It's a black '39 Buick, four door."

Smith looked at Jones. "Go see what you can find," he said curtly.

Jones left hurriedly, and Smith returned his focus to Sully. "Where are the guns, Hawken? You're not leaving here until I find out."

"Who told you I bought them in the first place?"

"The Hanger Hotel night clerk…Who do you think kept them stashed for Spence? The old man told us about your buying the .45s and ammo the minute I threatened to lock him up."

Sully thought desperately for an answer. "…I dropped both guns in the sewer. I figured it was a mistake to buy them, so I ditched them."

Smith looked at him doubtfully. "If you're yanking my chain, Hawken, you can *count* on everything in the book being thrown at you…We're in the process of checking out yours and Gregory's houses this very moment and if either of those pistols show up, you're paying the price."

Sully sat quietly for a moment. "…Tell me something?" he asked. "What were you looking for the first time you went into my house? There was nothing there that would help in your investigation."

"Nothing in particular. We were just trying to get a lead on what happened to you and Moran; that's all."

"…I guess I could have told you earlier, but there's somebody else who thinks I had something of value. The day I came out of a coma, somebody else broke into the house looking for something."

Smith looked surprised. "I wasn't aware of that," he said, then added quickly as if to cover up something. "It was probably kids."

"They weren't kids," Sully said. "Whoever did it was deliberate."

"What do you mean?"

"No kid alive would leave the house without snatching the few bucks I had in the cookie tin. The way I see it, whoever broke in wanted to go through my personal papers. They were laid out on the kitchen table along with the money...The money's still there. Whoever was there was looking for something specific. When they didn't find it, they vandalized the place trying to make it look like kids."

The phone rang just as Jones walked up to the desk. Smith picked up the receiver. "This is he," he said, then went silent. "Okay?... Yeah, I got it." He hung up and turned to Jones who was puffing feverishly. "What'd you find?"

"Nothing! It's clean."

Smith looked at Sully. "All right, Hawken, you're off the hook for a while. That call was from the guys that I sent to your place...You can thank your lucky stars they didn't find anything."

"I *told* you what I did with the guns," Sully said boldly, but still wondered how Fred managed to hide the pistol he gave him.

"Just exactly what sewer did you dump the guns in?" Smith asked pointedly. "We're putting somebody in it right now."

Sully had to think fast; a thoughtful look came on his face. "The best I remember, it was on Edgewood...Somewhere around Prior Street."

"We'd better find them, Hawken. If we don't, I'm coming after you."

Sully stood to leave. "My time's run out on the meter; don't need to break any more laws," he said with a smirk. "...Oh, yeah, what about Fred?"

"He stays where he's at," Jones butted in. "He ain't going nowhere as long as I got anything to do with it."

Sully looked at Smith. "Is that the last word?"

"Looks like it," Smith replied. "He's *still* mad about what happened."

Sully just shook his head. "Have you ever told him that if he weren't such a jerk, people wouldn't want to kick his head in all the time?"

Jones became furious at that remark. He withdrew his slapjack and began pounding it hard in the palm of his hand.

Sully did not see humor in the tirade. He told Smith, "If Fred's not on the street in seventy-two hours, I coming back with a lawyer."

Jones kicked the wall and cursed.

Sully left the police station after that and quickly stepped across the street to his car. A small slip of paper was under the windshield wiper; it was a ticket for letting the meter run out. He got into the car, leaned forward, then pulled out what had been ripping into his back for an hour. He laid the cumbersome .45 on the passenger seat, then drove directly to Five Points. The sobering thought that Smith and Jones weren't playing around anymore, hit him hard. They were in the process of hanging a murder rap on him. Then it all came together: Not only was Red brutally beaten and thrown into the river alive, something else had happened: Somebody had filled him full of .45 slugs as well. That was why Smith and Jones were so desperate for the weapons he got from G.W. Somehow they were going to link the bullets in Red to one of those weapons…Those two cops were playing a deadly game, and from the looks of things, he was the door prize. They were after his hide and would achieve success using whatever means possible. There *had* to be a purpose for wanting him out of the picture so badly. Sully needed to know what that reason was.

# CHAPTER SIXTEEN

Sully didn't like walking out of the Decatur Street jail without Fred, but there was little choice in the matter. The undiscovered .45 automatic he pulled from his pants now meant a trip to jail. He had to put as much distance as he could from the station, and do it without hesitation. If he and Fred were both behind bars, nothing would be accomplished. Not only would it hinder finding Jigs' killer, he would be put in a position of facing trumped-up charges. Entering the Five Point's intersection, he did a U-turn sharply onto Edgewood Avenue. When he reached the Pryor Street intersection, he quickly discovered what was necessary: A manhole by the curb. On the opposite side of the street was a wide drain with an iron grill to catch the larger debris. He double-parked the car, jammed the forty-five under his belt and then crossed the street rapidly to the manhole. He stood on the sidewalk and then bent over the drain and made sickening sounds like he was sick. Pedestrians turned away from the nauseating sight. Sully then dropped the .45 in the drain. A splash fifteen feet down told him the gun had hit bottom.

He worked back across through traffic, wanting to get away from the scene before the police had a chance to spot him. At least he had accomplished getting one of the weapons where it was supposed to be. Just as he pulled away, a glance in the rearview mirror revealed a number of squad cars pulling into the intersection. Their tires were screaming from braking so hard. The police immediately closed off all traffic. Sully thought they would easily find his gun, but what had Fred done with his? A lot depended on what happened to that gun and where it was.

Sully drove south down Boulevard Drive some minutes later, then slowed to a crawl in front of the Georgia Baptist Hospital. He parked across the street and then began walking toward a small, one-story building a block away. When he reached the structure of small businesses, he scanned the signs of the establishments. Garan T. Jewels, Attorney At Law, appeared on a window. He found what he wanted.

Sully stepped from the sidewalk directly into the attorney's office. He quickly canvassed the interior. It was dark, musty, and the distinct odor of cigar smoke burnt his nostrils. Two desks were prominent: The one in front for the secretary and another one behind an antique handrail in the dark. The rail was purposely there to prevent people from venturing further uninvited.

Sully spoke to the secretary, working diligently at the first desk. "Is Mister Jewels here?" he asked her.

"Garan!" she deadpanned over her shoulder. "You gonna be around long enough to talk to this guy?"

Sully looked to the rear of the darkened office and tried to visualize the person seated at the other desk. He could make out a reclined shadowy figure with his legs resting on the desk. A small glow came from a cigar each time it was drawn on. A desk lamp was switched on and the figure sat upright. "Come in, Hawken," Jewels said with familiarity. "Been expecting you...Virginia said you'd be by."

Sully didn't recall meeting the attorney, but with a year of his life blotted out, it was possible that their paths had crossed...

Garan T. Jewels wasted no time in retrieving a folder full of legal documents from the top desk drawer. He spread the papers out and handed Sully a pen. "Everywhere there's an X, sign," he said. "I'll take care of everything else tomorrow. You can pick up your check then...After you put your signature on these, I'm calling it a day."

Sully laid the pen on the desk and stood. "Then, we'll wait until you *do* have time. Actually, it's not the reason I came by...I need your help on another matter."

The lawyer smiled. "...Read the documents, and if you're satisfied, sign them. If not, I'll make the changes you like...If it will ease your suspicion, I had Jigs' trust a long time before this tragedy. So relax, I'm only doing what he asked."

Sully sat back down, then began reading and signing. A look of confusion crossed his face as he signed a document. "There's nothing here about a fee...Why is that?"

"There isn't one," Jewels replied. "It was taken care of beforehand." He reached in a drawer, withdrew a checkbook, and began writing a check. He handed it to Sully when through. It was for fifteen thousand dollars.

"This is a lot of money," Sully said, viewing the check. "You sure this is right?  These are big numbers."

"It's right!  Trust me!" Jewels said, then handed him more papers. "This document verifies you've received the inheritance...This one is necessary for the IRS." He handed Sully the copies he had already signed then slid two more across the desk, along with a large envelope. "This is the title to the Buick and the tag receipt."

Sully folded the documents and placed them in the envelope. "What about the help I asked for earlier?" he asked.  "Are you available?"

"Well, I am a lawyer...I don't see why not."

"I should warn you up front; it could get sticky."

Jewels smiled.  "The stickier, the better...My reputation as a person who gouges the establishment precedes me.  It's how I gained such a loathing over the years."

"I didn't know people disliked you so much...Maybe I've got the wrong lawyer?"

Jewels smiled broadly.  "I am *adored* by my clients," he said flatly. "The people who don't are the ones I oppose in court."

Sully grinned at the boisterous lawyer.  It was easy to see why Jigs chose him over other high-profiled attorneys.  Garan T. Jewels not only had charisma, but thoroughly enjoyed doing his job.  He was a poor man's dream.

"Tell me about your dilemma," Jewels asked seriously for the first time.  "Perhaps we can do something about this tonight."

"It's a long story."

"It's more challenging that way."

Sully eased back in the chair.  "The first thing you should know is, it's for a Negro friend...I don't know if it makes any difference, but..."

Jewels interrupted him.  "It doesn't matter in the least...It only makes the knife cut deeper into a bigot's belly.  Actually, it's an edge. That sort of thing creates anger in some people, which in turn, brings on a multitude of errors, usually in my favor. No, Mister Hawken, it does not bother me...Please continue."

Sully immediately told him the story of Fred's troubles, about the guns that were purchased, the disposal of one of them, and about the one he hoped Fred had hidden. He then said why he thought that Red Ward was shot with a forty-five caliber weapon.

Jewels listened attentively as the tale unwound, but his interest wasn't fully aroused until the charges against Fred were mentioned. The questions were demanding after that. "Let's get this straight," he said. "Gregory, was at home for a full thirty minutes before the police arrived, correct?"

"According to his mother...I haven't talked to him."

"Then, who in Heaven's name saw all these traffic violations? It wasn't the police; they would have followed him to his doorstep and arrested him on the spot. If there were witnesses other than the police, they would have had to trail Gregory to the house. On both accounts, someone should have recognized the car Gregory was driving. They didn't! That indicates only one thing: The police involved are lying...When they first arrived on the scene, they had no idea what kind of vehicle Gregory was driving. If they had, the Buick in the driveway would have been impounded. That one item eliminates the police as viable witnesses, as well as private citizens."

"That takes care of the traffic violations, but what about the other charges? Can you do anything about them?"

"Well, let's see—Resisting Arrest; a misdemeanor. He can be released on bond for that. The same goes for the assault charge. As far as attempted murder being a charge, that's a joke. They'll be thrown out post haste. The count of murder may be something different...Let's talk about that."

"I can only tell you that Fred was by my side for two days after we left Red's pool room. He would have never left me alone in bed."

"Can you account for any of that time? Could you provide someone to verify that you and Gregory were at your home the day that Ward was killed?"

Sully thought a minute. "It might be difficult," he admitted. "I slept around the clock that day."

"What about neighbors, friends, acquaintances? Could anyone have stopped by to check on you? Someone who could say without a doubt, that you and Gregory were at the house the entire time?"

"...I know people who will say anything I want them to."

"They'd lie for you?"

"In one sense, yes...In another, no."

"Very commendable, Hawken. You'd place your friend's welfare on the block by asking them to commit perjury."

"They wouldn't be committing a crime in my eyes. They'd be telling the truth as I told it to them."

"But," Jewels said smiling, "they would not have witnessed it personally."

"They know I wouldn't lie...That gives them a clear conscience."

"Not in the eyes of the law."

"Well, it's all I've got."

Jewels smiled. "It's all I need," he said, then stood and took his jacket from the rack. "...You have just hired yourself a lawyer."

"What about my phony witness?"

"We may not have to use him if things go as planned."

"Suppose my witness is a her?"

"That makes it even more intriguing," Jewels said, sliding an arm into the jacket. "Now, let's go get your friend out of jail."

# CHAPTER SEVENTEEN

When Sully and Garan Jewels arrived at the Decatur Street station, it was apparent that the lawyer was not a stranger there.  Every officer they met spoke to Jewels as they walked to the side of the building.  Sully was encouraged by the recognition; Fred's dismal predicament suddenly took a turn for the better.  Jewels quietly led the way down the cobblestone driveway in back where all in-coming prisoners are booked.  He opened the door, then stepped to the side and ushered Sully through first.

The officer behind the counter recognized Jewels immediately.  He reached across the counter and extended his hand.  "How are you doing, Garan?" he asked like they were old friends.  "What brings you out this late at night?"

"Got some business to take care of, Billy," Jewels said, taking the sergeant's hand.  "Like for you to meet a friend of mine...This is Sully Hawken."

The sergeant put out his hand.  "I'm Billy MacBurnette...You're that heavyweight fighter, aren't you?"

"I was!  But I don't fight anymore."

"I read about that," the sergeant said.  "That's a bad break...I thought a hometown boy was gonna be champ for a while."

"...I let a lot of people down."

"You didn't let *anybody* down, Hawken...It wasn't your fault some nut with a gun was on the prowl."

"I hope everybody feels that way," Sully said.

"They do!" the sergeant emphasized, turning to Jewels, "Now! What's going on?  You're not here to pass the time of day."

"As much as I'd like to say that," Jewels said elegantly, "I cannot...We are here in hope of extracting a guest."

"Who is it you're looking for?" the sergeant asked.

"A fellow by the name of Fred Gregory.  Who incidentally, is being held on numerous trumped-up allegations."

The sergeant grinned.  "Not everyone in the world is innocent, Garan.  I think you've picked yourself a loser this time."

"You can stop right there, Billy," Jewels said harshly, "That's a pretty damning statement for a man you know absolutely nothing about."

"I don't mean to be negative, Garan, but this guy didn't just run a red-light somewhere. He's in serious trouble. He's got five felony counts each for assault and attempted murder, plus murder-one hanging over his head. With *that* and all the traffic violations, he'll be lucky if he *ever* sees daylight again."

"I know a superior court judge who'll be more than happy to change your mind about that," Jewels said indignantly.

"You know what I think doesn't count, Garan...Besides, Gregory has already been transferred to the Tower. I don't think the governor could make the DA spring him."

Sully's eyes darted to Jewels. "What does that mean?"

"It *means* that Gregory has been sent to Fulton Tower. When a prisoner goes there, they are usually considered a flight risk and is denied bond.

"Isn't there anything we can do?" Sully asked.

"I'm afraid that Gregory has already been arraigned and is now waiting on a grand jury indictment. That would mean the DA has enough for a conviction...It's as Billy says: *Your friend is in a lot of trouble.*"

"How can they do that without legal council?"

Jewels tone turned serious with concern. "It was probably through a court appointed attorney. If a lawyer went along with this, he had to be handpicked by the prosecution. From the looks of things, I'd say the system has just declared war on Gregory...And it's just beginning."

MacBurnette threw his hands up. "I just work here...Don't blame me!"

"Maybe so, Billy, but until Fred Gregory is released from custody, every person in this building is my enemy."

Sully looked at Jewels. "What do we do now?"

"The first thing is to install me as Gregory's attorney. Then, we fire that attorney the courts provided him with." Jewels was testy as he addressed MacBurnette behind the desk. "How long has it been since Gregory was moved to the tower?"

"Quit acting like this is all my fault, Garan," the Sergeant said. "You know I have to do what I'm told...I can't go against orders."

"That's what they said at Nuremberg. If you remember, they hung those murderers...Now, how long has it been?"

"Two marshals came by and picked him up about an hour ago," MacBurnette said. "They were only here a few minutes...Sure didn't look right...I'll swear they acted like they were pulling a fast one..."

Jewels grabbed Sully by the arm and rushed him toward the door. "We have to move fast, Hawken. The courts have moved your friend for a precise reason: They intend to hide him somewhere in the system. It's there way of getting a death sentence without undue interference."

"Can it be stopped?" Sully asked. "...Don't they have to tell us where he is?"

"If I were his council, I would have the privilege of knowing."

"Then you have to be appointed his lawyer before they take him away, right?"

"If it's possible!" Jewels said, walking swiftly to the car. "If we're going to accomplish this, it has to be now...Before they have time to move him."

Sully was in the Buick and pulling away from the curb before Jewels was able to close the car door. He ignored all traffic laws during the six-block trip to Fulton Tower and made it in less than two minutes...They were just in time.

# CHAPTER EIGHTEEN

Sully stopped in the middle of the street and pointed to the front steps of the antiquated Fulton Tower Correctional Facility. "Over on the left," he barked to Jewels. "...It's Fred with those two policemen."

"Find a place to park," Jewels said, springing from the car. "And I want you over there as quickly as possible. Gregory will need a familiar face around when this starts."

Sully found a parking spot a quarter of a block away, then hurriedly trotted back to the loud confrontation taking place. The automobile was left precariously parked with the front end up on the curb.

Jewels turned just as Sully came breathlessly on the scene. "...And Mister Hawken will be witness to this transfer of council," he said loudly, flailing some papers in his hands.

Fred looked at Sully in total confusion. "What goin' on heah, boss?"

"You need to sign those papers, Fred," Sully said. "...I've asked Mister Jewels to be your lawyer."

"He's not *signing* anything," a marshal said harshly. "This is illegal and it's *not* going to happen. I have specific orders how this prisoner is to be handled and nobody's changing 'em."

"You are taking this man's constitutional rights away by denying him proper representation," Jewels exploded. "If you stop me from representing Mister Gregory, Superior Court Judge, Beuregard L. Langtree, will be notified within a matter of minutes...It's your call."

Jewels knew he had made his point when the officer blinked. "Over here, Hawken," he said, moving to Fred's side. "Give us your back..."

Sully turned around and Jewels laid the papers across his back.

Jewels handed Fred the pen. "Sign where the Xs are, Gregory, and you have a new attorney...It's that simple."

Fred had difficulty signing the documents with both arms and legs shackled and when through, the two marshals began mumbling. They grabbed Fred under the arms and drug him toward their vehicle.

"*Just* a minute," Jewels said strongly. "Our *business* is not over."

"We have a job to do, Jewels," one of the officers said disgustedly, "and we'd like to get it done sometime tonight."

Jewels handed Sully the papers. "Witness the signatures, Hawken. There are still a few questions to be answered before we are finished here."

Sully walked to the police car, placed the papers on the hood and began signing.

Jewels stared at the marshals menacingly, "Now, where do you intend to take my client under the cover of darkness? And let me *warn* you: If you deprive me of that information, it would be more erroneous than the offenses you've already committed."

"Tell him where he's going," one marshal said. "If they broke the law, it's no skin off our noses...Let the captain handle it."

"Sound advice," Jewels said, now thoroughly in control.

The marshal replied reluctantly, "We're taking him to the facility in Fairburn...It was supposed to be done secretly in an effort to protect him."

"Protect him?" Jewels ridiculed. "Just what is it you're supposed to be protecting him from?"

The officer shook his head in disgust. It was hard matching words with a lawyer such as Jewels. "As hard as it is for you to comprehend, Jewels, not everyone sees things as you do. To the people in the state of Georgia, this man has committed an unforgivable crime; he's murdered a white man. He's in constant danger of being taken from his cell by a mob and lynched. It's our job, regardless of what people think, to protect him to the best of our ability."

Jewels went uncharacteristically quiet. He had finally overstated his argument. "Sorry, gentlemen," he said, stepping back. "Sometimes, I tend to forget other people have something to contribute ...Please continue on your journey."

Sully watched the marshal's car speed off with Fred, "You think they're telling the truth about where they're taking him?"

"They didn't have a choice! The judge I mentioned is not imaginary. He's a very important jurist here in Atlanta. They know better than to go against his kind of power...Langtree and I go way back. He's one member of the bar I can count on for a favor."

"Sounds like you have something on him."

"I do," Jewels smiled. "But it's not as damning as he thinks. We just happened to attend the same college, that's all. He was caught partaking in an embarrassing incident but the charges were dropped when it went to court. He felt a stigma was attached to the situation and came to Georgia to escape the guilty stares. You can imagine the joy I felt when he became a superior court judge."

"What did he do?"

"It's best you don't know...If I told you, it might compromise my advantage." "Do you blackmail him?"

"I do *not!*" Jewels protested. "The only thing I have done that would be considered unethical is to smile knowingly while in his company. It makes him so nervous he does his best to avoid me. Most times he's relieved I just ask for a favor."

"And how often is that?"

"This would have been the third time."

"Over how long a period?"

"Seven years," Jewels said. "As you see, I do not bother him unless it's important...And for the record, I consider this an important item."

"I think I'm witnessing the dark and underhanded side of you," Sully said. "It may not be flagrant, but it's still there."

"Possibly, you're right," Jewels agreed without argument. "But sometimes, there's no alternative if you seek satisfactory results."

Sully sat down in the Buick and turned the ignition key. "Where to now?" he asked. "Do we head for Fairburn or call it a night?"

"I think Fairburn," Jewels said. "I need to confirm some things with Gregory before we venture further. It will give me something to start on early in the morning. And, at the moment, I feel time is of the essence. I happen to agree completely with what the marshal said: Gregory's life is definitely in danger."

"You really think somebody would drag him out of jail like that?"

Jewels was quiet a moment. "Honestly, I fear the police more than the people who would go to such extremes. I will say this: I don't doubt a word you've said so far, but if everything you've revealed *is* accurate, a lot of policemen would be lying. The size of such a conspiracy would have to be almost unbelievable."

"I don't care what the number is, it's *exactly* what's happening."

"I estimate the number of policemen it would take at six!" Jewels said. "But what's their motive? Why would so many decide to crush Gregory for no apparent reason other than prejudice? There's no explanation."

"Maybe Fred's just the springboard and they intend to drag me into it somehow?"

"That's a possibility, but again, the question of *why* arises. There's no doubt Smith and Jones have designated you as their primary target, but why didn't they go after you from the beginning? Why even *bother* with Gregory?"

"Maybe it's like I said, they just settled for Fred right now... There's something else that needs looking into while we're at it: The proof concerning that .45 slug they found in Red's body."

"You think they may try to tie it to the one you threw in the sewer?"

"Exactly! But I think I know where the .45 is that *really* killed him."

"What are you talking about?"

"Let me handle it," Sully said quietly. "If it doesn't turn out right, nothing's lost...Besides, you're better off not knowing."

"Is it illegal?"

"Somebody could get killed."

"Will it help our case?"

"Definitely!" Sully said, putting the car in gear.

"Then, by all means do it," Jewels said. "We'll deal with the illegalities as they surface. Now, on to Fairburn, Mister Hawken... Gregory is waiting."

# CHAPTER NINETEEN

Sully drove into the Town Square of Fairburn at a quarter to three in the morning. He had taken route 29 all the way from Atlanta before turning at the highway 92 intersection. Jewels instructed him to head for the police station and park there. The building was half a block away.

"Think it's all right? There's nothing but cop cars there?"

"All they can do is tell us to move."

Sully agreed with that simple logic and pulled into the lot. Stepping from the car, he looked across the hood at Jewels. "How long do you think this will take?"

"Hopefully, not long," Jewels said gruffly. "I'm wearing down a bit; it's been a long day."

They entered the small two-story jail, and noticed quickly that it was no where equal to the facilities in Atlanta. The small front chamber they entered was barely furnished. Other than a few wood benches scattered around, a single desk was at the rear of the room.

A short, overweight policeman sat there with his head drooping. He nodded, then lazily looked up; he was almost asleep. Startled by the intrusion, he came to his feet surprisingly fast. His eyes were wide with excitement as his hand dropped to the .38 on his hip. He glared at Sully and Jewels. "What do you want this late at night?" he barked, wiping the sleep from his eyes.

"I'm Fred Gregory's attorney, Garan Jewels...We'd like to—"

"Ain't nobody here by that name," the officer said sharply.

"I suggest you re-check your night's business," Jewels said quietly. We are parked outside beside the vehicle that brought him here."

"I ain't checking nothing," the officer growled. "I said, he ain't here!"

"Young man!" Jewels said indignantly. "I am Fred Gregory's legal council. I have the right to talk to the man any time I choose. I will invoke that right whether you approve or not."

A marshal stepped through the side door just as the officer was about to respond. "I thought that sounded like you making all that noise...A little late for this, isn't it, Jewels? It could've have waited until tomorrow."

"My schedule doesn't have hours," Jewels shot back. "Now, explain it to this *officer* that I can see Gregory any time I choose."

"...Let 'em in, Buddy," the marshal said. "They've got legal passage."

"You said nobody was supposed to know..."

"I know what I said, but I didn't figure they would be here tonight. Lawyers aren't the kind to stay up all night; he fooled me."

"You still said it," the officer said, insisting it was a matter of right or wrong.

"I did, and I'm sorry for misleading you," the marshal said. "We'll straighten things out in the morning. Everybody here will know that Gregory can see his lawyer whenever he pleases...All right?"

The officer took a large key ring from his belt, and stepped to the steel door on his right. "You should've said that to begin with," he pouted. "Now, I ain't nothing but a hick cop as far as they're concerned."

"Not true, "Jewels praised him. "We are well aware of your precarious position. If I were in your shoes, the response would be no different. I consider your action commendable."

The obese officer melted under the unexpected compliment. The harsh attitude had all but vanished when he opened the door. "I'll take Gregory to a holding cell; it'll be a few minutes...Follow me. I'll show you the way."

Sully was amazed at how easily the officer had been disarmed by simple flattery. They were quickly guided to a windowless room with a table and four chairs. The only way in or out, was through the one door. They sat and waited.

A marshal stepped in a few minutes later and instructed them to face the wall and place their hands overhead. "You have to be patted down," the marshal said yawning. "I know you're Gregory's attorney, Jewels, but until I talk to the DA, we're doing things like they're supposed to be done."

"I understand," Jewels said. "You don't know the legalities yet, and until you do, precaution is naturally the most desired path."

"You can save that garbage for Buddy," the marshal said. "Now, up against the wall if you want to see the prisoner,

"We have no objections," Jewels said, leaning against the wall,

The marshal looked at Sully, "What interest you have in this?" he asked, motioning for him to face the wall.

"Gregory works for me." Sully replied.

The marshal informed Sully of his status while shaking him down. "And, since you're a private citizen, every time you see the prisoner, we'll be going through this procedure—unless he's behind the wire."

"No problem," Sully said easily.

The marshal made a notation on his clipboard and pointed to the chairs. "Have a seat if you like. It'll take Gregory a while to get down the stairs with shackles on."

Sully sat, closed his eyes and eased his head against the wall. Jewels paced the floor nervously beside the table. The flamboyant lawyer began mumbling as if he were in front of a jury. It was then that Sully wondered if Garan T. Jewels was the person that he presented himself to be.

When Fred was ushered into the interrogation room, he was heavily laden with shackles. He could barely take a step without stumbling.

Sully had trouble holding his temper. "How can they get away that?" he growled.

"Injustice runs rampant in *all* law enforcement agencies," Jewels said flatly. "...It has for years."

"It can't be like this everywhere...There has to be a decent cop somewhere."

"Oh, there's plenty of fine officers...Problem is, they ignore the bad ones. And doing that makes them contributors to a corrupted system. The fraternity that refuses to police its own ranks, creates nothing but malfeasance."

Fred sat down, his face showing signs of strain. "What these folks trying to do, boss?" he asked Sully. "They knows I ain't killed nobody."

"I know, Fred," Sully said, "but calm down...Jewels is a good lawyer and if things work out, you'll be on the streets in no time."

Jewels looked at the marshal by the door. "Could we have some privacy?" He asked. "It's best for Mister Gregory."

"Don't see why not," The marshal replied, looking at the obese turnkey. "Let's go Buddy! Need to give these people some time to themselves."

The turnkey waddled away from the door. "You gonna hang around a while I get a bite?" He asked. "It's 'bout break time."

"I'll take care of things," the marshal replied, following him out.

Jewels sat down and immediately began the questioning. "This has to be asked, Gregory, and I want the truth…To *what* extent are the charges filed against you, true?"

"I knows they's lying if they says I murdered that Red Ward fella. They gots me on some other stuff too, but I ain't sho' what…I don't 'member doin' nothin' wrong."

"Didn't that court-appointed attorney tell you anything?"

"Nawsuh! He jes come in, write some things down and leave. He didn't talk to me hardly t'all while he heah."

"He didn't ask for an alibi, or talk about the evidence?"

"Nawsuh! Nothing like it."

"One thing, Fred: On the day Ward was killed, did you for any reason, leave Sully's house?"

"Never stepped out the do', boss…I's right there wit' him all the time he in bed."

"Did anyone stop by the house during that time?"

"Jes' that lady nex' do'. She check on Mister Sully to see if he be needin' anythin'."

"Did you tell the police that?"

"Truth is, I forgot 'bout it."

"What was the lady's name?"

"Miss Gabby," Fred said, looking at Sully. "She yo' friend, ain't she, boss?"

"Most of the time," Sully grinned thinly. "She can be a real pain when she wants to…But the answer is, yes…She is a friend."

"What time was she there?" Jewels persisted. "It's very important."

"The first time, 'bout lunch."

"Be more specific, Fred."

"It 'bout one thirty in the afternoon."

"What time did she come by after that?"

"'Bout six-thirty! It jes 'fore dark. She brought over some food."

"What time did she leave?"

"Real late; it *way* after dark. She kept waitin' for him to wake up, and he jes' keep on sleepin'...He's wore out that day."

"I think I have enough to keep me busy tomorrow," Jewels said standing and examining his notepad. "A shower and a nap should get me off to a good start."

"You sure that's all you need?" Sully asked. "It doesn't seem like an awful lot"

"There'll be more questions, but the answers I've gotten tonight are probably the most critical. Tomorrow's schedule will include a visit to the arresting detectives, and we will discuss the charges and the evidence in the case. If the gun you *think* is involved, ballistics and fingerprints will be checked again thoroughly. After that, it's on to the coroner's office. Time of death and actual cause is critical. Then, I'll pay your neighbor a visit. While all this is going on, everyone involved will be signing statements cementing them to their word...As you can see, my day will be full. A considerable amount of time is expected to achieve these goals."

"Sounds like a lot to me."

"Well, for every question answered, five more were created— henceforth, the numbers escalate...Now, on with business if we hope to get your friend out of here."

"...I have a few questions, you mind?" Sully asked.

"Not at all," Jewels said. "I have to jot some things anyway... Would it bother you if I listen?"

Sully nodded approval and turned to Fred. "When they first jailed you, did they ask anything about your .45?

"Right off the bat. Firs' think they do is lay this automatic on the table. It look jes' like one them you gots in Hapeville."

"Was it muddy, slimy, dirty? Anything like that?"

"Naw! Nothin' likes that. This gun clean as a whistle. It wrapped up in blitz cloth; likes the one I gots at home."

"Who were the cops?"

"It was them same two what was at the hospital...They's the ones what worked me over and throwed me in jail."

"Smith and Jones?"

"Tha's them!"

"Think about this hard...Did either one of them touch the gun before they handed it to you?"

"Never did!  That Smith fella helt the gun in one hand and uncovered it wit' t'other.  He ask me if I ever see the gun, an' I tol' him, *no*.  He shove it in my face and tol' me to look harder.  I did what he say, an' tol' him *no* again.  Then, he get nasty...He scream at me to take the gun an' make sure."

"Did you take it out of his hands?"

"Yassuh, I's getting tired of his mouthin', so I did it so's he shut up."

"The gun he shoved in your face...Was it the one I gave you?"

"Nawsuh!  I hid that gun good."

"Why hide it?  You didn't know they were coming after you."

"Mama don't like no guns 'roun' the house.  Have to keep that sort o' thing outside.  But, it ain't the only reason I hides it, boss...I's a felon, an' if they catches me with a gun, I goes back to Reidsville."

"Why didn't you tell me about this *before* I put a gun in your hands?"

"I did, boss!  I tol' you I was down to Tatnall County for killin' that fella."

"You said they *dropped* those charges."

"Nawsuh!  The God's truth is, all they done was parole me.  It's still there."

"What about the other times you were jailed...Weren't you afraid of going back to prison?"

"My parole officer wouldn't let 'em take me back...He knew I's railroaded."

"...Where *is* the gun I gave you, Fred?"

"You 'member where the Buick 's parked the night I's locked up?"

Sully nodded.

"Step through that bush 'gainst the back of the house. 'Bout two foot from the corner, lift out that bottom board. Ain't no nails so it come easy. The gun jes' 'hind that board—'les the polices foun' it...It wrapped up an' should be dry as a bone."

"I hope they haven't found it," Sully said, then walked to the door and knocked softly. "If they haven't, and it's still behind that board, I *know* what's going on."

The marshal opened the door. "You folks ready to leave?"

"I think we have enough for the moment," Jewels said.

*"Buddy!"* the marshal summoned the turnkey. "You need to take the prisoner upstairs...I'm stepping outside with these people."

The turnkey shuffled into the room with half a sandwich in his mouth. "Might'a known they'd want to leave as soon's I sat down to eat."

The marshal grinned once they were outside. "Can't pay any attention to him...To hear him tell it, he never has time for a meal."

When Sully drove away from the Fairburn jail, it was nearly daylight. "You may not see me for a while," he told Jewels. "I have some things to sort out."

"I won't be hard to find," Jewels said. "Everything else will be put on hold while I'm working this case."

Sully thought silently of Beverly the remainder of the trip.

# CHAPTER TWENTY

Sully dropped Jewels off, then drove south on Boulevard heading for home. A sliver of sunlight broke through the dense clouds just minutes from the house and startled him. The unexpected glare caused him to swerve erratically down the empty street. Being so weary, it was difficult to stay between the curbs. What had kept him awake this long was the thought of being so close to a bed. The strength he had earlier in the night had completely vanished. He turned at the top of the hill for the final two blocks, but before reaching the house, turned again. An ever so light message convinced him to circle the block and come in from the opposite direction. It would cost nothing but time, and little of that since the distance was minimal. He followed his instincts and the moment he turned onto Marion Avenue, it became obvious that fate had favored him again.

Sully did not recognize the empty, black, 88' Oldsmobile, parked just up the street. He slid down in the seat to give the appearance of a smaller man, and drove slowly by the house. He glanced down the driveway to the rear of the house, then blinked as if slapped in the face. Two very recognizable figures stood there engrossed in conversation. He recognized Judson Fletcher and Toni Gracci so easily that it stunned him. Instantly, a sea of memories flooded his brain like a dam had burst. He remembered intricate details of the past within seconds. The most important recollection was of the problem he once had with the two men. He had berated them unmercifully in the past, and had made bitter enemies of the two. He never thought at the time, that he would be too weak to stand up for himself. The situation was suddenly uncomfortable to deal with. He lacked the strength to take them on, and his only protection was a dull pocketknife. If he had to face two men loaded with animosity and armed to the teeth, the odds were definitely not in his favor. With Fred no longer available to help, the only thing to do was to get out of there.

Sully pulled past the house slowly, hoping the car would not attract the attention of Fletcher and Gracci. He held his breath going by Gabby's house. Luckily, she wasn't on the porch drinking coffee as she often did early in the morning. The house was dark so apparently she was still in bed. He breathed easily after getting by without being seen. His luck was still holding.

He eased to the opposite curb a block away and killed the engine. The decision was made to stay put until the Oldsmobile was gone. He slid down in the seat, adjusted the rearview mirror to monitor the situation, and then made himself comfortable. He settled in for what was expected to be a long vigil. An hour later, he disregarded the danger and the will to stay awake faded.

Sully awoke to the rat-a-tat-tat tapping on the window. He jerked upright disoriented, then looked sleepily at the policeman by the car.

The patrolman stared grimly at him while thumping the Billy-stick in his hand. He motioned for Sully to roll the window down.

Sully cranked the window halfway down. "Something wrong?" he asked groggily.

"The car has to be moved, mister," the patrolman said sternly. "The neighbors are complaining about it being parked here."

"I didn't know there was a law against parking."

"There isn't, but these folks were getting antsy about it. They're thinking you're a burglar up to no good. I told them it's probably a drunk sleeping a bender off, but they prefer you do it somewhere else."

Sully glanced toward his house and noticed the black Oldsmobile was no longer there. "I live down the street officer, and I assure you I'm not a criminal," he said, "Truth is, I'm having trouble with an old girlfriend. She's been going in the house and rearranging things."

"Have you reported it?"

"Naw," Sully replied. "I don't think that's necessary...She's not a bad kid."

"Tell you what," the officer said. "If your driver's license checks out, we'll let this slide...But you have to park in front of your own house."

Sully opened his billfold and handed the officer his driver's license.

"...Well, I'll be! Sully Hawken!" the patrolman said, looking a long time at the license. "Been reading about you...Tell you what!

Go home and work this out, and I'll do what I can to make the neighbors happy."

Sully thanked him, started the Buick and turned around to leave. Just as he parked in front of his house, an angry expression came on his face. *"No way I'm putting up with this,"* he mumbled under his breath. *"They're the ones who'll be looking over their shoulders from here on in."*

Sully turned the car around and headed in the direction of downtown. He was irritated for running scared and would reverse the situation once Fred's .45 was in his hand. He turned into the Gregory home driveway fifteen minutes later, and parked. He walked briskly to the rear of the house, then stepped behind the large hedge where Fred said his .45 would be. He went to one knee, grabbed the bottom board, and lifted it out. The automatic weapon was still there, safely wrapped in a blitz-cloth. It was proof-positive that the police forced Fred to put his fingerprints on the .45 they had. The weapon that killed Red Ward was definitely not one that he purchased. He jammed Fred's .45 in his belt and quickly returned to the car. The next move would have to be accomplished without delay. He would go home, pack, and then find a place out of the way to bed down. He wasn't afraid of Fletcher and Gracci catching him at home alone, but it would definitely upset the plans he had for them. What he needed at the moment was a place to stay where no one would suspect him to be.

*First things first,* he thought driving wildly back to the house. He would pack some clothes and get away from the house as quickly as possible. He'd worry about where to go once on the road. Once that was accomplished, additional changes would be made concerning secrecy.

# CHAPTER TWENTY ONE

Sully shoved open the front door not in the least concerned with the possible consequences of returning home. If Fletcher and Gracci had harbored an urge to kill him before, their motivation was about to become even greater. The .45 in his belt wasn't the difference; it was simply that he was ready to put *them* on the defensive.

Sully stepped inside and went about gathering up belongings he would need while gone. He quickly filled a duffel bag with clothes and threw it over his shoulder. He turned to leave, but before taking a step, a soft creak on the front room floor caused him to pause. He withdrew the .45 very quietly and aimed it at the door leading into the living room. With his finger firmly on the trigger, he slowly squeezed. If either Fletcher or Gracci appeared in that doorway, they were about to become very dead.

He waited patiently for movement for what seemed to be several minutes. The rationalization was that whoever was there, had no business coming in unannounced. He sensed the motion of someone moving across the floor and gripped the .45 even tighter.

"Sully!" a squeaky cried out when she saw the gun aimed at her head. "What are you doing with that gun?"

Sully quickly slid the .45 under his belt. "What are you doing here, Beverly?" he asked, not in the mood for a delay.

"I came to straighten something out," she said softly. "We need to talk."

"This is a bad time," he said, trying to get her away from the house. "I'll come by the hospital one day and we'll discuss it then. I'm in a hurry right now."

Beverly didn't budge. "*No!*" she said emphatically. "We're going to talk about it *right* now...This has been put off long enough!"

He grabbed her by the arm, rushed her through the living room and out the front door. "How'd you get here?" he growled, stepping onto the porch and searching the street for her car.

"You're hurting me, Sully," she protested, trying to get free from his grip. "Let me go...You're scaring me."

"Dammit, woman, you don't realize what you've just stepped into," he snapped. "Now, how'd you get here?"

"By bus," she said meekly. "My car's in the shop...What's the difference?"

He opened the driver's door and threw his duffel bag over the seat into the rear. "Get in," he said, nudging her across the front seat. "I'll explain when we're out of here."

"What's going on, Sully?" she asked, moving across to the passenger side. "You're acting like somebody's after you."

Cranking the Buick, Sully jammed it in gear with a loud grind then lurched forward. "Somebody *is* after me, and you don't need to get mixed up in it. Now, where can I drop you?"

She looked straight ahead and didn't say a word for several minutes. "...I'm already involved...A lot more than you realize. You see, I've known all along about you and Dorothy Haygood; it's the reason I came to you in the hospital."

Memories of Dorothy Haygood suddenly burst into his head. It was all there, except for a few days before he was shot. "Just what is it you think went on between Dorothy and me?" he asked sarcastically.

"I know you had an affair with her," Beverly replied. "That's why she wanted information about you. When something suspicious happened, I decided not to go through with it. It was too underhanded to suit me."

Sully eased his foot off the accelerator and slowed down. They were far enough away from the house to relax a moment. "You need to understand this right now," he said, glancing in her direction. "Dorothy had a long list of men she saw regularly, and *I* wasn't on it...Truth of the matter is, I didn't like the way she treated Jigs."

"That's not what I was told," Beverly said. "She said you were intimate lovers and was quite graphic about everything."

Sully shook his head in disgust. "If you know Dorothy at all, you have to know what a liar she is. Fact is, I despised her...For the first time in his life, Jigs was in love. And all she ever thought of was ways to destroy him...Now, where can I take you? You're in danger every minute you're with me."

"I'm going where you're going," she said. "There are things we have to discuss and it has to be done the right way."

"I don't know where this is headed—or where I'm going for that matter," he said calmly, "but one thing's for sure, you won't be with me. I've got a couple of goons looking for me that would like nothing better than to rip my head off. If they find me while you're around, it could turn into a very bad situation."

"Come to my place, Sully," she said without hesitation. "It'll be safe there."

"You didn't listen to what I said, Beverly. The people are trying to kill me...Besides, what about your doctor friend? I really don't think he'd like it."

"He won't say anything," Beverly answered. "We've gone our separate ways."

"I'm sorry," Sully said with a blank expression. "...I didn't mean to pry."

"No need to apologize," she assured him. "It's been over for some time. Now, let's go to my apartment. No one would ever think of looking for you there."

Sully still wasn't convinced. He had to make sure she understood the gravity of his dilemma. "It's not wise, Beverly. You're taking a big chance hooking up with me. It's like asking for grief. If these guys find out where I am, nothing will stop them. They'll be on your doorsteps in a heartbeat—and they don't leave witnesses."

"Let me worry about that," she said flatly. "Besides, no one would ever believe you're staying at my place. I sure won't tell anyone, will you?"

Sully looked straight ahead, trying to suppress the fantasies creeping into his mind. Curiosity ultimately kicked in. "Where is this place I'll feel so protected?" he asked. "I need to know it's safe before I go along with *anything*."

Beverly's eyes were glued to him. "Take Peachtree to the first street beyond the hospital. There's a parking lot by the building. Pull in back as far away from the street as you can...We'll go in the rear entrance."

Sully drove up Ponce De Leon, turned onto Peachtree, then passed Crawford Long. He turned in the first street and cruised slowly by the building. A *NURSES QUARTERS* sign caught his attention as they went by the front entrance. A string of rules were listed below. *No Visitors Overnight* was in bold print.

Sully moved slowly to the rear of the lot and found an empty space. It was just ten feet from the rear entrance. "You sure about this?" he asked, once again having doubts. "It could get you booted out of here...According to the sign, there's a tight set of rules. If that's the case, they're bound to figure it out."

"Just do as I say and everything will be all right," Beverly said. "Even if they do catch us, it won't be the end of the world...We'll deal with what we have to."

Sully reached into the back seat and retrieved his bag. "Lead the way," he said, waving his arm. He still wasn't sure it was the smart thing to do.

Beverly withdrew a set of keys from her pocketbook. "This door is always locked. I'll give you my key and I'll use the front entrance. Make a duplicate when you can. And don't worry too much about being seen here. All the nurses who have boyfriends use this door. The other nurses just turn their heads."

"What if I am seen?"

"Just act like you belong. The men who use this door, come and go without incident. I don't think you'll be challenged."

They stepped into the building and were at the very end of the hallway. "This is it," Beverly said, opening the door. "A corner apartment on the bottom floor. How convenient is that?"

Sully followed her into the apartment and placed his bag on the kitchen floor. It was a one bedroom efficiency apartment and very compact. "It's going to get crowded in here," he said softly.

"Do you approve?" she asked.

He relaxed and sat down in one of the chairs by the dinette. "If you still feel comfortable with this, you've got yourself a roommate."

She walked over to the stove and lifted a key from a key-organizer and handed it to him. "*This* is a spare key; not a key to my bedroom... Your place is on the couch."

Sully hadn't expected anything and was quick to reply. "It's your place; we go by your rules…Don't give it another thought."

"Now that that's settled, how about a bite to eat?"

Sully nodded approval.

"Well, if it's going to be anytime soon, I'll have to go to the grocery store. It may take a while so make yourself at home while I'm gone."

Sully slipped from his jacket and rolled it into a ball for a pillow, then moved toward the couch. "Give me a shake when you get back. I'll help with the cooking," he said sleepily. "Hope you don't mind, but I had a long night…"

"I've got a pillow," she said, opening the closet door. She then picked up her purse without saying another word and left. Sully had already fallen asleep.

# CHAPTER TWENTY TWO

Sully awoke to soothing music from behind the closed bedroom door. He sat up on the sofa and stretched. He turned on the light and glanced at the time; it was nine-thirty. The sun had long since dropped over the horizon. *It was late*, he thought, but not too late to accomplish what he had in mind earlier. The next step to take was to get up from the sofa and get moving. He opened the duffel bag and pulled out an aged leather jacket first. He laid it on the couch then dug deeper for a wrinkled fedora. The hats form had diminished terribly from years of neglect. He eased it onto the back of his head and reached for some old shoes.

Beverly heard the disturbance and opened the bedroom door. She stepped into the kitchen with the bedroom light directly behind her. The light outlined her body perfectly through her sheer negligee. The living room light was just dim enough to create a noticeable contrast. It made what was underneath highly visible.

Sully's eyes moved slowly down to her hips where her legs were set slightly apart. He swallowed hard upon noticing there were no underclothes.

"I heard you stirring," she said. "If you want something to eat, there's plenty in the refrigerator. Won't take but a few minutes to rustle something up."

Sully looked her straight in the eye trying to hide the embarrassment. "Not tonight...Maybe tomorrow? I've got a few things to take care of before morning." He wanted to kick himself for even thinking of leaving,

"I'll be in about six if you can make it."

Sully began tying his shoes, but this time couldn't avert his eyes. Beverly just stood there without making an attempt to hide her attributes. "I should be," he said, with his eyes glued to her body. "If everything goes like it should, I'll be here by early afternoon."

Beverly's face turned crimson, realizing that very instant what Sully was glaring at. The furthest thing from her mind was to arouse him and she quickly left the room. She returned several moments later with her body covered with a full-length robe. She made an effort to explain. "I've lived alone for a long time, Sully…You'll have to excuse me."

"If you think I'm complaining," he said, standing up, "forget it!"

Beverly wrapped the robe even tighter around her waist. "Then, tomorrow it is."

"I can't promise anything," he said, sliding one arm in the leather jacket, "but if I'm here early, maybe I can have a hot meal waiting on you."

"I hope what's happened doesn't put anything in your head," she said, still red-faced. "…You know the rules."

"Never crossed my mind," he said, stepping into the hallway. In the stairwell, he whispered quietly under his breath, *Not much, anyway.*"

Sully drove past Big Town's poolroom and surveyed the heavy pedestrian traffic. He pulled into an alley several blocks away and parked. A lot of people milling about that late at night meant only one thing: He knew most of them and didn't want them to know he was there. The only hope he had of getting into the poolroom without being detected was through the side entrance in the alley. The problem was finding it open. The custodian usually locked that door to clean up after the boxing crowd left. The gym shuts their doors regularly at nine and it was now ten-thirty, an hour and a half past closing. If the door were open, it would be a stroke of luck. If it wasn't, he'd just have to cancel out. He didn't want to walk in the door from the street side. Besides, a clear picture of Beverly standing in the doorway half-naked, was making that choice more appealing.

Sully cocked the old fedora over his eyes and turned up his jacket collar to avoid being recognized. He walked slowly toward the poolroom alley, changing his normal gate in the guise. Turning into the alley, the immediate thought was it was too late; all but a few cars had left for the evening.

Sully looked through the porthole of the pool room door and saw a faint light coming from a table in the middle of the hall. There were a dozen silent men crowded around the one table; it was the only light in the entire room. Two men were playing pool and the rest were gambling heavily on the side. He was too far away to recognize anyone from where he was and had to get closer. He tried the door and to his good fortune, it was unlocked. He quickly stepped inside and went against the darkened wall. The gym entrance to the right was closed and dark inside. The boxing people had left for the night, just as he had figured. He moved quietly toward the bathroom, which protruded ten feet out from the wall completely hidden from view. He stopped fifty feet from the gathering and peered around the corner of the restroom.

Judson Fletcher was waving around a hand full of bills and looking for bets. Tony Gracci was nowhere in sight. The strange part was, they were *always* together. This was highly out of the ordinary.

Sully stood in the dark for over an hour watching one patron after the other use the restroom, and Gracci still didn't show his face. The decision was made to go after Fletcher the instant that the gangster made a trip to the facilities. Sully would have to worry about Gracci later. This opportunity could not be passed up.

As if on que, Fletcher walked away from the crowd and headed for the restroom. He was alone; Gracci was still nowhere to be found.

Sully eased the .45 from under his belt, feeling it was the right time to make a move. He snapped the safety down without cocking it just after Fletcher stepped into the restroom. He looked around carefully to make sure that there would be no interference. His confidence soared quickly, realizing that being alone with Fletcher was greatly to his advantage. He felt much better about dealing with them one at a time with the odds in his favor.

Sully walked up behind Fletcher as he was using the urinal and tapped him gently on the shoulder. "Hello, Fletcher," he said softly.

"Yeah," Fletcher growled and turned around. He was zipping his pants up and did not recognize Sully.

Sully placed the cold barrel of the .45 up against Fletcher's neck and said menacingly, "Raise your right arm, tough guy." He cocked the weapon and squeezed the trigger lightly.

Fletcher's jaw dropped in fear upon realizing who he was dealing with. "What's this about, Hawken?" he asked with a quivering voice. "You've got no call to do this."

"Put the arm out," Sully snarled, easing a knife from his pocket.

The blade to the knife sprang open with a sharp click, startling Fletcher as he raised his arm.

Sully slid the razor-sharp knife inside of Fletcher's cuff and sliced the jacket up to the elbow. When the cloth fell from the arm, it revealed a small device with a .45 caliber Derringer attached. "My, aren't we the cute one," Sully tantalized.

"Who told you about that?" Fletcher asked shakily. "There ain't but three people on this planet who knew about that...Me, Gracci and the guy I bought it from."

Sully ignored the question. "Why'd you have to kill a nice guy like Red Ward?" he asked, snatching the small Derringer from its' holder. "He was just trying to make things easier on everybody...You didn't have to do that."

Fletcher began shivering when he saw Sully's trigger finger tighten on the .45. "C'mon, Hawken," he said with chattering teeth, "ease up on that thing. I don't know who told you I killed Ward, but they're lying. I ain't killed nobody."

Sully slammed the barrel of the .45 against Fletcher's head as hard as he could. Surprisingly, the big man didn't go down from the first strike, but the second one took him to his knees. Sully didn't let up after that. He swung viciously, time and time again at Fletcher's now bloodied head. Looking at Fletcher laying in a pool of blood on the floor, left little doubt the mobster was dead. Sully quickly wiped the bloody .45 off on his pants and shoved it into his pocket. He'd wasted a lot of time and it was necessary to get out of there before someone came in the restroom.

Sully bent over and hastily put his fingers to Fletcher's throat feeling for a pulse. He was disappointed that the maimed figure was still alive. He thought for a minute of finishing the job, but the time element was too critical. Fletcher would most likely die from the severe pounding, so why bother. He yanked a handkerchief from his jacket and placed the small Derringer in it. He immediately wiped the weapon free of his prints, then bent over and placed the gun in Fletcher's hand. He wrapped the unconscious man's hand around the gun so that only his fingerprints would be on it. He then ran a pencil into the top barrel of the weapon and gently laid it back in the handkerchief. He wrapped it up and put in his jacket pocket.

Then everything went strangely white.

Sully didn't go all the way out, but he was definitely down. He couldn't see the person who had hit him or what he was being hit with, but easily recognized the gruff voice that was speaking.

"Figured you'd pull something like this," Tony Gracci said, catching Sully with another savage stroke. "It's too bad I couldn't get here in time to help Judson...Looks like you done him."

Sully had trouble protecting himself from the onslaught that followed. He couldn't move, couldn't see or talk, and was completely without coordination. So, he did the only thing he remembered to do whenever hurt in a fight: He reached upward and covered his head with both arms.

Gracci laughed at the feeble attempt to ward off the blows and continued kicking him viciously in a portion of his exposed chest.

Sully felt his ribs crack after several kicks and his arms began to sag under the brutal beating. He drifted off and lost consciousness. Then, everything was eerily silent. He was relieved the kicking had stopped when he came to, but still felt dazed and disoriented. He had no idea how long he had been on the floor, but remembered something that happened just before he passed out. He had heard muffled voices, but was too far out of it to understand what was said.

Someone in the shadows said softly, "You okay, Sully?"

"Hector?" Sully mumbled, recognizing the voice. "Where'd you come from?"

"I came over to give the restroom one last cleaning and I found Gracci standing over you, lettin' you have it big time. So, I took a piece of pipe and give it to him upside the head...Never liked the guy anyway."

"Is he out of it?" Sully asked, trying to get to his feet.

"He's more than that," Hector grinned, "I think he's dead."

"Did you check to see if he was?"

"Don't make no difference to me how it goes...Both the bastards ought to be dead anyhow. This has been a long time coming."

"Does anybody else know what went on in here?" Sully asked, his eyes strangely moving around the room.

"Naw," Hector said. "Everybody's gone; I'm the only one left. The rest of 'em went over to Luckie Street without knowing what happened. They're over at Leb's grabbing a bite."

Unsure of his footing, Sully stood and said almost in a whisper, "We've been friends a long time, Hector...I don't want to put you behind the eight ball, but I'm in a lot of trouble..."

"Looks like I'm in as deep as you are now, Sully. Besides, I owe you...If it wasn't for for you and Jigs looking out for me when I was down, no tellin' where I'd have wound up. I couldn't even get a job as a sparring partner until you guys put me to work. My family would've starved if it hadn't been for that."

"Don't make it more than it was, Hector. You were a first rate sparring partner back then. But this is different! This could cost you a lot more than just a little trouble. If certain people find out you helped me, they'd come after you...You know I wouldn't ask if I could do for myself."

"Don't worry about it," Hector said. "I'll take care of everything for you. Just relax, you're in good hands..."

"That's not it," Sully said.

"What's wrong, then?"

"I'm blind as a bat, Hector...I've lost my sight."

"You can't see nothin'?" Hector asked, momentarily shocked.

"Just a bright background with silver stars bursting in it."

"I better get you to a hospital, man."

"No hospital," Sully insisted. "I'll be fine...The big thing right now is getting these bodies out of here and dumping them. We don't need any of this linked to you if we can help it. It could come back and haunt us."

"I'll take care of it," Hector assured him. "There's an alley down the street I can dump 'em. I'll drop 'em off there and come back and clean this up. My pickup's just outside, so stay put until I get back...You gonna' be all right?"

"I'll be fine," Sully said, listening to the bodies being dragged away. He sat patiently until Hector returned fifteen minutes later, then waited even longer for Hector to mop and clean the restroom.

"It's done," Hector said easily. "Now let's close up and get out of here."

"What about the bodies? Did you cover 'em up?"

"Yeah! I used some trash in the alley…They won't be found for a couple of days—unless they start smelling."

Sully walked slowly as he was lead from the pool hall. His body ached from the pains in his head and chest. "You don't sound like this bothers you very much," he said. "I would've thought it'd shake you a little."

There was a grim look on Hector's face. "If I'm supposed to feel pity for these guys, I hate to disappoint you. This should have happened a long time ago."

"You're not worried at all?"

"Are you?"

Sully suppressed a smile and leaned against the building outside. His mused over how easily Hector had disposed of the bodies.

Hector interrupted his thoughts. "Where's your car parked, Sully?" he asked. "We need to get it out of here. I'll have to leave my truck here and pick it up later…Nobody'll ever know you were here." He came back minutes later and rushed Sully, wincing in pain and holding his ribs tightly, into the passenger's seat.

Sully told Hector to head for Crawford Long. "…When you get to the hospital—go around back—to the Nurses' quarters." he said haltingly, then reached into his pockets for Beverly's keys. "A friend there has a few of my things in her apartment…I don't want her caught up in this if it can be avoided."

Hector drove into the nurses quarters and parked, then quickly entered the back door. He was gone just minutes before returning. He opened the passenger side door. "That girl's a handful, Sully…You know that?"

"What'd she say?" Sully asked, not realizing what had transpired. "She's not mad, is she?"

"Sounded like it to me," Hector said. "She said if you wanted anything to come inside and get it yourself. She said you were avoiding her, whatever that means. I can't imagine you *not* wanting to see her though; she's as pretty as they come."

"Just take me on home," Sully said. "I'll pick my things up later."

Beverly was standing by the passenger door with a scowl on her face before they realized she was there. She was stunned at the sight of Sully's face. "...My Lord!" she said meekly. "What happened?"

Sully tried to place his eyes in the direction her voice came from but failed miserably. "I don't want you getting involved in this, Beverly, so just let us be on our way...I'll talk to you when I can."

"Sully," She said weakly, "You're blind." She turned to Hector. "Get him in the apartment right now...I'll take care of him...He'll be fine."

# CHAPTER TWENTY THREE

Hector put his hand under Sully's arm and lifted him gently from the car. "This don't look good, Sully...Man, you can't even walk without stumblin' all over the place...You *ought* to be in the hospital;"

Beverly entwined her arm with Sully's on the other side, and then she and Hector slowly walked him to the back door. Once inside, they went quietly to the apartment and opened the door using Sully's key. "Hector's right, Sully. You should be in a hospital...This is as bad as it can get."

"No hospitals," Sully replied firmly. "The cops are going to find Fletcher and Gracci before long, and when they do, they'll hit the hospitals to see if anybody else was hurt. They know all about the bad blood between us, and if I'm in the hospital beat up, they'll know that I had something to do with it. There isn't any doubt I'd be at the top of their suspects list."

"You're gonna be there anyway," Hector said, guiding him into the bedroom. "Those bums didn't make no secret o' bein' after your hide."

"I don't care!...*No* hospitals," Sully said strongly, "and that's final!"

"You're making a big mistake," Hector said, easing Sully onto the edge of the bed. "You don't realize what could happen...Man, you could die." He turned to Beverly for support. "Do something, lady. My friend's going south, and he won't listen."

"All we can do is make him comfortable," Beverly said, knowing Sully's mind was closed to any thoughts of being hospitalized. "Help me get him undressed and maybe things will be all right? Only time will tell."

Hector bent over and removed the blood-soaked socks and shoes, then carefully removed the equally blood-covered jacket and shirt, along with the undershirt.

Beverly stared at Sully's grotesquely bruised and beaten upper torso; there was severe discoloration. She steadied Sully and undid his belt. "We have to get these pants off," she looked at Hector, "and it's going to hurt."

Sully felt the sudden sensation of being horizontal and his pants dropping to his ankles. Beverly was right: The excruciating pain shot up through his back and intensified in the rib cage. When the aching in his chest finally began to subside somewhat, his head exploded into a nightmare of bursting stars. He was losing consciousness at a frightful pace and his demeanor was turning to hopelessness. "Better hurry," he said weakly. "...I'm nearly out of it!"

They eased Sully into a comfortable position on the bed, ignoring the fact that he wasn't wearing underwear...It was not the time to be embarrassed.

Sully felt that he had to explain. "Sorry, don't—like—shorts," he said meekly. "...Don't like—to—do laundry..."

Beverly ran her fingers across the massive bruises on his chest and side. She turned to Hector. "Get a towel and fill it with ice from the refrigerator."

Hector moved quickly to the kitchen.

"You've got to stay awake a little bit longer, Sully" Beverly said. "The ribs have to be wrapped and you have to help me. If you go out now, there could be complications...You've got at least six cracked ribs and four more compounded and separated. I can't tell without an X-ray, but if I'm right, a wrong move could make a splintered rib puncture something—if it hasn't already. You have to let me know the instant the pain accelerates."

Sully had difficulty breathing and whispered, "You better hurry...I can't take much more of this."

Beverly stood up quickly when Hector returned with the ice. "Keep him still until I get back," she said sharply and raced out of the room. She yelled in from the kitchen. "Apply that ice to his head, and whatever you do, don't let him fall asleep." She returned immediately with an armload of bandages and began carefully wrapping Sully's battered rib cage. She spoke loudly to be well understood, "I know this is difficult but don't cave in on me now! We're almost there."

"Better—hurry," Sully said haltingly. "...Don't know—how long..."

Beverly finished wrapping his ribs and gently rolled him over. She wrapped the blood pressure tester band around his arm. Getting an alarmingly low count, she told Sully the bad news. "There's damage on the inside of the rib cage, Sully, and it's causing internal bleeding."

"Am—I going—to—live?" Sully joked weakly after the wrap was removed.

"Don't ask questions like that," she said, noticeably irritated. "I don't care if you are kidding."

"Who's kidding?" he grinned painfully.

Beverly tried to be professional but was slowly buckling under the stress. She couldn't understand why Sully's injuries were bothering her so much; she had seen a lot worse at the hospital. "Sully, I can't pinpoint the internal bleeding...Only a hospital can do that...You need proper care or you're going to die."

"Do what—you can—but no—hospital!"

Beverly tried to get his attention once more before he passed out. "Sully," she said loudly. "Is there pressure behind the eyes?"

"Yeah—lots of—it...I cant..." It was all he said before drifting off.

Hector quickly covered him with a blanket. "What about his head?" he asked, placing the ice package on his forehead. "Is he busted up inside his head too?"

"He's got a concussion," she replied, "and it's a bad one. The swelling has created pressure on the optic nerves and it's shut down his sight. If he doesn't get the right attention soon, it might be permanent."

"But, there *is* a chance he'll see again, *right*?"

"For this type of injury, it doesn't look good. But then, I'm not a doctor."

"What else can we do to help him?"

"Not much, I'm afraid," she said, walking toward the kitchen. "If he were in a hospital, the skull pressure could be relieved by drilling a hole. Even that's not a sure thing. The eyes are a different matter. To keep him from going totally blind, they'd have to insert a needle in the side of the eye to lower the pressure." She walked into the kitchen and retrieved an ice bag and filled it with more ice.

"What's that for?" Hector asked.

"His rib cage," she replied, then went back into the bedroom and laid the ice pack over Sully's chest. "It'll reduce the swelling and relieve some of the pain. He won't notice the difference until he wakes up though."

Hector was silent a moment. "...Who's going to take care of him when you're at work? He can't do nothin' here by himself...Maybe me and the wife could come by and stay with him?"

"You won't have to," Beverly said. "...I'm taking some vacation time. I'll be here all the time."

"You mind if I come by and check on him from time to time?" Hector asked timidly. "I've been owing him a long time. He took me off the streets when I couldn't get a job...I wouldn't have made it without him."

"...Come anytime you want—just don't tell anyone."

"Well, if you have things under control, I've got to go...Got some things to do before I head home."

"What really happened tonight?" Beverly asked, following him to the door. "What kind of animal would beat another person so badly?"

Hector hesitated before answering, then decided if Sully had trusted her to such an extent, there was no harm in revealing what took place. "It was a couple of guys that ain't got nothin' but blind hate for Sully," he began.

Beverly's eyes were wide with astonishment by the time the story was over. "Are you sure those men are dead?"

"I didn't look that close," Hector said without remorse, "but when I dropped 'em in the alley, they didn't look like they was breathing...If I were you, I wouldn't fret too much about them anyway. The world's better off without that pair. They wasn't nothin' but thieving murderers who had it coming. Besides, if I hadn't stepped in, they would've killed Sully without a second thought."

"*Why* did it happen, Hector? Surely there was another way."

"Not to them two...It's hard to figure their kind, ma'am, especially to someone like yourself. I told you how Sully had thoughts that they might be the ones who shot him and Jigs. Well, the word on the streets is that they've been trying to track Sully down and finish the job. Those two been after him ever since he got out of the hospital. He just turned the tables on 'em tonight, that's all."

"Why would they want to kill him in the first place? Sully doesn't seem to be the kind of person that would invoke that kind of anger."

"I reckon its cause Sully never was very friendly to 'em. He would've probably taken their heads off the first time they come around if it hadn't been for Jigs. At any rate, word has it that Jigs made a deal with some mobsters out of Chicago. When it fell through, they put them two thugs on Jigs and Sully to even the score."

"I can't believe Sully would get mixed up in anything like that. He appears way too smart."

"I don't think Sully did the mixing. All he ever did was back Jigs up. He just watched over the little man to make sure nobody hurt him. Of course, what I've told you come from the streets...That ain't always reliable. If you want to know what really happened, you'll have to ask Sully...*Me*—I don't want to know."

"What about your truck? How are you going to get to it this late," Beverly asked. "...I can't leave, and the trolleys are down for the night."

"I'll work it out somehow...Whatever I do, I'll leave the Buick parked here with the keys under the mat. I'll get a friend to follow me back with my truck before daylight sets in.

Beverly returned to the apartment secure with the knowledge that everything would be taken care of trouble free. She immediately picked up the phone and dialed the hospital. Within minutes, she had two weeks vacation.

# CHAPTER TWENTY FOUR

Sully awoke instantly with a jerk. Like a miraculous switch was tripped, his eyesight was back to normal. The troublesome white void from being pulverized had miraculously disappeared during the night. He sat on the side of the bed and stared out the window into the still dark morning. A cool breeze from the open window made him shiver slightly. He glanced at the illuminated clock on the nightstand; it was 4:30. Beverly snored softly on the bed. He wanted to wake her and tell her of the good news, but changed his mind at the last moment. He didn't want to bother her so early. He thought of how he had come to feel for her, and how difficult it was becoming to contain those feelings. It was frustrating and very bazaar to fall in love with someone, who, as far as he knew, was totally unaware of how he felt. Strangely, there was resentment toward her for the confusion in his life.

He eased off the edge of the bed, careful not to be a disturbance, then stepped into the kitchen. He quietly pulled the door to behind him, then went to the stove and put a pot of coffee on. He shivered from a chill again and decided something was needed to ward off the cold. He rummaged briefly through the duffel bag and found a pair of pajamas that he had packed away. He slid into the pajamas, then went back to the duffel for a razor and a toothbrush. The thing he needed most were slippers though. His bare feet were numb from the freezing floor. He grinned and decided not to go after them, beings how frostbite was highly unlucky at that time of the year. *And*, since the shoes were under the bed in the next room, it might wake Beverly.

He stepped into the bathroom, turned on the hot water in the sink and then let it run a few minutes. Once the water was hot, he lathered his face and shaved away what looked like a month's growth of beard. He ran his hand over his clean-shaven face examining the swollen areas that were still there from the beating. He felt the stitches on the right side of his head, then twisted around so he could see the other side in the mirror. He was shaved clean in two places and both had neatly sewn sutures to accommodate the wounds. He was impressed how Beverly had taken such good care of him. He would also have to thank her for keeping him out of the hospital. He brushed his teeth quickly then borrowed some mouthwash. He poured it into a paper cup, swished it around vigorously, and then stepped to the shower. He turned it on and waited patiently for the water to warm. When the steam became thick, he draped his pajamas over a chair and stepped in the stall. The burning sensation was intense. Ten minutes of the piping hot water all but eliminated the reeking soreness in his body. Except for the dull pain in his chest, the upper torso felt as good as ever.

He turned the water off and stepped from the shower. He took a towel from the rack, dried off, and then slid back into his pajamas. As the coffee began to perk loudly, he decided to go for the house shoes in the bedroom. His feet were becoming numb again. He silently eased his feet into the slippers, still wary of waking Beverly, then stepped back to the kitchen just as the coffee boiled over onto the hot eye. He quickly turned the eye off and wiped up the mess. He poured a cup of coffee but it was too hot to drink. He placed the cup under the faucet and cooled it with some tap water.

The sound of Beverly stirring about came from the bedroom. "*Sully!*" she screamed out in panic, then burst abruptly into the kitchen.

"Take it easy," he said, trying to quiet her. "...I'm fine."

Her eyes were wide with surprise while staring at him. "Your *head* doesn't hurt? You can see? This is amazing!"

"Everything's all right...Except for the pain in my ribs, I feel great."

"...I need a minute to adjust," she said, taking a deep breath. She poured a cup of coffee and was still laboring from the trauma. "I can't believe you're acting so calm; it's like you were never hurt."

"Hey, it's a shock to me too. I didn't figure on getting well this quick...I thought it would be a lot longer."

Beverly stood there, taking no notice of the sheer nightgown she wore and took a sip of the coffee "It's been twelve days, Sully, but even at that, it's hard to believe."

Sully avoided looking at her and turned away. "You mind putting something on? I see right through that thing and it's taking a toll on me."

Up until that moment, Beverly had no idea what she had done. She raced from the kitchen in embarrassment, then returned in a minute with a housecoat wrapped snugly around her waist. "I'm sorry, Sully," she said, sitting down red-faced. "I didn't think you'd get your sight back so quickly...You weren't supposed to see that."

"No need to be sorry...You haven't done anything wrong," Sully said softly. "It's just something I don't deal with very good. *And*, before it gets worse, it's probably best I move on."

"You don't have to do that," Beverly said. "I don't think you understand the situation fully."

"What's there to understand?" he asked, packing his belongings in the duffel bag. "All this time, I've had things scratching around in my head that shouldn't be there...You shouldn't be put in a situation like that."

"Listen to me, Sully," she began. "For two years I was with Thurman Haygood, a doctor at the hospital...He..."

"Are you talking about Dorothy Haygood's husband?" he interrupted.

"Yes!"

"When you said you came to me in the hospital because of Dorothy, I thought you were friends. I didn't know it was anything like that."

"Did you know Thurman?"

"As far as I know, I never met the man. About the only thing I heard was how he felt about the men in Dorothy's life."

"Did you know he was on duty the day you came out of a coma?"

"No, I didn't," Sully said, squinting, wondering what the conversation was leading to. "...Nobody told me."

"I don't have proof," Beverly said, choosing her words carefully, "but I believe Thurman felt that what happened to you and Mister Moran, was connected to Dorothy in some way. He never did come right out and say that, but he hinted at it when your names came up in our conversations. A lot of times our talks were about money, but it always turned to the men Dorothy was involved with, including you."

Sully felt the need to defend himself. "Anybody in town could have told you about ~~Beverly's~~ *her* bed hopping; it's not much of a secret. Everybody knows the woman's a shark and people with any sense, stay clear of her."

"Thurman thought you were seeing Dorothy while she was having an affair with Mister Moran, did you know that?"

Sully's mood darkened. "I can't help what other people think...Like I said before, I didn't fool around with the lady...And I told you why...Besides, she would have been scraping the bottom of the barrel if she figured on getting anything from me."

"You were worth fifty thousand dollars before you were hurt, and that was before you received a portion of the Moran estate...Sounds like a good enough reason to me!"

"All I can say is, when she made a move on me, I went straight to Jigs. Sad part was, he'd sluff it off and say she was just trying to make him jealous."

"Didn't you try to convince him otherwise?"

"Hey, I made an effort. What else could I do? It didn't matter what I said; he'd already made up his mind about her. I *always* thought she was nothing but trouble...I told him enough times."

As Beverly absorbed what was said, a strange thought entered her mind: Her feelings toward Sully were no longer platonic She decided that very moment that it *was* best he leave.

Sully stepped in the bathroom, dressed into street clothes and then returned to the kitchen. He picked up the duffel, slid his arm under the strap and threw it over his shoulder. He walked toward the front door and turned to her grimly. "Where did all this stuff come from? I've never heard such junk..."

"Some came from Thurman and Dorothy and some from Virginia Moran. I added two and two from the little I got from you."

"And when did all the math start?"

"When ~~Beverly~~ *Dorothy* started talking about you while you were in a coma."

"What about Haygood? You still seeing him?"

"No!…That came to an end a while back."

"But you're still talking to him?"

"It's kind of hard not to, seeing him at the hospital every day."

"What about Dorothy? I'd think she would hold a grudge for what went on between you and the doctor?"

"Strangely, it wasn't like that at all…She couldn't have cared less. I quit hanging around her because of the problems she might cause. I felt she was about to involve me in something out of bounds so I kept my distance."

"Can't blame you there!" Sully said. "There's no telling what she was up to. If you were *that* suspicious, you can bet you did the right thing…Besides, your situation with that pair was hopeless to begin with. There's no way Dorothy would give up her husband to anybody…His being loaded and her having a share of everything, pretty much stops that."

Beverly stood motionless a moment. "…There are some things that have become even more confused…I've been trying to understand why Dorothy would wait until you were completely defenseless before starting to cut you to ribbons. It's like she was trying to turn me against you?"

"She was! She knew that when I came out of the coma, that you'd be one of the first persons I'd talk to. She wanted you skeptical of anything I said…She didn't know at the time that my memory was going to give me so much trouble."

"Why would she do such a thing?"

"She must believe I know something I'm not supposed to. If I do, I sure can't remember it."

Beverly grabbed his arm roughly as he stepped away. "Be careful, Sully," she said, gripping tighter. "…There's more to this than what's surfacing. It looks to me like your problems are just beginning."

Sully glanced to the east before sitting in the Buick. Daylight was barely visible on the horizon. He threw the duffel in the back and sat down…Wondering how things would work out made it an even longer morning.

# CHAPTER TWENTY FIVE

Sully turned into the parking lot of Mammy Shanty's restaurant by the fork at West Peachtree and Peachtree. It was just past six; the sun had yet to break cleanly through the overcast. There was no reason to feel threatened at the popular diner on the north side of town, so he dispensed the .45 into the glove box. Not yet ready to completely throw caution to the wind, he surveyed the surroundings for several minutes before entering the restaurant. If someone had followed him and had intentions to harm him, what better place could they possibly find than an isolated parking lot; especially early in the morning.

The breakfast crowd, which usually didn't show until 6:30, had yet to arrive. He was the first customer in the door. The employees were busily scurrying about getting ready for the heavy workload ahead.

Sully found a booth and waited patiently, careful not to disturb them as they prepared for that first meal.

Several minutes later, a waitress wearing an apron and an infectious smile came up. "Bet you thought we weren't going to wait on you, didn't you?"

"I didn't think that at all," Sully said, teasing her. "You'd go broke in a hurry if you didn't take care of customers."

"Sorry it took so long to get here…Getting this meal out of the way is always the biggest part of our day."

"Take your time," Sully said. "I'm in no hurry."

"You care for a cup of coffee till we get the grill going?"

"Sounds good! And when you can, throw some eggs and bacon on for me…Maybe a couple of biscuits."

"Be back in a minute with the coffee," she said, walking away and looking over her shoulder. "Might take a while for the food." She returned exactly a minute later with a six-cup pot of coffee.

Sully thanked her, poured a hot cup and relaxed back against the cushioned seat.

"The cook's got your order and if you want to read the morning paper, I'm through with mine."

"Sure you don't mind?"

"It was going in the garbage anyway."

Before he completed that first cup of coffee, the house was full of patrons looking for their initial meal of the day. Sully relaxed after eating and was on his third cup of coffee when he spread the paper out on the booth table. He had a ritual of reading the headlines first, then the sports and the remaining smaller stories in the rest of the paper. When he came upon an article buried deep in the back pages, a shiver went up his spine. Almost unnoticeable, a one-paragraph announcement read: *"Local janitor survives being shot seven times at his place of employment."*

Sully read the few sentences about the attack on Hector Santana over and over. *Hector*, the article said, had been shot seven times while sitting in his truck alone. He was found in an alley beside Big Town's poolroom, his place of employment. No motive or suspects had been uncovered at the time of the story. Sully wondered if the killing of Fletcher and Gracci had anything to do with Hector's being shot. He dismissed the thought quickly. Hector was far too street wise to say anything about that to anyone. It had to be unrelated since there were no live witnesses and there was no one who could place him on the scene. Sully looked at the time; it was after seven-thirty and the sun was up. He paid the tab at the front counter, then walked back to the booth and left a nice tip. After exiting the restaurant, he fought the early morning traffic heading in the general direction of Georgia Baptist Hospital on Boulevard Drive. He looked for a parking spot in front of the hospital unsuccessfully, but when someone pulled away from the curb down the street, he pounced on it. The parking spot just happened to be directly across from Garan T. Jewels' place of business. He parked quickly, then walked briskly across the busy thoroughfare trying to avoid the speedy traffic. He stopped at the plate glass window in front the lawyer's office and peered inside; the door was locked and no one was there. *Maybe he was early? It was just eight o'clock.* He dodged the fast-moving automobiles that seemed to be trying to run him down, returning to the other side of the street. Safely getting back to the sidewalk on the other side, Sully then made his way to the Emergency Room of the hospital.

Sully stepped into the empty waiting room and looked around for a nurse. Not seeing one, he went to the window that had an *"Admissions"* sign hanging above it. There was no one in sight so he waited.

A nurse noticed him shortly there after with his chin resting lazily on his chest. She asked pleasantly, "Can I help you?"

Sully jerked his head up. Caught unaware, his thoughts were momentarily in another world. "Hope so," he said, standing and gathering himself. "You mind taking a look at these stitches? I think they need to come out?"

She opened the door under the *"Hospital Personnel Only"* sign and peered out of the doorway into the quiet hallway. "Come on in," she smiled easily. "We're pretty busy but I think we can squeeze you in."

Sully sat and turned his head so the nurse could see the sutures. "Is it time for them to come out?"

"Wouldn't have hurt for them to be taken out sooner but there's no harm done. Just relax," she said, "this won't take long." she reached into a tray for scissors and a pair of tweezers and began snipping.

Sully felt a sting like someone pricked him with a needle every time a stitch was clipped. The extraction of the sutures took less than two minutes.

Swabbing the wounds with alcohol, the nurse smiled again. "Believe it or not, I think you're going to survive."

Sully stood and rubbed his itchy scalp. "How much do I owe you?"

"Not a thing," she said. "We do this on a regular basis as long as we're not busy…It's not unusual in this part of town. But, before you go, tell me who thought of using fishing line to sew you up?"

"A friend," he replied. "Did she do a good job?"

"Yes, she did. So good in fact, I thought a doctor had sewn you up. The fishing line shot that theory down."

Sully left the Emergency Room and went to the front of the hospital. He glanced at the time; it was after nine o'clock. Jewels should be in his office by now. He crossed the busy street again, flagrantly jaywalking for the third time in just over an hour. He went to the entrance of Jewels' office and looked inside for the second time; the interior was still dark. He sat on the steps at the base of the front door and laid his head back against the cold glass. For the moment, he'd gone as far as he could go without Jewels. There was little choice left but to wait. Grady Hospital would be the next place to go after he was through with Jewels. The paper had mentioned Hector was there. If the cops weren't crawling all over Intensive Care, maybe he could get an update on how his friend was doing?

As morning wore on, a drowsy feeling enticed Sully to doze occasionally. The sun breaking through, along with the boredom of waiting, forced him to relax in the slowly decreasing chill.

"Mister Hawken!" a voice said loudly, shaking him from his slumber.

Sully looked up and recognized Jewels' secretary. He stood then stepped to the side, allowing her to get to the door. "You folks are running late, aren't you?" he asked, glancing at his watch; it was after ten.

"There was a matter to take care of at the courthouse this morning," she replied. "Your friend, Mister Gregory, was indicted by the grand jury on a *Murder One* charge and Garan had to be there to represent him."

Sully was bothered by that announcement; the legal persecution of Fred was completely out of hand. Something had to be done to grind that to a halt. "Where's Jewels now?" he asked, knowing he was helpless without the flamboyant lawyer. "Is he coming back to the office?"

"He'll be along shortly. He had a few calls to make at the court house."

Sully wondered why the lawyer didn't make the calls from his office.

The secretary quickly explained after noticing the curiosity on Sully's face. "It's really not that unusual. When Garan wants to keep things private, he finds a way to separate us."

Sully did not question her account of the calls, but *was* curious about what took place in the morning's proceedings. "What about

Fred? Was he in the courtroom with Jewels while this hearing was going on?"

"Of course…He *had* to be."

"Did Jewels put him on the stand?"

"For a while."

"What did he ask him about?"

"The weapon that was supposedly used in the crime, was the largest topic. Garan *was* going to call you as a witness since Gregory spent the day of the murder with you. The problem was, we couldn't find you. But—we weren't by ourselves there; half of Atlanta's been looking for you."

"*Who's* been looking for me?"

"A couple of detectives came by *several* times; then there were the uniformed policemen…Oh, yes, two guys with their heads all bandaged up dropped by…I hope they never come back."

"What did *they* look like?"

"I really can't say," she said. "The bandages covered most of their faces. "Big, I guess…One bigger than the other; a little on the fat side."

"Their faces! Did it look like they had been beaten?"

"I don't know about that, but, something definitely unpleasant had happened to them…It looked like they had been badly disfigured in an automobile accident."

*That* disclosure raised questions about something thought to be history. If Fletcher and Gracci had miraculously survived and were still alive, it was a distinct possibility that *they* had gunned down Hector. If that were so, Sully knew for a fact that he would be next. "The detectives? Do you happen to remember their names?"

"One of their names was Jones," she said, reaching into her purse. "Give me a minute to find their card."

"No need," Sully said. "I'm betting one was tall and thin and the other one was short and stocky?"

"Yes, do you know them?"

"Yeah," Sully said, walking to Jewels' desk and sitting. "We've crossed paths a few times." He took the automatic from his belt and eased the slide back. Sure a bullet was in the chamber, he eased the slide forward until it clicked. He pushed the slide safety up until it was firmly in place then dropped the gun back under his belt. There would be no more surprises for the remainder of the day.

# CHAPTER TWENTY SIX

When Jewels walked in his office, the first thing he spied was Sully stretched out in a chair with his feet up on his desk. He opened the banister gate and stepped through to what was supposed to be his private sector. "Well, Hawken," he said stiffly, laying a mountain of paperwork on the desk. "I see you've made yourself at home...Gone two weeks without a word and the first day back, it's like all's right in the world."

Sully got up from Jewels' chair and sat in one beside the desk. "I wasn't trying to take over your territory, Garan, but after sitting out front on the bricks for three hours, it figured I had something comfortable coming...If that's being rude, I apologize."

"You've been here that long?"

"Didn't have much of a choice! When I read about Hector Santana getting shot this morning, I thought it'd be best to see you as quick as possible."

"Who, pray tell, is Hector Santana? And what does his being shot have to do with me? I've never heard of him."

"He's the guy that pulled my fat out of the fire a few weeks ago. And, if I'm thinking right, almost got himself killed for the trouble."

"I have no earthly idea what you're talking about, young man. Would you mind explaining what this is all about?"

"Do you remember anything about a couple of hoods coming in here looking for me recently? They had their heads all wrapped up in bandages."

"It would be hard to forget those two," Jewels said. "It was not a pleasant experience. From the moment they walked in the door, I felt threatened."

"Do you remember how badly they were beat up?"

"I do," Jewels said. "Did you do that?"

"I had a little help."

"This Santana? Was he your partner in the endeavor?"

"Yes, he was," Sully said. "...And when they were dropped in an alley, they were supposed to be dead. Apparently they weren't!"

"Then you think these two men shot your friend in retaliation."

"If their names were Fletcher and Gracci, I'd bet my life on it."

"Since that's exactly what their names are, I'd say you already have. I have a memo in my desk confirming it…I had no intention of ever forgetting them!"

"They seem to have a way of leaving a lasting impression every place they go," Sully said. "I think they get a kick out of it!"

"When you walk through life, always confident you are a man as I have, then someone walks up and within minutes makes you a sniveling coward. *Yes*, I would have to say I've been impressed."

"Sorry you had to deal with that, Jewels. I'll take the blame for them coming here and pushing you around. If I'd have been in shape to take care of business to begin with, it never would've happened."

"You would've killed them both?"

"And never give it a thought!"

"I never dreamed you had such a callous side, Hawken."

"I don't have feelings where those two are concerned," Sully said. "They've already killed one friend, maybe two, and tried to kill another. They've had their shot at ending my days. They won't walk away from our next meeting so easily."

Jewels sat heavily in his chair, letting out a huge breath of air. "Now that we have your character flaws sufficiently summarized, I suggest we lay out a strategy to extract Mister Gregory from his imprisonment. I'm afraid your friend is one step short of being lost forever."

"That's about to change," Sully said. "I have something in my pocket that should get Fred released in a hurry—if certain people will listen."

Jewels looked suspiciously at him. "*Who* did you have in mind?"

"You said you were on friendly terms with Chief Jenkins. Do you suppose you could set up a meeting with just the three of us?"

"It's according to what you intend to lay on the table," Jewels replied. "That will determine whether I call him or not."

Sully pulled out the .45 Derringer he had taken from Judson Fletcher and laid it on the table. He peeled back the handkerchief covering it. "I believe this is the gun that killed Red Ward. With a little help, I think I can prove it. And, if the chief will listen to what I have to say, it could reveal a conspiracy in the police department."

"This meeting isn't supposed to be about police wrong-doing, Hawken...Our concern is with Mister Gregory!"

"That's the way it *has* to be, Jewels," Sully said. "It's the only way Fred will be able to get out of this mess. Do you remember telling me it would take at least six men in the police department to put Fred in the electric chair? Well, this is the way to expose them. If just one cop will come forward with what they know, it would prove the evidence was fabricated. It could put some bad policemen behind bars, if Jenkins decides to do the right thing."

"You don't actually think Herbert Jenkins will approve of something this drastic, do you? Good Lord, Hawken, these are cops who worship the ground he walks on...He'd never agree to anything that would destroy their loyalty."

"If he's a decent cop, he will," Sully said, refusing to accept the philosophy of police solidarity. "I can't see the chief supporting law enforcement brotherhood when something like this is going on."

Jewels reached for the telephone. "You know of course, this whole thing could backfire and blow up in our face. If it does, all hope is lost for Gregory."

"Call the Chief," Sully said. "Let's get this moving." He stood and walked to the front of the office, giving Jewels the freedom to explain the complexity of the situation. Gazing out the front glass window, he heard an angry outburst from Jewels. He wondered what the police chief said that provoked Jewels like that.

Jewels hung up and walked to the front of the office where Sully was. "Got some bad news, Hawken," he said. "The only way he'll give us an audience is for some officers come by and pick us up. We'll be under guard, something similar to an arrest. I told him you wouldn't agree, so we argued."

"You told him wrong," Sully said. "I don't care what the circumstances are, this is the only chance Fred has. There's no way I'll pass that up...Call him back! Ask him not to tell anyone of our coming, and to give me time to explain what I think happened without interruptions."

Jewels picked up the phone and made the call. He returned several minutes later with a grim look on his face. "A car will be here shortly...I hope you know what you're doing."

"Me too," Sully said and laid his head back on the chair.

# CHAPTER TWENTY SEVEN

Jewels stood quietly outside waiting for the arrival of the patrol car. Sully lingered inside thinking of how he would present his case to Chief Jenkins. Convincing the chief there was a conspiracy had to be a success in order to establish Fred's innocence. If he failed, the evidence would be wasted entirely. The whole venture would be defeated before it started. The fact that Jenkins was a hard sell wasn't the only reason he expected difficulty. There was more to it than that: If the chief went after the officers involved, the possibility exists that the department's loyalty would be lost forever. The charismatic *Top-Cop* was not about to put that commodity on the block unless he was dead certain of the outcome…Especially where a black man is indicted for murdering a white man. He knew first hand that Jenkins *wasn't* a hard-line prejudicial, but the current mindset in time had to be considered. The chief's survival depended on his ability to protect his officers, and above all, keep their fraternity intact. If Jenkins *were* to take up the cause of a Negro heading to the gallows, it would definitely be the test of his metal. Jewels now had the un-enviable job of changing that aspect of the powerful policeman's reasoning. No matter *how* strong the evidence was, he was not too confident.

A white, four-door Lincoln, with two uniformed police officers inside, double-parked in front of the office. The automobile had *Chief of Police* printed in small letters on the door. The smartly dressed officer stepped from the passenger side and asked Jewels, "Are you Jewels?"

"I am!" Jewels replied easily. "Hawken is inside." He stepped to the front door and asked Sully, "Are you ready?"

Sully thought negatively, *I hope I am.*

Jewels opened the rear door to the staff car and looked back at Sully. "You know of course, this trip has to end on a positive note," he said, sliding across the seat. "…For your sake and Gregory's."

The officer in the front seat turned to face them as they pulled away, "I'm Captain Otis Randall," he said, "Chief Jenkins' aide."

"Tell me something, Randall," Sully said. "Why did Jenkins insist on sending his personal car for us? I thought we had an agreement that our presence at the station wasn't supposed to be known."

"Nothing has changed, Hawken. No one will know you're in the building. Just leave it in our hands...It'll make for a shorter day!"

"Let's take another look at this, captain," Sully said, "you guys come here in a car that stands out like a sore thumb. Doing that and then being dressed to the hilt in uniform, is not good judgment. I'm having a hard time going along with broadcasting importance that can't be ignored."

Randall turned around with a frown creasing his tight lips. "Maybe you don't realize it, Hawken, but you're in no position to dictate to *anyone* at the moment. I've read a number of reports recently; all with serious charges pending against *you*. If I were you, I'd be thankful to get an audience instead of being in the lock up."

Sully's face went flush with redness. He leaned forward and was about to respond but was pulled back by Jewels.

"This isn't the time," Jewels said quietly. "Losing your temper is a waste of emotion at the moment...Save it for when it's needed."

Randall looked over his shoulder wondering why Jewels would say something like that. He never realized how close he came to being throttled from behind.

Sully remained silent the remainder of the trip to mask his infuriation. To calm himself, he thought intently of ways to handle things without being the subject of abject consequences. He gritted his teeth and opted to accept his fate if he did wind up doing the wrong thing. He fully understood that after all was said and done, hindsight was always the most attractive. But cold hard reality is, Fred's welfare, and his, depended primarily on how well this case was presented.

The Lincoln stopped and parked on a side street, adjacent to the front of the police station. The driver patiently viewed the pedestrians nearby until the streets were clear. He stepped from the car once he was satisfied there were no prying eyes. "It's clear!" he said, then walked toward a steel door that led into the station. The captain opened the entrance, obviously private because of its impregnable nature, and everyone moved inside.

With the door locked behind them, the foursome walked up the stairwell to the second level. At the top of the stairs, Captain Randall opened the lone door there and invited everyone into the chief's private office.

Herbert Jenkins sat behind his desk silently, perceiving the situation with the people who had entered his domain. There was a dark scowl on his face.

Captain Randall asked everyone to be seated and then waited until they were all comfortable. "...Now," he said easily, "let's introduce ourselves properly before we get this meeting under way."

Sully and Jewels remained silent. They would let the captain handle the introductions as he saw fit.

"This is Chief Jenkins," Randall said, then pointed at Sully. "This is Sully Hawken, chief...I believe you know Mister Jewels."

Jewels and the chief acknowledged their association by nodding.

The room was quiet a moment as Chief Jenkins glared intensely at Sully. He was apparently looking for a sign of weakness but found nothing. The initial proceedings began with an abrupt statement by Jenkins. "All right, Hawken, you asked for my attention...Now you have it! I suggest you make the most of it."

"First of all," Sully began, "I don't want you thinking I'm here with allegations of police corruption without anything to back it up."

Jenkins stiffened. "Be very aware of what you say today, Hawken. You're making some pretty wild charges against some of the best investigators here. Understand this, young man; I will not put up with unwarranted accusations against them until the full truth of the matter is known."

"I understand that, but don't I have the right to be heard?" Sully asked with respect. His tone was such so as not to become an adversary. He certainly didn't want to waste the opportunity of talking to the top law enforcement man in Atlanta.

Jenkins motioned for Sully to continue.

"I'll start with the *most* damning thing concerning the charges against Gregory."

"Easy, Hawken," Jenkins warned him. "I've told you what I'll put up with, so present your case without indictments or you're out of here."

"How familiar are you with the Gregory case?" Sully asked politely. "It'd keep me from covering a lot of unnecessary ground if I knew."

"Because of the implications," Jenkins responded, "I made it a point to know every aspect of the case. To be honest; I don't think you have anything that will change my opinion of the charges against him."

"The murder weapon," Sully said. "Do you know about it?"

"I *read* the report!"

"Did you know that the gun was sparkling clean when the prints were lifted?"

A frown crossed Jenkins' face. "So?"

"Then you have to know the weapon was pulled from a sewer just blocks away while Fred Gregory was sitting in a cell?"

Jenkins frowned coldly. He hadn't taken that into consideration and was embarrassed by the oversight.

"If you know that, you're aware of the impossibility of extracting prints from a weapon covered with grime and sediment. The gun was cleaned, then deliberately forced upon Gregory in his cell. After Fred handled the weapon, it was delivered to your fingerprint people covered with his prints."

Jenkins raised his right hand and rubbed his cheek. "Randall!" he said. "Get whoever lifted those prints in the office. I don't want anyone outside of this office knowing why he's being brought in…Not a word, understood?"

"Give me a few minutes," Randall said and then stepped out. He returned a few minutes later and took a seat. "He'll be here shortly," he told Jenkins. "He's got a report he's finishing up…"

"No one took notice?" Jenkins asked.

"No sir!" Randall replied.

There was a knock on the door almost immediately.

Randall went to the door and opened it. "Come in, Stewart," he said, then guided the officer to a chair. "We have a few questions."

Officer Stewart looked confused.

"This Gregory case," Randall said. "We have something that doesn't seem to add up…We're hoping you can straighten things out."

Stewart looked around nervously. "I'll do what I can, but I had little to do with that investigation."

Chief Jenkins leaned forward. "Did you pull the prints from the murder weapon in question?"

"Yes sir," Stewart replied, "but that was the extent of my involvement."

"Then you were *very* involved! What kind of shape was the gun in when you received it?"

Stewart swallowed hard, obviously uneasy at the line of questioning. "I don't understand…It was just a gun tagged to have prints removed."

Jenkins frowned. "Was the gun clean or was it covered with filth?"

"It was a clean weapon," Stewart said, becoming more uncomfortable.

"Who placed the gun in your hands?"

"Homicide, sir."

"Don't play dumb with me," Jenkins exploded. "I want to know the name of the investigator who gave the weapon to you."

Stewart winced; he was beginning to feel the weight of being asked questions that might involve him in criminal conspiracy. By being grilled in such an intent manner, there was little doubt that the chief already had the answers. "The officer in charge of the investigation," he said shakily, "was Detective Smith in Homicide."

Jenkins stood up rigidly, his face full of anger. "And you're standing here in front of me saying that you received a weapon straight from the sewers of Atlanta without a trace of grime on it."

"I…I didn't know it was pulled from a sewer," Stewart replied weakly.

"How is it that every officer in the investigation knew where the gun had been and you didn't?" Jenkins demanded, then glowered at the officer with contempt. "It's your job to know these things. You'd better think very carefully before you give me an answer, Stewart. The road you're about to take is very critical."

Stewart bowed his head in resignation. "...You're right, I did know the gun was pulled from the sewer. There's not much I can do about it now, but when I let that get by me, I knew it was nothing but trouble. It's not much of an excuse, but I figured at the time that homicide knew what they were doing..."

Jenkins lost the hardness in his voice after realizing he might have to break a good officer. "Did Gregory being a Negro have anything to do your decision?"

"It had a lot to do with it," Stewart said honestly, unable to look the chief in the eye. "This sounds bad, I know, but I was brought up where folks didn't cotton to colored people's foolishness. I looked at it that the way when Smith brought the gun in to be dusted. I figured Gregory was guilty of something anyway, so why *not* hang him out to dry? It probably doesn't matter now, but I know that I should've told somebody about the gun. I guess it'll mean my badge."

"We'll worry about that later," Jenkins said, leaning back in the chair. "Now, when you returned the weapon to Smith, was it in the same condition it was when you received it?"

"It was still spotless!"

Jenkins looked at Stewart thoughtfully. "This might not be as unforgiving as you think," he said. "There'll be charges, make no mistake...And you'll answer to them. Just remember that whatever the outcome, *I* have the final say. The way you've conducted yourself today will definitely have a bearing on the decision..."

"Do I keep working, sir?" Stewart asked, "Or am I on suspension?"

"You go back to work as if nothing happened. Captain Randall will inform you when a statement is necessary. In the meantime, not a word of this is to be repeated outside of these walls. Is that clear?"

"Yes, sir!" Stewart said, then quietly left the office.

When the door closed, Jenkins turned to Sully. "What's else is there?" he asked, no longer in doubt of what was being presented.

Sully moved on to what he perceived to happen next. "I think the next thing to look into is, the route the weapon took once it was in the building. The second place the gun should have gone was to ballistics. I know this is far-fetched, but I don't believe the bullets used as evidence are the ones that killed Red Ward. If I'm correct, the original bullets were replaced with some from the .45 Smith and Jones cleaned up."

Jenkins did not react negatively to this allegation as he had previously. He put both hands on the desk and stood. He paced several minutes before turning to Randall. "Get Collingsworth." he growled.

"There are other officers on the ballistics detail beside Collingsworth," Randall said. "You sure you don't want them all?"

"Just Collingsworth will do; I have my reasons. He's the man Smith would approach with something like this."

Randall left the office wondering why the chief made that statement, but knowing it would be disclosed after Collingsworth joined the meeting. Both men returned shortly and the detective was instructed to have a seat.

Collingsworth felt tension in the atmosphere and was instantly ill at ease. He had noticed the look on Detective Stewart's face when he returned to his desk and had a good idea of what was happening.

Jenkins began questioning the officer, but not in the manner that he had approached Officer Stewart. This line of questioning was delivered with compassion and thoughtfulness. "How long have you been here, Collingsworth?" he asked quietly. "Ten—eleven years now?"

"No, sir! Just six!"

"You came here from California, right?"

"Yes sir! Long Beach!"

"Why did you leave your post there and seek a job in Atlanta?"

The question seemed to embarrass the sergeant. "Can we discuss this privately, sir?" he asked with spasmodically blinking eyes.

"The answer's unimportant," Jenkins said. "I just want you to know I've known for some time why you transferred to Atlanta."

Collingsworth glanced from side to side, noticeably disturbed. "What's this about, Chief? Have I done something wrong?"

"We'll know in a moment," Jenkins said. "Right now, I want you to answer Mister Hawken's questions as honestly as you can."

"Yes sir," he said, almost unintelligible. "I'll do my best."

Sully looked straight at the sergeant, the notion firmly planted to approach the officer in the same fashion Chief Jenkins had. "Sergeant, how familiar are you with the Gregory case?"

Collingsworth did not answer right away. "...I've been expecting this," he said dejectedly. "I knew there'd be trouble the very minute those bastards came to my desk."

Jenkins leaned forward, his face taking on a crimson color again. "...I'm assuming you mean Homicide Detectives Smith and Jones?"

"Yes sir," Collingsworth mumbled.

"Just wanted to get it straight! Was it the first time they asked you for a favor?"

"Favor!" the sergeant said through clinched teeth. "Is that what you think it was? They've been blackmailing me for years. This was the third time they forced me to do something like this. They didn't make no bones about ruining my career if I didn't cooperate. It wasn't like I had a choice."

"You could have come to me," Jenkins said. "...But besides that, didn't the idea of sending an innocent black man to the electric chair bother you?"

"They said he was guilty."

"And you believed them?"

"I certainly wanted to. They just didn't give me an alternative."

Jenkins was quiet for a moment. "...Son, do this: Explain what you know about the Gregory case, and we'll get back to those other incidents when the time's right."

Collingsworth eased forward in the chair. "...It was about a month ago when this business about Gregory started. I was at my desk one afternoon, trying to catch up on some late reports. Then Smith and Jones came to me with the gun. As usual, they had a cocky attitude because they have something detrimental on me. It's something I'd rather not talk about...They knew I couldn't turn them down. They dropped the .45 on the desk and told me to fire two rounds from it. They wanted me to exchange those bullets with the ones that came out of Red Ward's body. I did what they told me to, and those bullets are now ballistic evidence in the case."

Jenkins stood and began pacing back and forth to a quiet audience. He stopped mid-stride and pointed at Collingsworth. "Do you still have the original bullets that came out of Red Ward?"

"Yes sir," Collingsworth said. "I thought it best to hang onto the truth."

Jenkins looked away but kept his finger pointing at Collingsworth. "Exchange those bullets back, and put them in their proper prospective. In the meantime, nothing is to be said of this meeting. I'll handle this from here on in. Go back to your desk as if nothing happened."

"What kind of charges are going to be brought against me, Chief? I've got a family...I need to make plans."

"I'll talk with the district attorney and I.A. and we'll see what comes of it. I will say this: your coming clean with this is positively in your favor. And the fact that you were blackmailed, will certainly be discussed."

When Collingsworth left the office, Sully quickly turned the meeting to Fred's incarceration. "Don't you think there's enough proof on the table to release Fred today?" He asked Jenkins. "He's been behind bars long enough for something he didn't do."

"I agree," Jenkins said, "but due process has to be observed. The DA and a superior court judge will have to be informed so it can be dealt with properly."

Sully stood and then placed the neatly wrapped .45 Derringer on the desk. "If you want something that could clear things up this very minute, I think this is it," he said, uncovering the weapon. "This is a Derringer I took off a guy named Judson Fletcher. His prints are on it. If you run it through ballistics, I think you'll find the bullets from this gun match the ones taken out of Red Ward."

Randall interrupted. "So it was you who put those two in the hospital? I knew something was fishy when they refused to tell us anything."

"The truth is, I didn't have the strength to handle it myself. I probably wouldn't have survived if it hadn't been for a friend pulling them off of me. I was completely helpless until that happened."

"What's your friend's name?" Randall asked. "We need to talk to him."

"His name is Hector Santana; but you won't be able to question him for a while. He's at Grady and in pretty bad shape. Fletcher and Gracci filled him full of bullets because he stopped them from killing me."

"Do you have proof of that?" Randall asked. "We can't just add these charges on without it, you know."

"Just my word," Sully said. "But they did it. And if you don't want to indict them, I'll take care of it myself."

Randall stared hard at Sully. "Wipe those kind of thoughts from your mind right now, Hawken. This station is full of officers who are quite capable of handling the situation. You don't have that prerogative."

"If we're through here," Sully looked to Jenkins, would you mind getting us back to Jewels' office? I have to find a place to lay my head that's safe. With Fletcher and Gracci out there looking for me, it's a safe bet that I'll have Smith and Jones hot on my trail too. When *they* find out who put them behind the eight ball, the odds of one of them catching up with me aren't favorable."

"Take Hawken and Jewels where they want to go," Jenkins told his driver, "And I don't want anything happening to either of them."

Sully stepped to the exit leading to the side street, expecting Jewels to follow.

Jewels remained seated. "I think I'll stay a while...It might be best to remain here for Gregory's release. I'm sure he'll appreciate it."

Sully said nothing as he followed the driver down the steps and to the automobile. He had wondered during the meeting why Jewels' had gone so uncharacteristically quiet. There had to be a reason for that kind of behavior. The lawyer was usually outspoken to the degree of absurdity, but he had been almost completely silent the entire afternoon. Then, to announce he was staying behind for Fred's release seemed totally unnecessary. It could take hours, but Fred was capable of being discharged without assistance. Sully was confused, and was becoming more suspicious of the flamboyant lawyer's actions as the day lengthened.

# CHAPTER TWENTY EIGHT

Sully stepped from the car in front of Jewels' office and warily looked around. Without a doubt, the best thing to do at the moment was to avoid the men who were bent on extracting revenge. After a little soul-searching, he settled on allowing the police department time to do their job. If they wouldn't, or couldn't by a certain date, then he would revert to his original plans of dealing with them. The turn of events had made him so cautious, it was beginning to be too much. With Fletcher and Gracci, plus the two detectives searching for him simultaneously, the odds of *not* being found were not in his favor. They could be anywhere. Hopeful they were not watching his car at the moment, he glanced around and then walked cautiously to where the Buick was parked. Cranking the car, he pulled away from the curb and drove toward town.

Sully pulled off onto a side street two blocks from Grady Hospital. He walked slowly toward the hospital, observing everything on the way carefully. There was always the outside chance that someone would be there looking for him. His friendship with Hector was well known and he would naturally be expected to check on his friend. He would do just that, but not in a way that would be obvious. Sully went to the rear of the building and waited patiently by a locked basement door with a *for employees only* sign. Twenty minutes later, the door swung open and two nurses stepped out without giving him a glance. He caught the door before it closed and slipped quietly inside. To his good fortune, there was no one in the hall to question his going against house rules. He took the stairwell to the first floor, stepped in and went to the closest nurses' station. He asked the nurse on duty what floor Intensive Care was on, then went back to the stairs and walked up to the third floor. A point was made to be very quiet as he took each step. He certainly didn't want to walk up on somebody with a gun in their hand; especially someone looking for him. He eased the door to the third floor open and looked carefully in both directions. He saw only hospital personnel. He lingered a while longer then dropped his fedora down over his eyes and turned his jacket collar up. On one swift movement, he went out the door and walked quickly to the ICU waiting room. It was deserted. He sat in the corner to easily survey all traffic in and out and waited. His right hand rested comfortably on the .45 under his belt.

When Cissi Santana walked into the empty room, she did a double-take. "Sully, what on earth are you here? Don't you realize the danger you're in?"

"I wanted to see about Hector!"

"He's doing fine! But you won't be if those men find you. They were at the end of the hall yesterday with their heads all covered in bandages...I recognized them at once. Hector figured they'd be here looking for you and warned me...You'd better leave!"

"They didn't bother you or Hector, did they?"

"I don't think they'll do anything with so many witnesses around."

"Maybe not to you, but it won't mean a thing if they walk up on me. Listen, cissi, Hector's all right and my being here could be a problem. Tell him I'll be back when things lighten up." He handed her a fist full of bills and left before she could object.

Sully found himself pulling into the parking area of the nurse's quarters. He parked and just stared at Beverly's apartment window. He sat behind the wheel a long time before coming to a conclusion. Finally, he reached over the seat and grabbed his bag. He threw it over a shoulder and then made his way toward the building. There were only two things to face: Acceptance or rejection. It was in her hands now. He was ready to accept whatever choice she made. He held Beverly's keys in one hand and his bag in the other when he knocked on the door.

Beverly stood in the door for a moment and stared. Without saying a word, she took the bag from his shoulder and walked into the kitchen. "I was beginning to wonder if you were coming in at all," she said quietly. "I've been watching from the window."

"I'm not very good at being confused," Sully said, following her into the kitchen. "I have these feelings for you, and I don't think you want anything like that."

"I wouldn't let you in the apartment if that were the case."

"Why didn't you tell me that before I made such a fool of myself this morning? It hasn't made for a good day!"

"That would have been hard to do, Sully...You were out the door and gone before I had a chance to think...Maybe I've just gotten used to your company, I don't know? Maybe I care more than I'm willing to admit?"

Sully looked at her as if for the first time. Her hair was unkempt and her eyes were red from crying and rubbing them. She held the housecoat tightly with both hands to make sure it was completely covering her. Without warning, she let go of the garment and it tumbled to the floor. She faced him completely naked.

"I was about to take a shower when I heard the knock," she said seductively.

Sully smiled. Less than a minute ago she was looking at him from the window. She abruptly stepped toward the shower and her effortless movement across the floor complimented her magnificent figure. It was all he could do to keep from following her.

Beverly suddenly had doubts if she was handling the situation correctly. The thoughts were still there when she reached in and turned on the shower. When the water reached the right temperature, she stepped in and began lathering her body. When the wash rag was down to her hips, the shower curtain was roughly drawn to the side.

"Let me do that," Sully said gruffly, stepping in with her.

Beverly put both hands on his chest and pushed him away, but after a matter of seconds crumbled under the onslaught. She had never been taken to such heights so quickly, and surrendered without further protest. As the steaming water rained sensuously down on them, they remained wrapped in each other's arms for over an hour. They were trapped in a sea of ecstasy.

Sully stepped away after the long soaking, looked at his wrinkled hands and smiled. "We'll look like a pair of prunes if we don't get out of the shower," he said, kissing her. "...You mind?"

She cut the water off and reached for a towel. "No," she smiled. "There are things to do other than getting squeaky clean." It was obvious that when Beverly made a decision, it was the complete package. It was not a parcel at a time.

Sully followed her from the shower and then sat down without bothering to dry off. Her perfect body and flawless skin had him mesmerized. While she dried off facing him, he reached out and pulled her toward him. He stood quickly and lifted her into his arms. With her head on his shoulder, he clumsily reached for the doorknob. Turning it, he eased the door back with his foot. He shifted Beverly sideways to keep from hitting her head, then went into the bedroom. He laid her across the edge of the bed, then feasted his eyes on her gorgeous figure again. She lay there quietly and did not move. In his entire life, Sully was never with a woman capable of moving him to such distraction. He was completely speechless. He turned out the lights, then stepped to the bed and lay beside her. They were locked in a sensuous embrace almost instantly. After that, all sense of time was lost. At seven o'clock the next morning, without a word passing between them, they drifted off to sleep in a sea of contentment.

# CHAPTER TWENTY NINE

"Wake up, Sully" Beverly shook him gently. "We need to talk before I leave."

Sully opened his eyes to the soft tugging, then rolled over. "What time is it?" he asked, groggily fumbling for the clock.

"It's after five-thirty," she said, running her hand through his hair. "I have to be on the floor in less than an hour."

"You're going back to work today?" he asked, sitting upright in the bed.

"It's been over two weeks," she said. "You're better now, and I can't just sit around here without good reason. Being out of work all the time can create a problem at the hospital."

Still dazed, Sully stared into empty space. "I didn't expect it to end so soon...I was hoping we'd have a little more time together..."

"C'mon, Sully, we haven't been out of bed for three days except to eat," she said, kissing him on the nose. "We can't stay locked up in a fit of passion forever."

"Don't see why not," he said, throwing his legs over the side of the bed and sliding his feet into his slippers. "I'm enjoying it. Aren't you?"

"Immensely!" she said. "But there comes a time when the good life has to be earned. Just living it isn't enough."

"How about *that*," Sully said, faking disappointment. "A guy finally gets happy and all the lady does is spout philosophy."

"This isn't the time for jokes, Sully," she said in a somber tone. "We have serious matters to discuss...Now, listen to me."

Sully grew silent when the seriousness in her voice became evident. "...I hope this isn't about what I think it is," he said quietly.

She stroked his cheek gently. "More than likely, it is," she said. "Do you remember the last time I tried to explain about Virginia Moran and Dorothy Haygood? You didn't want to hear it then, but now, there isn't a choice. There are things that you *have* to know about me."

"I wasn't trying to avoid the issue, Beverly. You were uncomfortable discussing it, so I changed the subject; it's no big mystery."

"Well, I want you to listen this time. I feel like I've done nothing but present a false front and I'm beginning to feel guilty."

"To be honest, I'd rather *not* hear about something that happened before I met you. I'm all right with things as they are. Do you realize that if I told you everything I'm guilty of, we'd never even have a relationship."

"There's a lot more to it than that," she said, standing. "I've been involved in things that you might have trouble dealing with."

Sully stood and put his hands on her shoulders. "You're selling me short, lady…You haven't learned a whole lot about me since we've been together. Now, go to work," he said, guiding her to the door, "and forget this nonsense."

She whirled at the entrance and threw her arms around his neck. "I didn't think I'd fall in love with you," she said. "It's making all this *very* complex."

"It always does," he said, pushing her gently into the hallway. "Now relax! I'll try to be here when you get back."

Sully showered lazily after Beverly left, then went into the kitchen and poured a cup of coffee. He took the coffee into the bedroom, sat it on the night table and then began dressing. By the time he was ready for the day, slivers of daylight broke through the window shades. He walked out into the parking lot, got into the Buick, turned the ignition key on and pressed his foot hard on the floor starter. He let the Buick idle a few minutes, then left the parking area heading in the general direction of downtown. He drove down Pryor Street into mid-town, then took a hard left at Auburn Avenue. He slowed down as he approached the alley leading to the Gregory home. He glanced quickly down the muddy dead-end street to see if there was any activity close by. Nothing considered troublesome was there but he decided to make another pass just to be on the safe side. Convinced there was no stakeout, he drove into the quagmire. Still not wanting to make a wrong move, he pulled the .45 from his belt and checked the chamber. A live round was in the barrel and the safety was off; it was ready to fire. Stopping in front of the house, he glanced around once more while standing by the car door, then cautiously stepped up on the porch. With his hand locked tightly on the handle of the automatic, he knocked on the door. He heard heavy footsteps coming across the floor inside, and was sure Fred was going to open the door.

The door opened partially, then suddenly, a huge revolver was thrust into Sully's face. "What you want, man?" the enormous black man said contemptuously.

Sully jerked back in surprise, then his face tightened in anger. "You take that piece away from my face, and we'll talk about it," he snarled.

"Mister Sully?" he heard Fred's voice in the background. "Is that you?"

"Yeah, it's me!" Sully said, looking past the man blocking the doorway. "Now tell this gorilla to step aside."

"Let him in, brother," Fred said, coming toward the door. "It my boss!"

"What's this about?" Sully asked Fred. "Are you okay?"

"I's fine...But I think you's in trouble."

"What do you mean?" Sully asked. "...Is there something I don't know about?"

Fred placed his hand over his brother's revolver and pushed it to the side. "C'mon inside, boss," he said. "You ain't 'posed to be runnin' 'round in the open like this. 'Sides, if you knew what happnin', you wouldn't be here at all."

Sully stepped inside avoiding Fred's frowning brother. "...Okay, now tell me what this is all about?"

Fred paused a moment. "...You 'member t'other night when I got outta jail?"

"I wasn't there," Sully said. "I left before they released you. Jewels said he was going to hang around until they released you, so I took off..."

"Well, that fella' Jewels took care of them legal matters all right, jes like he 'posed to. But I was doin' some listenin' while that was goin' on. I heard all 'bout them 'tectives bein' in trouble for makin' all that stuff up 'bout me. An' they's talkin' about them two gangsters and how you and yo' friend busted 'em up and put 'em in the hospital. They say that's why yo' friend was shot all up…An you was bein' sent a message that you's gon' to be nex.'"

"I'm aware of all that, *now,* what's happened that's got *you* so upset?"

"It's that lawyer, boss. You best be on yo' toes from now on."

"What'd he do?"

"All that time I's in jail, that man act funny 'round me. Can't 'xactly put my finger to it, but first time I sees him at Fulton Tower, I knew somethin' weren't right."

"You sure you're not seeing something that's not there, Fred? Granted, Jewels is a little quirky, but there's no reason to doubt him."

"You's 'bout to change yo' way of thinkin' on that," Fred said easily. "You 'member that night he got me outta the lock-up. He got us a taxi when we outside, then we head fo'the house. I thank him fo' what he did and went inside to talk to Mama 'fore she went to bed. She ain't been sleeping too good, me not bein' 'round, so's talkin' a lil' put her to ease. Once she still, I steps out to the porch an look up to the stars. Well, that taxi what brought me home had been gone a long time and I figured that Jewels fella' had left with it…But he didn't! He were standin' down to the corner under the streetlight. Plain as day, he was talkin' to them two 'tectives everybody out lookin' for."

"The light at the end of the alley is fifty yards away, Fred. Are you sure it was them?"

"I knows what I saw, boss, and I ain't wrong. Them 'tectives was chummy as all getout with Jewels, jes like I say."

"Smith and Jones, right?"

"Yassuh, it were them two. Plain as the nose on your face."

"With Jewels?"

"Yassuh!"

A look of concern crossed Sully's face. "If that's the case, and Jewels is tied to them somehow, I've got myself in a mess."

"That ain't all you's got to worry about," Fred said. "Sides them two comin' 'round all the time, they's been two other men here askin' questions. Didn't bother me none, but it got mama to worryin'. She don' like me leavin' the house at all now."

Sully aimed a thumb in the direction of the Fred's huge brother standing by the door. "Is that why he's answering the door?"

"He jes *one* of the brothers stayin' here. Mama didn't like what was goin' on so she ask 'em to hang 'round a spell."

"How many brothers do you have?"

"Countin' me, they's five. Rest of 'em sleepin' in the back right now. One of 'em is always up here by the door."

"I can't understand why your family is so upset though," Sully said. "That bunch is after my hide, not yours."

"Boss, they's the same ones what wanted to fry my hide just to get to you. And they damn nigh had me, even without a dime's worth of proof. If you hadn't a' foun' that gun, I'd have wound up sittin' in 'Ol Sparky for sure. It different on my side of the fence, boss. Black folk fight you gun and knife: we ain't scairt of that. When we gets spooked is when white folks come at us with blood in their eyes. We knows we's gon' lose that battle; ain't nothin' we can do. We jes bunch up like rabbits trapped in a hole and hide. We knows we's gon' be some hound's breakfast fo' long."

Sully reached in his pocket and pulled out his billfold; his association with the Gregory family had created a lot of pain for them and it was time to bring it to a halt. He handed Fred a wad of bills amounting to over two hundred dollars. "It's all I have right now," he said. "It'll have to do until I get to the bank."

Fred handed the money back. "You don't owes me nothin', boss. You the only white friend I got, and I don't need no pay for helping a friend."

"You wouldn't be in such a mess if it wasn't for me encouraging you with money," Sully said, trying in vain to force the cash on Fred.

"That weren't none of your doin', boss. People what don't like coloreds is the cause of my troubles. We jes call it even!"

Sully pocketed the money reluctantly. "You going back to work at the hospital now?" he asked, turning to leave.

"I gon' jes' stay with mama right now, I's worry'd 'nex' time them lawdogs come 'roun, they might sho' 'nough get me in that hot seat at Reidsville."

Sully was extremely agitated when he left by what Fred's family had been put through unnecessarily.  He would make it a point to discuss things with Captain Randall.  Fred and his family should be protected better.

# CHAPTER THIRTY

By the time Sully entered the Decatur Street station, the frustration had subsided enough to where the subject would be approached rationally. He decided to give the benefit of doubt to the police for their failure to bring in Smith and Jones. He stepped in the precinct and searched for the one policeman who would give him the truth. An abrasive plainclothes walked up behind him and tapped him roughly on the shoulder.

"You looking for somebody in particular, Hawken?" the officer asked icily.

"Captain Randall," he replied, returning the cop's stony glare.

"Over there," the officer said sourly, pointing to a glass-enclosed office at the rear of the large chamber.

Sully walked through a maze of busy officers, curious as to why all eyes were focused intently on him. Then, it dawned on him: The hostility was so thick because he was responsible for the downfall of two detectives. They didn't stop to think that the evidence he presented was the key factor, or that an innocent man was saved from the electric chair. They only focused on a single fact: One of their own had been taken down due to an outsider's efforts. It was all that was necessary to trigger such a response.

Sully ignored the angry stares and moved through the crowd into Randall's office. It was empty. He opted to wait and took a seat by the desk. Several minutes later, he saw Randall walking toward his office shouting angrily at the officers that they had a job to do and to get back to work.

Randall came in the office with a smile on his face. "Don't pay any attention to those guys," he said, shaking Sully's hand. "They're uneasy about what's going on. One of 'em gets hurt and they all feel the pain. It makes them want to retaliate."

"I figured that's what it was…I'm a little dense at times; it took a few seconds."

Randall walked around the cubicle and closed the blinds. "I know you wouldn't be here unless it was something important, so let's do this in privacy." He sat down and faced Sully. "Now, what's on your mind?"

"I've got a long list...You got the time?"

"I'll *make* the time."

"Well, first of all, I don't understand how Smith and Jones are still able to walk the streets with so many cops out there looking for them. The Gregory family is being terrorized by those two, and nothing is being done about it. They watched the Gregory home for days in hopes of my showing up, and luckily, when I did go there, they had already left...Tell me something: Why weren't they put behind bars the same day Jewels and I had that meeting with Jenkins? I presented enough evidence that some kind of action should have been warranted; you *certainly* had reason to do something."

"We had '*Just Cause*,' no getting around that," Randall agreed. "The problem was, certain aspects of the law had to be conducted before we could do anything. First of all, the Stewart and Collingsworth statements had to be presented to a judge. That took two hours to accomplish. By then, Smith and Jones got wind of what we were doing. It had spread through the department quickly and someone got the word to them...They haven't been seen since."

"I don't think anybody's looking very hard," Sully said sarcastically.

"What do you expect of me, Hawken? I *do* know what's happening, but *you* have to understand that this investigation isn't the most popular thing around here. These people don't like seeing a cop go down under any circumstances."

"Is it going to take somebody else getting killed to get cops off their butts?" Sully snapped. "Hell, man, Smith and Jones have been after me from the very day I got out of that coma. And now that I've become a problem, they'll be coming after me even harder...And nobody's doing anything."

"I can supply you with police protection," Randall said, "but I can't guarantee it'll be much help the way things are."

"You said it yourself, no cop *likes* seeing another cop in trouble. Any guard you put with me would probably turn his head at the first sign of difficulty. They'd step aside and let me deal with it alone. I'm better off looking out for myself."

"I'm sorry, Hawken, but it's the best I have to offer…And that's with every cop in this precinct knowing I'd fire them for not doing their job. Pure and simple, the majority of them don't care. They'd forego their pensions, their jobs, even spend time in prison before turning in a fellow officer. It's a stacked deck. And I have no idea how to combat it…Do you?"

"I guess I'm going to get the short end of the stick no matter what happens," Sully said, knowing he'd been stonewalled. "Bare this in mind, Randall: If I ever face off against those two, I don't care if they are cops, I'm taking care of business…Even if it means putting 'em in their graves."

Randall pondered Sully's sudden hard stance. "You've made your point," he said softly. "And I do sympathize with your thinking in terms of self preservation. I *definitely* feel you have the right to defend yourself if the department won't do it for you. I could never go public with a statement like that, but you have my solemn oath I will stand behind your actions if it comes to that."

Sully wondered what motivated a declaration like that. If he understood correctly, Randall had just given him the green light to go after two rogue cops in any fashion he pleased. But, even with those blessings, Sully realized they were only words that could be easily recanted. "What about Judson Fletcher and Toni Gracci?" he asked. "Did you know they've been showing up at the Gregory home looking for me also? And the Derringer I turned over to you? It's supposed to be the gun that killed Red…What's being done about that?"

"The prints we lifted from the gun *were* Fletcher's and the ballistics match proved it was the weapon that killed Red Ward. He's definitely our man, but Toni Gracci is somewhat of a problem; we don't have a thing on him…He's clean."

Disappointed Gracci would still be free if Fletcher were arrested, Sully sought another angle. "Since there's a good chance those two killed Jigs and shot me, what's the law say about bringing Gracci in on that?"

"That's not possible: They were both somewhere else that night; it's already checked out. Besides, the bullet that killed your friend, Moran, doesn't match those involved in the Ward killing. We've got Fletcher dead to rights, but we have absolutely nothing on Gracci, not even a motive."

"You're saying a quarter of a million bucks isn't reason enough? A lot of people would kill for money like that and not lose an ounce of sleep."

"What are you talking about?" Randall said, leaning forward in the chair. "What quarter of a million dollars?"

"That's how much money Jigs had on him the night he was murdered. Didn't you read the reports? Surely Smith and Jones wrote that down. They certainly talked to the people who knew about it."

"There's nothing about money mentioned in any of those reports," Randall said, showing unusual interest. "You were with Moran that night...Can't you remember why he had that kind of money on him?"

"I have my memory back all right, with the exception of a few days before and after the Gerklin fight...That's still a mystery."

"Then how did you find out about the money Moran had on him?"

"I talked to a guy who was with Jigs at the Kimbell House the night he was killed. He said Jigs had a money belt crammed full of hundred dollar bills. He also had a bag of jewelry tied in under his shoulder...I talked to Jigs' sister about it later, and she said the same thing. Only she told me exactly what he was carrying; it was something like a quarter of a million dollars in cash and jewels."

"I'm *assuming* you're talking about Virginia Moran?" Randall said.

"That's right; he had only the one sister."

"How did she found out about her brother carrying all that money, or maybe why he'd do such a stupid thing?"

"You should probably talk to her about that," Sully said. "When I talked to her, she didn't exactly make a secret of anything, but, she might have thought I'd keep my mouth shut at the time. Personally, I don't think Jigs wanted *anybody* knowing about the fortune he carried around that night...But, that's just common sense."

Randall sat back easily. "I'll call Miss Moran later," he said, "and see what she has to say…Now let's get back to this Gracci and Fletcher thing. Up front, you should know that we're making a solid effort to get those two behind bars. We've staked out people at all of their old haunts; the pool halls, the restaurants, things like that. We've got men day and night at the Dinkler Plaza where they've holed up in the past. So far, they haven't showed their faces, but it doesn't mean they won't. Then there's a possibility that they've already skipped town; it'd suit me fine if they have. Even if we do bring Fletcher in, it won't help your situation much; Gracci will be coming after you the instant he finds out there's no charges against him."

Sully thanked Randall for his time and stood, satisfied all his questions had been answered with the exception of one. "The Gregory family?" he asked. "What are you going to do for them?"

"They'll be fine," Randall said. "I'm sending some people out to watch their house periodically. "Are you interested in what's going to happen to Smith and Jones when we bring them in? Do you want to know the charges they'll be facing?"

Sully looked at the police captain cynically. "Coming in to face charges sounds like you're not too sure of *anything* being done."

"I didn't mean for it to sound that way," Randall said. "…With the evidence we have, they'll both wind up behind bars for at least twenty years. There are three counts of blackmail pending, plus tampering and numerous charges of falsifying and manufacturing evidence. If the charges stand up, they'll be gone a long time. If they find a way to worm out of *this*, I'll be very surprised."

Sully walked out of the police station with a feeling that things were finally turning in his favor. The only thing left keeping him from rooting out Jigs' killer was Smith and Jones, the *very* men who might have killed him in the first place. Taking that into consideration, he came to a deadly conclusion: If the police weren't going after the two detectives, he would—and it wouldn't be pleasant.

# CHAPTER THIRTY ONE

Sully eased into the downtown area and turned on Pryor Street. He pulled up to the curb in the alley behind Big Town's poolroom. He checked the .45 before getting out into the darkened alleyway. There wasn't much light between the buildings and the shadows made it look threatening. He didn't see anything that warranted his leaving and went straight to the entrance that led into the gymnasium. He took a quick glance through the glass portal in the door before going inside. At the rear of the room by the closed poolroom door, a throng of spectators was concentrated heavily around the center ring. He didn't see anyone that could pose a threat and stepped quietly into the smoke-filled chamber. A dozen men watched intensely as a pair of sweaty boxers fought back and forth. The only source of light was a solitary hundred-watt bulb, which filtered eerily down through the smoke to the ring.

Sully walked slowly toward the crowd gathered around the elevated platform. All eyes were on the fighters until Sully came under the light. One gambler recognized him, then the entire crowd flocked around and greeted him. The two boxers stopped fighting after the distraction and reached through the ropes grasping for his hand. It was the first time Sully had been there since Jigs died and it was a good feeling. The only time he had been near the gym since then was the night he and Hector took down Fletcher and Gracci—and that was in the poolroom next door.

He stood silently among the people who knew him, supported him, and were closest to him, but strangely, all he thought of was Jigs. The impact the man had made on his life was overwhelming. He never had a closer friend. After ten minutes of embarrassing adulation, Sully was relieved when Calvin, the gym manager, motioned for him to come into his office.

Calvin was the type who made it a point to know everything about everybody and that suited Sully just fine. The first question he intended to find out was where his old cut man, Bumpy Webster, lived. He knew Bumpy would give him the full truth and that's what he needed before making a move on Smith and Jones. He also wanted to know if seeking Webster out would create a problem for Calvin. He didn't want to drag his friend into a situation that was harmful.

Calvin put his hand on Sully's shoulder as they walked away from the assemblage. "There are a couple of things you should never do, Sully," he said soberly, "and one of 'em is coming in here like you ain't got a worry in the world...It ain't the smartest move you've ever made."

"I appreciate the concern," Sully said as they walked toward the enclosed office to the rear wall, "but I'm not quite as dumb as you think I am."

"You must know something I don't, because everything here points to your getting the pure hell kicked out of you."

Sully took a seat in the office. "I really don't think Fletcher or Gracci will be coming around. I've heard that they might've blown town with the cops nipping at their heels. And I don't believe those two homicide cops are foolish enough to come around. I got it from the station that at least a dozen warrants were issued for them. If they hang around one spot too long, their own people will be forced to arrest them."

"You may be right, but..."

Sully cut him short. "Relax, Calvin, none of those guys are a problem here at the gym. Fletcher and Gracci are out of the picture and Smith and Jones aren't about to show their faces here."

"...I take it you haven't heard who's in town?"

"Apparently not!" Sully said, a touch of doubt seeping through.

"Carmine Anoletti showed up with a army of thugs a few days ago, and guess who they're out pounding the pavement looking for?"

Sully didn't expect that. "Why would they be on the prod for me? I wouldn't think Anoletti would come after me because a couple of his guys got slapped around. If Fletcher and Gracci had wound up dead, I could understand his getting hot...All we did was put 'em in the hospital for a few days."

"Jesus!" Calvin said, taken aback. "It was *you* who took those two apart?" It was the first he had heard of Sully having a hand in the beating of Fletcher and Gracci.

170

"I didn't do it by myself," Sully said. "If Hector hadn't walked in when he did, they would've probably killed me. I was out of it at the time."

Calvin shook his head in disbelief. "So that's why Hector was shot all to pieces? I knew the cops were lying when they said it was robbery…Who the hell would rob a poor Mexican that ain't got a dime to his name?"

"For what it's worth, it's why they went after him. Hector made himself a target the minute he pulled my fat out of the fire."

"The cops don't know anything about this, do they?"

"They do now! I *told* 'em! And the truth is, up until Hector was shot, I thought Fletcher and Gracci were dead. I didn't know they were recuperating in the hospital. Hector must have thought the same thing. It's the only way they could catch him off guard that easily. That's probably why they didn't tell the cops anything. They wanted to get even when they got back on the streets."

"You did your level best to kill 'em, didn't you?" Calvin asked, then answered his own question, "You really did…"

"I thought about it all right," Sully said, "but it didn't go that far for one reason: I was stopped short… the important thing was getting the gun Fletcher used to kill Red Ward with."

"That's probably why Anoletti has his boys out looking for you? I knew you had to do *something* to put him on your case."

"I don't know what Anoletti is thinking, but he's going to have to wait…I've got other things to deal with right now."

"Be careful, boy. If you mess around any of your old hangouts, eventually, they'll run into you. I'm surprised it didn't happen today. They've been in and out of here all day long."

"I'll be leaving in just a few minutes," Sully said. "I just wanted to find out where my old cut man was."

"You talking about Bumpy Webster?"

"Yeah! I wanted to talk to him about some things."

"…Like your climb up through the heavyweight ranks, I suppose?"

"How'd you know that?"

"It's my place to know what goes on around here, Sully. What bothers me is that you never knew about the tank jobs. Didn't you even *suspect* anything when Jigs hooked up with those people from Chicago? Jesus, man, you were the main attraction. Somebody had to say something."

"I found out about it just recently. Before that, I didn't have a clue. You know me well enough to know that I wouldn't go along with a tank job of any kind. Not even for Jigs! It isn't my style! Especially in that Gerklin fight; that was too important to me...I really thought I had a chance at the crown."

Calvin suddenly became jittery. He felt that he had overstepped his boundaries by divulging so much. He had revealed things that only a hand full of people were privy to, and was beginning to squirm from the possible repercussions. "Sully," he said, fighting the thoughts down, "I'm going to tell you some things, but if anybody finds out about it, I could wind up in a bad light."

"Your words are safe with me, Calvin. They won't go any further."

Calvin took a deep breath, already regretting what he was going to disclose. "It was a fix from the very beginning," he said slowly. "Every fight you had with the top contenders was rigged!"

"You're trying to say I knocked out four top heavyweights, and that all of the fights were fixed?"

"I ain't *trying* to tell you anything, Sully," Calvin said, "It's what happened! And I was in on it to a degree."

"You were mixed up in it too?" Sully asked, not believing it.

"Not the whole thing, but I knew enough to read between the lines."

"How many more were in on it?"

"Bumpy Webster and me were the most informed. There's a few that might know a little something, but not many...This was kept pretty quiet, kid. Everybody was too afraid to open their traps."

"Where's Bumpy staying?" Sully asked grimly.

"You go easy on him, Sully," Calvin said sternly. "He's an old man and doesn't need to get involved."

"You let me worry about that," Sully said, without changing his attitude. He didn't intend to spare anyone if it meant finding Jigs' killer.

"He's at the Capitol Hotel, across from the Doctor's building," Calvin said reluctantly. "He's got a room on the first floor. He's been afraid to go any higher ever since the Winecoff fire."

"I know where it is," Sully said, then turned and walked out of the office into the gym. Calvin was right behind him.

"Keep me out of this if you can," Calvin pleaded, walking alongside. "I don't need that crowd after me."

"Relax," Sully assured him. "I've already told you what I'd do."

Calvin kept up with Sully's fast pace until he glanced at the ring thirty feet in front of them. He froze in his tracks when he recognized the two men standing there. "Oh, hell," he said weakly. "It's them!"

Sully walked directly toward the pair as if they weren't in the room. Dipping his hand into his jacket pocket, he tightly gripped the .45. His days of being pushed around were over. Just as he walked past the two men heading for the rear door, a huge hand reached out and gripped his jacket, spinning him around roughly.

The man growled "Not so fast, tough guy…Mister Anoletti wants to…"

Sully swung his forearm upward, breaking the hold on his jacket, then brought the .45 down on the thug's temple. With one blow, the gangster fell to the floor in a heap. Sully aimed the weapon at the other man's head. "You tell your boss, when I get time we'll talk about anything he wants to. Until then, stay out of my way."

The second man showed no fear but was smart enough to know it would be senseless to make a move on someone who clearly had the upper hand. "You keep this up, pal, you're a dead man," he said easily.

Backing out of the gym door, Sully said calmly, "I think Anoletti already has his mind made up about that."

"You'd be dead if that was the case, kid."

Sully moved quickly to his car and when no one followed, took his time driving out of the alley. He knew the hotel where Bumpy was staying and headed North on Peachtree. Three blocks away, he pulled into the parking lot beside the Doctor's Building. He backed the Buick into a parking space for the seclusion it offered, then cautiously moved across the street to the Capitol Hotel. He stepped inside the stench-ridden flophouse and went to a small counter in the narrow hallway. An elderly man was seated there reading the Constitution and smoking a gigantic black cigar. That solved the riddle of where the foul odor came from.

"Yes sir?" the old man said, looking up and sporting a toothless grin.

"Is Bumpy Webster in?" Sully asked.

"If he is, he's in 104...It's just down the hall."

Sully walked down the dimly lit hallway until he reached room 104. He knocked softly on the door. "Bumpy! It's Sully Hawkin! You got a minute?"

There was a slow shuffling of feet behind the flimsy door, then the door opened until the chain latch caught it. A wrinkled old face peered through the opening. "Sully?" a squeaky voice, asked. "What you doing here?"

"Open up, Bumpy. We need to talk."

Bumpy unhitched the chain and stepped back from the door. "C'mon in," he said pleasantly. "It's been a while."

Sully stepped inside the one room apartment and sat in one of the two chairs by a small table. "You don't mind me taking a load off, do you?" he asked.

"Don't mind at all," Bumpy said. "Want some coffee? It's a fresh pot!"

"Maybe some other time," Sully said somberly. "Right now, I need the answers to a few questions and I'll be on my way."

The old man was quiet for a moment. "It's about that mess Jigs and I drug you into, isn't it?"

"You knew all along, didn't you?"

"I had to! Jigs couldn't have pulled it off without me in your corner."

"Why didn't you tell me what was going on?"

"Jigs didn't want it that way. He figured it best to keep everything from you...Said you wouldn't go along with it and told me to keep my trap shut."

"He was right...I'd have walked away."

"That's what Jigs said...But he always had you in mind. You know what he told me before the fight? He said he was gonna make you rich whether you liked it or not."

"Well, he did stick a lot of money in the bank for me, but I'm not sure I deserve any of it."

"Take an old man's advice, son: Keep quiet about the money. Don't make no difference where it comes from; if it's green, it spends."

Sully looked forlornly at Bumpy. "Did I even have a chance in those fights?"

"None at all!" Bumpy said apologetically. "...Sorry, kid! You didn't have the make-up to be a contender. Any one of those guys could have taken you out if they'd had the notion."

"Wait a minute! If I was such a pushover, how did I knock out Bull Gerklin? He's one of the best heavyweights in the country."

"Damned if I know, kid...All I know is, you were getting ripped to pieces one minute, then from out of the blue you caught him with a right. Jigs already had the towel in his hand when Gerklin's head hit the canvas. He had intended to end it before you got too badly beat up. There's no way he could've stopped the fight after that; the crowd would've killed him."

"Jigs might have been wrong, you know...Maybe I *was* good enough to take on top contenders?"

"You weren't, Sully! Take my word for it. Ain't no doubt that you can knock out any heavyweight alive. The rub is, the other guy has to stand still so's you can hit him. That don't happen fighting the big boys."

"Were they *all* that much faster than me?"

"Those ranked were! You could hold your own in club fighting, but that's as far as you could go."

"It's tough on the ego thinking you've knocked out top fighters like that...I really thought I was doing something."

"To Jigs way of thinking, you *were*. That was to be your last fight and he wanted you to retire feeling good about your career. That's why he asked Anoletti to hold Gerklin back. He had that crook's word you wouldn't have your head handed to you."

"*Retirement*! I never heard anything about that."

"It was Jigs' plan. He didn't want you to know anything about what was going on. Think about it: If you'd have looked halfway decent losing that fight, you could've walked away a top heavyweight. But Anoletti threw a broomstick in the spokes. He didn't *tell* Gerklin to back off. From the minute that bum got in the ring, we knew he came to cut you to ribbons."

"Why would he want to rip *me* up? I never had any problems with him."

"*I* think Anoletti told him to…You didn't exactly keep it a secret how you felt about that gang. The bad part came when you were unfriendly to Anoletti. He took *that* personal. It was payback time for that disrespect…You made the wrong people mad, and they wanted their due."

"There's an outside chance that he did more than just sic a fighter on me. He might be responsible for Jigs death."

"He's ruthless, not much doubt bout it," Bumpy said. "And after he lost all that money on the fight, I wouldn't put much of anything past him."

"What did you get out of all this, Bumpy? Surely, you didn't do it for nothing."

"By my standards, I suppose I made out pretty good. Those first three fights were good paydays for me. But, if I'd have placed my bets on Gerklin like I was supposed to, I'd have lost my shirt. Turns out, I made a few bucks. It don't amount to much, but it comes in handy now that I ain't working the ring."

"I hope you didn't quit because I dumped Gerklin that night…I know it upset a lot of people's plans…And it looks like it might be the very reason Jigs was killed."

"Forget that nonsense, boy! It was none of your fault. We were the ones who brought you into that crap blind. We didn't have to go along with Anoletti when he came to us waving all that money. The truth is, he had us pegged right off the bat. When he saw the dollar signs lighting up in our eyes, he knew he had us."

"Has Anoletti been to see you since he came to town?" Sully said, standing.

"I know he's in town, but he ain't been here."

"Would you have *any* idea why he's set his sights so hard on me?"

"No I don't, but you can bet it's about money somehow or other."

"Tell me this: What did Anoletti do to *you* after the Gerklin fight?"

"He put his boys on me after Jigs slipped out…They asked a lot of questions about what went wrong and I told 'em. They slapped me around a little and sent me home with bloody face…That was about it."

"Did they say anything about killing Jigs while they were working on you?"

"Oh, yeah! But it was mostly temper talking. I don't think they intended to murder Jigs outright, if that's what you mean."

Sully thanked him, said goodbye, then stepped out into the dimming twilight; it had been a long day. With darkness approaching, his thoughts settled on one more task that had to be taken care: Garan T. Jewels, the human question mark. He hoped that mystery would be solved shortly.

# CHAPTER THIRTY TWO

With nighttime swiftly coming about, Sully drove through the dwindling traffic at a maddening pace.  If he were going to reach Jewels' office before he left for the day, it was going to be difficult.  He gunned the Buick down Forrest Avenue hoping to make the single traffic light that would impede his effort.  That was five blocks away at the corner of boulevard.  He made it in a matter of minutes.

He slowed down just as he reached Boulevard and glanced into Jewels' office window.  Three figures stood talking just inside the entrance.  He could not see who the men were because of the dim lighting and darkness.  Sully crossed the intersection just as an unmarked patrol car pulled up and stopped by the curb.  The officers waved at the men when the siren sounded playfully for a moment.  The men inside smiled and stepped out to acknowledge the greeting.  Sully's jaw went stiff upon seeing Jewels walk from the shadows with Smith and Jones as if nothing were wrong.  His blood was boiling by the time he got through the crossing.  It was no wonder that everyone was acting as if there were nothing to worry about; there wasn't!  The friendly gesture by the officers in the car proved that.  What bothered Sully most was that the men in the car had to be either detectives or high-ranking officers.  Unmarked vehicles are specifically for one or the other.  It was common knowledge that Smith and Jones had warrants out for them and these cops were deliberately ignoring that mandate.  Such a flagrant violation sent a clear message to Sully: There was only Otis Randall to turn to.  Smith and Jones would never be brought down under these circumstances.  He gritted his teeth as the patrol car moved slowly away and honked its horn.  Atlanta police had done nothing other than turn the investigation into a joke.

Sully backed into a parking spot on Forrest Avenue then stepped from the car and looked up the street.  His face was red with anger.  The situation was complex enough and having to face it without support was not something he looked forward to.  The odds were stacked against him but there was no longer an option.  It was quite obvious that the Atlanta police were not going to arrest Smith and Jones for anything.

Sully jerked out the .45 and quickly checked it. He immediately crossed the street and began walking up the other side. A streetlight suddenly illuminated the entire corner; that made things more to his liking. Smith and Jones would no longer be just standing around in the dark. His reasoning now was to simply confront Smith and Jones and hold them until Randall could get on the scene; the good captain could take over from there. He stopped at the corner momentarily, gripped the .45, then swirled around the corner with the gun leveled chest high. He pulled back quickly when no one was seen. Where could they have gone so quickly? He stepped back around the corner and moved carefully toward Jewels' office. Everything seemed to have danger lurking behind it. He reached the window at Jewels' office, took a quick look inside and jerked back. Jewels was alone. Neither his secretary nor Smith and Jones were anywhere in sight.

Sully stepped through the front door with the .45 dangling at his side. He wondered how the lawyer's betrayal could be dealt with but knew there was only one way. The lawyer would simply have to pay the price if he could not come up with the right answers. How far it would go would basically depend on his cooperation.

Jewels was in no way prepared for Sully's unannounced appearance. The sudden visit made him glance around nervously for an escape route. He looked shakily at the .45 in Sully's hand. "…What—what are you doing here?"

"I *was* going to talk to your friends," Sully said sarcastically, "but I missed them somehow. You know where they might have gone?"

Jewels' face was ashen. "I was told—it would be best if I didn't know," he said with a quivering voice. "They said if I knew where they were, it would not be in their best interest. I could never feel comfortable under those circumstances. I'm quite sure they would make an effort to extract revenge in retaliation…The problems accompanying such an awkward position would not be pleasant."

"How about harboring fugitives? Think you're *slick* enough to handle something like that?"

"*Good Lord, Hawken!* The men just walked in the door for legal counseling. It takes time to work things out."

"Is that what you call it? Counseling? To set the record straight, I know you were with them the night you took Fred home from jail...You've had plenty of time, pal."

"I can explain that," Jewels said, once again looking at Sully's gun. "I represent them just as I represented Mister Gregory. I have to work out a way so that they can surrender to the authorities *without* facing so many charges. Can't you see their side? If they go in now, their lives will be over."

"So what's the big deal? The kind of grief they spread around, they *deserve* to be cooked—well done."

"It takes time to work things out legally, Hawken. I can't jump into something of this magnitude blindly. I have to have a workable presentation. It's my job to carry clients through bad situations."

"Tell me something, Jewels," Sully snapped. "Have you talked to the police about this so-called proposal of yours?"

"...Not yet," Jewels blinked spasmodically. "There hasn't been sufficient time."

Sully turned and walked toward the front door without looking back. "In case you forget, or you don't find the time, I'm giving Randall a call tonight. He'll be thrilled to hear you have something to offer."

Jewels sat down heavily in the chair. The air rushing from his mouth made his lungs sound like they were collapsing. Sully looked in the window after stepping outside. The lawyer's face was that of a man drowning in a sea of troubles.

Sully walked into the night, unable to comprehend the strange cohesion that bonded Jewels and the two detectives so tightly together. If a seed of distrust had somehow been planted during the short meeting, maybe a crack in their solidarity would be forthcoming. He sat quietly in the car for a few minutes, wondering if anything had been accomplished from coming down so hard on Jewels. Smith and Jones hadn't been there, but at least now, there was some pressure on Jewels to clean up his act. It *was* a victory of sorts, and might possibly be the one it takes to keep the two detectives off his back. If he were lucky, maybe they would stay out of his hair for a while?  Hopefully, he could find time to piece more of the puzzle together?

# CHAPTER THIRTY THREE

Sully stepped through the door expecting Beverly to greet him but the apartment was empty. It was after nine o'clock. She should have been home hours earlier. The kitchen was cold and dark with only the one small night-light above the stove on. It gave off just enough brightness to see the light switch.

Beverly had said something about going back to work this morning and would likely spend long hours at the hospital, but this was ridiculous. It was after nine o'clock and she had been on the job for fourteen hours. There was no need in that. Maybe three weeks of vacation had pushed her backlog to its limit, but the attempt to catch it all up in one day irritated him.

Sully turned some soft music on the radio and put coffee on the stove. He rested easily on the bed, dozing lightly until the pot made the telltale noise of being ready. He cut the stove down just as the coffee began to boil over. He wiped the mess up quickly with a paper towel then poured a cup and sat down and relaxed. His stomach growled angrily when he took a sip. It was the first thing that had gone into his stomach since early that morning. He opened the refrigerator door and poked around, looking for something decent to eat. Unable to find anything that would satisfy the hunger, he sat back down to wait for Beverly. If she weren't too tired, they could go out and have a late evening meal somewhere.

It was after one o'clock when Beverly awoke him. He looked up, then slid his head up against the headboard and relaxed. "You okay?" he asked groggily, wiping the sleep from his eyes.

"I'm fine! You?"

"A little hungry, but it can wait."

"I was stuck at the hospital longer than expected. There were several bad accidents tonight and Grady was swamped...They asked us to take a few off their hands. Several more were diverted to Piedmont. Having to deal with that and being so far behind with my own work is why I'm late."

"You hungry?" he asked, running his hand up her thigh, stopping after touching bare skin beyond where the nylons were hooked.

"Starved," she said, putting a hand on his cheek. "Could you stand some bacon and eggs?"

"You're going to cook this late?"

"No, but I know a place close by that's open."

Sully eased his legs off the side of the bed and guided his feet into his slippers. "Where are we going?"

"The Greyhound station. They're the only folks in town that stay up all night."

He stood, yawned and stretched. "Give me a few minutes! I'll throw some water in my face and slip into some shoes."

"I'll clean the coffee pot in the meantime."

Sully quickly washed his face and brushed his teeth, then stepped back into the kitchen. He looked at Beverly with concern while she stood at the sink cleaning the coffeepot. "You'll never make it to work this morning without sleep? Don't you think you're stretching it a bit?"

"I have the day off," she said easily. "The hospital decided it would be best for the people who worked through the night get a little rest. They knew a few of hours of sleep wouldn't be enough."

Sully stood, then slipped into his jacket and walked into the bedroom.

"Where are you going?"

"I don't like going anywhere without the .45…You mind?"

"Sully! It's two o'clock in the morning…Don't be so paranoid!"

Sully gave in reluctantly and shoved the weapon under a pillow for her sake. He knew how uncomfortable she felt around guns. He knew it was a mistake the instant he opened the door to leave.

Four men burst in the moment the door cracked, knocking Beverly to the floor. Sully turned to run for the .45 in the bedroom but was stopped short. One of the men slammed him hard against the wall, then directed his attention to Beverly laying dazed on the floor. "If you want to see this pug alive again, I suggest you keep your trap shut about this…No cops, lady!"

Beverly shook the cobwebs from her head and bounced to her feet, no longer afraid of consequences. "You leave him alone," she screamed, charging the four men in anger. The moment she got to the man talking, he threw a punch at her that drove her halfway across the room into a heap.

Sully went berserk when he saw the blood covering her face. He jerked one arm free for a second, then lashed out wildly at the men holding him. He managed to land several strong punches before he was hit from behind. A blow from the butt of a gun sent him reeling into a state of semi-consciousness.

The four men drug Sully's limp form from the apartment and moved toward a black sedan in the lot. Beverly stepped from the building with Sully's .45 in her hand. She waved the automatic back and forth frantically trying to pull the trigger. They shoved Sully in the back seat of the sedan and one of the men said coldly, "Get rid of that broad before she gets somebody's attention."

"*You* get rid of her," another man said. "The boss said no complications. You pop a cap on her and that's what we got—complications!"

"Get in," the man replied, getting into the back seat. "And you'd better hope she don't figure out how to shoot that damn thing."

The sedan left the parking lot in a cloud of smoke with its engine screaming. Beverly chased the car until it was out of sight, then sank to her knees and wept in frustration. She had done all she could do. "*Next* time, things will be different," she said convincingly. *Next time she'd know how to fire the .45 in her hands.* She was helpless at the moment though; they had Sully and there was nothing she could do about it. She had to do what they said. They had been very clear what would happen if there were a problem of any kind. Sully's life was in the balance.

She walked slowly back to the apartment a defeated woman. The unsuccessful effort she had made to help Sully initiated a silent vow: *This is not going to happen again. In the future, I'll know what to do.*

# CHAPTER THIRTY FOUR

Sully was addled for a moment but somehow had managed to avoid damaging his delicate vision. He looked out of the rear window helplessly as the sedan sped down the deserted street. He watched Beverly slump to the pavement, powerless to do anything. He felt an enormous pride in her for striking out the very instant danger was apparent. The fiery way she had come to his defense impressed him immensely. She had revealed something at the same time that had not been so conspicuous before hand. She showed feelings for him beyond what he had imagined. If he were able to survive what was in store for him tonight, that loyalty, or love, whatever it may be, would not be forgotten.

"Where are you taking me?" Sully asked through a blood-splattered mouth. "…At least tell me what's going on."

"Shut your mouth, bum" the man next to him growled. "You'll learn soon enough!…You're lucky you're still breathing."

Sully glanced in the gruff man's direction. "I heard your friend over there say there wasn't supposed to be complications…That tells me your boss wants me in good health a little bit longer."

"My friend's got himself a big mouth."

"What's your boss going to say when I tell him you almost killed my girlfriend? You think he'll pat you on the back for that?"

The man drew back as if to hit Sully. The passenger in front turned and stuck a revolver in his face. "Knock it off," he threatened, cocking the weapon. "You tear his head off, we *all* pay the price. Anoletti said how he wanted things and that's how it's gonna be. Now relax; we got a long ride."

"I'm running this show," the thug in back replied arrogantly, leaning forward until the gun touched his chin. "If you don't like it, pull the trigger."

The man withdrew the revolver and turned back around. "You gotta cool it, man," he said, suddenly realizing his rank. "You're gonna get us *all* dead."

"Carmine's my uncle," the thug retorted. "What's he gonna do? Shoot me?"

"He may not shoot you, but he won't mind taking it out on us if we let you do something stupid. Now lighten up, or you'll wind up slinging hash in south Chicago like your cousin."

"Well, I ain't no Toni Gracci," the thug said sarcastically, leaning back in the seat. "I'm a lot more important than that piece of garbage."

The conversation dried up after that statement. But what was said did give Sully an insight as to what happened to Toni Gracci. Apparently, Gracci's way of handling things in Atlanta had brought disapproval from his superiors in Chicago. His being kin to Anoletti had probably been the only thing that saved him from a fate worse than death. He wondered what they had done to Judson Fletcher. Fifteen minutes north of Buckhead, the sedan turned off and eased into a manicured graveled driveway. The tree-covered path led to a house two hundred yards from the entrance and could not be seen from the road. The dwelling was never visible until they were within fifty feet. The huge sedan came gently to a halt and Sully was roughly taken from the back seat. His eyes already adjusted to the dark; he took in the lush surroundings as best he could for possible future references. He made out an immaculate estate with at least three armed guards watching the front of the premises. He had to imagine that the rear of the rambling structure was protected just as well.

Sully was ushered down a well-lit hall, then led into a darkened room and seated against the wall. A wall lamp was turned on and he immediately marveled at the enormity of the eloquent study. Three of the four walls in the room had books that reached all the way to the ten-foot ceiling. The remaining wall was a row of windows that stretched some forty feet across. It was wealth at its most extravagant.

Sully sat with his eyes closed while the four men stood alertly close by. They were making sure he was not going anywhere. All four men were noticeably quiet; it was as if speaking might disturb their night's work. A half an hour dredged by slowly and Sully's face was beginning to bother him. Besides having to deal with a broken nose, the blood covering his face and neck had crept down inside his shirt and had became uncomfortable. The pain was intense but he wasn't about to give those responsible, satisfaction of a complaint.

The door cracked open slowly and the elderly Carmine Anoletti walked in with a disgusted look on his face; he was alone. He never took his eyes from the floor. He sat heavily in the leather chair behind the desk with his glasses on the tip of his nose. He looked at Sully's disfigured face with a frown. "Who did this?" he growled sternly.

"I did," the boisterous nephew said, stepping forward. "Him and that broad gave us some trouble so I slapped 'em around a little."

Anoletti was silent a moment, then opened the middle drawer of his desk. He pulled out a gold plated .32 automatic, jacked a shell into its chamber and laid it on the desk within reach. "Everybody out in the hall," he said gently, changing his demeanor. "I want to talk to Mister Hawken alone."

The four men stepped to the door but Anoletti stopped them in their tracks with a thundering voice. "Nephew!... Since you're the one who felt this had to be done to our guest, you can be the one to furnish him some hot water and a wash rag." He wasn't asking—he was ordering.

The nephew strode out of the room in a huff. He did not appreciate being talked to like that in front of his men. He thought it was an insult for a man of his position to be put down in front of Sully. Angrily, he slammed the door behind him.

As the nephew past the men in the hallway, one of his men commented dryly, "He keeps that up, he's gonna wind up fish-food like Fletcher."

"What happened to Fletcher?" Sully asked, hoping he had heard right.

"...That's none of your concern, Hawken," Anoletti said sourly. "You're here to answer questions, not ask them."

Sully responded in a like fashion. "You kill my best friend," he blurted out indignantly, "put a bullet in my brain, then expect me to roll over and act like some puppy dog. Well, if it's all the same to you, I'd like some answers myself."

Just as Anoletti was about to reply, the door was opened. His nephew stepped in the study, only this time it was with an entirely different attitude. The brash young gangster knew he had overstepped his boundaries minutes earlier by showing his temper. The time to make amends couldn't wait if he was going to survive that show of disrespect. His fury completely diminished, he placed the pan of hot water, along with a towel and washrag beside Sully. "Uncle Carmine," he said, "I'm..."

Anoletti cut him short without ever looking at him. It was obvious the young man had severely touched a nerve with his uncle. "Get out of here," he said, his voice rising slightly. "We will discuss this in private."

The rattled nephew left the room with his head lowered; he was greeted outside with silence. Everyone in the hall was aware that the impetuous underling would have to atone for how he had acted toward his uncle. It was no secret that the ultimate offense was committed in their demanding organization.

After the door closed, Anoletti turned to Sully with fire in his eyes. "Get one thing straight, Hawken! Not me, or anyone associated with this organization, was responsible for Jigs Moran's death. It would be very stupid of me to kill a man that was bringing $250,000 dollars to my doorsteps?"

Sully eyed him with suspicion. "Bringing you $250,000? How do you figure that money was yours?"

"It was a gesture of good faith," Anoletti said calmly, "since he was directly responsible for wrecking a very profitable business deal of mine."

"So that's why he was carrying all that money; he was buying his life back. You were going to kill him, weren't you?"

"It crossed my mind, I'll have to admit," Anoletti said. "But when Moran came to me and apologized, saying he would repay the money he had cost me, I had to relent. Needless to say, my associates were as disturbed as I was at the time, but under the circumstances, we decided to leave Moran alone."

"This $250,000 dollars! Was it going to satisfy the debt, or was it just beginning?

"It was a down payment."

"How much more were you going to milk him for? A million, two, more?"

"More likely, in the neighborhood of two million." Anoletti said quietly, then glared menacingly across the desk. "...And before you go jumping to conclusions, it was Moran who approached me with a proposal of making good our losses. Our people in Chicago had already agreed to cut our losses and leave it alone."

"That was mighty generous of them," Sully smirked. "I'm curious as to what brought that on. Not too many people would just walk away from a big loss without blowing their stack."

"It wasn't generosity, I assure you" Anoletti said. "It was *necessary!* We didn't want anything to happen to Moran at the time because it would have been placed squarely on our shoulders. And his death proved us right; everybody came after our organization when you and Moran were shot down. The first thing the boxing community thought was that it was a tank job that went wrong. They were right of course, and it certainly gave credit to their thoughts. They all attributed the murder to us because we were the ones who lost so much money on the fight. From the very beginning, our only purpose was to transfer the gambler's money from the bookie's pocket to ours, nothing more. It wasn't like we were out to break the bookie's backs or anything like that. That would have been lunacy; they're the backbone of our operations. It was supposed to be a simple move, accomplished every day in our circles. It's the way we operate, always with the odds in our favor."

"You're telling me that you wanted Jigs to stay healthy for the sole purpose of proving a fix wasn't on?"

"That's the sum of it."

Sully's jaw went rigid before asking his next question. "So, where do we go from here? You've brought me here in the middle of the night for something...What is it?"

"Common sense tells me that Moran never told you anything about our partnership. That's the only reason this conversation is being carried on so freely. It's certainly not because I feel any pity for you. What I expect of you is nothing more than what you're already doing:

Find Moran's killer. You do that for me and you'll be amply compensated in return."

"Why don't you turn your own people loose on this? They'd do just as good a job as I could."

"This is your town, Hawken. People here know you and trust you. There's a certain element here that would never open up to us like they would to you. That's the advantage you have and you should be able to find the person responsible in time. When you do, just give me a call. I'll take care of it and you'll never be involved."

"What is this, revenge? Money? What's so important about getting your hands on this guy?"

"...In my business," Anoletti said, "control, discipline, and absolute loyalty are necessary to maintain power. No one, and I stress *no one,* in our ranks or outside, can be allowed to walk away after doing something like this. This person, or persons, will have to pay the ultimate price."

"So you're sending the message out that if people do you wrong, they wind up in the trunk of a car, right?"

"Crudely put, but precise...Do we have a deal?"

"No restrictions?"

"None that I'm aware of."

"And I won't have to worry about guys like Fletcher and Gracci breathing down my neck?"

"Not any more you won't."

"Then we have a deal," Sully said.

"I'm glad you agreed," Anoletti said. "If you hadn't, I might have been forced to do something I wouldn't relish."

Sully knew he never had a choice. Before the words were ever spoken, it was quite obvious that he would either go to work for Anoletti or his days were over. It was *crystal* clear. "Before I go," he said. "Could you clear one thing up for me? What was the purpose of Fletcher and Gracci making a career out of coming after me when we both wanted the same thing?"

"Simple! I wasn't aware of what was going on down here. When I first heard of your friend, Ward's murder, I knew something wasn't right. That's when I decided to look into things a little deeper. What I found was that there was a revenge factor. It seems you had insulted Fletcher and my nephew, Toni, for so long, you had made deadly enemies of them. They would never forget that kind of abuse. And since they were in control of the operation here when you got out of the hospital, they wanted some payback. When I found out about they're dogging you, I put a stop to it. If they had killed you on top of doing in Ward, it would've drawn too much attention. It had a lot to do with my decision."

Sully stood up unsteadily from the strain. "If you're through with me, do you think we can call it a day? I need an ice bag and a warm bed."

"Would you like to go back to your lady friend's apartment? I can arrange it."

"It's the only place I can go," Sully replied, stepping toward the door. He stopped halfway there and turned. "Tell me something: How were your people able to find me when nobody else could?"

"The people you rent your house from. They gave us that nurse's name at the hospital and my boys followed her home. They just waited for you to show up. It didn't take a lot of intelligence to figure that one out."

"There's some cops downtown who couldn't do it."

"That should tell you something about law enforcement. And while we're discussing it, if those two cops are a problem, I want to know about it." Anoletti then escorted Sully to the door and instructed his men where to take him.

Sully walked outside and got into the back seat of the lush sedan. He relaxed for a moment and was almost dozing when the full impact of what Carmine Anoletti said hit him. He couldn't believe that a simple complaint by him would send Smith and Jones directly to their graves. The power of life and death was something he felt uncomfortable with. If the two cops had to die, he would rather it be by his hand than some unconscionable thug.

# CHAPTER THIRTY FIVE

Sully opened the door and stepped into the apartment wondering why every light there was on. He quietly walked through the kitchen and into the bedroom, in case Beverly had settled in for the night. She had not been in the bedroom because the bed was still made from that morning. He looked around to see if she had left a note. Not seeing one, he went back to the kitchen. He heard water trickling in the shower as he walked by the bathroom. The water had to be barely turned on since the sound wasn't very loud.

The bathroom door was slightly ajar. "Beverly?" he asked and didn't get a response. He stepped in and pulled the shower curtain back. Beverly was sitting directly under the showerhead with cold water drizzling down on her head. She was fully clothed and shivering intensely. He wondered if it was fear or the chilly water.

He turned off the faucet and knelt beside her. "You okay?" he asked softly.

She looked at him without an expression on her face. There was no surprise, no joy; it was if she was in a stupor of some kind. "I'm fine," she finally said. The words came out like they meant nothing.

Sully knew she was far from all right. It was obvious that she was in shock from what had happened earlier. He reached into the tub and cradled her into his arms, then gently lifted her out of the frigid water. "Let's get you out of these wet clothes, then we'll get you in a nice warm bed."

Beverly obeyed every suggestion as if it were a command. She stood very still while he removed the wet clothes and wrapped a dry towel around her.

Sully quickly carried her to the bedroom and laid her across the bed. He began dressing her in some warm pajamas. During the short moment she was completely exposed, his mind became enthralled in other emotions. During that one weak moment, the thought of lying beside her and drawing her body close came to mind. He stopped short! *Who was he kidding,* he thought. It was his comfort he was thinking of, not hers. He pulled the covers up to her neck satisfied it was the best thing all around. She was asleep the instant her head became comfortable on the soft pillow. He doubled an extra blanket from the closet and then laid it over her for more warmth. He quietly turned out the lights, then went to the bathroom and began taking off his bloody clothes. He piled them in a neat stack on the floor, then turned on the cold shower and stepped in. Thirty minutes later, he went into the bedroom and lay beside Beverly. He snuggled up tightly to her back and eased one arm under her neck and the other across her waist. He was asleep almost at once.

He jerked upright after sleeping for what seemed to be only a few seconds; he was wide awake. He glanced at the clock. It was a quarter till three; he had slept for seven straight hours. If he hurried, there was still enough time to catch Randall at the station before he left for the day. He looked around for Beverly while dressing, then remembered she had to be at work at noon. Satisfied things were all right, he left the apartment on the run. He quickly cranked the Buick and left the lot on two wheels. If he could get to the station before 4:00 o'clock, perhaps Randall could advise him on certain matters. The captain had to have connections, considering his high rank in the department.

The one most important thing to discuss was Jewels: he was hoping Randall could somehow finagle an in-depth report on Garan T. Jewels' finances. Then there were the two ex-detectives, Smith and Jones; he needed to find out how they were linked to Jewels? Maybe a summary of all their bank accounts could tie them together? He would check with Randall and see if he had a better approach?

Sully pulled up to the Decatur Street Precinct and glanced at his watch; it was 3:30 PM. He parked hurriedly, then raced up the front steps, three at a time. He glanced around quickly once inside, but did not see Captain Randall. Sully went straight to his office on the far side of the inner chamber. He looked in Randall's office, but it was strangely void of any of his belongings. There was nothing to indicate that the cubicle was occupied by anyone. Randall's name wasn't on the door and the walls were completely bare of his pictures and awards.

Sully caught an officer by the arm as he walked by. "Where's Captain Randall?" he asked. "...Has his office been moved?"

The officer had trouble looking him in the eye. "Captain Randall's been retired...He left the station for good yesterday."

Sully glanced around the entire room; not a single eye would acknowledge his presence. "What's going on here?" he demanded. "I talked to Randall two days ago; there was nothing said about any retirement."

"We've been instructed not to discuss the captain with anyone, Mister Hawken. The chief said he'd fire anyone who broke that order."

Sully glared at the officer with contempt. "How do you know who I am?"

"Everybody here knows who you are."

"And *why* is that?"

"C'mon, Hawken, you're making things difficult."

"Well, I'll be damned," Sully said, realizing what had happened. "Randall got a pink slip because he sided with me, didn't he?"

The officer made an effort to withdraw himself from the conversation. "I've got work to take care of, mister. You have to excuse me?"

Sully lashed out at all the bowed heads ignoring him. "Now that you've cost the best cop in the building his job, I hope the *lot* of you are satisfied."

A disturbed Chief Jenkins stood at the rear of the room with a scowl on his face. His arms folded tightly in front of him indicated he was furious.

Sully walked over to the desk sergeant immediately after the rant. "You know who I am?" he growled.

"Yeah, I know!" the sergeant said, looking in Jenkins' direction.

"Never mind him," Sully spat out. "*You* give me Randall's home address."

The sergeant looked at Jenkins again without fulfilling the request.

Sully heard heavy footsteps approaching from behind. Jenkins was deliberately stomping his feet in anger. He turned and looked at the imposing chief of police.

"I want you out of this precinct Hawken," Jenkins said strongly, "and you'd best be quick about it."

Sully didn't budge. "That won't be a problem if I get what I want."

Jenkins looked at the sergeant. "Did anybody here misunderstand my orders? I thought I made it quite clear how things were going to be."

"Mister Hawken wanted Captain Randall's home address, sir."

"Did you give it to him?"

"No sir!"

"Then *give* it to him," Jenkins snapped and walked away.

The sergeant wrote down Randall's address and handed it to Sully. "Tell Captain Randall we're behind him," the officer whispered when Jenkins was out of earshot, "but you see how it is. Our hands are tied."

"Oh yeah, I see!" Sully sneered. "You protect a couple of dirty cops like they're heroes, then dump a stand-up guy like Randall... Hard to miss that."

# CHAPTER THIRTY SIX

After leaving the police station, Sully drove past the Capital building still in somewhat of turmoil. He turned east on Memorial Drive and twenty minutes later was on East Lake Drive, deep into the suburbs of east Fulton County. His temper had calmed down considerably by the time he pulled into Otis Randalls' driveway. The East Lake neighborhood was a showcase of homes built in the twenties and thirties and Randall's home was no different. They all showed individualism and were immaculately maintained.

Sully pulled to a stop on the two strip concrete driveway, parking close to a flower-bordered path. He stepped from the car and moved slowly up the walk, then stepped onto the porch and rang the bell. He heard footsteps coming down the inner hall, then the door was slightly cracked open.

A large Negro woman eyed him suspiciously, but was very respectful. "Can I help you?" she asked politely.

"Is Captain Randall home?...I'd like to speak to him if he is...Tell him it's Sully Hawken!"

"Just a moment," she said, then closed the door and locked it.

Sully grinned at her lack of trust.

A minute later, Randall opened the door and greeted him. "C'mon in and take a load off, Hawken! Glad you dropped by!"

Sully followed him through the house to a small office at the end of the hallway; they both took a seat.

"How'd you get the address?" Randall asked. "I'm not in the book."

"Chief Jenkins made a cop give it to me. It's not a inconvenience, is it?"

"Not in this case," Randall said, "but there are not a lot of people, especially the ones I put away, that I'd want here at the house...Some of them would give their eye teeth to know where I lived."

"Jenkins probably didn't consider me a threat," Sully said. "And for what it's worth, that sergeant wouldn't give it out until he was ordered to."

"No harm, I suppose...I'm sure Jenkins looked at it that way."

Sully was quiet a moment. "I'm guessing siding with me against Smith and Jones created a problem...If that's what cost you your job, I'm sorry!"

Randall smiled. "You've got an over-active imagination, Hawken. That had nothing to do with my being fired. Jenkins forced me into retirement because of problems we had going back twenty years. I just left him without a choice this time...If I weren't ready to retire, It would've never happened."

"You don't think our association had anything to do with it."

"To a degree, I suppose, but it wasn't the sole reason. When I talked to Jenkins a few days ago, I was far from pleasant. Things came unraveled when I complained about the department not being aggressive enough with Smith and Jones. When I told him about their driving a city vehicle around like they were still on the force, he blew his stack. I could've kept my mouth shut, I suppose, but I didn't... This would've all blown over if I hadn't antagonized him, so relax; none of it's your fault."

"...About Smith and Jones driving a city car around: How can they do that without creating problems for other cops? There's bound to be complications?"

"Up to now, no officers have been confronted about ignoring the car. As long as that goes on, they *won't* do a thing..."

"I know! I was a witness to it yesterday when I went by Jewels' office. Smith and Jones were out on the sidewalk talking to him when two cops came by and waved. They hit the siren like it was old home week."

"Jewels was talking with those two out in the open?"

"As close as you and I are..."

"Things are more out of control than I thought, then," Randall said thoughtfully. "It looks like our friend Jewels has something working that we're not aware of..."

"If you'll do something for me, I think I can come up with the answer."

"A word of advice before this go any further."

"...What's that?"

"Give Jewels a long leash for the moment…He's made no secret of being in bed with Smith and Jones, so lets feed him a little rope. I've got a few things in mind that might prove beneficial…By the way, did you confront Jewels about what you saw?"

"Oh, yeah," Sully replied. "I thought they were still there when I went in the door, but that wasn't the case. I intended to hold Smith and Jones until you could get there."

"What was Jewels' explanation for their being there? Was he caught off guard?"

"Oh, yeah! He had no idea I'd be coming by his office…He said the reason they were talking was that they were his clients. He said they were negotiating a surrender."

"Do you believe that?"

"No way! It doesn't add up. He's had more than enough time to arrange that because he was seen in their company two blocks from Fred's house the very night Fred was released. All three of them were standing under a streetlight talking away. That's been quite a while back."

"What did Jewels say about that?"

"I didn't tell him much…I figured the less he thinks I know, the easier it'll be to nail him down the road. Besides, I've already given him something to chew on. I told him I was going to tell you about Smith and Jones wanting to give up…"

"How'd he take that?"

"Not very good. He turned white as a sheet."

"The moment he finds out I'm off the force, he'll feel he's off the hook. That'll be the end of his worries."

"…You don't particularly like Jewels. Do you?"

Randall smiled. "He's hard to tolerate at times!"

"There has to be a reason."

"It's probably childish, but the day I laid eyes on the man, I despised him. He's never done the first thing to earn such animosity, but it's there…"

"I don't think it's childish," Sully said. "Most everybody's met someone like that at one time or the other…I have!"

Randall leaned forward in his chair. "Now, back to business! How I can help?"

Sully pulled his organizer and opened it. "...The list is long."

"We won't worry about that for the time being. Just walk me through it; we'll discuss each item as we go along."

"Before this goes any further, you should know what I intend to do."

"You sure you want to do that?" Randall questioned. "It'll mean my being privy to your entire endeavor..."

"I'll have to trust somebody sooner or later anyway. If I can't trust you, I'm in a lot of trouble."

"Just wanted to make sure we're on the same page, that's all."

"Here's what I had in mind. First of all, I'm going to get Fred Gregory to tail Jewels full time. He may be able to uncover something of value, you never know...There's always that chance."

"It's an excellent idea," Randall said. "Now, what do you want from me?"

"I want a rundown on Jewels' finances: his checking accounts, his savings, any stocks and bonds that might be lying around...Can you do that?"

"I can't, but I know someone who can...Now, the bank accounts? How *far* back do you want to go?"

"At *least* sixteen months! It should tell me what I want to know."

"You want every transaction made? Deposits, withdrawals, transferred funds?"

"I want to know about every dime that comes in and goes out, including the names associated with each move."

"This person I know can get you that and a lot more, *if* you want it."

"I want more," Sully said.

Randall took a pad and pen from the desk. "All right, let's have it all!"

"I want the same information on four other people:...Virginia Moran, Dorothy Haygood, and Smith and Jones. Is that possible?"

"If it's a problem, I'll be in touch."

"*That* might be hard to do...I've been keeping my whereabouts secret lately."

"Would you rather contact me?"

"Yeah, I'd like to keep things as they are?"

Randall handed him a business card. "This is my number here; it's private and unlisted. Barring something unexpected, I should be here around the clock."

"How long do you think it'll take your friend to work this up?"

"Three, maybe four days, at the least. It'll take that long to find the banks involved. After that, it's just a matter of copying records."

"Sounds like you've been involved in this kind of thing before."

"Several times!...We never could use it in a court of law, but it always opened other doors. Things usually fell in place after the *who, where* and *how* was figured out. Once the *why* came to light, it went to the prosecutor's office. Juries love it when you give them a motive."

Sully stood and put his jacket on. "...I had some doubts for a while. If I'd had somewhere else to go, I'd probably have gone there."

"Then you're satisfied with our arrangement?"

"That's a fair assumption."

"Then *sit* back down," Randall commanded gruffly. "You have some things to explain and there's no time like now to get started."

"Where do you want me to start?"

"Let's try sixteen months ago; that seems to be when all this *bullshit* started."

Sully began from the beginning, revealing everything in detail, leaving nothing out.

# CHAPTER THIRTY SEVEN

There wasn't a light on in the apartment and Sully wondered if Beverly had gone to bed for the night. It was unusual for her not to have a night light on. Maybe she was still at the hospital, but it was unlikely. This would be the second night in a row she would have worked long hours. That's not a good practice for nurses. But, there's always the chance that circumstances demanded it? Her Ford convertible was parked outside, but that meant nothing either; it was less than a five-minute walk to the hospital. Except on special occasions, the car was hardly used. There was no getting around it; Beverly had never returned to the apartment.

Once inside the apartment, it was obvious that nothing had changed since she had left that morning. Everything remained exactly as it was then. She hadn't disturbed him when she went to work, and that was definitely out of character for her. His mind began churning the possibilities as he raced out of the building.

He circled the block quickly to the hospital, then caught the elevator to the fifth floor. He approached the nurse's station breathing heavily. "Beverly Johnson!" he said to a seated nurse. "...Is she working?"

The nurse looked at him suspiciously. "What kind of business do you have with her?" the nurse asked protectively.

"I know it's late, but she was supposed to meet me earlier and never showed. When I went by her place, there was no one there and I got concerned."

"When's the last time you saw her, Mister Hawken?"

"Earlier today!" he lied, then wondered how she knew him. "...Do I know you?"

"Probably not, but I'm familiar with you."

"Is it because I was a patient here for three months?"

"That's one reason, but the fact that I'm Beverly's friend is the other."

"She's *told* you about me?" Sully asked, until then thinking that Beverly would never discuss him with anyone.

"Not as much as I'd like to hear," the nurse said, "but enough to let me know how she feels."

"And how's that?"

"Until this afternoon, I'd say you were an important part of her life."

"What's that supposed to mean?" Sully asked. "I don't know of anything that's changed since then."

"I guess beating up on a woman means nothing to you," the nurse railed out. "...It takes a real tough guy to do something like that?"

"Lady, I don't know what bathroom wall you got that from, but if I were you, I'd get a bucket of soap and clean it up. Now *where's* Beverly?"

"I think you should talk to the supervisor before this goes any further."

"You've got one minute...After that, I'll find her on my own."

"I suppose you'll knock us around like you did Beverly, if we try and stop you?

"You never heard her say I did anything like that."

"I didn't have to; I have eyes."

"That doesn't mean you saw anything."

She started to reply then turned to the to the telephone and dialed quickly. She paused a moment. "...Mrs. Jordan," she began, "Hawken is here, just like I said."

Sully's face turned red with anger. The only crime committed was getting Beverly involved in something that wasn't her concern. Now he was being accused of battering her. He gritted his teeth in an attempt to keep control.

A stout nurse, possibly in her fifties, came through the elevator door with a uniformed policeman at her side. They walked up next to Sully.

"Don't you start with me, lady," Sully threatened softly. "I've had it with you people. One more wild accusation and it's going to get sticky around here."

The policeman put a hand on his nightstick. "If *I* were you, I'd be quiet and listen to what she has to say."

Sully stared at the cop menacingly. "...Well, you *ain't* me, pal. And before you yank that stick out, you'd better make damn sure you got things right...And just so you ain't surprised, I get nasty when I'm threatened."

"*Hold on a second, boys*," the supervisor said, interceding. She turned to the night nurse. "Janice, you said this was the man that hurt Beverly. Where did that come from?"

"Well, *nobody* told me! I knew Beverly was seeing him and it's pretty obvious he hit her...Good Lord! Just look at him...He had to have done it."

The supervisor waved her hand at Sully's face. "Janice, do you really believe that Beverly could do something like that to this man? Condemning someone with nothing but a guess is not very smart. Now, go back to work; I'll handle this." She patted the policeman on the shoulder. "You can go back downstairs, Charley."

"You sure?" the cop replied eyeing Sully suspiciously.

"I'm sure," she said. "...Now get out of here."

The policeman stared back at Sully while walking slowly to the elevator. He still wasn't sure he should leave.

"I don't think he likes me," Sully said, watching the cop get into the elevator. The supervisor did not comment. "...Let's go over to the waiting room. We should talk before you see Beverly."

Sully followed her to the ICU waiting area and took a seat facing her. "Is she all right?" he asked, now thinking things were worse than he originally thought.

"She's fine, Mister Hawken. The only problem is, she came to work this morning in a daze. *Naturally*, we became concerned and ran some tests. We discovered she had experienced a mild concussion. We put her to bed rather than let her go on the floor. There was plenty of room, so we gave her an ICU bed."

"Did you admit her, or is that a nurses perk?"

"No, we didn't admit her, and it's not something we normally do. It was the only way she'd agree to stay. She flew into hysterics when she heard a police report would have to be filed, and the only way we could calm her down was *not* register her."

"Can I see her? I'd feel better about this if I could."

"I don't see why not," the supervisor said. "Just be quiet...She's asleep from the medication and we'd rather not disturb her just yet."

Sully followed the night supervisor into an ICU cubicle at the rear of the chamber. He walked to the side of the bed and looked at Beverly; he took a step back. He was stunned at the condition she was in. Both eyes were swollen shut and black. He didn't remember her being hit that hard. "Did she say anything about how this happened?"

"Not a word! I think she was hiding something."

Sully bent over and kissed her on the cheek, then straightened up and turned to leave. He was satisfied she was in good hands.

"Sully!" Beverly said weakly. "What happened—to you—last night?"

Sully felt guilty for awakening her. "How long you been awake?"

"Since the—argument in—the hall...Couldn't help but hear that."

"Sorry about that!...I was getting a little uptight."

"You didn't bother me. If anything, it helped me get awake. I was just waiting for the medication to wear off...That stuff gives me a horrible hangover."

"I could've held it down...You should've said something."

"I would have if it had gotten out of hand, but you handled it fine...It was nice to know you'd be in here eventually."

Sully looked over his shoulder; the supervisor had left the room. "How'd you get a concussion?" he asked quietly. "When those goons took me out of the apartment, except for being mad as hell, you seemed okay."

"When that man knocked me down, my head hit the floor pretty hard. There was a delayed reaction. I didn't even know I had a concussion until I was at work...I remember very little."

"Do you remember me taking you out of the shower?"

"Vaguely," she replied. "...And I remember coming to the hospital with my head in a fog...That's when they put me to bed."

"What did you tell them happened?"

"That I walked into a closet door and fell backward on the floor."

Sully smiled. "I don't think they bought it."

"I *know* they didn't! And if I hadn't pitched such a fit, they'd have filed a police report...I certainly didn't want that; I didn't know what kind of trouble you were in."

"You did the right thing; and it keeps you out of it."

Beverly took a deep breath and closed her eyes. "What happened after they took you away? I remember thinking, I'd never see you again."

"It was a strange night, and that's putting it mildly. They were the very people I thought wanted to kill me. I wound up at their bosses' house, and guess what? The old man asked me to find Jigs' killer...He said I could do anything up to, and including *murder,* in the effort. Said he'd back me all the way."

Beverly blinked nervously. "Good Lord, Sully! What kind of people are you dealing with? If they're saying it's okay to commit murder, what's next?"

"Take it easy, kid" Sully said gently. "You know I wouldn't do anything like that; it's not the way I operate. I don't think I should've told you about this...It has nothing to do with you."

Beverly didn't like being considered an outsider and railed out. "I can't believe you said that. Not only did I miss weeks of work nursing you back to health, but I could've been wound up in serious trouble hurt during the process...Then there's the matter of getting socked around and winding up with a concussion...All that, and you say I don't need to know anything...I think I have the right to know *everything!*"

"You don't understand, Beverly," Sully said meekly. "It's for your own good."

Beverly let the words sink in and her face softened. "I *am* thankful for what you're trying to do, but believe me, secrets are a two-way street. Whether you like it or not, there *are* things you need to know about me."

Sully downplayed her flight to confession. "I think it's best, things stay as they are. I get uncomfortable knowing too much about a person."

"I'll be home early; wait for me," Beverly said, showing more alertness. "Before this goes any further, we need to sit down and have a long talk. After that, I want to know about the trouble you're in."

"That sounds like an ultimatum!"

"It is! The air has to be cleared."

Sully left the hospital having trouble believing something could bother her to such an extent. She was adamant that *nothing* could be resolved until *everything* was out in the open. It was *not* to his liking.

# CHAPTER THIRTY EIGHT

The night was noticeably chilly standing in front of the hospital. Sully shivered slightly as a cold gust of air whistled under his jacket. Except for the one strong breeze, there was very little wind. He stood still in the star-lit night a few moments, allowing his body to get adjusted to the cold, then walked back around to Beverly's apartment. He'd wait for her there like she asked him to.

He went straight to the apartment, kicked off his shoes and laid across the bed fully clothed. The day's events had completely worn him down. He covered up with a comforter and quickly gave in to the drowsiness. He was too tired to reverse the restless slumber and quietly dozed off.

It was after five when he woke up. Slightly disoriented, he was sure he had slept longer than that. It was still an hour and a half before daylight. Knowing he'd never get back to sleep under the circumstances, he threw his feet over the side of the bed and sat there a moment trying to get awake. He found his shoes in the dark, stood and stretched widely, then staggered in to the bathroom. He brushed his teeth with his eyes closed, then splashed cold water on his face trying to disperse the grogginess. He left the apartment still thinking of going back to bed, but knew it wasn't in the cards. There was still a situation to be dealt with concerning Fred Gregory; maybe it could be finished before Beverly came in.

Sully parked in the Gregory driveway just as daylight began to break through on the horizon. A light was on in the living room. He wondered who would be up and about that early in the morning. He stepped up onto the porch and knocked softly on the door. Not hearing a sound inside, he pounded the door harder the second time. There was an immediate response.

Sully took a step backwards when he heard an unfamiliar voice cursing as they stomped down the hallway. He expected an enormous person to answer the door and he was right.

A large Negro man snatched the door open angrily. He stood there, noticeably irritated from being disturbed so early. "What you want, man?" he barked threateningly.

"I need to talk to Fred," Sully said, still back on his heels.

"If you a damn cop, this *could'a* waited."

"I'm *not* a cop...Fred's a friend of mine!" Sully said. "I don't mean to disturb anyone, but this is important...Sorry!"

"Who is you, man?"

"Sully Hawken!"

"The huge man's face mellowed somewhat. When he spoke, the hardness was gone from his voice. "C'mon in and set yo'self down. I'll go gets him out ta' bed...An' if you's wonderin', I's his brother, Zack."

Sully stepped inside and took a seat on the sofa. He didn't recall Fred ever mentioning his brother before and wondered why it was never brought up.

Zack's voice thundered from down the hall, "Wake up, Fred!" he said loudly. "Mistuh Hawken here! He want to see you!"

Sully heard movement in the rear of the house for a few minutes, then silence. In a few minutes, Fred came down the hall fully clothed and looking drowsy.

"Mornin" Mister Sully," Fred said easily, sitting beside him. "Is anythin' wrong?"

"No, but I do need a little help on something"

"Don' knows 'bout dat, boss. Even tho'them polices ain't been around fo' a few days, I still gots to worry 'bout 'em. *All* my brothers is leavin' soon an' ain't no one gon' be heah to watch after mama. I needs to go back to work at the hospital."

"If that's what you want, it's fine with me...By the way, why is it, you never mentioned Zack before?"

"...Cause they jes' let him out a few days' ago."

"Let him out of where?"

"The city farm...Over on Constitution road, jes' befo' you gets to South River."

"I know where it is...Been there a few times myself."

Fred's eyes widened. "You's been to jail? I didn' knows that."

"Just as a visitor," Sully smiled. "I took cigarettes and candy to some friends. It means a lot to a person in the lock-up."

Fred's face went blank. "I *knows*."

"...Sorry I didn't get to do more for you while you were in jail, but my world was upside down at the time. I was hiding from some people and it was all I could do to stay out of their way."

"I weren't thinking that, boss. My mind was on the troubles I had while I's in jail...I made me a promise that if'n I got out of that place alive, ain't nobody ever gon' lock me up again."

Zack walked in the room then with three cups of hot coffee, passed them out and sat down.

Sully asked Fred. "When are you figuring on going back to work?"

"Don't know, jes' yet. Supposed to call 'em this week."

"Think you could postpone it for another week? I sure do need someone to keep an eye on our friend, Jewels."

"I can probably do that!...Is he up to somethin?"

"I think so; it sure looks like it anyway! When you saw him at the end of the alley talking with Smith and Jones, it started me thinking."

"Thought dat was strange myself."

"Well, he's spending more time than ever with them now...I saw the three of them scheming about something the other night in front of Jewels' office."

"If them cops was black, they wouldn't get away wit' anythin' like dat."

"Probably not!" Sully agreed. "...Now listen carefully! If Smith and Jones do happen to come around while you're on Jewels trail, stay away from them. Those two have absolutely nothing to lose. If they got it in their head you were tailing *them,* they wouldn't hesitate to come after you."

"Don't bother me none if they does...I ain't gon' turn t'other cheek to 'em ever again. But it sho' don't soun' like you be getting' much fo' yo' money."

"Well, I am! I need to know what Jewels is up to, especially now. I think he knows something about Jigs death, *and* the money that disappeared."

"You minds if Zack tag along wit' me? I kin pays him. A little money'll get him back on his feet."

"I don't mind!...Just don't let your presence be known...You have to promise me you'll keep your distance."

Zack spoke up for the first time. "Suppose they spots us and we can't get away? What we supposed to do then?"

"In that case, do what you have to...You won't have a choice in the matter."

"Well, I gon' tote hardware. I don' knows 'bout Fred but I don' likes looking down the barrel of a gun with nothin' but nickels in my pockets."

"How do you feel about that, Fred?" Sully asked.

"Same as Zack! I knows how tickled them cops would be to corner me up."

"Are you a felon like Fred?" Sully asked Zack.

"Yassuh!"

"You do know what the price is for a felon carrying a pistol, don't you? It could mean a lot of hard time."

Zack philosophized with an old saying "D'ruther be judged by twelve than carried by six."

"Just wanted you to know what you're setting yourselves up for."

"We knows, Boss," Fred said. "I done tol' you how I feels. Come hell or high water, I ain't goin' back to no jail."

Sully wondered to what extent Fred would carry out that declaration and showed concern with a frown.

"We *gon'* carry the guns," Fred said, noticing the uncertainty on Sully's face. "We keep our distance likes you says, boss. The only way them pistols comes out is if they comes after us."

"If that's the best I can get, I guess I'll have to be satisfied with it," Sully said, handing his car keys to Fred. "Do you know where Jewels' office is?"

"Yassuh! Jes' 'cross from Georgia Baptist Hospital."

"Have you been there before?"

"Yassuh!...One time!"

"Think you can find it again?"

"Should be able to."

"Okay, here's what I want you to do: Drop me off at the Nurses quarters behind Crawford Long, then take the Buick and camp out close to Jewels' office. I need to know who goes in and out of his office. I want an exact description of all visitors. If he leaves at any time, I want him followed. Stay close on his tail, but back far enough so he doesn't notice. If he makes you, pull out...There's always the next day."

"What we do when he knock off for the day?"

"Follow him then, *especially*. It's probably the best time of all. That's when he'll feel at ease the most..."

"You ready to go now?" Fred said, standing. "It's daylight! We needs to find a good watchin' spot befo' Jewels go to work." He looked at his brother, Zack. "Get the guns from under the house...We meet you in front."

Stepping to the car, Fred looked at Sully. "How we gon' get in touch if somethin' come up?"

"I'll show you where I've been staying, but I don't want anyone to know. I'd prefer the person I'm with, not to be involved...I should be in most nights by midnight, so run me down about that time. Things usually die down by then."

"I'll fill Zack in when we gets gone."

Zack walked up to the car and handed Fred a five shot .44 Magnum revolver. He eased a .357 Magnum in his own belt. "...We ready?"

Sully looked at Fred as they crawled into the automobile. "Where'd you come up with cannons like that?"

"A friend of mine sol' 'em to me. He bought 'em, then somethin' happen an' he has to gets rid of 'em...I bought 'em fo' sixty dollars."

"Who did you get them from?"

"You 'member dat night we in Hapeville?"

"Yes! What about it?"

"This man I knows, bought the guns fum that same fella you saw at t' hotel. I never seed him, but I sho 'membered his name."

"G.W. Spence?"

"Yassuh! That were his name, and he deal in guns."

Sully eased back in the car seat. What would bring G.W. back to Atlanta knowing full well it may present a problem for him? He couldn't have known about Gracci and Fletcher being out of the picture—unless someone had contacted him in Florida. He wasn't the type to show back up unless it was safe all around. Sully wondered who knew where G.W. was and had called him?

Sully handed Fred a key after they parked. "This is for the back door; I have another one. Anytime you need me, the apartment's at the top of the stairs, first door to the left."

"Boss, that's where the nurses stays," he protested. "Ain't no man 'posed to go in there, specially me!"

"That's true, but in my case, I didn't exactly have a choice. A lot people were on the streets trying to run me down at the time."

Fred did not like the idea of going into the Nurses quarters in the middle of the night, key or no key—and kept voicing his opinion going out of the parking lot.

Sully glanced at the time going in the back entrance; it was almost eight o'clock. He'd put on some coffee for Beverly, then make breakfast when she came home...Life was definitely looking up!

# CHAPTER THIRTY NINE

Sully sat down to a hot cup of coffee at Beverly's apartment and relaxed. He was sure finding Jigs' killer was within reach now. And it looked like that achievement might be made through none other than the enigmatic Garan T. Jewels. With Fred following the lawyer twenty-four hours a day, and Captain Randall on his financial trail, some positive results should be forthcoming in a matter of days.

It was now after nine-thirty and Beverly still hadn't come in from the hospital. Sully was beginning to become concerned. At eleven, he had had enough. He left the dormitory in a hurry and went straight to the hospital.

At the ICU nurse's station on the fifth floor, he asked a floor nurse, "Is Beverly Johnson still here?...I'm a friend!"

Looking at his broken nose and battered face, she hesitated. "...She left at shift change...But that was at seven o'clock."

"We were supposed to meet earlier and somehow I missed her," Sully said, hoping the concern was for nothing.

The nurse was unaware of the problem during the night and began asking questions as he walked away. "What do you think has happened?" she asked inquisitively, trailing behind.

"I don't know! But, if anything comes up, get word to me at her apartment."

"You have a key to *her* apartment?"

Sully didn't answer at first, picking up the pace to the elevator. "I've stopped by to pick her up a few times...She leaves the door unlocked for me."

"I didn't know she had a friend like that...I would've thought she'd told me."

Sully rang the bell for the elevator, mildly irritated by the rude prying. When the elevator door slid open, Beverly stood there with two grocery bags in her arms.

"Sully!" Beverly said. "What are you doing here?"

"I was looking for you...I was worried."

Beverly smiled sheepishly. "You won't *believe* what happened after I left the hospital this morning. It was so strange…One minute I was walking down Ponce De Leon in a daze, then all of a sudden I realized that I was heading to an apartment I lived in years ago. I was okay once I realized it was the concussion, so I turned around and headed home. I stopped by a grocery store for a few things on the way back. When I got to the apartment, I realized I didn't have my keys." She handed Sully the groceries. "Hold these! I'll be back in a minute."

Sully took the bags and stepped to the side.

Beverly hurried toward the nurse's station, ignoring the prying nurse walking close behind. She returned moments later waving the keys as if it were treasure. "…Right where I left them."

They boarded the elevator, went downstairs, then walked around to the nurses' quarters. Beverly opened the door to the apartment allowing Sully to pass with the groceries. "Put that stuff on the table," she said. "I'll put it up in a few minutes. This is the second day in this uniform and I've got to get out of it *now*…I look a mess."

Sully did as he was told and set the bag of groceries on the table. He then sat and waited for her to return.

She walked in the kitchen shortly thereafter in a housecoat and slippers. She quietly began putting the food away.

Sully watched her move around the room gracefully, then smiled… He wondered if she were wearing anything underneath the housecoat. "…I need a favor," he finally said, setting his mind on another course. You mind my using the Ford for a while? "Fred's doing some work for me and has the Buick. I need some transportation."

Beverly found the keys in her pocketbook, then handed them to him." "It hasn't been cranked in a while…It may not even run."

Sully put the keys his pocket. "…You're sure you don't mind?"

"If I did, I'd say so."

He took a step toward the door. "You need some privacy, and this is a good time since I've got things to do…Think you'll need me for anything?"

"*Sit down*, Sully," Beverly said abruptly, then clasped her hands with her elbows on the table. She stared intensely at him. "This has gone far enough. It's time we put things on the table."

"I've told you how I felt about confessions and I haven't changed my mind."

"...I *won't* rest until this is out in the open."

It was obvious by Beverly's voice that she had something significant to say. she was bound and determined to reveal whatever it was, and there was nothing he could do. He sat in silence.

"...Do you remember the night we discussed my association with Dorothy Haygood and Virginia Moran?" she asked.

"The only thing I remember was you weren't having anything else to do with them. That was enough for me."

"Well, that's not altogether true. I've been misleading you from the very day we met. Good Lord, Sully! Even that was a set-up."

"Why would they do that?...There's no purpose!"

"I'll start from the beginning...The first time I met Dorothy was at Scottish Rite Hospital; that was two years ago. We became friends. As the friendship grew, we began doing everything together. During that time, I was always a third person. I closed my eyes to what she did *until* she began introducing me to some men she knew. That's when our friendship began to unravel. I dated some of the men until I found out that Dorothy was offering me as the prize. I won't go into what happened, but it wasn't pretty."

"When did all this take place?"

"A couple of months after I met her. We were never good friends after that...Especially after she pushed me into a relationship with her husband."

"Doc Haygood?"

"Yes! I dated him for a while, but the truth is, I just felt sorry for the man. It was a hopeless affair; I don't know why I did it. There certainly wasn't a big attraction...Thurman didn't exactly hide the fact that he was still in love with Dorothy."

"Do you think there was a purpose behind her shoving you at him?"

"Absolutely! She thought Thurman wouldn't be able to watch her so closely if he was with me."

"How long did it last?"

"Till you came out of the coma."

Sully leaned back and relaxed. "It's not necessary I know about your past life, Beverly...This hasn't changed a thing. It was a lot of heartache for nothing."

"There's more!...A lot more!"

"If it's about someone pushing you in my direction, I won't object to that."

"No one's doing that anymore, Sully. It's just that I think you should know certain things. It all started some month's back when Dorothy introduced me to Virginia Moran. They came right out and asked me if I would get cozy with you if you survived. It was an odd request, but I agreed; I didn't see any harm in it at the time. I never dreamed there was a devious motive."

Sully frowned. "I wonder why they wanted to keep such close tabs on me? My life's not exactly an open book, but I don't have anything to hide."

"It has something to do with an unrecorded will. From what I overheard, you were in Mister Moran's will, and Virginia desperately wanted to find it before anyone else did...I think she intended to destroy it."

"That's strange!...I received fifteen thousand dollars from Jigs' estate...Garan Jewels wrote the check."

"It involves a lot more than that, Sully. Otherwise, Virginia wouldn't have given me five thousand dollars to look for it."

"You took five thousand bucks from Virginia? When did that happen?"

"The day the hospital confirmed you were okay...I was pretty confused at the time, or it never would've happened. I wanted to leave Atlanta and that money was going to be my ticket out of here. I felt like I was coming apart; I wasn't of course, but the thought was there just the same."

"What made you change your mind?"

"You!...One day I thought escape was the only solution and a week later, everything was different."

"You stayed because of me?"

"Yes! You brought something fresh into my life."

"...Let's talk about that will for a minute," Sully said, grasping her hand "The first time you went to my house: Is that what you were looking for?"

"Yes, but nothing was there...The only papers I found were in a cookie tin in the bedroom. Nothing there even resembled a will."

"It seems strange that I'm just now hearing about this will. Jigs may have mentioned it; I *just* don't know. My memory hasn't been all that reliable lately. One thing for certain: If Virginia puts that much stock in there being a will, there is one. And that pretty much explains why she's been dogging me."

"Something else!...Did you know that Detectives Smith and Jones visited the Moran mansion regularly?"

"I heard about that! I just thought they were investigating Jigs' murder."

"This was before Jigs was killed."

"You're kidding! Was Jigs ever there when it happened?"

"Never! I think Virginia was paying them to keep an eye on Mister Moran and didn't want him to find out."

"What about Garan Jewels? Did he ever come around when the cops were there?"

"Only one time that I remember. I did hear that it went on regularly, but then, I wasn't exactly an everyday guest at the house."

"And this was all before Jigs was killed?"

"The day I saw them together was a month before his death."

"I wonder what that was about? Tell me, did you ever tell anyone that I was at your apartment when I lost my sight?"

"I wouldn't have done that under any circumstances...By then I had figured out there was a conspiracy of some kind; I just didn't know what."

"Have you been in contact with any of them since Hector brought me to your apartment that night?"

"A few times...I told them I'd lost contact with you."

"Did they believe you?"

"They seemed to."

Sully was silent a moment. "...When you were tight with Dorothy, was she laying up with anyone besides Jigs?"

"There were four men. She changed bed partners regularly back then. The names were different from one month to the next."

"Who was in the picture while Jigs was alive?"

"Other than Mister Moran, there was Garan Jewels, a wealthy bank official whose name I don't have, and a man called G.W. Spence. There was also a high-ranking police official; I don't have his name either. That was Dorothy's regulars when Mister Moran was killed. I don't know how she kept them separated."

Sully's eyes narrowed after G.W.'s name was mentioned. His old friend had failed to mention anything about his shacking up with Dorothy Haygood the last time they were together. That needed to be looked into.

"Do you see now, why I had to tell you this? It wasn't because I wanted to clear my conscience; you needed to know what you're up against."

"I know this: If certain people find out I've been here, you could be in danger. It wouldn't take a lot of brains to figure out you told me things."

"I'm not worried as long as you're here," she said, standing and dropping the robe. She stepped toward the shower. "...You coming?"

He had thought right; there was nothing under the robe.

# CHAPTER FORTY

Sully left the next morning leaving Beverly in bed still sleeping soundly. He could not remember *when* a woman was more giving or tuned in to his needs. It was difficult to walk away without saying a word. He knew if he awoke her, he would not have the will to leave if she asked him to stay.

Beverly's Ford convertible had been terribly neglected, judging from the dust in the car's interior. Sully wondered if there was enough strength in the battery to turn the engine over. It took a few minutes in the driver's seat to get familiar enough with the vehicle to try and start it. The switch-key was easy enough; so was the manual choke. He closed the choke all the way, patted the foot-feed several times, and then pressed the starter button on the dash. The engine turned over sluggishly a few times but wouldn't crank; the battery was too weak. He waited a minute, patted the accelerator a few more times and then pushed the starter button again. Well primed now, the engine turned over twice very slowly, then belched angrily through the carburetor for being disturbed. It still didn't crank. The battery was almost gone; there was possibly one more attempt left before it died completely. He patted the accelerator once again, then pressed the starter button for a final try. The engine caught on the second turn, coughing and sputtering from lack of running, then settled into a smooth hum. Sully eased the choke in slowly, then as the engine warmed, opened it completely. Sully was never a Henry Ford fan until that very moment; he'd have to concede that the man knew how to build a reliable product.

As the engine warmed, Sully's curiosity ran rampant on how to deal with G.W. Spence. Did G.W. lie about Fletcher and Gracci wanting to kill him? Keeping a low profile now that those two were out of the picture didn't make any sense. It didn't look like G.W. was ever in any danger…Why the charade?

When G.W. left town heading for Florida, he had acted terrified of what Gracci and Fletcher would do to him. He was back in town now, but strangely enough, doesn't feel comfortable in the mainstream.

He's selling guns again, like he always has, but finds it necessary to stay out of sight. He's acting as if someone is after him. Who could be frightening him to that extent?

Sully scratched his head in confusion; hopefully the answers would come when he found G.W. The first stop was at York's Poolroom; Sully carefully scanned the streets before approaching the entrance. It was not the time to run in to Smith and Jones accidentally. He closely observed the crowd inside from the doorway. Not seeing the detectives, he went inside and began asking if anyone had seen G.W.? They hadn't, and he left quickly. It was not wise to stay in one spot too long.

He got the same answers at Big Towns: No one had seen or had contact with G.W. lately. He repeated the pattern of leaving hurriedly. The Kimball House was next on the list. That was a brick wall also. The Peachtree Arcade restaurant was the next stop; it was just across the street at street level. No one had seen G.W. in weeks. He went to the basement cafeteria in the Arcade. It was the same answer: G.W. was a no-show and had been. Sully began systematically checking the downtown hotels that G.W. frequented. He went to the Dinkler Plaza and the Owl Room upstairs, then the Winecoff and finally the Henry Grady. The restaurants and watering holes were visited at each location. He went to three restaurants that G.W. had liked: The Ship Ahoy, Leb's and Herron's. Sully had covered the entire metro area without a single person seeing G.W. The search would have to be moved away from downtown, to places G.W. was known to go at times.

Sully left early the next morning, moving methodically down a list he had drawn up. The first stop was the Georgian Terrace Hotel, then west down North Avenue to the Q' Room above the Varsity. The Cotton Patch, Pilgreens and the Yellow Jacket Inn on the other side of Grant Field were to follow. He doubled back to the Biltmore on West Peachtree and then to Joe Cotton's Rhythm Ranch. He had doled out $120.00 looking for information for nothing! Discouraged by the two-day lack of success, he drove to Mamie Shanties' restaurant in North Atlanta for the final destination.

Striking out at there, he gave up and headed for Beverly's apartment.

Beverly looked at her watch when he came in the door; it was just before eight and already dark. "Looks like you had a long day," she said soothingly. "I'll put on some coffee on if you like?"

Sully sat heavily in a chair and let out a sigh of relief. "You sure it's no bother?" After two days of pounding the pavement, the nicks and quirks were gaining ground on his wore-down frame. The daytime spent looking for G.W. and staying with Beverly at night was beginning to take its' toll. Half of that was pleasurable, but he had to rest sometimes.

Beverly moved to the stove when the coffee began perking. She poured a cup for him, then sat down and took his free hand. "Tell me if something's wrong, Sully...My head's clear now...Maybe I can help?"

"I'm just tired...I'm spending a lot of time looking for G. W...He hasn't been to any of his old hangouts and I can't figure out why."

"Why is he so important to you?"

Sully took a sip of the hot coffee and whistled when it burnt his tongue. "I think he knows something about Jigs's death. I'm not sure if he was involved yet, but for the last couple of days, it's been on my mind. It's crazy! Just before he left town, he was doing fine. Twenty-four hours later, he was running for his life. He came by the house the night after I saw him. He told me this story about Fletcher and Gracci gunning for him. He was heading for Florida to beat the heat. I don't believe now that they were *ever* after him...Somebody had to tell those hoods about the guns I bought, and it couldn't have been anyone other than G.W....Maybe I'm the one he's afraid of? If that's the case, I need to know why."

"That would mean Dorothy Haygood is involved."

"I thought about that! It might be the reason G.W. kept their relationship a secret from me. If he's so much in love with Dorothy, he'd do most anything to satisfy her."

"You think he would kill for her?"

"Maybe? I don't know? There's a possibility that they both know something about Jigs murder and are afraid to say anything."

"Are you going to see Dorothy?"

"When I get things straightened out with G.W., I will...There's something I need to talk to her about."

"...If you say something about her being your lover, she'll know *exactly* where it came from. You can count on those two cops getting the word after that. All they'll have to do is park on my doorsteps... That's the way those gangsters found you."

"Maybe I should put her on the back burner for a while...I don't know?"

Beverly walked over behind him and began massaging his shoulders. "...I have a question: Do you believe Virginia Moran had anything to do with her brother's death?"

"To be honest, I wouldn't put anything past her. She has a love of money that's almost perverse. If Jigs had made her angry enough by wanting to give so much money to Carmine Anoletti, it could've happened...I can imagine what went through her head when this will business surfaced."

"Do you love me, Sully?"

"As much as a man can, I suppose. Why do you ask?"

"I don't know? I have this feeling you're going to walk away one day...I don't know if you'll be able handle the things I'm guilty of."

Sully jerked his head around angrily. "You see what I was talking about? This is what happens when people open up about their personal lives...Nothing's going to change!...Absolutely nothing!"

"A lot went on that I haven't told you about, Sully; there are things that will hurt...I didn't give you the whole picture. It's the same as lying."

"...Why bring it up now?"

"You'll hear the truth one of these days, and it's not pretty."

Sully stood, then walked into the bedroom shedding his clothes. "We'll see!" he said, yanking down the covers. "...Now let it rest!"

Beverly cleaned the coffeepot and the few dishes, then followed him into the bedroom. Within a few minutes she was up against his back running a hand slowly over his chest. He was already asleep.

# CHAPTER FORTY ONE

Sully awoke the next morning after 11:30. He had slept fourteen straight hours and every muscle in his body was aching. Sleeping hard effected him that way. He was more tired now than when he went to sleep. He sat groggily on the edge of the bed trying to get awake, then realized that the apartment was quiet. Then it came to him: Beverly was at work. After the ritual of rubbing eyes and stretching limbs, he staggered into the kitchen. A note was positioned on the table where it wouldn't be overlooked.

*You were sleeping and I didn't want to bother you. Coffee's on the stove. Just heat. Be home around dark!*
*Beverly*

Sully turned on the stove and went back into the bedroom. He laid out some clothes, then pulled the .45 from his jacket on the bedpost. He eased back the slide making sure a bullet was in the chamber. Releasing it, he engaged the safety and put it on the dresser. Satisfied everything was in working order, he downed a quick cup of coffee and headed for the shower. He was out of the apartment by noon. It had taken less than thirty minutes from waking up to walking out.

After a stop at the bank for money, he drove down Auburn Avenue toward Fred's house. He and Zack could only be one of two places at that time of day: Either at home or watching Jewels' office. He'd go to the house first since it was the closest.

He drove slowly up the alley toward the Gregory home; there was no sign of the Buick in front. A quick look in the driveway revealed it wasn't there either. They had to be at Jewels. Sully turned around and headed straight for Boulevard Drive.

He began checking the parked cars for Fred and his brother, a block away from Georgia Baptist Hospital. He drove slowly past the light at Forrest Avenue without finding them, then turned around and came back. He found a parking spot a half block from the corner and pulled into it. He wondered where Fred and Zack were? He turned the engine off and slid down in the seat. He could easily see Jewels' front window from there without being spotted.

Ten minutes later, a knock on the passenger's window startled him. The .45 came around cocked and ready to fire in the same instant.

"Whoa, boss!" Fred said, backing away and throwing his hands up. He eased in beside Sully. "You's mighty quick about snatchin' that thing out these days."

"I wasn't expecting anyone to be here, that's all. You caught me off guard...I had my mind on Jewel's place. I thought something might've gone wrong when I didn't see the Buick."

"Ain't nothin' happened up to now, boss, but eva'thing under control. Me and Zack park where nobody sees us. We's better off that way."

"What if Jewels decides to take off in a hurry? Can you act fast enough?"

"Ain't no problem, boss," Fred said, pointing his thumb toward an apartment building on the hill. "Look up there!"

Sully leaned over and looked at the building. Zack, was resting comfortably on a bench in front of the apartments.

"See that driveway by Zack?"

Sully nodded.

"The car up there out of sight. Ain't no way Jewels gon' go sneakin' off wit'out us catchin' up. We gots him in a lock!"

Comfortable that Fred had things well in hand, Sully asked about his friend who bought the guns from G.W. "This friend of yours—the one you got the guns from...He got a name?"

"His name Jesse Cole. He stay at the corner out on Auburn Avenue."

"Down the alley?"

"Yassuh! Same side of the street."

"You think he's home?"

"Not likely. Zack say the law come fo'him t'other night. He say they cuff him an' take him to the farm."

"How did he know that's where they were going?"

"Cause Zack was at the farm wit' him las' month. He say Jesse up and walk off wit'out sayin' nothin' to nobody. He still had six months to do; he gon' get mo' fo' running off. They jes' gon' take him back."

"Do you think I could see him if I went to the farm?" Sully asked. "I want to know where he did business with G.W."

"You don' needs Jesse for that, boss. I knows where they meet… You knows dat alley 'hind the Biltmore."

"Is that where they hooked up?"

"Yassuh! He says that Spence fella stay there. He say when Spence went afta' them guns, he go back in the hotel fo' 'bout fifteen minutes."

"Do you know what entrance he used?"

"It were the one the help use out by the corner. He say Spence come out the same do' wit' the guns."

"Where was Jesse waiting?"

"At the garbage rack, 'bout mid-way ta' alley."

Sully understood now why G.W.'s name wasn't in the hotel registry when he had asked the day before. He was in the hotel with somebody else or under an assumed name. He had been on a wild goose chase then, but now things were different; there was no doubt where G.W. was. *Today is Friday*, he thought. Maybe G.W. was more comfortable about moving around on the weekend. If he did leave the hotel, the alley and main entrance were the only two places he would use; both could be seen easily from across the street.

Sully thought a minute. "…You say Jewels hasn't made any moves out of the ordinary since you've been here?"

"Yassuh! He goin' home ever' night—'cept fo' las' night. He stop by dat Moran lady's house fo' a while."

"That's it?"

"Other than that, he be quiet as a mouse."

Sully filed that away. As long as Jewels was unaware of what was going on, the more apt he would be to make a mistake. He told Fred when he would be in touch, said goodbye, and then left. There were more stops to make before the day was over.

# CHAPTER FORTY TWO

It is not out of the ordinary for a lawyer to spend a lot of time at a client's home, especially if there is great wealth involved. When Virginia Moran's brother Jigs died, her holdings almost doubled when his assets temporarily rolled over into her hands. Those inherited entities had to be dealt with by an attorney, regardless of background or the sleaze they were involved in. Sully felt the bottom of the barrel had been scraped when it was learned that Garan Jewels was Virginia Moran's legal advisor. She had definitely found an attorney who would satisfy her needs.

Sully accepted the fact that Jewels was handling the Moran estate under Virginia's control, but then, no quicker than he gave in to that logic, it was rejected. Any other lawyer would have used a telephone to keep everything in order. There was no need to do so in person.

Sully turned right off Ponce De Leon onto East Lake Road without ever slowing down. There was still a ten-mile drive to negotiate before the Randall house came into view. Fifteen minutes later, he was in the Randall driveway. A sudden chill caused him to think he was coming down with a virus; the doctors had warned him to be careful before leaving the hospital. His body wasn't up to battling any kind of illness. He stepped from the warm car into the cold air and shivered a second time more violently. He stepped quickly up on the porch. The unforgiving shivering began again, but this time it wouldn't stop. He knocked hard on the door, hoping someone inside would notice the urgency in the assault. At a quick glance, the dark interior of the house gave the appearance that no one was home. Sully knew one thing: He had to either get in the house or get back in the car, and it had to be quick. He wasn't going to last much longer. He shook uncontrollably and knocked even harder the second time.

A light brightened up the hallway and Pearl Randall came down the hallway. "Just a minute," she said softly, then opened the door.

Sully stood there shaking. "You mind if I come in for a minute?" he smiled nervously. "I think I'm freezing to death."

"Good heavens, Mister Hawken," she said, opening the door wider and drawing him inside. "You're pale as a sheet!"

Sully rubbed his arms briskly. "I wasn't expecting the cold air to cut through me like that. That temperature dropped fast."

Pearl eased the door to. "You go on back to Otis' office; I'll put some coffee on. You sure look like you could use some...He was hoping you'd drop by today; said he wanted to talk some things over with you."

Sully walked down the hall to Randall's office still shaking from the chill, and then knocked on Randall's office door. He stepped inside without waiting for an invitation. He sat down heavily and grinned sheepishly. "Don't mean to barge in like this, but I need to get off my feet."

Randall picked up a blanket from the bench behind him and handed it to Sully. "I get the chills myself...I keep this handy."

The soft threads of the blanket had an immediate effect. Sully quit shaking the second the warm cloth was around his shoulders.

Pearl Randall came in carrying an elegant silver tray with a pot of coffee and two cups. "I brought you a cup too," she told her husband.

"We thank you, Pearl," Randall smiled. "...I'm sure Sully does."

"I do!" Sully said. "It will probably save my life."

Pearl Randall left the room a vision of domestic satisfaction. A guest had come into her home and felt the grace of true southern hospitality.

"I think my Pearl likes you," Randall said after she was out of earshot. "As a rule, she's gracious to everyone, but it's been a while since our best silver has been out."

"A guy *could* get attached to that kind of treatment."

"All right," Randall said dramatically, running his fingers over his notes, "Time to get down to business. I have some things that will be hard for you to believe."

"You think it's wise to leave something that sensitive here at the house?"

"The things I've written down aren't a problem. What I intend to keep a secret are best left to memory. So, in the future, if memory fails you, call me; I don't forget anything. You have to understand that all the information obtained by illegal methods has to be kept quiet. We couldn't afford to face something like that in court." Randall reminded Sully of the card with his private number. "Very seldom do I leave the premises these days, so if you have to call at an odd hour, don't consider it an imposition. I'm usually available day or night. Remember, I'm an ex cop...Pearl and I have dealt with that sort of inconvenience our entire life."

Sully reached for a pen in his shirt pocket, then clipped it back. "Like you said:...Trust everything to memory."

"It's best," Randall said, "and you're about to see why...We'll start with Garan Jewels' finances, then go down the list. First of all, we *know* he's a thief. Maybe not as big as we first thought, but nevertheless, a swindler without conscience. Somehow, he's convinced Virginia Moran to give him the power of attorney over a portion of her estate. At present, he has the power to manipulate that money without fear of criminal charges. It goes like this: Every three months, the Moran estate automatically transfers money into a general fund under Jewels' control, leveling it off at $25,000. The deposits are anywhere from $2,000 to $20,000. Jewels is smart enough to never let the fund dip below $5,000 dollars. He drains the account systematically under the pretense of handling the estate and various pet projects for her. He hasn't made a dent in her holdings yet, but he *has* lined his pockets to the tune of $240,000 over the past sixteen months. That amounts to five hundred bucks a day. I also found out that his savings account has a balance of over $3,000,000 dollars. How much of that money came from Moran properties, I haven't a clue."

"Did you tell Virginia what you found out?"

"I didn't even bother to call her. All this information was obtained illegally and couldn't be used. If it went before a judge, he'd have to throw it out; the agreement as much as says that Jewels can do what he wants with that money...I'd just be setting myself up for criminal charges if it were brought into a court."

"For curiosity's sake, what's the Moran fortune worth now?"

"Cash on hand, over $17,000,000...Stocks, bonds and holdings are at least equal to that—or more."

"Maybe she knows what Jewels is doing?  Maybe she's fattening up that fund so that he'll do her dirty work?...It's something to think about!"

"It is, but I see Jewels as an impetuous rogue."

"He might be a lot more than that."

"What makes you say that?"

"I've learned recently that Jigs might have made a will out that hasn't been found.  I'm supposed to be the chief benefactor to a large portion of his estate.  If that's true, it explains the break-ins at my house.  It could also mean that Jewels is being paid under the table to find the will and destroy it."

"If that's what this is about," Randall said slowly, "and the will isn't found before long, it could lead to more drastic measures."

"That's right," Sully said.  "And I believe that Smith and Jones are just looking for the opportunity to take me out of the picture.  Maybe if Jewels finds the will and gets rid of it, they'll back off...I don't know. I think the only reason I'm alive today is because they haven't been lucky enough to run me down."

Randall thumbed through a few notes and turned them around for Sully to see.  "That would explain this!  Note that every day Jewels made a withdrawal from that account, both Smith and Jones made deposits for the same amount or close to it on the same day.  I'd say that puts them on the payroll."

"How far back do those deposits go?"

"About a year!"

"It sounds like those two botched a double homicide when I survived.  Virginia must have gone ballistic when she found out what Jigs was going to do with that money.  That, on top of this will, had to have put her head in a spin.  That must have been when she asked Jewels to make me history."

"Don't jump to that conclusion just yet...We've got a long way to go before we can prove anything."

"I can't help what I feel.  I think that woman wanted me included in a double murder, and I want her put where she belongs."

"In the meantime, whatever you decide to do, let me know beforehand.  If you go off half-cocked, we could both wind up behind bars. Do you realize the predicament we'd be in if it got out how I obtained this information?"

"I won't do a thing unless I talk to you," Sully replied softly. "...I promise!"

"Fine," Randall said, somewhat relieved. "Now let's get to Dorothy Haygood...Looks like she's clean; we came up with nothing. She had her own money to start and that never changed. Neither did the money she controls through her husband's estate. No trace of money or anything else was found that connects her directly to Virginia Moran or Garan Jewels."

"Is there anything else I could use? I've got to be up early in the morning and I need to be on the road. I'm in the process of running down a guy named G.W. Spence. You ever hear of him?"

"I know him," Randall said, a little too quickly. "...And I have something else that you'll find interesting:...It seems that our friend, Jewels was never associated with Jigs Moran in any capacity, much less being his lawyer. I doubt if Moran ever met him."

"Now, that is a surprise...Did you find out *who* Jigs' lawyer was?"

"His name's Jerimiah Woodard. Took a while but we finally ran him down in Avondale Estates. He has a small practice there, and up to now, I hadn't thought of involving him. But, with this will business surfacing, I think we should."

"Absolutely," Sully agreed, then paused. "...This Woodard character had to have known about Jigs death? And, if he did, why didn't he step forward before now? Isn't it a lawyer's responsibility to carry on a person's wishes after his death?"

"Only if he has the legal right to...It is possible that Woodard is in the dark about what's going on."

Sully got out of the chair and stretched. "Tell you what: Let me handle Woodard if you don't mind."

"That's fine; just keep me posted."

"Something else: Could you run a check on Spence? I've got a strong suspicion that he's a piece of the puzzle."

"Consider it done."

The meeting over, Sully bade the Randall's goodbye and returned to Beverly's apartment for a good night's rest. He had to be at his best for the up-coming day.

# CHAPTER FORTY THREE

Traffic at six a.m. on a Saturday morning was usually nonexistent in front of the Biltmore hotel. This particular day, Sully was surprised to see a clamor of activity just as the sun came up on the horizon. The hotel entrance was full of people getting an early start on celebrating the attraction of the day: Georgia Tech's gridiron classic with the University of Georgia. The game was scheduled for early afternoon at Grant Field. Of all days to start looking for G.W., this one had to be the worst. The majority of the crowd was most likely Alumni from both Tech and the University of Georgia that had been up all night championing their loyalties. There were many fans that had simply got out of bed after finding it impossible to sleep from all the noise downstairs. Then, there were the early birds who couldn't get a decent night's rest because of the excitement. They enjoyed watching the crowd grow at the stadium. Whatever reasons the gathering had for being awake so early, they had made Sully's day miserable.

He tried unsuccessfully to find G.W. in the throng of people with field glasses for hours and by 11 o'clock, the streets were relatively empty. Latecomers were on the scene as expected and several drunks staggered aimlessly toward cabs for a ride to the game. The crowd had thinned now to where he could easily spot G.W. if he came around. At 1:00 o'clock, Sully leaned forward in surprise. A familiar figure came hurriedly around the corner onto West Peachtree. He braced his elbows on the dash and focused the binoculars on the side street by the hotel. It was Dorothy Haygood, making her way swiftly toward the main entrance. *That's why the desk clerk didn't have a record of G.W. being in the hotel before,* Sully thought. *They were there sharing a room under her name, not his.*

Sully jumped from the car just as she entered the entrance, then crossed the street in a dead run. If he could catch a glimpse of her before she got on the elevator, maybe it could be narrowed down to what floor they were on. Once she was inside, several minutes went by before he got to the lobby. He looked around feverishly for her but she was nowhere in sight. She had already boarded an elevator on the upper level, and since all were busy, it was impossible to know which one she was on.

Sully recognized the clerk he had talked to a day earlier behind a large marble laden counter in the lobby. He stepped over and asked quietly, "You remember me? I'm the guy who asked about G.W. Spence."

The clerk stared down his nose. "I do…Nothing has changed. He still doesn't reside here."

Sully's expression grew rigid. "Do you even know G.W. Spence?"

"I know who stays at this hotel and who doesn't."

A bellhop walked up and nervously interrupted. "Cap'n, we gots us 'bout six sets of luggage whut needs room numbers. If we gon' put 'em rooms 'fore that game over, we bes' get it done in a hurry."

Sully cut the clerk short before he could respond. "I saw Dorothy Haygood come in a few minutes ago. I'm in a hurry, so give me the room number and I'm out of here." Annoyed at the gruff demand, the clerk turned to the porter angrily, "I'll be there in a minute!…We'll straighten it out then!"

The bellhop walked away with a sour look on his face.

"The room number, man!" Sully demanded. "I haven't got all day."

"I can't do that…It's against regulations."

"You didn't mention that when I greased your palm the other day."

"But this is a lady…I can't!"

"I'm going to fold two twenties together," Sully said, "and by the time they hit the counter, I'd better have her number. I'm running out of patience, pal, so do yourself a favor and take the money before this gets ugly."

Just as the two twenties fell on the counter, the clerk said nervously, "…They have two rooms: 318 and 320."

Sully turned and walked away without bothering to thank him, then went to the elevators on the upper level. "Three!" he told the black attendant, then leaned back against the inner rail.

The aged operator closed the gates slowly and eased the control forward. When the elevator came to a halt, the man said softly, "Third flo'," and opened the gates.

Sully stepped into the hall, then walked hurriedly toward 318 and 320. He wondered why they would choose rooms facing east over the ones in the rear. The back side of the hotel was the best way to get away from the late evening sun...And why the two rooms? If there were just two of them, why all that extra space? He knocked at 318, then waited a decent interval and knocked again.

"Just a minute," a voice said happily before the door was opened. It was obvious that Dorothy Haygood was expecting someone else. She was immediately distant when she recognized Sully. "What are you doing here?"

"We have something to talk about."

"I'm expecting someone," she said irritably, then tried to close the door. "This is not a good time, Sully...See me next week."

Sully shoved the door back, forcing her to stumble clumsily. "I'll leave when I get some answers," he said flatly, "not before."

"I'm calling the police," she said angrily reaching for the telephone.

"Go ahead," Sully challenged, then looked around the room. He had no idea what he was looking for. "The cops will be glad to hear you're hooking at the Biltmore...So will the hotel!" It was nothing but a threat, but the instant the alternative was presented, her protests halted. That convinced Sully this was the room she hooked from while next door was used for her and G.W.'s privacy. "Where is he?" he asked, moving things around and not looking at her.

"What—what do you want with G.W.?"

"I want to ask him about a few things, that's all. I want to know why he's staying off the streets, especially after everybody thought he'd left Atlanta for good. It makes people think bad things."

"What's wrong with his coming back? He knew it was safe," she said defensively. "Those two men aren't after him anymore."

"Who told him?"

"I don't know! G.W. said the police found what was left of Judson Fletcher washed up on the bank in the Chattahoochee."

"When was that?" Sully asked, already knowing the answer.

"I don't know what day…It was earlier this week."

"Why hasn't it been on the radio or in the paper? Things like that aren't kept quiet unless it's for a reason."

Dorothy looked sheepish, then unwittingly revealed what she knew. "Maybe the cops don't want anyone to know about it yet? I don't know!"

"That means G.W. got his information from a cop, and I've got a pretty good idea who it is."

Dorothy suddenly became indignant about being found so easily. "Who told you I was staying here, *Beverly?*"

"…That nurse at the hospital? The one that ran a few errands for me when I was laid up."

"…That's exactly who I'm talking about. That, oh so innocent lady, used this room just as much as I did at one time. She's not exactly a member of the church choir, you know."

"I'll tell you this," Sully seethed, "right now, I'm convinced you and G.W. are mixed up in Jigs' death somehow. And if this Beverly *does* know something, I have ways of digging it out of her." He regretted the words instantly. He might have unintentionally put Beverly in danger.

The blunt accusation momentarily set Dorothy aback; it was obvious the message had shaken her. Fear registered on her face the instant the accusation of murder was delivered. It seemed clear now that she and G.W. were either involved in the killing or knew something about it. When she realized what happened, Dorothy went very quiet. Sully knew he would never get a straight answer after that and gave up trying…Besides, G.W. was a much easier target.

A knock at the door startled them both. Dorothy walked nervously to the door and opened it. A large man, slightly overweight, bald, roughly fifty and dressed very smartly, stepped inside grinning broadly. "Hi, Dorothy," he said, then took a step back when he saw Sully in the background. He was immediately intimidated. "Look, Maybe this is bad timing…I think I should leave."

"There's no need for that," Dorothy said angrily. "He was just leaving."

"One thing before I get out of here: What's the banker's name you and Virginia are such big friends with now?"

"How—how did you know about him?"

"I get around," Sully replied, "Now what's the name?"

Dorothy was hesitant to reveal the name at first, but knew if Sully was that knowledgeable, it was just a matter of time. "...Thomas Cantrell," she finally said.

"What bank?"

"Fulton National," she said nervously. "I'm warning you, Sully, don't involve him...He hasn't done a thing!"

"We'll just have to wait and see about that, won't we?" Sully said, walking past the bald man and pulling the door to.

Sully stepped next door and knocked hard on the door, but no one answered. If G.W. had been there and heard the loud arguing, he was bound to have left in a hurry. There was no need to brace him right away anyway; Dorothy had already given it away that they knew something. He could get the whole story from G.W. at a later date. The problem of Beverly was another matter. He had vowed that nothing would ever change his feelings about her, but he was wrong. When Dorothy revealed Beverly was involved with her in prostitution, it had ripped the life out of him. He hoped he had hid that hurt. If Dorothy had picked up on what he was thinking, she might relay it to someone who would do Beverly harm. It was evident she had to go into hiding for a while.

# CHAPTER FORTY FOUR

Thoughts of regret were now churning uncontrollably in Sully's gut. Not only had he became highly disturbed after finding out about Beverly's involvement in prostitution, but an even greater mistake might have been made. If he had accidentally revealed to Dorothy Haygood how he felt about Beverly, disastrous consequences might be in the offering. A distinct possibility existed now that Beverly would have to face Smith and Jones alone one day. She had to be taken out of harm's way under these circumstances. The only problem with warning her of the danger was having to wait until she came in from work. He could probably drop by the hospital, but that would serve no purpose other than worrying her the rest of the day The big question now was, how long it took Dorothy to relay the message to Garan Jewels or Virginia Moran? That determined how much time there was to get Beverly away from the apartment.

With the afternoon before him and nothing to do, Sully dropped by the Lucky Seven Club between the Peachtrees. He parked on a side street a block away, then went around the corner and went inside. He sat in a booth at the rear and ordered a drink. He listened to the soft music for several hours, then abruptly stood and dropped a wad of bills on the table for the tab. The next stop was the Farmer's Market on Murphy Avenue. He turned onto Sylvan Road and drove to a gas station at the rear entrance. The noticeably deceptive filling station had thrived for years by filling the alcohol needs of people, rather than servicing automobiles. He parked alongside a rusty pump that had never sold the first gallon of gasoline, then stepped inside.

"A pint of first run," Sully said thickly.

The attendant passed a bottle across the counter. "You at the right place, champ," he said. "You doin' allright?"

Sully smiled and nodded. The previous drinks had mellowed him slightly.

"Haven't seen you in a while…You ever think about going back in the ring?"

"Doubt if that'll ever happen it," Sully said, reaching in the cooler for a soft drink. "My health isn't that great!"

"Read about that in the Journal; it said you was having a hard time in the hospital. Everybody was talking about how you weren't gonna make it, but I knew better...I tol' 'em you was a tough nut...Comin' in that door is proof of that."

Sully turned up the pint of 180 proof moonshine, drank half of it, then washed it down with a portion of coke. A burning sensation went down his throat and into his stomach. He eased the bottle of liquid fire into his jacket pocket. "You don't know how close your friends came to being right."

"That was bad about Moran," the attendant said while buffing the counter slowly. "He was stand-up...They ever catch who did it?"

"Not yet!" Sully replied. "But, they will...Things are beginning to fall in place."

"...You know something?"

"Nothing but what's on the streets," Sully said, downing the rest of the pint. "You know how reliable that is."

The attendant continued wiping. "In my day, I'd believe what came out of the alley quicker than what those cops downtown said."

Sully set the empty bottle on the counter. "Things *have* changed! Nowadays, almost *everybody's* a liar...Figuring out the truth has become an art form."

"Sounds like you're having to deal with that."

"I've put up with quite a bit lately," Sully admitted, then for reasons he couldn't explain, wanted to get away from the inquisitive attendant. "...Give me another pint of that, *'who shot John'*? and I'll be on my way."

"You sure? That stuff is liable to put you back in the hospital."

"You're right, bonded is good enough...I don't need to get *too* loose." Sully laid a ten on the counter to pay for the two bottles."

"You owe me a nickel," The attendant said easing the second pint on the counter.

Sully dropped a quarter on the counter with questionable look on his face.

"It's for the coke!" the attendant said, sliding twenty cents toward him.

"Keep it," Sully said, then walked out into the crisp night.

Sully drove to the nurse's quarters, thoroughly braced for the visit with Beverly. He had practiced his approach the entire way and wondered how Beverly would react to the position he had put her in. One thing was for certain: He needed to wait until the white lightning had diminished. His thoughts went back to Dorothy Haygood for a moment; if she had picked up on what he was thinking while at the Biltmore, it was his responsibility to keep Beverly out of it if possible. He pulled into the apartment parking lot, still feeling the effects of the alcohol.

He had trouble focusing his eyesight after stepping from the car, but strangely, his equilibrium was just the opposite. He was steady on his feet. Sully was normally a social drinker who refused to indulge beyond a light buzz. This was one of the times that rule was ignored. Oddly enough, a thick tongue and a slurred voice is the only thing that will give away the heavy drinking; providing he is a good ten feet away.

Sully waited a few minutes in the car, then glanced at his watch; it was after 7:00 o'clock. It had been dark for half an hour. He went inside and began digging clumsily in his pockets for the key to the door. Remembering it was on the keyring, he singled it out and slid it into the door. A light came from under the door when he turned the key.

Beverly was sitting at the dinette table, staring at him. "Looks like you've been drinking," she said without emotion. "What's that about?"

"What gave me away?" Sully said, avoiding her glare.

"For somebody who's been sober since I met them, it's not too difficult...Now, what's going on?"

"...I'm afraid I've put you on the spot, Beverly...I didn't mean to, but that's what happened."

"What are you talking about?"

"I talked to Dorothy Haygood earlier today."

"Why is it I already had that feeling?...Where did you see her?"

"The Biltmore! I was looking for G.W. when she popped up."

"Did she tell you about the things I was involved in?"

"Yeah," Sully said soberly. "I kind of lost it when she did...I didn't think anything could bother me where you're concerned, but I was wrong."

"Does she know you've been staying with me?"

"I tried not to let it out of the bag, but I don't think I did a very good job. If she passes it on to Smith and Jones that I've been here, you can bet they'll be on their way shortly. What you need to do is pack your bags and get out of here...If they catch us here together, there's a good chance they'll hurt you, trying to get to me. You know, it's possible these are the people that killed Jigs, and they might want to finish the job by taking me out. I'd like to postpone that for a while, if I can!"

Beverly grabbed a single satchel and began packing. "...Do you think this could relate to the things I've told you?"

"It has *something* to do with it, I'm sure. Why else would Virginia turn her dogs loose on me? I never had anything she wanted before."

Beverly placed the satchel on the kitchen table. "Would you take this out to the car? I need to get an overnight bag from the closet."

Sully stepped outside, opened the trunk of the Ford and laid the bag inside. He closed the lid, then sat down under the steering wheel and waited patiently. Minutes later, Beverly stepped through the exit to the parking lot.

She walked hurriedly to the car, laid the overnight bag in the seat between them, and sat down. "We need to talk, Sully...We can't part like this."

Sully said nothing. He turned on the switch and pressed the starter button; the engine immediately came to life. Just as he was about to turn on the lights, he killed the engine. He pushed her roughly down in the seat. "Stay down," he said, crouching beside her. He pulled the .45 from his waist and released the safety. "We've got company."

An unmarked police car with its' headlights off, came into the parking lot quietly and came to a halt two parking spaces away. Smith and Jones stepped from the car with their weapons drawn. They headed directly for Beverly's apartment.

Once they were out of sight, Sully started the engine and pulled away. He didn't turn on the lights until they were a block away. "Nothing's going to stop them now, short of a bullet. I was hoping it wouldn't happen this way."

"...Is all this necessary, Sully?"

"They came here for a purpose, Beverly: They want to kill me. And if you think they'll leave a witness to something like that, you'd better think again. They know now I've been here, and that makes you a threat. We have to find a place that's safe for you until all this quiets down?"

"...I have a sister in Acworth; she lives the other side of Marietta off old 41. It's about an hour's drive. Nobody knows her and it should all right there."

Sully pulled a wad of bills from his billfold and handed them to her. "I have a couple of hundred...Take it! You might need it!"

"I'm all right," Beverly said and pushed his hand away.

He reluctantly put the money back in his wallet and drove in silence. Forty-five minutes later, they were at the outskirts of Marietta.

Once through the heart of the small city, Beverly spoke for the first time in thirty minutes. "...I quit way before I met you, Sully. It wasn't the kind of life I wanted."

Sully said nothing.

"It was when Dorothy dumped her husband on me that I took a good look at myself."

He still didn't answer.

"She did her level best to get me back in the business, but I'd made up my mind it was over. The only reason I agreed to spy on you was because I thought I owed her something. It was a stupid thing to do."

"What made you stop?"

"I suppose—it was the way I grew to feel about you. The guilt was almost unbearable. Between that and fear of losing you, I don't know which was worse."

"Did Dorothy ever say just what it was she wanted to know?"

"Never! She just told me to stay close and find out where you went and who you spent time with."

Sully slowed down when the Acworth city limits sign appeared by the road. "I'll need directions from here on in."

Beverly's face was drawn when they pulled into the driveway. "This is it, isn't it?"

Sully's jaw tightened. "I don't know...I know how I feel about you, but that may not be enough...Let's let the dust settle for a while!"

Beverly opened the car door and stepped out into the night. "That says it all," she said, picking up the overnight bag. "Get my bag from the trunk and you can be on your way."

Sully stepped to the rear of the car and pulled out the satchel and walked toward the house. "I'll put this on the porch."

A light came on at the front of the house. The door cracked open and a young woman looked out from behind the screen.

"Just leave it, Sully," Beverly said, "It's late, and they'll be wondering what all this is about. I'll take care of things from here."

Sully returned to the Ford and eased into the driver's seat. He started the engine and listened to it purr softly.

A young man came out into the yard and confronted Beverly in an unfriendly manner. He glanced momentarily at Sully then turned his attention back to Beverly; they did not make a move toward the house.

*A strange way for family to act,* Sully thought and began backing out of the driveway. He rolled down the window after a few yards. "I'll leave the car at the apartment...Allright?"

She waved without looking.

Sully took the hint and drove off into the night.

# CHAPTER FORTY FIVE

Sully drove into the outskirts of Atlanta with a monumental hangover. The long harrowing day was winding down and strangely enough, the feeling that it was just beginning began to bother him. Learning of Beverly's involvement in prostitution certainly hadn't helped, but getting saturated with alcohol on top of that had his stomach churning. By the time he reached Beverly's apartment, sobering brought on a raunchy headache along with the turmoil raging in his head. That impulsive leap into drunkenness had not only wasted time, but may have set Beverly up as a potential target. They had been within seconds of colliding head on with Smith and Jones in the parking lot. If the two detectives had been a minute earlier, the day's events could have turned out very different. This time, it wasn't to be. But he couldn't afford to leave things in the hands of destiny in the future. It was too unpredictable.

Sully drove by Jewels' office with the hope of finding Fred and Zack still watching and waiting; they were nowhere in sight. Luck smiled on him for the second time that day. As he drove slowly past Jewels' office, a dim light in the back caught his attention. He quickly parked across the street in front of the hospital, then rolled down the window and slid down in the seat. He adjusted the rearview mirror to get a good view of Jewels' front door.

It didn't take long for the night air to start the shivering again, reminding him of what had happened earlier in Randall's driveway. He didn't want to repeat that incident and decided to go to the hospital lobby where it was warm.

Sully got out on the passenger side, never taking his eyes from Jewels' entrance, then walked hurriedly to the main entrance. He stepped inside and leaned against a pillar in the darkened interior. He looked across the street and his head began to nod; a losing battle with sleep slowly began to overtake him. His eyelids gave way to exhaustion in the next few minutes; it was too comfortable in the warm surroundings of the hospital lobby. He steps out into the cold night air, with the hope that it will somehow revive him.

Jewels' office went dark suddenly and Sully was alert instantly. Jewels emerged moments later and got into his car; a few minutes after that, he drove away.

Sully raced down the steps three at a time. He wondered where Jewels was headed and tried to stay focused on which way the lawyer went. He wondered why Fred and Zack weren't there watching his every move as they should be. It wasn't like them not to be on the job; maybe something had gone wrong?

Sully jerked open the door of the Ford with the intention of following Jewels, but just as he was about to get in the car, an automobile came barreling down the street at a high rate of speed. He watched from the shadows as the unmarked police car went roaring by. There was suddenly a new priority: a familiar police car with a pair of bright headlights to follow.

He cranked the Ford quickly, then pulled out of the parking spot on two wheels. He didn't turn the lights on and stayed well behind to avoid detection. When the patrol car turned into the alley where Fred lived, Sully knew there was about to be trouble. He drove past the alley and parked a block away. He was out of the car and yanking the .45 from his waist in a matter of seconds. He entered the alleyway on a dead run, cocking the weapon in stride. He kept to the dark shadows in front of the houses, trying to avoid the mud puddles as best he could. All it would take is one loud splash to draw the attention away from the Gregory home. Smith and Jones would more than likely come to see what the noise was about. If that happened, the trouble could be his.

Sully saw the front porch light on at the Gregory home from three houses away. The unmarked police car was parked directly in front of the house, but it was empty. He wondered if Fred and Zack were home, and if so, why? The answer came when he heard loud voices coming from inside the living room. There was little doubt that the disagreement was already out of hand. Sully ran up to the front porch having no idea what to expect. He quietly slid to his knees and leveled the .45 at the front door. He aimed the barrel of the automatic at the backs of Smith and Jones. Zack and his mother watched helplessly as Fred kneeled on the floor cursing the two detectives through a bloody mouth. The two ex-cops stood over him threateningly with their weapons drawn.

"Get yo' ass out dis house," Fred screamed. "You ain't even cops now. I knows 'bout you two and the troubles you's in, an' when I gets up from here, I goin' downtown an' tell 'em what you be doin'."

"One more time, *nigger*," Jones said through clinched teeth. "You either tell us where Hawken is, or you get a bullet in the head."

Sully drew in on Jones instantly. If the cops' trigger finger tightened at all, it would be the last thing he ever did. He was the one making most of the noise, and Sully knew the demented cop was fully capable of killing Fred without giving it another thought.

Jones then took his finger from the trigger and swatted Fred beside the ear with the butt of his pistol. Blood began to flow profusely.

"Better tell him what he wants to know," Smith taunted. "He ain't playing with you. He wouldn't think no more of killing you than he would a damn cockroach."

Sully watched silently when the unpredictable Jones violently jammed the weapon into the holster. The cop had no idea how close he had just come to being shot in the back of the head.

Jones kicked the wall in a fit of anger. "Let's get out of here," he growled. "They don't know nothin'. Even if they do, they ain't gonna tell us…We'll wind up killing these bastards and still get nothin'."

Smith looked over his shoulder as they turned to leave. "We'll be back!" he spat through clenched teeth. "A lot sooner'n you think, too."

With nowhere to hide, Sully stood erect; he hadn't given the first thought of what to do when Smith and Jones decided to leave. He would be in a very precarious position if he had to square off against the two detectives without backup. Fred and Zack couldn't help because their weapons were probably under the house. Their mother had forbid guns *in* the house, and being good sons, they didn't question her wisdom.

Sully drew a stance with the .45, anticipating an all-out gun battle. Then, providence intervened once again.

Zack spotted Sully and called out to the detectives to draw their attention. "Hey, boss!" he said as if remembering something. If he could stopping them from leaving by distracting them momentarily, maybe Sully could get around the side of the house and out of sight.

"What you want, *boy*?" Jones asked angrily.

Sully understood what Zack was doing and immediately skirted around the porch to the rear of the house.

Once Sully moved to safety, Zack smiled apologetically. "It ain't 'portant, cap'n. It weren't nothin' at all."

"Don't you be playing with me none," Jones railed out viciously. "I'll give you some of what your brother got."

"Yassuh!" Zack said timidly. "I jes' thought if'n I hear anything about that Hawken fella, I be lettin' you know the nex' time you comes by."

Sully ran quietly to the rear of the driveway where Fred had parked the Buick, then slid down and laid the .45 across the fender. He squeezed the trigger lightly, then watched silently in the dark until Smith and Jones drove away.

Satisfied they had left for the night, Sully went to the front of the house and up on the porch. He stepped inside and closed the door behind him. Zack already had Fred up from the floor and resting comfortably on the sofa.

Fred spoke through swollen bloody lips when he spotted Sully. "Hey, boss! Where you come from?"

"He been here," Zack said knowingly. "He damn nigh killed that cop what aimed his gun at you."

A smile grew on Fred's puffy face. "Might as well have pulled that trigger, boss. It gon' happen sooner or later anyhow; should'a jes' went ahead an' got it on over with."

Alice Gregory came into the room with a bowl of hot water and a rag. "How long were you out there, Mister Hawken?"

"A few minutes...Just long enough to figure out what was about to happen."

"If you could've been a tad quicker, maybe you could have stopped them detectives from beating up my boy like that."

"I think Fred handled things pretty good under the circumstances."

She looked at the .45 in Sully's hand. "With *that* gun, you could've done something. I don't like my boys being treated like this and from now on, things are going to be different...Zack! Go get them guns! I know you have 'em hid somewhere under this house. From this day forward, whoever walks in that door better have good intentions. If they don't, I want you boys to shoot 'em." What was an ugly incident from the outset had now evolved into a deadly event.

Sully knew the power Mrs. Gregory held over her sons, and she had just turned them loose on Smith and Jones. By all standards, she had declared war.

Zack left the room and returned in a matter of minutes with the two revolvers from under the house. He handed Fred one and slid the other into his back pocket, pulling the shirt over it for concealment.

Fred tucked his gun in the waist band out front; he didn't bother hiding it. "We knows where they at," he said without emotion. "Might as well get it done...They's had their way long enough."

"...You know where they are?"

"Sho' do...We followed Jewels to where them two been hiding early on in the day. He weren't there long, but long enough to set a fire underneath 'em. They come out that front door actin' all crazy an' such. They's flashing them guns, hollering something back and forth at Jewels. When they leave, it were so fast, they's out of sight 'fore we could turn around. We figured they was going after you. We didn't have no chance of catching up with 'em, and 'bout the only thing left to do was follow Jewels. But, by the time we turn around, he gone too. We went by yo' 'partment looking fo' you. When no one come to da door, we jes' come on home. We knew you'd be by here sooner or later...It were the only way we could warn you."

Sully wasn't very satisfied with what was accomplished during the last twenty-four hours. He had started the day off on the wrong foot when he went after Dorothy Haygood for answers. Not only was Beverly set up as a target for that stupidity, but now, the Gregory family was in danger as well. It all started when he saw the fear in Dorothy Haygood's eyes earlier. His accusations had to be close to the truth to warrant that kind of reaction. She must have called Jewels after that, and when Jewels got the message, he drove straight to Smith and Jones with what he had. They didn't have any trouble finding Beverly's apartment once they found out he had been staying there. Dorothy and Beverly had been friends in the past and all Dorothy had to do was give them the address. For Beverly's sake, he hoped she remained out of sight for a while.

"Fred," Sully said, "I want you and Zack to stay home for a while…At least until I can get back with you. There are people I have to see, and I don't want this getting out of hand just yet."

A frown came across Fred's face. "I gots a score to settle, boss, an' sittin' 'roun here ain't the way to get even."

Zack was of the same mind. He didn't like being pushed around without any retaliation. He wanted things brought to a head quickly. "Whut you reckon them cops gon' do when somebody slap 'em in the face wit' a hog-leg? I think they gon' mess in they britches."

"Stay home, please, Zack," Sully asked again. "Give it a few days and then we'll take care of business."

"We need to crack heads now, boss," Fred said. "We wait too long an' it gon' wind up bein' trouble. What's gon' happen if they run you down while me an' Zack ain't there? They put you in yo' grave, for sho'."

"It won't be happening any time soon, I assure you. For the next couple of days, I'll be in a world they don't even know exists."

"What world that, boss?" Fred asked.

"One of legal lawyers and bankers with integrity."

Zack sat down clumsily beside Fred. "We give you three days…After that, we do what we gotta do…"

"You feel the same way?" Sully asked Fred.

"I's with Zack on this, boss."

"You guys are supposed to be working for me," Sully said, "or at least I thought you were. What's changed?"

"We still works for you, boss," Fred said, "but you jes' gon' hafta take us off the clock fo' a while…It done gon' too far this time."

"…There's not a whole lot I can do if your minds are made up. Just promise me you'll wait three days before doing anything. If I can finish my business by then, we'll take care of those two together."

"We ain't waitin' no longer 'n Wednesday," fred said. "We don' hear nothin' by then, we goin' wit'out you."

"That's all I ask," Sully said. "Now which one of you is going to drive the Buick to Beverly's apartment?"

Zack looked at Sully puzzled. "We gon' need the car, boss. We can't do nothin' without wheels."

Fred eyed Sully with suspicion. "You doin' this to keep us home?"

"I wouldn't do that, Fred," Sully replied. "I'm going to need the car because I promised Beverly I'd park hers at the apartment."

"That's it?"

"That's all there is to it."

"Follow him to the 'partment," Fred told Zack. "He kin bring you back here. If we has to, we kin find another way to take care o' them two."

"You won't have to," Sully said. "I'll be here by Wednesday, I promise!"

# CHAPTER FORTY SIX

To most Avondale Estates residents, their small village has not changed since the early twenties. The people, who built the town just east of Decatur, evidently had strong ties with Swiss backgrounds. The architecture reeked with inspiration from the mountainside chalets in Switzerland. The buildings on the main thoroughfare have such distinct features, it always makes one think of the faraway land.

Jeremiah Woodard was fifty-nine at the time he moved to Avondale Estates in 1924. That was twenty-five years earlier. Prior to that, he had spent 30 years practicing law in the city of Atlanta. Woodard's initial intent was to work in semi-retirement and blend into the environment as a country gentleman. The Stock Market crash in '29 brought him back to reality. The choice was made to work until he could no longer function. Now eighty-three and still in good health, he continued to frequent his office on a daily basis. The only way to describe his modern day practice was caution and distrust. His advice to brokers and investors was simple: If they had not personally experienced the crash of '29, they were fools to think that it could not happen again.

On a rain-soaked Monday morning, Woodard looked nostalgically out of his second story office window. Christmas was just weeks away and the first present had yet to be purchased. As he soaked in the dismal weather outside, a loud knock interrupted his thoughts.

"There's a young man here to see you, dad," a woman's voice said softly…"He doesn't have an appointment."

Woodard smiled. "Am I so busy that people need one?"

"There is such a thing as professionalism," she scolded him. "Now do you want to see him or not?"

Woodard laughed at his daughter's serious nature. She was still trying to hold the family dignity together after all these years. "Does the young man have a name?"

"He says his name is Sully Hawken—a friend of Jigs Moran."

The smile left Woodard's face instantly. "Show him in," he said. "…And keep all calls on hold."

Woodard's daughter walked out of the office and sat at her desk. "Would you step inside, Mister Hawken. My father will see you now."

Sully went into Jeremiah Woodard's sanctuary and immediately glanced around the room in surprise. Except for a few diplomas, only photos from the past were on the walls. "You have pictures of a lot important people here...I'm impressed!"

"The ones I prize most are on the cabinet by the wall," Woodard said, pointing to a twelve-foot wide, solid walnut cabinet. "You may recognize someone in those pictures...At least you should."

Sully gazed intently at the ancient pictures, but recognized no one. "I'm sorry, but," he said, then stopped mid-sentence when he saw a faded picture of a golfer with his caddie. "...He couldn't have been over twenty then, could he?"

Woodard leaned forward over the desk, resting his elbows on the edge. "He was sixteen...He caddied for me in those days. It was before his father became wealthy with Coca Cola stock."

"Well, I'll be! I always thought the money came from Jigs' grandfather," Sully said thoughtfully.

"It did. But old man Moran saw fit to withhold his belongings from the family until he died. They got very little before that happened. They had to scratch for a living like everybody else...It was the elder Moran's way of keeping control."

"And Jigs had to earn his way following golfers around?"

"Only one golfer, Hawken...Me! Where do you think Jigs got his love of gambling and the seedy side of life? By the time he was twenty years old, he knew the odds of every gambling event that existed. He was a phenomenal individual."

"...This is strange," Sully said. "All the years I was with Jigs, your name was never mentioned. Yesterday was the first time I ever heard of you...Why would he keep something like that from me?"

"It's not that difficult to understand. If you could comprehend Jigs' complex way of looking at things, it was easy to see. The boy was simply ashamed of his heritage, which came about from my indiscretions...It was all, well before he was born, but it lasted until his mother died. Years ago, Mrs. Moran and I had a torrid affair.

Someone in the family made a terrible mistake and told Jigs I was his father. He was very young at the time and it had a profound effect on him; he carried that stigma to the grave."

Sully admired the frank honesty of the aged gentleman. "Why are you telling me this? It couldn't be a very well-known story, or I would've heard about it."

"This is the first time it's been discussed in probably thirty years, with the exception of Jigs and my daughter, And, since all of the people involved are dead except for Virginia Moran, I see no harm in talking about it—especially to someone I know won't repeat it."

"Did Virginia ever know her brother was by a different father, or was it kept from her too?"

"She may not have known in the early days, but she'd have to have that knowledge now, the way things are shaping up. And it could wind up being a powerful tool in court. If it could be proved that Jigs wasn't a legal heir, or cast a doubt on his parentage, it could tie up the estate for years, with her at the helm."

"What's the purpose of telling me this now?" Sully asked. "It doesn't have a bearing on me at all."

"Oh, but it does," Woodard corrected. "When Jigs wrote you into that will, he insisted that you know everything. He had predicted Virginia's reaction to your being a beneficiary. This will keeps her from eliminating you as an heir apparent. Jigs knew that if he didn't do things legally, Virginia would receive the entire Moran fortune uncontested. That's why the paperwork was drawn up here in the office. If that will disappeared or was somehow forgotten, the courts would have no choice but to place the entire estate in her hands. He wanted his portion of that fortune to go to you, his longtime friend. It's what Jigs asked me to do...You represented the son he never had; this meant a better life for you. The logic is suspect to some, but the only thing Jigs ever wanted was to pass on his legacy."

"...Do you know where the will is?"

"Of course I do!" Woodard said. "It's in a secure safety deposit box down the street. It's listed in both yours and Jigs' name. We put it there month's ago. The problem is, Virginia Moran and her vultures have found its whereabouts also."

Sully became upset that Woodard knew of his existence all along, but never made an effort to contact him. He felt he should have been informed of the will as soon as he got out of the hospital. "If you were so familiar with the will's contents, why wasn't I told about it before now?"

"I was bound by law not to tell anyone about the document until after it was probated. Only the family held the right to be informed of the will's actuality."

"Then it was you who told Virginia about the will? That's what everybody was looking for when they broke into my house."

Woodard was quiet a moment then explained. "I did tell her...It's the law. But, I never revealed its location."

"That explains a few things."

"There's another matter of law we have to discuss," Woodard said. "Even though I was appointed executor of the will, it still has to be delivered to the Fulton County Probate Court. And, since no one other than you has access to that box, it's your responsibility. Once the probate court rules the will legitimate, a judge will return the document to me for enactment. That's when the beneficiaries are to be legally notified."

"You mean to say this will has been sitting in a safety deposit box all this time, without ever being recorded?"

"That's right! Jigs was murdered before he could take care of it."

"Why didn't you do it for him? You knew the contents and how important it was to him."

"I knew, but the will was in the bank vault...I couldn't say or do anything while the family looked over my shoulders."

"I think I should know what's in that will, don't you? I've got people who want to bury me because of it."

"I wish I could help but the way things are, my hands are tied. I've stretched the law about as far as I can for one day. I'm not supposed to discuss the will with anyone other than the family...That particular rule has taken a terrible beating today."

"At least tell me what bank the will is in? I'd like to see what's causing all this trouble."

Woodard rose from his chair and smiled. "...Now, if you were to retain me as your attorney, I could do a lot of things...Escorting you to the bank is one of them."

"Where do I sign?"

"Caroline!" Woodard shouted loudly and gathered some papers together.

Caroline entered the office promptly with a pad and pen.

"We now represent Mister Hawken," Woodard said. "I want the papers drawn up and ready to sign when we return. We should be back in about an hour."

"I'll have it ready," she said, and left the office.

"Now Mister Hawken, if you'll accompany me, we'll create enough heat to dry out this weary day."

"My Buick is out front," Sully said, ascending the staircase. "We can go in it."

"There's no need," Woodard said, then stepped out into the rain and opened a huge, black Manhattan umbrella. "It's just a few doors down the street."

Sully took refuge under the umbrella with Woodard. "Where'd you get this thing?" he asked, pointing overhead. "We've got room for a few more under here."

"Bought it up north a few years back...Always wanted one; just never had the opportunity to acquire it until I actually went there. Quite a place, that New York. Have you ever been there?"

"No, never quite made it. The closest I ever came was when Jigs lined up a fight in Jersey once...It looked nice from across the river, though."

"It's even nicer when you get to walk the streets. You should have gone there when you had the chance. I'm surprised Jigs didn't take you over on the ferry. When he was younger, he enjoyed adventures like that."

"We had something working back in Atlanta at the time. I do remember we caught *The Southerner* out of Jersey afterwards to come home."

Woodard smiled at the mention of the railroad run. "I've been on that line," he said, opening the door to the bank. "Only stops in Washington going both ways. Best ride on the eastern seaboard."

Sully stepped in ahead of Woodard, then glanced around the small marble covered interior of the bank. It was a simple but costly design. Expense and caution had been ignored when the building was constructed. From the carved marble statues to the solid marble ceiling, the establishment was a show of blatant extravagance. *"A terrible waste of money,"* he thought.

Woodard placed the wet umbrella in a corner to dry, the stepped up to a teller's cage. "Is Walter here?" he asked the elderly woman.

"He's at the drugstore," she smiled graciously. "Hasn't been gone more than a minute. He should be back shortly. If you like, have a seat and I can call and tell him you're here."

"No need, dear," Woodard said politely. "Walter's not the type to wander off. The bank's too important for that."

A few minutes later, Walter Wiley, a fit man in his eighties and President of the First National Bank of Avondale, walked in. "Jeremiah!" he said, recognizing Woodard. "Have you been waiting for me?"

"Not long!" Woodard replied. "Don't concern yourself...My client and I just wanted to discuss a few things with you, if you have time."

"Privately?"

"Preferably!"

Wiley motioned to the rear of bank. "...Suppose we step back to the office and close the door...It's quiet back there." Wiley invited Woodard and Sully to join him after easing the door shut, then eased back in a chair. "Now, how can I be of service, gentlemen?"

"This, is Sully Hawken, Walter," Woodard said as if the banker were familiar with the name.

Wiley stood, then walked to the door and opened it. "Judy! I don't want to be disturbed. Keep people at bay, if you will."

"Yes sir!" the teller replied.

Wiley sat back down. "It seems, Mister Hawken, that we have been grossly misinformed about your state of health. We have been told that you were in the hospital and that your demise was inevitable."

"When was that?" Sully asked.

"The first time was about six weeks ago. Since then, the same story has been repeated several times. The last time was just days ago."

"Were they trying to get into Jigs' safety deposit box?"

"They were!"

"You didn't give it to them?"

"Absolutely not!" Wiley replied. "The only way they could gain entry, would be with your death certificate, which would leave Virginia Moran as the sole heir. Even with that, it would take a court order. The extent these people went to, to get at that box, bordered on ridiculous when they presented a court order signed by a superior court judge in Atlanta."

"What was the judges name?"

"It was Beauregard L. Langtree," Woodard answered for the banker. "A puppet of Garan T. Jewels, who just happens to be the director of Virginian Moran's estate."

Sully wondered if Woodard knew that the judge had been blackmailed by Jewels from time to time. "Were you here at the bank when the court order was delivered?" he asked Woodard.

"Yes!" Woodard replied. "And I have to admit that Jewels and his companions presented a strong case."

"The companions?" Sully asked. "Who were they?"

"Their spokesman was naturally Garan Jewels," Wiley said, pulling a document from his desk. "Virginia Moran and a banker from Atlanta were with him. The banker was Thomas Cantrell. He works at Fulton National where Miss Moran banks."

"And you ignored their requests?"

"There was never a choice in the matter. I am bound by law that the contents of the box are yours, unless your death is confirmed. And, since such a document wasn't available, the box has to be held in our care. If the bank had relented and gave the box to them, can you imagine the troubles we would have now..."

"Well, let's take a look at it. I'd like to know what's so important that it drives people to murder."

"Positive ID first, then we'll go in the vault."

Sully presented his driver's license, his boxing license and an entry card to the gymnasium. "Is that enough?"

"It's fine," Wiley said. "Now, do you have a key to the box?"

"I didn't even know the box existed until an hour ago," Sully replied. "Is it a problem?"

"That would be up to one of our legal advisors," Wiley said. "With their approval, you can gain immediate access."

"How do we get in touch with them?"

Wiley smiled. "The chairman is seated just to your right. And, since he represents the bank as well as you, I'd venture to say that you'll know exactly what's in the box in a matter of minutes."

Woodard was grinning also. "You see how simple things can be," he said. "Hell, I knew you were alive all along...It was just a matter of time before you found your way to my office. In the meantime, I wasn't about to let those people come in and act as if Jigs' life was meaningless."

"Now Mister Hawken, to the vault," Wiley said. "It's time for your moment of truth."

They immediately went into the open vault. Wiley opened a stainless steel cage door that led to the safety deposit boxes stacked neatly in the rear. He took a key from his ring and handed it to Sully. "Use the counter over there," he said, removing a steel box from a shelf. "Take your time; we'll be just outside."

"If you don't mind, I'd rather you hang around. I don't have any secrets, and I'll probably need some help understanding the legal terms."

Both men agreed and waited for Sully to unlock the rectangular steel cover. On top, neatly folded in a manila envelope, was a number of legal papers. Sully emptied the packet on the counter and began thumbing through the contents. When he got to *"The Last Will and Testament of Jigs Moran,"* he stopped. He unfolded the document and laid it to the side. The first few sentences were meaningless legal jargon, but after that, it was straight to the point. The wording was simple and easy to understand. Jigs had deliberately drawn the document up in language that anyone could understand. Sully was to be the recipient of 1.8 million dollars from Jigs' estate, plus ownership of all stocks enclosed in the packet.

Sully looked bewildered and waved the contents in front of Woodard. "Virginia Moran went crazy over that? She's sitting on millions of dollars, and she's trying to have me killed for this?"

"Not so hastily," Woodard said. "Let me explain what you have."

Sully handed the papers to him and shook his head in disgust. "Because of this woman's greediness, she's coming after me with fire in her eyes. It doesn't make sense. Why does she consider me such a threat?"

"Because you are," Woodard said, laying the papers out on the counter. "The holdings that Jigs left you have an annual income of over a million dollars. The gross worth of the stock is a little over nine million dollars. You're a rich man, Mister Hawken, like it or not."

"...That may be so, but it won't stop me from going after the people responsible for Jigs death..."

"I don't know if I can contribute much along that line," Woodard said easily, "but with the files I've accumulated recently, there is more than enough to attract a prosecutor's attention. They involve most notably, your friend Jewels, Virginia Moran, Mister Cantrell and his honor, Judge Langtree. Now, if you want to add anything, or anyone, to that list, it most certainly won't hurt our cause."

"All I have are the documents that Jewels asked me to sign when I got out of the hospital. Those papers are probably as phony as he is...I do have a friend who's been helping at times; maybe he has something to contribute? You'd have to be very careful with what he has though. It wasn't all acquired by using legal methods and could create a very delicate situation. A portion of it concerns how Virginia Moran cooked up this scheme in a attempt to pacify me. She figured if I was satisfied with what she gave me, I'd ride off into the sunset."

"Get the information to me as quick as you can. You have my word; its source or how it was obtained will not be revealed. Your friend's name won't be mentioned under any circumstances. Now, the next step is to deliver what I have to the grand jury, hopefully by Christmas…Things have been dormant far too long."

Sully suddenly thought of Smith and Jones; there wasn't much time left. "…Other than dropping the will off at the probate court, can you take care of everything without me? I have things to do before Wednesday rolls around."

"Walter and I will take care of it," Woodard said. "Just get what you can to the office as promptly as possible. There's nothing left to do now, other than signing the papers in my office."

Sully thanked them both, but they never heard a word. They were too busy hovering over the stack of legal papers. He then went to Woodard's office, signed the Power of Attorney sheet and left.

# CHAPTER FORTY SEVEN

The Fulton National Bank drive-in parking facility faced Marietta Street a block west of downtown Five Points. Sully entered the ramp of the building, then went to the fourth level area and parked. He took to the stairwell rather than waiting on the elevator. He walked out onto a wide balcony that overlooked the main chamber, a floor short. The circular informational counter was on the bottom level.

The woman attendant was on the telephone briefly, then turned to Sully. "May I help you, sir?" she asked.

Sully thought a moment. "...I'm looking for Thomas Cantrell. Is he in?"

The woman pointed to a row of enclosed offices away from the main lobby. "Third door on the left," she offered. "His secretary is out front."

Sully thanked her, then walked quickly to the office. He opened the door with Cantrell's name on it and stepped inside.

The lady sitting at the desk greeted him questionably while thumbing through her log. "Do you have an appointment today, sir?" she asked. "There's nothing lined up on the calendar."

"It's not necessary," Sully said, charm dripping from his lips, "Tom's expecting me...Is he in?"

The secretary was confused momentarily, then became suspicious. "I seem to have forgotten your name," she said, no longer in a receptive mood. "Perhaps I should talk to Mister Cantrell?"

"Tell him Sully Hawken is here."

The secretary hit the intercom, ringing it one time.

"Yes!" a voice, said.

"Sully Hawken is here...He says you were expecting him."

A long silence over the intercom put tension in the air. "...Send him in," the voice eventually said.

"You can go in," the secretary said, wondering if she had done things correctly.

Sully stepped into Cantrell's office, closed the door behind him and then took a seat without being asked.

"Mister Hawken!" Cantrell said, reaching across the desk to shake his hand. "I'm Thomas Cantrell." The banker was apparently disturbed by the unannounced visit.

"I wouldn't act too proud of it if I were you," Sully said, taking the hand. "I know a few people who would knock you on your butt if they heard it. I'd probably be one of them, if this meeting wasn't in your office."

Cantrell became even more upset by the rebuff. "I'm at a loss for words, Hawken...I don't understand!"

"You knew the right words when it came to Jigs Moran's safety deposit box."

Cantrell suddenly had the revelation that Sully knew of his improprieties. If the knowledge of the well-kept secret became public, troubling consequences were bound to follow. The bank would naturally have to investigate him, but the implication alone would be enough to ruin him.

"I know where this is headed, Hawken," Cantrell said, as sweat ran down his collar. "And you are correct: I illegally gave information about that particular box to a friend. It was a favor! There was no malice intended. I had no idea anyone would be hurt...Or it wouldn't have happened..."

"If you're looking for sympathy," Sully said coldly, "You're not getting it from me...I can't help you at all, pal. Otis Randall is the one you have to worry about. He's the guy that has your number. He's also the guy I report to...In case you don't know, he was Chief Jenkin's second-in-command until just recently.

"Then, what's the purpose of this visit if I'm already convicted?"

"I wanted to meet the man that could do the things you did, and keep a clear conscience. Did you know that you might be responsible for the death of one man and indirectly the cause of another? Those killings and at least two attempts on my life, are in part, attributed to your lack of integrity."

Cantrell sank down in the chair. "If I could turn back the clock, I would," he said dejectedly. "...If I gave you answers, answers that would be beneficial, would it help me at all?"

"You'd have to do it on your own...The way I look at it; you've been caught with your hand in the cookie jar and will do anything to get off the hook. If you'd have come forward with this before people started dying, it might've helped. But, you didn't...You even took it a step further and went with Jewels and Virginia Moran to that Avondale bank."

Cantrell looked at the floor; there was no place to hide.

"Who was the first to approach you about Jigs' box?" Sully asked, taking advantage of the banker's sudden vulnerability.

"Dorothy Haygood! We were very close friends at the time...She wanted me to check things out as a favor for Miss Moran."

"Was that the first time you dealt with Virginia?"

"No, we had a lot of meetings concerning her finances; investments; things of that nature. But up to that point, everything had been above board."

"What kind of relationship did you have with Dorothy?"

"...We were friends!"

"That doesn't say anything...What kind of friends? Were you acquaintances, business associates, occasional bed partners or all-out lovers?"

"I suppose I'm guilty of it all...Without realizing it, I had the misfortune to become deeply infatuated with Dorothy. It's not an easy thing to deal with, you know. A woman like that can light the world up if they have a hold on you. In my case, it was a smothering death grip I had no control of."

"Do you know how many men felt that at the same time?"

"...Four," Cantrell said, "including me...I fantasized regularly about being the one she would eventually chose."

"That's only four you know of, right?" Sully asked. "The woman has a talent for finding men for a precise purpose, then dropping them. All she had to do was get you in bed; a man like you didn't have a chance. You were probably promised the moon and would have done anything for her—up to and including murder."

"Hold it, Hawken," Cantrell protested. "I've never been a party to anything like that...I may have been naive to the point of bad judgment, but I'd never let myself get involved in murder."

"Your actions say otherwise...What were you thinking when you went into that Avondale Estates bank to illegally gain entry to a safety deposit box? You had to know it was against the law...Explain that!"

"Dorothy said you were on your death-bed...I saw no harm."

"That's not the point, Cantrell! You should've brought this whole thing to a halt the minute Dorothy asked you to find Jigs' box...If I were you, I'd make it a point to go to the authorities and tell them what you did. It may not help since you're so deeply involved, but there's always that chance...Maybe the courts will be lenient if everything is put on the table...I don't know?"

"...I tried, you know," Cantrell said, "but Dorothy kept me from doing anything. I followed her around like a moon-struck child for the longest...It may wind up putting me behind bars for years."

"Tell me something, Cantrell? Was there anything else they wanted from the box? Was it *only* the will?"

"Yes...Finding that will was the most important item from the very start. When Mister Moran died, it became a priority."

"Then she knew about the will all along?"

"Oh, yes. Mister Moran had mentioned it to Dorothy weeks before and revealed that you were a major beneficiary. He said that the document was still in a safety deposit box and had to be recorded."

"And she went to Virginia with that information?"

"Yes, but Miss Moran didn't quite know what to think of it at the time. When a lawyer named Jeremiah Woodard contacted her after Mister Moran's death, she knew it was true. The lawyer confirmed that a new will had been drawn up. It had an unbelievable effect on her; the very thought that part of the Moran fortune was going to someone else floored her."

"What did she do when she found out for sure?"

"She wanted to see the will, but Woodard said he didn't know its whereabouts. Mister Moran had left his office with the document weeks earlier and never approached the subject again."

"Did you believe Woodard?"

"I didn't know what to believe! That was when it dawned on me what was behind getting into that box...Jewels, Virginia and Dorothy were conspiring to keep the will from being probated. They were trying to keep the Moran estate under one roof. It's speculation of course, but I believe Virginia had her brother killed in hopes that the will would be found and destroyed. You have to understand that a huge portion of what I've told you, was kept from me in the beginning. I was considered an outsider until I became so involved...Watch your step, Mister Hawken, Virginia will spend millions to keep that fortune intact, and will stop at nothing to accomplish that goal."

"How did you find out where the will was to begin with? I didn't know about the box myself until this very day."

"Pure coincidence! I had run into a stone wall until, quite by accident, the Moran name came up in a conversation. I was talking to a bank examiner who had visited the Avondale Bank the day before...He thought it strange that a deposit box was listed under Jigs Moran's name without a checking or saving's account to accompany it. It caught his attention because you didn't have any accounts either."

"Is that when you contacted Dorothy?"

"I thought it appropriate at the time," Cantrell said. "I thought the will would be honored. But I had already changed my mind by the time we entered that bank..."

"What caused that?"

"I heard Dorothy talking to Jewels about how much they would receive for coming up with the will."

"How much was it?"

"Fifty thousand dollars, but I wasn't supposed to know about it...They were to get the money as soon as the will was placed in Miss Moran's hands."

"That's funny," Sully said sarcastically. "Jewels and Dorothy wanted to exclude you from the deal for a few lousy bucks. Those two have probably ripped that old lady off to the tune of a couple of million bucks over the years. The sad part is, Virginia doesn't care. As long as she's the one signing the checks, all's right in her world. It's a power thing to her."

"That's very possible…She's a hard person to read sometime."

"And you changed your mind about things when you heard Jewels and Dorothy deciding not to include you?"

"Yes!"

"Then why did you go to the bank with them? And with a court order on top of that…Just admitting you made a fool of yourself doesn't make you much of a victim. You brought this on yourself, pal…Especially when you lied to me about not receiving any compensation for finding the will. You see, Captain Randall found recent transactions on file where you made very large deposits; the money came from the Moran estate. How do you explain that to a jury?"

Sully knew the jab had struck home when Cantrell went pale. The motive all along had been to give the banker something to think about, and it had. Sully left the bank with the satisfaction that he had finally made someone squirm; and this was only the beginning. He checked his watch; it was 4:00 o'clock. There was still enough time to see a certain crooked lawyer.

# CHAPTER FORTY EIGHT

It was late that evening when Sully stepped quietly into Jewels office. The lawyer sat calmly behind his desk thumbing through documents, until Sully kicked the swinging gate between them off its hinges.

Jewels' secretary screamed and bolted for the front door when she saw the weapon in Sully's trousers, "Garan!" she yelled in terror. "He's got a gun!"

Jewels stood up and backed away in fear. He raised his hands as if to ward off the bullets he thought were coming.

"Sit down, you pompous ass," Sully said, and took a seat beside the desk. "I'm not going to kill you...Not just yet anyway! As much as I'd like to put you out of your misery, we're going to postpone it for a while. In the meantime, here's a little something for you to chew on. It's kind of like that garbage you've been feeding me lately."

"I don't understand?" Jewels said nervously. "If I've done something to upset you, it certainly wasn't intentional."

"I'm finding it hard to be civil to you right now, Jewels, so be careful what you say...I want you to know I'm aware of your association with Virginia Moran and Dorothy Haygood. I also know about your trying to use Thomas Cantrell and Judge Langtree to recover Jigs' will from the bank in Avondale. Then there's the matter of the two killers you put on Jigs and me after the Gerklin fight. It's taken a few months to figure this out, but things are finally coming together. Your days of being an attorney are about to come to a halt."

"You have this all wrong," Jewels said unconvincingly. "Smith and Jones were on Virginia's payroll years before I came on the scene; all I do is pay them...It's with her money, but that's the extent of my involvement. It's absurd to think I have any control over those two. I'm just a messenger!"

Sully grinned sardonically. "Do I look stupid, Garan? I've taken a bullet to the head, but thinking I don't know what you're doing, is an insult...You don't know yet what's been collected against you for an indictment, but rest assured, there's more than enough to put you away."

"What—what are you talking about?"

"You remember Captain Randall? Well, he's gathering information about the way that you've been handling certain aspects of the Moran estate. It consists mostly of the transactions you made in Virginia's account at Fulton National; specifically those concerning Smith, Jones and Thomas Cantrell. It's all being documented." Sully then said something totally false to see what Jewels' reaction would be. "Randall also found some things involving Dorothy Haygood and G.W. Spence...You left a trail a mile wide when you raided that $25,000 slush fund Virginia had set up for you. There's documented proof that you pocketed between $10,000 to $15,000 every month from that account. Those are big numbers, considering Virginia pays you a salary to go along with that thievery. Including what Jeremiah Woodard has worked up on you, there's probably a dozen felonies you'll be contending with."

"Why are you doing this?" Jewels asked. "I've twisted some of the rules, but there was never an intent to hurt anyone. I admit I knew about some things Smith and Jones did, but for the most part, I was kept in the dark."

Sully grinned thinly. "If I were you, I'd save the explanations. When you go before the grand jury, they might come in handy. *They* might believe you, but you're wasting your breath if you think I do."

"I'm—not rich—by any means," Jewels stuttered, "but I am somewhat wealthy. Whatever I have in the bank is yours...All you have to do is dispose of this evidence...You have my word it will be *very* beneficial."

"Your word isn't worth much these days, Jewels. Even if I wanted to, which I don't, I couldn't turn it around. Too many people want your scalp."

"Why are you doing this to me? I've done nothing to warrant this kind of treatment."

"You did it to yourself," Sully said, "but, you'll never be able to see it." He stepped out on the sidewalk when the sound of sirens was heard in the distance. "It looks like your secretary has called the cops…I'd best be on my way, but don't worry; I'll still drop by occasionally."

Jewels' jaw was slightly ajar as he watched Sully step away in the twilight. A hollow look covered his face. He was contemplating how to handle his bleak future when the answer burst into his mind like a breath of fresh air. There was no longer anything to worry about.

## CHAPTER FORTY NINE

The snow began to trickle lightly on the hood of the Buick and it gave the impression that a white Christmas could be forthcoming. Sully thought of the youthful years: The decorated trees, the atmosphere, the Christmas music at the small Methodist church he and his mother frequented. The nostalgic remembrance was cut short when painful memories of what was missed came to focus. He forced the thoughts from his mind as if they didn't exist.

The snow began to come down harder when he drove past the governor's mansion. The white flakes dropping on the lawn were illuminated by the outside decorations; it lit up the sky with brilliant sparkling crystals. The snow-covered yard turned the surroundings into a fairyland. He shook his head, aggravated for letting his mind drift; this was not the time for frivolity. Childish dreams could turn into a deadly distraction. He had enough to deal with at the moment, having two ex-cops intent on running him down and killing him.

Sully parked a block away from the Moran Mansion, cut the lights and let his eyes adjust to the dark. He turned the collar up on the jacket and forced the fedora firmly down on his head. He stepped from the car and walked slowly across the street to a streetlight halfway to the house. He removed the .45 from his belt and checked it. Once satisfied the weapon would be up to the task, it was replaced hurriedly. He stood in the shadows on the far sidewalk and took in the parameters of the estate intensely. There were no vehicles in front of the house or over by the driveway, which meant that Virginia Moran had to be home alone. He never had any intentions of harming her, other than to put a fright in her, but felt a certain degree of caution should be exercised. This was more than likely the woman who had her own brother murdered and had him ticketed for the same fate. He moved quietly onto the front porch and looked through the window by the door. A lamp in the hallway was on and another light came from under the door of the study. That particular room had only been used for business purposes in the past. He gently tried the door handle but it was locked. He decided to enter the house unannounced and slid a plastic card from his billfold between the lock-bolt and the plate. He jiggled the card until the bolt was forced back. He eased the door open, then quietly stepped inside and closed it. He moved slowly down the hall toward the study at the far end. His right hand went to the .45 just as he reached the study. He stood silently by the door and listened as Virginia Moran railed at someone on the phone.

"You blundering idiot," she screamed and slammed the telephone down in a fit of temper.

Sully wondered who she had been talking to in such a derogatory manner. He cracked the door slightly to make sure she was alone. The door squeaked softly and drew her attention. Seeing that she was by herself, he took his hand from the .45.

Virginia Moran looked up when he entered the room. Her eyes were riveted on him: no fear, no surprise, just anger. "What do you think you're doing, coming in here at this time of the night?" she asked sarcastically. "Skulking around like a thief...I've a mind to call the police."

Sully sat opposite her. "Why don't you call Smith or Jones? They'd probably be glad to know I dropped by."

"I might do just that! It's about time somebody put you in your place."

"I'm assuming a casket is what you prefer?"

"Assume what you like, only do it somewhere else, young man. I don't like having visitors this late, especially those who aren't invited."

"You're right, Virginia, I did break in. But you're the cause of that. I couldn't just walk in while those two thugs are on the loose, now, could I?"

"My name happens to be *Miss Moran*...I do not appreciate your calling me Virginia...On top of that, I have no idea what you're talking about. Now please leave!"

"There are a few things you should know before I make my exit, *Virginia*. It's well documented that Smith and Jones have been on your payroll for some time. And we also know what you've told them to do once they catch up with me. Sad part is, even if they succeed, you won't gain a thing...I've already found the will you've broken every law in the book to get to, and it's in a probate court judge's hand right now. If things go accordingly, the evidence we have should be enough to put you and your friends in a cell. Smith, Jones, Jewels, Cantrell, Judge Langtree, Dorothy Haygood and G.W. Spence; we've got every one of you in a vise"

"Who is *we*?" Virginia growled defiantly.

"Otis Randall and a slick old lawyer named Jeremiah Woodard. Do you remember him? Between them, they have enough hard evidence to shut you down for life...Some of your pals have already started jumping ship; Jewels was kind enough to name you as the ringleader. How do you suppose that will sound in court?"

"I haven't murdered anyone!" she exclaimed loudly. "And you have no proof that says otherwise. I sit here in my own house, mind my own business while Jewels handles my affairs. If Garan has done things to plunder this estate, I will be the most surprised person in the courtroom when it is presented. How many juries do you think would convict an elderly woman who was robbed blindly for years, and is then accused by the thief of murder?"

"...I can't believe this!" Sully grimaced. "You were planning Jigs' death all along, weren't you? That money never meant a thing. All you ever wanted was to keep it out of his hands. You had your own brother killed because of *that*? It takes a pretty sick person to have those kind of thoughts."

"You are entitled to an opinion, I suppose, but at least get the facts straight: Jigs was not a Moran...And I did *not* kill him!"

"...Get used to it, Virginia! Jigs is your legal sibling where the law's concerned. You had the same mother and father, and it's in the books whether you approve or not. Regardless of his status in your eyes, it didn't give you the right to have him shot down like a rabid dog."

"For the last time, I had nothing to do with his death," she said angrily. "He was a thief and stole from my inheritance...He didn't deserve to die like he did, but it doesn't change the fact that he was a common criminal."

"Did Jigs know how you felt about this when he was alive?"

"He did! I made no apologies...I told him years ago that he would never inherit a penny from this estate, and I was right; he collected nothing."

"That's where you're wrong, lady. The courts protect his wealth and the will is very specific about where the money will go. That's the way Jigs wanted it and as far as I'm concerned, that's the way it'll be..."

"You haven't received anything to date, Mister Hawken...I wouldn't count on it too heavily if I were you."

"You're a complex person, *Virginia*. Here you are a woman in her late sixties, the only surviving member of a wealthy family, with more than enough to last a dozen lifetimes. What do you think will happen to the estate when you die? I don't think it will be buried alongside you? Once you're covered with dirt, lawyers and state officials will wind up with the bulk of it."

"At least those who don't deserve anything will benefit," she snarled.

Sully shook his head in disbelief. "...And to think that all those years Jigs tolerated the hate and spite simply because you were *his* sister. You always came first and you repay him the way you did. The man never said an unkind word about you...You've got quite a resume to present to your Maker, lady. I wouldn't want to be in your shoes."

"Get out of this house!" Virginia growled viscously and began shaking uncontrollably.

"You know this conversation will be repeated in a courtroom one of these days," Sully said. "A jury is going to hear every word of it."

"I doubt it, Mister Hawken," Virginia replied slightly subdued. "What was said in this study never happened, and you'll never be able to prove otherwise. Now please vacate the premises."

Sully stepped to the door, then turned around and looked at Virginia Moran. His long time tormentor was still shaking when she stepped over in front of the window. He pulled the door to and instinctively felt a presence in the hall. He jerked hard to one side, and grasped the .45 in his belt.

272

A wispy figure stood there in a state of shock. Sarah, the household maid for over thirty years, was trembling with a hand over her mouth. She was crying. Apparently, she had heard enough to push her to that point.

Sully motioned for her to follow him outside; Virginia Moran didn't need to know her loyal servant had heard what was said in the study.

Sully stepped onto the porch and looked back down the hallway. "How long were you outside the room?"

"I walked over when you closed the door," she sniffled, unable to look him in the eye. "I was worried about Miss Virginia...I wanted to be close by in case she needed me. She doesn't usually have company this late without telling me."

"How much did you hear?" Sully asked, "...You may be in danger."

Sarah looked up tearfully. "...Did she really do those things? Did she really get Mister Jigs killed like you said?"

"It looks that way."

"Oh, Lord, Miss Virginia's gone mad, and I've got nowhere to go. I surely can't stay here no more."

"Settle down, Sarah. As long as Virginia knows nothing about this, you'll be fine. Just make sure she doesn't find out. It could turn into a major problem if she knew you were at the door."

"...She do get mad when I gets nosy."

"She'd do a lot more than get mad if you tell her anything."

Sarah began to tremble again. "Oh, me, I always know'd Miss Virginia had the fangs of a rattler, but I never dreamed it'd come to the likes of this."

"Do what I tell you and everything will be all right," Sully said, calming her. "Go back in the house and act as if nothing has happened. Deny knowing I was in the house until you saw me in the hall...Can you do that?"

"...If I can't, I'm leaving this house t'night."

"Just remember, deny everything! That's all there is to it," Sully said, then disappeared in the darkness.

Sarah suddenly realized that her world had come crashing down. "Oh, Lord!" she said softly. "What gon' happen to me now?"

# CHAPTER FIFTY

Sully turned slowly into the dark alley with the lights off, then withdrew the .45 and laid it on the seat. Considering he had never killed anyone before, he wondered if he'd have the stomach to pull the trigger. It was all on Smith and Jones' shoulders; if they drew him into a situation that forced him to shoot, that question would more than likely be answered instantly. If the two cops left him no choice, hopefully the problem would take care of itself.

He drove slowly past the house, looking intently in all directions. He knew that any sign of the detectives' presence would call for action, but not to the point of doing something foolish. He turned around at the end of the alley after the threat of danger passed and came back. He pulled in front of the Gregory home, got out of the car and stepped up on the porch; it was after 11:00 o'clock. He had to be careful; this was the time of night Smith and Jones were at their best. Their deadly intentions fit well under the darkness of the cloudy skies.

Sully knocked on the door. "Fred! Zack!" he said softly. "It's Sully!" The movement of someone stirring inside was heard and he stepped back. His hand dropped to the .45 in his belt.

Zack opened the door. "C'mon in, boss. We weren't s'pecting you till mo'nin. Howcum you here tonight?"

"I thought we'd give those cops a visit tonight, if you're up to it? They won't be expecting it and I'm ready to put this to an end."

"We was talkin' about that jus' 'fo you knock on the do'. But we give our word to wait, and that what we was doin'."

"What we doin'?" Fred said, walking into the room.

Zack turned to Fred. "Mistuh Sully wants to go after them two right now...What you think?"

"Well, they sho won't figure on anybody botherin' 'em where they's at, mos' specially in the middle of night."

"Then it's a go," Sully said.

"You sure 'bout this, Zack?" Fred asked his brother.

"My shoes is on and my pistol loaded."

Fred sat on the couch, removed his slippers and reached for his shoes. "I meets you at the car in a minute."

Sully stepped outside and waited for Fred as the engine warmed. Zack curled up in the back seat with the huge revolver across his thighs.

Fred stepped out on the porch and gazed at the snow. "Shame we gots to mess this pretty night up. Them two ain't never gon' see nothin' like this again."

"Save the sympathy for somebody who deserves it," Sully said callously. "There won't be any coming your way when we get there."

"Can't help it, boss. It the first Christmas I ever 'member wantin' to kill somebody...T'ain't right this time o' the year."

"Whut right," Zack said, "is taking care of business so's we don't have to worry 'bout them law dogs breathing down our neck fum now on."

"You right," Fred said, sitting heavily in the front seat. "But it sho' ruin everythin', mos' 'specially with all this snow."

Sully pulled out of the alley onto Auburn Avenue with the headlights still off. "Which way we headed?"

"You know anythin' 'bout Bellwood?" Fred asked.

"I know it's out Bankhead Highway by the old Exposition Cotton Mill...Is that where we're going?"

"Yassuh! You 'member where the ol' Boy's Club is?"

"Yeah, it's on Bankhead in front of the mill."

"Just past the club, take a right the second street and park. We walks to the house from there."

Sully pulled up to the curb fifteen minutes later, and killed the engine. He turned to face Fred and Zack. "I want your word that you won't take any chances when we go in there. I'm not in the mood to give your mother any bad news."

Neither man replied.

"I mean it," Sully said. "Either you agree or this isn't going down."

"We ain't chil'ren, boss," Fred said easily, "We ain't doin' this jus' for you, so set yo' conscience to ease. We gots minds of our own; it somethin' we has to do. I knows we started out helpin' you, but it different now…Them two is killers, an' wouldn't lose a minute's sleep if they was to shoot all three of us. It be like they's squashing a bug. Nawsuh, don' feels like you takin' 'vantage of anybody. We done talked 'bout this, an' them two gon' get whut they got comin' to 'em."

"All right then," Sully said. "Just remember: Once we're in, there won't be any turning back."

"Don' worry 'bout us, boss," Zack said. "It somethin' we was gon' do anyhow…Them two ain't gon' be bothering nobody ever again after tonight."

The reality of what was about to happen suddenly struck Sully. There was a good chance they would be involved in a killing before the night was over. It certainly wasn't the first time he tried to kill someone, but the attempt was unsuccessful when both men survived. It wound up being very costly after he nearly lost his eyesight and Hector came close to losing his life. The doubts began to mount and he wondered if he could handle the responsibility of another person's death. The thought of walking away came into play.

"It time, boss," Fred said, bringing him out of the trance.

Sully stepped from the car and jacked a round in the .45. "I go in first, understand?" he said. "Just follow me. If they don't give us a problem, we take 'em straight to Decatur Street. We're not going in there just to murder someone."

Zack had a different approach to the situation; he wanted to go in blazing away, then leave without a trace if possible. "We can't do it like that, boss. If them two walk out alive, we two dead niggers an' you knows it."

"He right, boss," Fred said. "You prob'ly gon' be all right, but what gon' happen to us? Who you think they goin' after when that bunch downtown put 'em back on the streets? It won't be you, for sho'. That mean we gon' have Smith 'an Jones and the whole police department down our throats. Nawsuh! It can't be but one way: Them two gots to go; it that simple!"

"I don't know if I can kill anyone like that—even if they do deserve it," Sully said. "It goes against every grain in my body."

"Then you on yo' own, boss! Me an' Zack ain't goin' in 'les it like that."

"It's probably best," Sully said. "I've put you behind the eight ball too many times as it is...Which house is it?"

"See the one with the light on the porch?"

Sully nodded.

"The one t'other side that is where they is."

Sully was quiet a moment. "...Let me take a shot at them first...If there's trouble and I can't handle it, do what you have to. If no ones there, I'll be back shortly and we'll take things from there."

"Yassuh," Fred said as if ignoring him.

"Are you listening to me, Fred?" Sully asked sharply.

"...I's listenin'."

"Zack?"

"Yassuh! I's listenin' too!"

Sully felt the frozen snow crunch softly under the weight of his shoes as he walked to the far side of the street. He held the .45 up to the streetlight and cocked the hammer. This episode was about to be put in its perspective once and for all. He walked slowly past the tenement houses that were like so many built earlier in the century for cotton mill workers. Small three room houses, maybe ten feet wide and thirty feet deep, cropped so close together that only a few feet of space separated them. In the south, it had been a way of life for mill workers to live in company houses. After the mills were closed, the textile companies had rented the dwellings as a source of income. The volume of the cheap structures not only made it profitable for the owners, but it was cheap housing for the poor as well.

Sully passed the house with the light, then stopped just beyond in the shadows. He looked down the narrow passageway beside the house Smith and Jones were supposed to be in. A dim light shined from under a shade at the rear. He raised the .45 above his head and slid quietly into the opening. He moved slowly toward the light, taking extra caution to be as quiet as possible. Each window was checked for signs of activity before they were passed by. Reaching the window with the light, he squatted slightly and looked under the drawn shade. Smith and Jones sat at the table involved in quiet conversation. He looked to the rear of the room and noticed that there was a flimsy door hanging precariously on loose hinges. He would go in there. The doorway would probably splinter with a sudden show of force. It would be the best way to quickly gain the upper hand. He moved silently to the rear of the house where the entrance would be made. He took a deep breath, then raised his foot and kicked the door down.

Smith and Jones jumped to their feet with their weapons already out when the door crashed to the floor. The element of surprise went out the window when both detectives began firing in his direction.

Sully was hit twice before he got a shot off; a bullet singed his neck and another scratched his cheek, splitting the earlobe. He dropped to the floor from the onslaught and began firing back rapidly. A volley of bullets behind him came as a welcome surprise. Jones went down hard and Smith stumbled toward the front of the house firing wildly over his shoulder. Sully was startled when Zack fell beside him spewing blood from a gaping chest wound. He scrambled to his feet and rammed another clip in the .45. The automatic clicked loudly when a live round went in the chamber. With Fred at his side, they raced to the front of the house where Smith had fled. By the time they got to the street, Smith was in his car and speeding away. They fired hopelessly from long range. The fleeing detective had escaped a deadly barrage by seconds.

"He won't go far," Fred said disgustedly.

"Why's that?" Sully asked, feeling the moist blood under his shirt.

"Cause I gots two good hits on him; both in the chest. He gon' be dead in a couple of hours, fo' sure."

"We better check on Zack," Sully said. "He's been hit pretty hard."

Fred raced back inside, knelt by his brother, then looked at Sully. "Better get the car, boss!" he said. "I think he's dying."

Sully noticed a suitcase on the kitchen table on his way to the car; he grabbed it and tucked it under an arm. He ran to the Buick and threw the suitcase in the front seat. After cranking the car, he returned quickly to the front of the house. He reached back and opened the rear door for Fred who came out of the house carrying Zack.

Fred eased the unconscious Zack into the back seat and slid in beside him. "Better head for Grady, boss. It's the closest hospital 'round heah. It ain't over ten minutes away this late at night."

Sully went around the corner with the tires screaming for mercy. He looked in the rearview mirror just as curious neighbors began turning their house lights on. The row of tenement houses gave off a strange glow that made it look like a fairyland in the snow. "I don't think anybody saw us," he said, pressing the accelerator to the floorboard. "Maybe we got away clean?"

"Don' make no difference, boss. That Smith fella hurt so bad he gon' have to go to a hospital. When he do, they gon' call the police. Them cops ain't dumb...They gon' know what happen an' they coming fo' us. You gots a chance, Mister Sully, but you gots to get out from here, right now."

Sully pulled up on the Grady Memorial Emergency ramp and looked at Fred. "You expect me to leave you after you risked your neck saving my hide. It's not going to happen that way, pal," he said, quickly jumping out of the car. "Come hell or high water, we're in this together."

"You don' understand, boss," Fred said, lifting his brother from the back seat. "I ain't goin' back to jail...You don' needs to be 'round me now."

Sully sat stunned as he watched Fred carry his brother into the emergency room. What he was just told was nothing short of a death statement.

Fred came out of the Emergency Room entrance minutes later and jumped in the car. "Bes' get outta hear, boss. The police is already in there. They tol' me to wait in the hall till they got Zack straightened away. They wantin' to ask me 'bout this. Soon's they turned they back, I's out the door."

"Did you tell them who Zack was or what happened to him?"

"I tol' 'em I didn't know who he was, an' that somebody shot him durin' a argument. It'll take 'em a couple of days to figure out who he is, and when they does, they be coming fo' me."

"When that happens, promise me you won't start shooting at them."

"Can't do that, boss...Last time I's in jail I wasn't worried 'bout nothin' cause I didn't do nothin'. It different this time. I jes' might have killed me two white men t'night, and they ain't gon' let that slide. I's a dead man fo' that...Ain't no way 'round it."

"What are you going to do now?"

"Jes' take me home...Whatever gon' happen, gon' hafta be there anyhow. Might as well spen' time with momma while I can."

Sully drove Fred to his home, let him out and drove away. He couldn't help but wonder how his friend would handle things. He thought of turning himself in to take the heat off of Fred, but it would be pointless. If Smith took himself to a hospital, the instant the police find out who Zack is, they'll come for Fred. The only other solution would be if Smith lay down and died somewhere. When the cops find Jones' body, they will more than likely figure the two had an argument and killed each other. Hopefully, it will happen that way; only time will tell.

Sully drove to his house in Grant Park, then stepped inside and went to the bedroom. He slid the suitcase under the bed, laid the .45 on the nightstand and began to shed the bloody clothes. He intended to take a scalding hot shower and bandage the wounds but it never happened; five minutes later, he was asleep across the bed. It was just past 4:00 a.m.

# CHAPTER FIFTY ONE

Fred and Zack would have to take care of themselves for the moment; Sully had to stay focused on the wounded Smith. If the ex-detective could be found before he died, he might reveal something of value; most especially the person who had killed Jigs. Sully hoped that riddle would be solved shortly. Sully laid across the bed to sleep but all he could do was toss and turn. The wounds were only superficial, but the nagging pain was enough to keep him from dozing. Finally dropping off into a deep slumber, he was jostled roughly a few hours later.

"Wake up, Sully," a voice demanded. "We gotta talk!"

Sully turned away from the disturbance, wanting it to go away. He had been without sleep too long and wasn't ready to be bothered with the outside world yet. He grunted heavily in discontent, ignoring the interference and then went back to sleep.

"C'mon Sully," the aggravating voice said and shook him harder. "Dammit, man, I gotta get out of here! Wake up!"

Sully groggily turned to the voice, then, in total surprise, jerked upright on the bed. "G.W.?...What are you doing here?"

"We need to talk," G.W. said nervously.

Sully grappled for the .45 that had been on the night table but it wasn't there. He turned to G.W. with puffy eyes full of apprehension. The thought of being shot to death in his own bed showed fully on his face.

G.W. held the barrel of the .45 in his hand and then laid it on the bed. "Easy, man, I ain't here to cause you no grief," he said. "I just didn't want you waking up and unloading that thing at me."

Sully closed his eyes and dropped his chin on his chest. He wondered what was behind G.W. coming to him? The gun-dealer had been thick as a thief with Dorothy Haygood for a long time, so why this sudden attention? "Find me a cold rag somewhere, G. W...I had a real bad night!"

G.W. stepped into the bathroom, wet a rag, and returned to the bedroom. He handed Sully the rag and sat on the side of the bed. "Get yourself together, man. We need to get this over with; I'm in a hurry."

Sully held the rag to his face "...You've already said that. If you were in such a hurry, maybe you should've started a little earlier. Now what's this about?"

"I got a call from Smith; he wanted a message delivered."

Sully reached for his shoes and socks and immediately began dressing. He checked the .45 then slid it under his belt. He stared hard at G.W. "So what's the big message, man? Times wasting!"

"He wants his suitcase!"

"How'd he know I had it? And what's so important about a beat up old suitcase?"

"Hell, I don't know, man...All I know is, after you guys swapped lead last night, he went back to the house to get it and it wasn't there. When he didn't see it, he must have figured you had it."

Sully looked through the shades and saw clouded daylight; the time was 7:30. "Is it morning or afternoon?" he asked.

"Morning!"

"What day?"

"Wednesday!"

"When did Smith call you?"

"About an hour ago!"

"Why didn't the bastard come and get the suitcase himself? If you can find me, he wouldn't have had much trouble."

"Man, he ain't in no shape to do nothin'. He's shot up pretty bad...Probably dead by now. He ain't getting out of that bed with all that lead you poured in him. Even if he could, soon's he showed his face, you'd open up on him. His best shot was sendin' me. I'm the only person left he can trust."

"Suppose I don't want to give him the suitcase? What's he going to do?"

"He figured you'd say that so he's going to give you something in return; answers to questions you never thought existed."

"There's only one question I need answered," Sully said. "If Smith can furnish that, we have a deal."

G.W. stood to leave. "Smith said there might be something else that would interest you."

"Yeah, and what's that?"

"An envelope full of stuff about Beverly Johnson. Whoever has it, supposedly decides whether she walks or not. It's all original; no copies anywhere!"

"...Where's Smith holed up?"

G.W. handed him a slip of paper. "You know where the Techwood Theater is at North and Techwood?"

"I know!"

"It's the third house from the theater, going toward the Varsity. He's in the front apartment on the left. Just step in the hall and knock on the door."

"Whose place is it?"

"An old girlfriends!"

"Will she be there?"

"I don't know, man...She might be at the coroners by now."

"Maybe you should go with me, just in case."

"That ain't gonna happen, Sully. The guy's desperate; he's shot all to pieces and might do something crazy. He's got it in his head that his only salvation is in that satchel."

"I'd feel better if you tagged along...If I have to kill somebody, I want to make sure you're the first to go."

"Well, I ain't going," G.W. said strongly. "I got me a train to catch."

Sully placed the .45 against G.W.'s temple and cocked the hammer. "Tell me what's got you so spooked, and we'll talk about you catching that train."

"Put that thing away Sully, you ain't no killer."

Sully lowered the gun. "Okay then, what's bothering you?"

"...It's Dorothy and the people she's dealing with. She caught me eavesdropping yesterday...I saw it in her eyes; she's gonna have me killed."

"What people? Give me some names!"

"You're gonna have to get that from her or maybe Smith! I've already said more than I should have."

"Smith may not be alive when I get there. Besides, what difference does it make? You're leaving, so who's to know?"

"These people got long arms, Sully. If I let anything out, I'd be a dead man in a matter of days. No matter what rock I crawled under, they'd find me."

"After all you and Dorothy meant to each other, the things you did together, why would she want to kill you?"

"I heard what I heard, Sully. I know what the woman's capable of...I've seen her do things that nobody would believe."

"If it was in her mind to kill you, don't you think it would've happened a long time ago?"

"Maybe! I don't know...But I do know it's in her head now."

A sardonic grin came on Sully's face. "It's hard to believe you're an innocent victim, G.W....Or that you and Dorothy had nothing to do with Jigs' death."

"There's stuff I don't want to tell you, Sully, and I got my reasons. I just want you to know that when Smith and Jones were sent after you, I called it quits. I ain't gonna be part of a murder for nobody!"

"What do you take me for, G.W.?" Sully asked sharply. "It's pretty clear that Jigs' death is linked to Dorothy and the Moran estate, and you're right in the middle of it. Virginia recruited all of you to help her get the estate under her control...And if you're trying to convince me you didn't know about it, you're not as smart as I thought. You've been holding hands with that bunch and that makes you an accomplice. No amount of explaining is going to wash it away."

"...You're wrong about Smith and Jones, you know...They didn't kill Jigs and didn't know who did...Every time that subject came up, it was a mystery to them too. Maybe things are different now, I don't know. Maybe when you see Smith he'll clear it all up. I know I ain't going to."

"You're testing my patience, G.W. I think the both of us should go to Smith" G.W. walked slowly to the door. "I've told you why I came here, and now I'm leaving. If you're gonna' shoot, you might as well go on and do it. I ain't got no life left anyway."

"Relax, G.W.," Sully said, following him to the door. "If Dorothy has you so afraid that you're willing to take a bullet just to get out the door, my chances of getting anything out of you are next to nothing."

G.W. turned to face Sully at the door. "We were friends a long time," he said wistfully. "It won't ever be that way again because you think I betrayed you and Jigs. Well, you might be right? I could probably come up with something to make things right, but I won't...Maybe one day you'll understand?"

Sully frowned. "What brought on this visit in the first place? It's certainly wasn't being an errand boy for Smith...And it's not because you think Dorothy is going to kill you; there has to be another explanation."

"I guess I had to warn you about what was coming...If you don't back off, Sully, a person you trust is going to catch you off guard."

"Does your leaving mean you're through with Dorothy?"

"Maybe I'll be back one day, I don't know...It's hard to understand the hold that Dorothy has on me. The fact is, I don't know if I can get over her...I was so wrapped up in her; it was miserable. According to her, when this was over, we'd be rolling in money. Look at me now; I'm near broke and running away with my tail between my legs, scared to death that some joker is going to pop a cap on me."

Sully watched G.W. disappear around the corner and out of sight. He had trouble mustering sympathy for his old friend.

## CHAPTER FIFTY TWO

Meeting with the critically wounded Smith was important but it would have to wait a little longer; Otis Randall had to be seen before that could be done. Sully turned on to East Lake Drive and drove hastily the rest of the way to the Randall home. Reaching the house, he pulled in the driveway, dodging the small patches of mud without getting onto the adjacent walkway. He stepped from the car just as the sun broke through the clouds. The early morning rise in temperature had already begun to melt the snow in the yard. He went to the porch, wiped the mud from his shoes, then knocked softly on the door. He waited patiently for a response, which didn't take long; Pearl Randall was at the door almost immediately greeting him with a smile. The time was 8:45; just forty-five minutes after G.W. had pulled away from his house in Grant Park.

As usual, Pearl Randall treated him as if he were a favorite relative. "Good morning, Mister Hawken!" she said with her deep southern accent. "What brings you here so early? You should be out enjoying this sunshine."

"I need to talk to your husband for a few minutes…Something has come up that he needs to know about."

"He was up late last night," she explained, quietly guiding Sully back to Captain Randall's home office. She asked him to have a seat. "He'll be a few minutes…Would you like a cup of coffee?"

"If it's no trouble."

"No cream or sugar, is that right?"

"Yes ma'am! Just hot and black."

Pearl Randall left the office and returned minutes later with a hot pot of coffee. She took a full cup from the tray and placed it on the desk. "Otis will be here in a few minutes; he's putting his robe on now."

"Thank you," Sully said, and raised the cup to his lips.

Randall stepped in the room just as his wife, Pearl left. She closed the door quietly behind her. "Hello, Sully," Randall said, sitting behind the desk. "Pearl tells me you have something."

"I'm not sure what I have, but G.W. Spence paid me a visit this morning. I think you should know what I'm about to get involved in...Somebody needs to follow this up in case things don't turn out like I hope."

"You want to tell me about it?"

"It has something to do with what happened last night."

"This sounds pretty serious! What did Spence have to say?"

"...It started around midnight last night when I decided to go after Smith and Jones; they were at a house in the Bellwood community. Fred Gregory and his brother were with me. We went in the house trying to catch them off guard, but it didn't work out like that...As soon as they recognized me, they started shooting. When the smoke cleared, Jones was dead and Smith was on the run; he was shot up pretty bad."

"What about Gregory and his brother? Did they make it out all right?"

"Zack didn't! He's at Grady now under an assumed name."

"And Fred?"

"He's okay! He's at home."

"How about you?"

"A few scratches...Nothing to worry about."

"What on God's earth possessed you to go after those two in the first place?"

"I didn't have a choice. Since I talked to you, I found out that Virginia Moran paid Smith and Jones to finish the job they tried to do back in July."

"You're absolutely sure they killed Moran—no doubts?"

"I have a few! G.W. said they didn't have anything to do with it, which got me to thinking...He sounded pretty sure of it."

"You know there might be a murder charge forthcoming concerning Jones."

"...They intended to kill me. What could I do? I'm hoping you'll have enough evidence to get me out of this, *if* I'm ever drug into court."

"*If*? What are you talking about, *if*? Of course you'll be charged."

"Maybe not? Smith and Jones are the only ones who had anything to complain about. Now Jones is dead and Smith won't say anything because he needs an out."

"What about me? I know you killed Jones."

"So does G.W. and the Gregorys, but they won't say anything... They've got too much to lose."

"And you expect me to keep quiet like them?"

"...I came here because I trust you to do the right thing...If you feel like it's an imposition, do what you have to."

Randall fell silent. "...You mentioned Smith wanting an out? Have you had any contact with him since last night?"

"No, but he talked to G.W....Seems he wants to see me. That's where I'm headed as soon as I leave here."

"How did Spence know where you'd be?" Randall said, his eyes squinting. "And how did he find you so quickly?"

"I asked G.W. about that, but he didn't say."

"How does Spence fit into all of this?"

"All I know is, he delivered the message this morning."

"I understand that! What I want to know is why Smith would go to Spence for anything? They travel different paths."

"I don't know about that!...From the way G.W. talked, they were pretty close. Maybe Smith thought it was all right because G.W. was about to leave town."

"What has that got to do with it?"

"Apparently he found out about Dorothy Haygood wanting G.W. dead. He knew G.W. would have to leave Atlanta and he was no longer in the picture."

"And Smith knew all about this?"

"He had to!"

"And who was going to kill Spence?"

"G.W. wouldn't say who; he just said some people. He said I'd find out soon enough and that those same people would be coming after me when they find out Smith hadn't finished the job."

"What else did Spence have to say?"

"He said Smith would answer questions I didn't even know existed, but that I had to give him back his suitcase."

Randall leaned forward in his chair, his eyes narrowing in concern. "This suitcase—did he say what was in it?"

"No! He just said he wanted it back." Sully replied.

"Did you open it?"

"Haven't had the time. Besides, Smith is history and there's nothing in that bag that concerns me. I figure it's his stash, and needs it to make tracks. It's got to be the only reason he wants it...G.W. did tell me that if I refused to take the suitcase back, Smith had some things on a friend that would send them to prison. I didn't want that so I agreed to deliver the goods."

"Do you have the suitcase with you?"

"It's in the trunk of the car."

"Bring it to me," Randall said. "I want to see what's in that bag."

"I can't do that, captain...If I let you go through the bag, it might jeopardize the agreement I made."

"How could you have an agreement with somebody you haven't even talked to? You haven't seen the man since last night, and if memory serves me correctly, he was doing his best to kill you at the time."

"You're right! And I agree it's stupid to put trust in someone like him...But, my friend means a lot to me."

"If you think for one minute that Beverly Johnson won't go to jail, you're sadly mistaken. She'll spend time, and nobody can stop it."

"How...How do you know I was talking about Beverly?" Sully stammered. "I never mentioned her name."

"I do my homework, Sully...Very little goes on that I don't know about. Now, go outside and get the suitcase."

Sully walked to the door in a state of shock, "Are you sure this is the way to handle things?" he asked tentatively.

"Damn right, I'm sure!" Randall said, leaning back in his chair.

Sully stepped out to the car, put the key in the ignition and turned it. He drove away just as Otis Randall came out of the house screaming obscenities.

# CHAPTER FIFTY THREE

Sully glanced in the rearview mirror halfway expecting Otis Randall to be there with fire in his eyes. By the time the outskirts of Kirkwood came into view, he had pushed it to the rear of his mind. There was a lot more to think about than Randall's hurt feelings. As a precautionary measure, he took to the side streets just in case someone *was* following. He took his time driving in the general direction of Memorial Drive, which was the main route to the downtown area. Once on Memorial, it would be critical to drive the speed limit and obey all traffic laws. A minor traffic violation had to be avoided at all costs. If the cops pulled him over and recognized him, it could create a distraction that would keep him from getting to Smith.

A mile past Kirkwood, the chance meeting of a patrol car almost became that very disaster. The police car jammed on its' brakes when the Buick was spotted, and one of the officers in the car pointed frantically in his direction. Sully jerked the wheel hard to the right and sped down a side street to put distance between them. The police were unable to pursue because of the snarled traffic and watched helplessly as Sully roared away. He wondered how the cops could be after him so quickly. As far as he knew, the only viable reason they had for chasing him was the killing of Detective Jones. Fred would never say anything, and neither would his brother, Jake. They'd be cutting their own throat. It wasn't G.W.; he was one person who didn't want to be in the spotlight. Especially now! He was too glad to get away in one piece. The only other person who knew of the gun battle was Otis Randall. It didn't take long for Sully to realize that he'd underestimated the anger in Randall's eyes. Randall had to have called an *All Points Bulletin* in, the instant he left the captain's house.

He had to give his situation more thought now. With every cop in town after him, it was a totally different scenario. If he were going to keep clear of the police, he would have to stop being so visible. That meant the Buick would have to be taken out of the picture quickly. It was what attracted the patrol car in the first place. Public transportation was out of the question also; it was probably being monitored by now. The only way left to get around was by taxi.

Sully kept to the back alleys and headed straight for Grant Park; if he could get to the lake pavilion before being spotted, he would dump the Buick there. It would probably be towed away sometime during the night, but there would be more than enough time to deal with Smith. If that could be accomplished by late afternoon, maybe he could get Randall to call off the manhunt. It was a razor-edged fence he sat on, but there was never a choice. No matter which way he fell, disaster was in the forcast; either cops or unknown killers would be waiting.

Sully drove to within fifty yards of the pavilion, then parked and opened the trunk. He took Smith's ragged suitcase, tucked it under his arm and then walked slowly toward the pavilion by the lake. There were several Veteran cabs parked beside the roundhouse. How could they expect to get fares on such a miserable day, especially from an isolated location like this? Not many people hung around the park on cold days. The answer came to him when he saw the cab drivers sitting and talking inside while drinking coffee. The main office downtown was probably transferring the calls to the roundhouse from there. *Pretty smart,* he thought. They were saving time and money by just kicking back and waiting for the telephone to ring. It worked fine for Sully since he intended to call a taxi from the roundhouse anyway.

Sully stepped inside and except for a few hacks inside, the building was empty. He walked to where the drivers were seated. "Anybody available for a trip to the corner of North and Techwood, over by Georgia Tech?"

A burly man recognized Sully and slid his cap back on his head. "Tell you what, champ: With three fares all day, it ain't like we're covered up. I was about to call it a day, and I had the next fare…That ought to tell you something."

"Then I'm lucky I got here when I did."

"…You could've waited a little bit longer?" a second driver joked. "I was next on the list!"

The first driver smiled. "Take the ride, Wally…I had a fare earlier. You got a house full of kids to worry about."

"Hey, man, I'm just joking around," the second driver said seriously. "I ain't taking your ride."

"Somebody better, cause I ain't leaving the pavilion," the huge driver said. "Too cold out there for this guy."

Sully dropped a twenty on the table in front of the burly driver. "That's for giving up the fare," he said, then slid another twenty in front of Wally. "You get that and the fare, if we're out of here in the next ten seconds."

Wally snatched up the twenty, donned his cap, and headed for the door in one motion. "If you're waiting on me, Hawken, you're backing up."

Sully slid into the back seat of the cab as Wally warmed the engine. He laid Smith's bag on the seat, then stared at it before unhooking the straps. He wondered momentarily what was so important about the contents of the satchel, and then opened it. He saw nothing at first but bundled cash, then dug underneath to find a handful of manila envelopes. He noticed each envelope had a name printed on it. When he saw Beverly's name, he went no further. Tempted to ignore it, he pulled the envelope and slowly began to examine the contents. The legal documents were without much interest, but some 8" by 10" nude photographs with the negatives attached, was clearly a surprise. He couldn't recognize the people in the photos to begin because of poor quality. They had been developed far too long and were out of focus. He stretched a picture out at arms length and his heart sank. There was no mistaking it was Beverly, locked in a tight embrace with a man. Several more pictures with other men stunned him into silence. It was several minutes before the pictures were placed back in the envelope. He didn't return the envelope to the suitcase though; instead, it was jammed inside his jacket pocket.

Sully came out of the trance when the driver turned down Techwood toward Grant Field. He leaned forward in the seat. "Pull over here!"

The driver eased up to the curb. "Why here?" the confused Wally asked. "We're still a couple of blocks away."

"I need a favor!"

"Name it, champ!"

"It was obvious at the park, that you and your buddies figured out who I was right off the bat. The problem is, I don't want anyone to know I hailed a cab there. If the cops tow my car in, they're going straight to the roundhouse and ask questions. I don't want *anyone* to know where I am, *especially* the cops. Can you take care of that? Maybe get the other drivers to back you up?"

"I'll make the call."

"There's a drugstore around the next corner. Use the pay phone there, then wait for me. I shouldn't be gone long, so keep the meter running."

"You sure?"

Sully dropped a ten spot in his lap. "Yeah! I'm sure."

Sully crossed North Avenue to the far side, then glanced at the laundromat and the theater across the street. The third house just beyond the theater was where Smith was holed up. He studied the three houses for a moment to get the layout. All three were of the same build: community porches on both ends and large hallways running from the street in front to the alley in back. There were a total of eight apartments in each building; four downstairs and four upstairs.

Sully walked up the far side of the street until he was even with the house Smith was in. The apartment where Smith was supposed to be had its shades drawn. Something told him not to walk up on the porch without caution. He would keep walking up the street and circle around to the alley in back; he'd enter the house from the back way. He meticulously examined the layout in the rear, especially the steps that led to the back porch. The crawl space underneath was covered with wood lattice and provided an ideal hiding place for the suitcase. He didn't like the idea of meeting Smith without something to equalize things. Smith could catch him flat-footed with the bag, and refuse to tell him what else he held over Beverly's head. He opened a small gate under the porch and shoved the suitcase inside, then looked around making sure there were no prying eyes.

He stepped through the soggy weeds that led to the porch, then slowly ascended the steps, trying to be careful of calling attention to his presence. He moved slowly down the hallway until he was at Smith's apartment door. He stood to one side and knocked softly; his right hand gripped the .45.

A moment of silence ensued, then a voice, noticeably wracked with pain and distrust answered, "Who is it?"

Sully backed further away from the door. The automatic slid from his belt with both hands firmly on the butt of the gun. "It's me," Sully said. "...Hawken!"

"C'mon in!" Smith said wearily. "The door's open."

Sully grabbed the door handle, staying well to the side and turned it ever so gently. He slid the door open with his foot, peeking inside cautiously. Smith was lying helplessly on the bed with blood and bruises covering his body. He was grossly swollen from his neck to his thighs. Smith had apparently suffered three bullet wounds from the night before.

*"Jesus!"* Sully said under his breath, stepping inside. "You need to be in a hospital, Smith. You're going to die if you stay here."

Smith wheezed with blood trickling from the corner of his mouth. "I'll worry about that when I get my bag...You have it, don't you?"

"It's right outside, but first, I have to know if it's worth going after."

"Dammit, can't you see I'm dying, Hawken?" Smith gurgled. "It's all I got!"

"Then we need to get this done in a hurry, don't we?"

"You wouldn't get away with this if I was a whole man," Smith said viciously. "I'd rip your damn heart out!"

"Another reason to get this behind us," Sully said without emotion. "I have plenty of time...You don't have that luxury."

Smith was quiet a moment, then surprised Sully with an unexpected admission. "You got it in your head that me and Jonesy killed your pal, Moran, don't you? I got news for you: we didn't pull the trigger on you or Moran...Never intended to either. Old lady Moran wanted us to, though."

"If you didn't kill Jigs, who did?"

"Beats the hell out of me," Smith said. "When me and Jonesy got there, we were too late. Virginia Moran had told us about the money and said we could have it all, after we took him down. Truth is, we never was gonna hurt him."

"A quarter a million dollars is a lot of money."

"Yeah, it is, but we didn't get it. We were just gonna put some masks on, rough him up and take the money…We sure as hell weren't going to kill anybody for it. It would've been easy enough to pull off since nobody knew us. Hell, who would suspect cops of a holdup?"

"Don't you think Virginia would have something to say?"

"What could she do? Hell, she was paying us to kill her own brother."

"What do you suppose happened to the money and the jewels?"

"I don't know, Hawken," Smith said, "and that's the God's truth. All I can tell you is, it looked like both of you were dead when we got there. I went through Moran's pockets pretty quick; did the same to you…Didn't find a thing!."

"After Jigs and I left the Kimball House, how far behind us were you?"

"Couldn't have been more than ten minutes. Somebody knew exactly how much time it would take for us to get there. They had it timed perfectly to get out of there before we got on the scene."

"Who else knew about this besides Virginia?"

"Nobody! I told Miss Moran if she said anything to anybody, the deal was off."

"Why is it I'm having trouble believing you?"

"You're thinking like Virginia Moran now. She had it in her mind we'd try to rip her off from the very beginning. Think about it, man: if I had that money, would I be hanging around just for a few extra bucks?"

"Let's say I believe you…What about this last attempt you made to get me out of the way? That's kind of hard to ignore."

"*What damn attempt?*" Smith growled, beginning to cough blood again. "You're the one who came after me."

"She paid you to kill me, didn't she?"

"Yeah, but we never got a dime. She didn't trust us anymore. She said she'd pay after you were dead and not before. That's when me and Jonesy cooked up this deal to milk a few more bucks out of her before we left town. I called the Journal the day you and your friends came after us. I gave them your obituary; it'll be in today's paper. The old lady wanted proof you were dead and we gave it to her. We were supposed to get $10,000 apiece for that article. We already had forty thousand in the bag; that would go a long way in Mexico."

Sully looked at his watch. "It's a little early for the Journal, but I can wait. If my name is in the obituaries, and you tell me a few things, the bag is yours."

"The first edition is already on the streets. There's a box at the corner. Go check it for yourself...I ain't going nowhere!"

Sully walked hurriedly to the corner, dropped a nickel in the box, and retrieved a first edition paper. He thumbed through to the obituaries until his name came up in print. *"Sully Hawken: promising heavyweight and local celebrity gunned down by unknown assailants."* He read the paper then threw it in a garbage can. When he re-entered the apartment, Smith was having trouble breathing. The rank smell of death filled the room. He shook the near comatose Smith and jarred him awake. He was sure that the ex-detective had little to look forward to. "I read the paper, Smith, but I still need to know about Beverly."

Smith's eyes blinked open momentarily. He opened his mouth but nothing came out. Then his eyes popped wide open. "My bag, Hawken...Gotta have that first!"

Sully looked at Smith, amazed that the man still had fantasies about getting away with a lot of money. How could a hardened detective harbor such insane thoughts? "You can have the satchel any time, Smith. But you have to tell me about Beverly Johnson...It's up to you!"

"Damn it Hawken, my whole life's in that bag; the money, the bus tickets, all I have on people; it's my protection; everything's there!"

"What about those photos of Beverly? What are they for?"

"They're for blackmail, but she didn't know about it. We took the pictures from behind a screen. Hell, she didn't even know they existed until a few days ago. That's when I offered to sell 'em to her...It meant a few more bucks!"

"Was she going to buy them?"

"She said she was! I told her I was leaving and wouldn't be back to cause her any more trouble. You kept us from closing the deal when you barged in on us last night. Now—my suitcase; I want to get out of here."

Sully walked to the door and stopped. "...You're sure that's all you have on her!"

"Yeah! I'm sure!" Smith said, then drew his service revolver with a blood covered hand. "I'm warning you, Hawken: If you're not back within a minute, I'm coming after you. And this time I will kill you."

"Relax," Sully said calmly, stepping out into the hallway. "All I wanted was what you had on Beverly. Everything else is yours."

Sully went to the back porch and quietly descended the stairs. He opened the gate to the crawl space and pulled out the satchel. He started for the steps, then froze when shots rang out. He heard Smith curse loudly, then more shots came from the hall upstairs. Someone was stumbling noisily down the hallway. Sully ducked out of sight under the steps, then pulled the .45. More shots were fired just as the person running reached the back porch. A lifeless body tumbled from the porch to the bottom of the stairs. Detective Smith, once the scourge of Atlanta law-breakers, had finally made the obituaries.

Sully eyes were glued to the cracks in the porch above. Another person was heard walking toward the back porch. The man stopped in the shadows above and cursed softly. Sully thought the voice was familiar but whoever it was, spoke so quietly, he couldn't place it. Before he could get a better look, the person turned and walked away. Sully quickly worked his way around the block to where the cab was waiting. What was in Smith's luggage, now, took on a whole new meaning.

# CHAPTER FIFTY FOUR

Sully dropped another twenty on the cabby and said he wanted off at Peachtree and Baker. "If the cops track you down and start asking questions, tell 'em I got out at Five Points, okay?"

"It's fine with me, champ," the driver said, then handed Sully a slip of paper with two telephone numbers on it. "Call me anytime you need a ride…One's the pavilion; the other's my house!"

"So long as nobody tracks me down, I'll get back to you. But what I do and where I go, *has* to be kept quiet."

Wally agreed to the conditions then pulled away slowly. He jammed the brakes before going ten yards, then backed up. "You forgot your bag, champ."

Sully retrieved the suitcase with an embarrassed smile. "You just saved me a lot of trouble, Wally…I'll be in touch!"

Sully walked down Baker Street towards the bus station then onto Spring Street. He turned on Luckie Street and headed for the YMCA. He signed in for three days but opted to keep the room longer. He still wasn't sure what he would do. He didn't use the elevator and walked up to the second floor; elevator operators had the ability to remember their passengers. When the night clerk failed to recognize him, he didn't want to test his luck further.

The room Sully got faced the front; it turned out to be more than expected. Easy access to the rear stairwell that led to the outer corridor, was the perfect escape route. He returned to the room and cracked the window slightly; the room temperature dropped considerably, but it was a minor concession. If he could hear what went on outside, hopefully there would be time to get to the stairwell undetected.

He stayed fully dressed so he would be out the door on a moment's notice; it would also ward off the chill. He laid Smith's suitcase on the bed; it was time to find out what the bag contained. He unhooked the leather bindings and opened it. Smith had said there was $40,000 in cash, but probably twice that amount was wrapped in $1,000 bundles. But Sully wasn't interested in the money; the envelopes came first. He laid the folders on the bed and read the names printed on them. He was startled by who they were; Dorothy Haygood, G.W. Spence, Garan Jewels, Virginia Moran, the banker, Thomas Cantrell and Judge Beauregard Langtree. The remainder were influential politicians and high-ranking police officers.

When Sully saw Otis Randall's name on the final envelope, it caught him by surprise. The thickness of the folder was even harder to fathom. What could an honest cop like Randall have done to warrant so much dirt? He was the best policeman he'd ever been associated with, in or out of uniform. What did they have on him? The captain was a friend, but everything would have to be looked at differently now. If Randall was a bad cop, that meant he had been lying all along. He had a lot of respect for the ex-policeman, but if that envelope held proof of Randall working against him, somebody had a lot of explaining to do. Sully read the documents for a full thirty minutes, through one damning piece of evidence after another, then sat on the edge of the bed stunned. The evidence against Randall and the others was almost unbelievable. Everything pointed to Smith living out his life on the shoulders of blackmail. Sully thumbed through the remainder of the envelopes looking for anything that could be held against Beverly but found nothing. Satisfied she would be all right, he put the remaining folders in the suitcase, then laid across the bed. It was just past four in the afternoon.

Sully awoke to loud traffic noise and quickly stepped to the window; it was 9:15 and darkness had settled in. He had slept soundly for five hours. He turned on the light, then went to the wash basin and vigorously splashed cold water in his face. Then it dawned on him: Dorothy Haygood had the answers. The papers in Randall's folder proved that Dorothy and G.W. were working with him. That's what G.W. had tried to tell him, but couldn't. It wasn't Dorothy he was afraid of; it was Otis Randall. Sully couldn't get to G.W. now because he had left town, and since going after Otis Randall was the wrong thing to do, he would settle for Dorothy—for the moment.

It was clear now that G.W. didn't kill Jigs. Virginia Moran didn't have anything to do with it either. She had paid Smith and Jones to do it, but they couldn't have.  One reason was they didn't have either the money or the jewels; the other was the obituary they had put in the Journal.  That was nothing more than an attempt to scam a little cash out of Virginia Moran.  Garan T. Jewels was a maggot beyond belief, but still lacked the courage to kill anyone.  The sleazy lawyer couldn't have accomplished anything as vile as murder.  Beverly was quickly ruled out; she was guilty of a lot of things, but certainly not of murder. The banker, Cantrell, wasn't even given a thought; he lacked the temperament of a killer.  Through a process of elimination that left only Dorothy Haygood and Otis Randall, Dorothy would be the one to receive the unannounced visit tonight.

Sully walked to the nearest trolley stop holding the suitcase tightly, then waited for a ride to Grant Park.  He knew the danger of public transportation was huge, but he had to get to the Buick before it was hauled in.  He took a back seat on the trolley when it arrived, then pulled his cap down over his eyes.  Getting off at Cherokee Avenue, he went straight to the Buick; it was still parked by the closed pavilion and covered with frost.  Sully had decided earlier, not to call Wally. The late hour was taken into consideration and besides, the cab driver had a family; he didn't need to get involved an anything dangerous. Sully didn't know what was going to happen when he went to see Dorothy but one thing was for sure: He didn't need an innocent cab-driver hanging around.  He wondered how much more the cab driver could be expected to keep quiet about.  If someone were to wind up dead at Dorothy's house, it would be difficult to ask a man he hardly knew to ignore it.

Sully drove away with one thing in mind: He had to avoid being spotted on the way to Dorothy's.  He skirted the downtown area by using back streets until he reached the east side of Piedmont Park; knowledge of the inner city had made it easy up until then.  He didn't see the first police car and decided to take Tenth Street straight to Peachtree.  There was only eight blocks of heavy traffic before he would turn.  It would be taking a chance, but he was pushed to be bolder.  Things had to be resolved and being cautious would do nothing but prolong the situation.

The feeling of well being was shattered the instant he pulled onto the main thoroughfare; his heart pounded vigorously upon spotting several patrol cars. He was somewhat surprised that the cops didn't make an attempt to pull him over. It wasn't that they hadn't seen him; they had looked directly at him several times. It was like nobody knew he was on the run.

It took from Tenth Street to where the Peachtrees merged before he could breathe a sigh of relief. He now wondered how long it would take the cops to figure things out; going unnoticed like that was a relief, but it couldn't last.

# CHAPTER FIFTY FIVE .

The Haygood home sat comfortably at the rear of a huge, well-manicured lawn. Bushes and trees covered the outer perimeter, while in contrast, little or no foliage was near or around the house. Sully slowly drove the long driveway trying to remember how the exterior was laid out. It became painfully clear that surprise was not going to be an ally. Sneaking up on this house, day or night, would not be accomplished easily. He had hoped to be a lot less obvious.

Sully came to a stop at the main entrance, then stepped away and looked around. The only light on in the house came from the living room in front. Luckily, a small light was on above the front steps; it would have been impossible to see in the night's blackness if it had been off. It was ironic that a ruthless woman like Dorothy Haygood would have consideration for anybody.

He went back to the car after sizing up the situation, then reached for the suitcase in the front seat. He stopped short; the bag might be cumbersome if he were put in an awkward position. He eased the door to softly, then stepped on to the porch; the huge front door was slightly ajar; something was not right. The light in the living room was shining out into the hallway past the partially opened door. He stood by the entranceway for a moment, then after hearing or seeing nothing out of the ordinary, stepped inside. He quietly closed the door, then walked slowly down the hallway toward nothing but dead silence. His hand dropped to the .45 tucked in his waist while his eyes stayed glued to the door leading into the living room. He moved forward silently.

"C'mon in, Sully?" a familiar voice said dryly from the living room.

"Captain Randall! Is that you? What are you doing here?" Sully asked, then entered the room cautiously.

"Yes, it's me," Randall replied. "I told you before, very little goes on in this town that I don't know about."

"How'd you know I'd be here?"

"That's not too hard to figure. You wanted answers and you needed to see the person who has them."

"If *you* knew that Dorothy had these answers, why wasn't something done about it before now?"

"I'm doing something this very minute; it's why I'm here."

"You want to tell me about it, or do I have to guess?"

"Before we go into that, did you bring Smith's luggage? That's what's needed to wind this up."

"…Just to let you know, I've gone through everything in the bag," Sully said, then added. "…How'd you know I still had the suitcase? The last time we talked, I made it clear I was giving it back to Smith in exchange for what he had on Beverly."

Randall's eyes narrowed. "Someone at the station called me about Smith being killed earlier this afternoon. The detectives went over his apartment with a fine tooth comb and didn't find the bag."

"That's odd," Sully said. "How'd they even know about the bag?"

"There's nothing odd about it at all. When the detective called, I told him to find the bag and deliver it to me. When he didn't come up with it, I figured at first that you might have killed Smith and kept the suitcase. But you wouldn't gain anything from that. You were too concerned with keeping Beverly out of trouble and killing Smith wouldn't have helped her at all. No, Sully! Other than your girlfriend, you're only interested in who killed Moran…Now get me the suitcase!"

"I'll be back in a minute," Sully said, "it's in the car!" He walked briskly out the door and returned quickly. He dropped the bag on the coffee table in the center of the room. "There it is! It's yours…Now who killed Jigs?"

Randall drew his .38 police special and aimed it directly at Sully's heart. He frowned and put the other hand around the satchel's handle. "This is the only thing left that would give me a problem."

"You killed Jigs, didn't you?…Why?"

"Sully, I didn't kill your friend—and there is no mysterious killer …Hell, boy, you did your partner in. It was an accident, but the fact is, your finger was on the trigger that night…It was all a regrettable mistake; nobody was supposed to get killed…It was just something that happened."

Sully threw a disgusted look at Randall. "What do you take me for, a complete idiot? Jigs Moran was my best friend. That's not much of an answer."

"It's what happened!"

"Where did you get that garbage from? It had to be from a sewer."

"From G.W. Spence! He was there!"

"You're going to have to come up with something better than that."

"I don't *have* to come up with anything, Sully...And it won't be important after tonight. But, for argument's sake, I'll tell you what Spence had to say...He said that he had left the Kimball house before you and Moran did that night...He was going to wait by the car and confront Moran about a money situation. Moran had advised him to place a lot of money on the Gerklin fight—against you...It was a sure thing! You didn't have a chance of winning. Moran also told three of his close friends the same thing. Problem was, you didn't know anything about the fix; Moran hadn't told you. When you knocked Gerklin out, it upset everybody's apple cart. Moran's wanting to let his close pals in on some easy money backfired and he had to make their losses good...He didn't have to, but that was Moran's way of doing things. What put Spence in such a bind was where he got the money for the bet in the first place. Fletcher and Gracci had loaned him a bundle and all of a sudden, they wanted their dough. Spence was running scared and when he found out Moran had all that cash, it was a way to get off the hook. He'd simply get Moran to pay off the debt; he was the cause of Spence's troubles anyway. Moran said he'd take care of it, but it had to be at a later date. Spence wouldn't take no for an answer and they began arguing...You were hearing all that crap for the first time and when you heard that Moran was in on the fix, you exploded. I suppose, going without sleep, plus popping Benzedrine and drinking like a fish had a lot to do with what happened. Anyway, when you threatened Spence and scared him, he came out with a pistol. While you two were tussling over the gun, Moran came over to keep you from doing anything stupid. That's when the gun went off; the bullet caught Moran in the chest; he was dead before he hit the ground. Spence said you sat down beside Moran in a stupor for a moment, then before he could stop you, you raised the pistol to your head and pulled the trigger…You shot yourself too, Sully."

"…Did you wind up with the jewels and the money?"

"…I don't have it yet, but it'll be here soon. Spence had taken it straight to Dorothy that night because he didn't know what to do. He thought you and Moran were dead, and he certainly didn't want to be brought up on a murder rap. Flashing money around would've have done that…That's why he didn't pay off Gracci and Fletcher."

"What happened to the gun?"

"Spence took it with him. It could be traced back to him."

"…Who has the money now?"

"Your girlfriend!"

"Beverly?

"Yes! She'll be here with it shortly."

"…Was she in on this from the beginning?"

"Not at all, but the law won't make any exceptions. She'll wind up behind bars the same as me if this becomes public."

"You're talking in circles, Randall! How could she *not* be mixed up in it and know what she knows?"

"Things happened that you don't know about."

"And what's that?"

"First of all, there's the money and the jewels; they've been at Beverly's apartment for months. She didn't know it, but that's where they were all along. Dorothy had gone to Beverly and asked her to keep the satchel for a while. She said the bag contained some personal things and to hide it until she came back for it. Beverly never asked any questions and simply put the bag in the kitchen closet. That's where it's been all this time."

"Wait just a minute," Sully said. "While I was staying with Beverly, half of Atlanta was looking for me. Dorothy had to know I was there. Why did she keep it a secret from everybody? She was definitely a person that wanted my hide."

"Fortunately for you, it didn't happen that way. Dorothy and G.W. knew where the bag was, but they had no idea you were staying with Beverly. You have Beverly to thank for keeping that quiet. She did a good job of protecting you while you were at her apartment…Most likely, if she had known what was taking place, she might not have been so secretive."

"What makes you say that?" Sully sneered.

"Some people just don't like to be *that* involved."

"I'll accept that for now, so where does that leave me?"

"It's not good, Sully! You've painted yourself in a corner and forced me to do something not to my liking."

"What about Beverly? What's going to happen to her?"

"I haven't got that worked out yet...She's about to start a new life somewhere...Hopefully she still can without a hitch?"

"What about G.W.? There's no ignoring him...*He* knows what you've done."

"Let's just say, I don't think Mister Spence will ever be heard from again," Randall said, then cocked the hammer of the revolver. "I don't like doing this, Sully...My wife Pearl and I thought the world of you...You should've let it go!"

Snatching at straws, Sully blurted out, "Before you pull that trigger, would you clear a few things up for me?"

Randall eased the hammer forward. "There's only a few minutes left; Beverly will be here any minute. You can't be alive when she gets here. It would be a problem if she knew that I killed you."

"You killed Smith, didn't you?"

"I didn't have a choice. When I got to his apartment, I thought you had already dropped off the suitcase. When I asked Smith for it, he went crazy and snatched a pistol out from under a pillow and fired at me. I couldn't leave a witness like that running loose, so I had to kill him. Besides, by then I had it figured that you'd eventually deliver it to me anyway."

"How'd you find out where Smith was holed up? Nobody, especially Dorothy, knew where he was...And G.W. said he didn't tell her."

"Smith's girlfriend let it out...When he showed up full of bullet holes, she panicked and telephoned Dorothy."

"And Dorothy called you?"

"She called early this morning and told me where he was...I had intended get the suitcase from Smith until you told me you had it."

"Tell me something, Randall: Did you call the cops off? Why did they only come after me that one time?

"I asked a few friends to watch out for you. I knew where you were headed and I told them. If they pulled you over, I wanted them to escort you back to the house. When I found out you lost them in traffic, I decided to give you time to deliver the suitcase...I could always drop by and relieve Smith of it later. I just didn't give you enough time."

Sully's jaw went rigid. "You know, the day will come when the scales tip the other way...I may not be around, but it's coming."

Randall cocked the hammer with a blank expression.

Sully had run the gauntlet; there were no more ways to stave off the inevitable. He could die quietly or fight feverishly for life. He came within a split second of making a move for his .45 when the protruding leg of a female behind the couch caught his eye. Fearful Randall had killed Beverly, he asked shakily, "Who is it?"

"...It's Dorothy," Randall finally said. "She presented herself as a problem and had to be dealt with. I'm afraid you'll be charged with her death."

"What about Beverly? She won't like this when she finds out."

"She'll be all right," Randall said, "if the killing stops here."

A sardonic look was etched into Sully's face. "Now, that's gall; how can you say something like that when you're about to commit another murder?"

Randall raised the revolver and tightened his finger on the trigger.

Sully dove hard to his left, jerking out the .45 just as Randall fired. He felt a single bullet rip deep into his side. He rolled violently and emptied the automatic blindly, completely missing Randall in the wild exchange. Out of bullets, he lay still against the wall, resigned to whatever fate had dealt him. He looked at Randall expecting the worst. When Randall's knees buckled and he fell to the floor, Sully could not believe his eyes. There was no way a bullet from his gun had found its target.

He stood up holding the gaping wound in his side, unable to conceive what had just taken place. By all rights, *he* should be dead, not Otis Randall. He held his breath and looked down at Randall's lifeless body. "...Must have been a ricochet?"

A soft voice came from the doorway. "Is he dead?"

Sully jerked around to face the figure in the shadows.

Beverly stood there with a smoking gun in her hand; she was trembling. "He was going to kill you, Sully. I couldn't let him do that. I swore the night those goons carried you away, I wouldn't let it happen again."

Sully was quiet a moment, then stared at Randall's lifeless body. "...How long were you at the door?"

"Long enough!...But it doesn't matter; I'm leaving as soon as I get an envelope from that bag," she said, pointing to Smith's suitcase."

"Where are you going?"

"As far as I possibly can...I want this over and done with."

"And that folder is supposed to let you off the hook?"

"No, it doesn't, Sully...I'll still have to live with myself. But at least I won't spend time in jail for something I had nothing to do with."

He reached into his jacket and handed her the envelope containing her name. "You were up to your ears in prostitution and blackmail; the photos show that."

Beverly's face sagged from embarrassment. "You saw the pictures?"

"Yeah! So how can you say you didn't do anything?"

"Because I didn't. They took those pictures without my knowledge, then used them to squeeze money and favors out of those people. You don't honestly believe I could do anything like that, do you?"

"...No, you wouldn't," Sully said, already regretting the accusation. He handed her the folder. "It's all there...I hope it helps."

There was silence for several minutes then Beverly meticulously wiped her gun free of fingerprints. She went behind the couch and placed the weapon in Dorothy's hand, wrapping the dead woman's fingers tightly around the pistol grip. She stepped over to Smith's satchel on the coffee table, opened it and laid the documents on the sofa. She extracted Otis Randall's file. "I'm taking this with me," she said softly.

"Why Randall's file? He's as dirty as they come!"

"He needs to be the hero this time," Beverly said, picking up Smith's suitcase that still held the money. "If all goes right, investigators will see these documents and realize they were used for blackmail purposes. Hopefully, they will think Dorothy shot Randall after being caught, and he shot back trying to protect himself."

"What about the bullets I filled the room with? What will explain that?"

"I don't know, Sully, but I'm sure they'll think a third party was involved; hopefully they won't think it was you. We should probably get rid of your gun, just to be on the safe side."

"What are you going to do with all that money?"

"It goes with me...If I have to run, it has to be far—and that takes money."

The searing pain bent Sully over. "Sounds like you've got everything under control," he said sarcastically.

Beverly helped him out of the house and sat him in the driver's side of the Buick. "Can you drive?"

"I think so."

"Follow me then; I have a place we can use for a few days. What we have to do now, is keep you out of the hospital and away from the police for a while. If this works, maybe Pearl Randall's pension will stay intact."

Sully looked confused. "How do you know Pearl?"

"I don't, but from what I've heard, she doesn't deserve the legacy of a crooked cop."

Sully leaned over the steering wheel. "Where's all this headed, Beverly?"

"I'm going to help you, Sully. I'll stay until you're all right..."

Mysteriously, the pain vanished. For a brief moment, he had forgotten that Beverly was a nurse of accomplished skills.

311

# EPILOGUE

Then she was gone. She was there only five short days before vanishing in the middle of the night without a word. Beverly had made sure his physical condition was in order before leaving, but the vascular aspect was a different story. Sully recovered from the bullet wound in time, but the mental spike in his chest wasn't so forgiving. It would take months for that pain to heal. But heal it did, as all affairs of the heart eventually do.

Sully did receive a degree of satisfaction while watching justice being dispensed over the following months. He listened intently to the saga of Garan Jewels and how the conniving lawyer had transferred all his holdings to a bank in the Bimini islands. Jewels had been devastated upon finding out that the courts had frozen the assets before he arrived there. Broke and stranded, he was forced to surrender meekly to local authorities. Sully was infuriated the following year when Jewels retained the bulk of his holdings and was re-established as an attorney. His old friend, Judge Langtree, was the person responsible for working out the deal.

Judge Langtree, under severe scrutiny, never lost control of his court. It had been a bitter disappointment to prosecuting attorneys when the jury returned with the *Not Guilty* verdict.

*The banker Thomas Cantrell did not fare that well. The court took a dim view of the way certain aspects of other people's affairs were handled, and he was sentenced to four years and a heavy fine. The politicians and police officers that were charged weathered the storm and all was forgotten inside a year.*

The height of Sully's satisfaction came when Virginia Moran learned half her fortune was awarded to him. The way she worshipped money and power, it was the ultimate deliverance of punishment.

Otis Randall became a household name because of the fake death scene Beverly had so cleverly created. Randall's widow, Pearl, was awarded countless tributes for her late husband's so-called *sacrifice* in the line-of-duty.

Dorothy Haygood was cast as the *sinful madam* who dealt with people's lives carelessly and then paid the supreme price when confronted by the heroic Randall.

Sully sat through the trials, one after the other, watching the guilty face their peers and receive their just rewards. It came as a surprise that Beverly's name was not mentioned the first time. The prosecution had apparently considered her too insignificant to be charged with anything. He felt comfortable that her safety was secure in whatever new world she had created for herself.

Sully finally came to the conclusion that Randall had murdered G.W. Spence the same night he shot Dorothy Haygood. It was the only way to account for why G.W. was never heard from again. Sully gave little thought to the fact that G.W. was the only person, other than Beverly, who knew the real story of Jigs' death. Otis Randall had found out after wrenching it from G.W., but the captain was no longer around to do anything about it. Sully did owe G.W. for keeping quiet as long as he could, and if the gunrunner ever came back, all would be forgiven.

Sully also held a debt of gratitude to the people who went to great lengths to help him through those dangerous times. Hector Santana, who had almost died for coming to his aid, was on the top of the list. Jake Gregory was equally important; Jake had taken a bullet in his behalf. Both were well rewarded once out of the hospital. Then, there was Fred: Sully probably owed him more than anyone. The trick was not to offend by being overly generous. The most relieving part was that the Gregory's were never charged, or implicated, in the shooting death of Detective Jones.

Sully's life evened out once everything was put in its proper prospective, but it had taken the better part of two years to achieve that goal. He bought the small house in Grant Park, still drove the old Buick, and daily ventured to the gym for workouts. His paltry physique had regained its original structure from the constant exercise, which was a solace of sorts but, the sad truth was, it was a lonely life. For a man of thirty-four, it was not the ideal existence.

No one was ever charged with Jigs' death and the murder eventually faded into oblivion. Sully was drawn inexplicably to his new councilor, Jeremiah Woodard, and made frequent stopovers thereafter to the lawyer's office in Avondale Estates. With each sojourn, Woodard would inadvertently reveal another trait he passed down to Jigs. The similarity was so close at times that it was like talking to Jigs himself.

When Beverly went away, it had left a huge void in Sully's life; not a day went by that he didn't think of her. In time, he learned to accept the punishing hurt with a minimum of anxiety; that is, until a postcard was delivered nearly four years later. The rumpled card was from the isle of Little Inagua, nestled on the southernmost tip of the Bahamas; a beautiful beach scene covered one side. The short message read, *"The island is paradise. I'll be here."* It came without a signature, but there was no mistaking who wrote it.

# ABOUT THE AUTHOR

Sixty-nine-years-of-age—married forty-eight years—three children and four grandchildren. Discharged honorably from the Air Force in 1955. With Korean War veteran rights, took courses with Famous Artist's School in Connecticut for three years. Hired by Owens-Illinois Glass Co. In 1957, spent thirty-five years on the payroll. During that period, went to school at Atlanta Tech for three years at the bequest of the company, ('73-'76.) Retired as a journeyman in 1992. Began writing in 1993 as a hobby. Took a self-study course in grammar in 1994. Began taking writing seriously in 1995. Still writes at his northwest Georgia home where he resides.